continued . . .

SERPENT'S KISS

Thea Harrison

BERKLEY SENSATION, NEW YORK

THE BERKLEY PUBLISHING GROUP
Published by the Penguin Group
Penguin Group (USA) Inc.
375 Hudson Street, New York, New York 10014, USA
Penguin Group (Canada), 90 Eglinton Avenue East, Suite 700, Toronto, Ontario M4P 2Y3, Canada
(a division of Pearson Penguin Canada Inc.)
Penguin Books Ltd., 80 Strand, London WC2R 0RL, England
Penguin Group Ireland, 25 St. Stephen's Green, Dublin 2, Ireland (a division of Penguin Books Ltd.)
Penguin Group (Australia), 250 Camberwell Road, Camberwell, Victoria 3124, Australia
(a division of Pearson Australia Group Pty. Ltd.)
Penguin Books India Pvt. Ltd., 11 Community Centre, Panchsheel Park, New Delhi—110 017, India
Penguin Group (NZ), 67 Apollo Drive, Rosedale, Auckland 0632, New Zealand
(a division of Pearson New Zealand Ltd.)
Penguin Books (South Africa) (Pty.) Ltd., 24 Sturdee Avenue, Rosebank, Johannesburg 2196,
South Africa

Penguin Books Ltd., Registered Offices: 80 Strand, London WC2R 0RL, England

This is a work of fiction. Names, characters, places, and incidents either are the product of the author's
imagination or are used fictitiously, and any resemblance to actual persons, living or dead, business
establishments, events, or locales is entirely coincidental. The publisher does not have any control
over and does not assume any responsibility for author or third-party websites or their content.

SERPENT'S KISS

A Berkley Sensation Book / published by arrangement with the author

PRINTING HISTORY
Berkley Sensation mass-market edition / October 2011

Copyright © 2011 by Teddy Harrison.
Excerpt from *Oracle's Moon* by Thea Harrison copyright © by Teddy Harrison.
Cover art by Tony Mauro.
Cover design by George Long.
Cover hand lettering by Ron Zinn.
Interior text design by Tiffany Estreicher.

ISBN: 978-0-425-24440-1

BERKLEY SENSATION®
Berkley Sensation Books are published by The Berkley Publishing Group,
a division of Penguin Group (USA) Inc.,
375 Hudson Street, New York, New York 10014.
BERKLEY SENSATION® is a registered trademark of Penguin Group (USA) Inc.
The "B" design is a trademark of Penguin Group (USA) Inc.

PRINTED IN THE UNITED STATES OF AMERICA

10 9 8 7 6 5 4 3 2 1

ACKNOWLEDGMENTS

Once again, I have a lot of people to thank:

To Luann Reed-Siegel, who has done an amazing job on copy-editing.

To publicist Erin Galloway at Penguin, who has been friendly, patient, informative, prompt, dedicated, and enthusiastic.

To Janet and Don, who offered.

To my beta readers Shawn, Kristin, Anne, and Fran for their prompt, intelligent feedback. You guys are awesome!

To Lorene and Carol, as always.

To Matt, for his continuing goodhearted, generous work on the website.

To my editor, Cindy Hwang, and my agent, Amy Boggs. Thank you again, for everything you do.

And last but most important, to you, the readers. Without you, none of this would be happening. I'm eternally grateful.

Politics, n. A strife of interests masquerading as a contest of principles.
The conduct of public affairs for private advantage.
For the Elder Races, this generally involves bloodshed of some sort and a spate of funerals.

—AMBROSE BIERCE ON REVISING *THE DEVIL'S DICTIONARY*

≈ ONE ≈

"I am a bad woman, of course," said Carling Severan, the Vampyre sorceress, in an absent tone of voice. "It is a fact that I made peace with many centuries ago. I calibrate everything I do, even the most generous-seeming gesture, in terms of how it may serve me."

Carling sat in her favorite armchair by a spacious window. The chair's butter-soft leather had long ago molded to the contours of her body. Outside the window lay a lush, well-tended garden that was ornamented with the subtle hues of the moonlit night. Her gaze was trained on the scene, but, like her face, the expression in her long almond-shaped eyes was blank.

"Why would you say such a thing?" Rhoswen asked. There were tears in the younger Vampyre's voice as she knelt beside the armchair, her blonde head turned up to Carling like a flower's to a midnight sun. "You're the most wonderful person in the world."

"That is very sweet of you." Carling kissed Rhoswen's forehead, since the other woman seemed to need it. Although the distance in Carling's gaze lessened, it did not entirely disappear. "But those are rather disturbing words. If you believe that of someone such as I, you must acquire more discernment."

Her servant's tears spilled over and streaked down a cameo-perfect face. Rhoswen threw her arms around Carling with a sob.

Carling's sleek eyebrows rose. "What is this?" she asked, her tone weary. "What have I said to upset you?"

Rhoswen shook her head and clung tighter.

Rhoswen was one of Carling's two youngest progeny. Carling had stopped creating Vampyres long ago, except for a few extraordinarily talented exceptions she had discovered in the latter part of the nineteenth century. Rhoswen had been part of a shabby Shakespearean theatre company, with a voice of pure gold and a fatal case of pulmonary tuberculosis. Carling had turned Rhoswen when she had been a frightened, dying eighteen-year-old. She allowed the younger woman greater liberties than she did her other servants. She endured Rhoswen's strangling hold as she thought.

She said, "We were talking about the events that led up to the Dark Fae Queen's coronation. You persist in believing that I did a good thing when I healed Niniane and her lover Tiago when they were injured. While the results might have been beneficial, I was merely pointing out what a selfish creature at heart I really am."

"Two days ago," Rhoswen said into her lap. "We had that conversation two days ago, and then you faded again."

"Did I?" She straightened her back, bracing herself against the news. "Well, we knew the deterioration was accelerating."

No one fully understood why very old Vampyres went through a period of increasing mental deterioration before they disintegrated into outright madness, then death. Since it was rare for Vampyres to achieve such an extreme old age, the phenomenon was little known outside the upper echelon of the Nightkind community. Vampyres lived violent lives, and they tended to die from other causes first.

Perhaps it was the inevitable progression of the disease itself. Perhaps, Carling thought, in the end our beginning contains the seeds of our eventual downfall. The souls that began as human were never meant to live the near-immortal life that the Vampyrism gave them.

Rhoswen's tear-streaked face lifted. "But you got better for a while! In Chicago, and later at the Dark Fae coronation, you were fully alert and functioning. You were present for every moment. We just have to keep you stimulated with new things."

Carling regarded her with a wry expression. Extraordinary experiences did seem to help, as they jolted one into alertness for a time. The problem was they only helped temporarily. To someone who has witnessed the passage of millennia, after a while even the extraordinary experiences became ordinary.

She sighed and admitted, "I had a couple of episodes I did not share with you."

The grief that filled Rhoswen's expression at that was positively Shakespearian. Carling's sense of wryness deepened as she looked upon the face of fanatic devotion and knew she had done nothing whatsoever to deserve it.

She had been born into obscurity so long ago the details of that time had faded from history. She had been kidnapped into slavery, whipped nearly to death and given as a concubine to an aging desert king, and she had sworn she would never let anyone take a lash to her again. She seduced the king into making her a queen and squandered an almost unimaginably long life in the acquisition of Power. She learned poisons, and warfare, and sorcery, how to rule and how to hold a grudge with all of her heart, and then she discovered Vampyrism, the serpent's kiss that had given her near immortality.

She had played chess with demons for human lives, counseled monarchs and warred with monsters. Throughout the unwinding scroll of centuries she had ruled more than one country with unwavering ruthlessness in her slender iron fist. She knew spells that were so secret the knowledge of their existence had all but passed from this earth, and she had seen things so wondrous the sight of them had brought proud men to their knees. She had conquered the darkness to walk in the full light of day, and she had lost, and lost, and lost so very many people and things that even grief failed to move her much anymore.

All of those fabulous experiences were now fading into the ornamented night.

There was simply nowhere else to take her life, no adventure so compelling she must fight above all else to survive and see it through, no mountaintop she had to scale. After everything she had done to survive, after fighting to live for so long and to rule, she had now become . . . disinterested.

And here was the final of all treasures, the last jewel in her casket of secrets that rested on top of the others, winking its onyx light.

The Power she had worked so hard to accumulate was

pulsing in rhythm with the accelerating deterioration of her mind. She saw it flare all around her in an exquisite transparent shimmer. It covered her in a shroud that sparkled like diamonds.

She had not expected that her death would be so lovely.

She had lost track of when it had begun. The past and the present intermingled in her mind. Time had become a riddle. Perhaps it had been a hundred years ago. Or perhaps it had been the entirety of her life, which held certain symmetry. That for which she had fought so hard, shed blood over, and cried tears of rage would be what consumed her in the end.

Another Power flare was building. She could sense its inevitability, like the oncoming crescendo in an immortal symphony, or the next intimate pulse of her long-abandoned, almost-forgotten heartbeat. The expression in her eyes turned vague as she focused her attention on that ravishing internal flame.

Just before it engulfed her again, she noticed an oddity. There was no sound in the house around them, no movement from other Vampyres, no spark of human emotion. There was nothing but Rhoswen's hitched breathing as the younger Vampyre knelt at her feet, and the small contented sounds of a dog nearby as he scratched at his ear then dug out a nesting place in his floor cushion. Carling had lived for a long time surrounded by jackals eager to feed from scraps that fell from the tables of those in Power, but sometime over the last week, all her usual attendants and sycophants had fled.

Some creatures had a well-developed sense of self-preservation, unlike others.

She said to Rhoswen, "I suggest you work harder on acquiring that sense of discernment."

Every little thing is going to be all right.

Recently Rune had quoted Bob Marley to Niniane Lorelle when she had been at a low point in her life. Niniane was young for a faerie, a sweet woman and had been a close friend of his for a long time. She also happened to be the Dark Fae Queen now and the newest entry on America's list of the top ten most powerful people in the country. Rune had brought Bob up in conversation to comfort her after an assassination attempt had been made on her life, in which a friend of hers had been killed, and her mate Tiago had nearly died as well.

And damn if that Marley song didn't keep running through his head ever since. It was one of those brain viruses, like a TV commercial or a musical theme from a movie that got stuck on perpetual replay, and he couldn't find an off switch for the sound system that was wired into his brain.

Not that, in the normal course of things, he didn't like Bob's music. Rune just wanted him to shut up for a little freaking while so he could get some shut-eye.

Instead Rune kept waking up in the middle of the night, staring at his ceiling as silk sheets sandpapered his oversensitive skin and mental snapshots of recent events shuttered against his mind's retina while Bob kept on playing.

Every little thing.

Snap, and Rune's other good friend Tiago was sprawled on his back in a forested clearing, gutted and drenched in his own blood, while Niniane knelt at his head and held on to him in perfect terror.

Snap, and Rune stared into the gorgeous blank expression of one of the most Powerful Nightkind rulers in history, as he grabbed Carling by the shoulders, shook her hard and roared point-blank in her face.

Snap, and he struck a bargain with Carling that saved Tiago's life but could very well end his own.

Snap, and Carling was walking naked out of the Adriyel River at twilight, deep in the heart of the Dark Fae land, drenched in silvery water that glistened in the dying day as if she wore a transparent gown of stars. The curves and hollows of her muscled body, the dark hair that lay slick against her shapely skull, her high-cheeked, inscrutable Egyptian face—they were all so fucking perfect. And one of the most perfect things about her was also one of the most tragic, for the lithe sensual beauty of her body had been marred with dozens of long white lash scars. When she had been a mortal human, she had been whipped with such force it must have been a ferocious cruelty, and yet she moved with the strong, sleek confident sensuality of a tiger. The sight of her had stopped his breath, stopped his thinking, stopped his soul, his everything, so that he needed some kind of cosmic reboot that hadn't happened yet because part of him was still caught frozen in that moment of epiphany.

Snap, and he bore witness as an antique gun simultaneously fired and exploded in the forest clearing, killing both a traitor and a good woman. A woman he had liked very much. A strong, funny, fragile human who shouldn't have lost her short precious life because he and his fellow sentinel Aryal had screwed up and left her to protect Niniane on her own.

Snap, and he saw Cameron's face when she had been alive. The human had had the long, strong body of an athlete, her spare features sprinkled with good humor and cinnamon-colored freckles.

Snap, and he saw Cameron that final time as the Dark Fae soldiers prepared and wrapped her body for transportation back to her family in Chicago. All the pretty cinnamon color had leached out of her freckles. The exploding gun she had shot to save Niniane's life had taken out a large chunk of her head. It was always so harsh when you saw a friend in that last, saddest state. They were okay. They didn't hurt anymore. At that point you were the one who was wounded.

Every little thing is going to be all right.

Except sometimes it wasn't, Bob. Sometimes things got so fucked up all you could do was send them home in a body bag.

Rune's temper grew short. Usually he was an easy-going kind of Wyr, but he started snapping off people's heads for no reason. Metaphorically, anyway. At least he hadn't started snapping off people's heads for real. Still, people started to avoid him.

"What's up your ass?" Aryal had asked after Niniane's coronation, when they had crossed over from Adriyel to Chicago and were en route back to New York.

They took their preferred method of travel and flew in their Wyr forms. Aryal was his fellow sentinel and a harpy, which meant she was a right royal bitch ninety percent of the time. Usually her snarky attitude cracked him up. At the moment it almost had him drop-kicking her into the side of a skyscraper.

"I'm being haunted by Marley's ghost," he told her.

Aryal slanted a dark eyebrow at him. When she was in her harpy form, the angles of her face were pronounced, upswept. Her gray-fade-to-black wings beat strongly in the hot summer wind that blew wild around them. "Which ghost?" the harpy asked. "The past, present or future?"

Huh? It took him a second to catch on. Then the Dickens connection happened in his head and he thought, Jacob Marley, not Bob. Aryal had gotten the Jacob Marley character and the three spirits of Christmas past, present and future all muddled up.

Time and time and time. What happened, what is, and what is yet to come.

He barked out a laugh. The sound was filled with ground glass. "All of them," he said. "I'm being haunted by all of them."

"Dude, give it up," said Aryal, in a mild tone that he recognized as a conciliatory one, coming as it was from her. "Believe in Christmas already."

The harpy looked almost delicate as he flew by her side. His Wyr form was that of a gryphon. He had the body of a lion and the head and wings of a golden eagle. His paws were the size of hubcaps and tipped with long wicked retractable claws, and his eagle's head had lion-colored eyes. His feline body had breadth and power across the chest, sleek strong haunches, and was the dun color of hot desert places. In his Wyr form he was immense, easily the size of an SUV, with a correspondingly huge wingspan.

In his human form, Rune stood six-foot-four, and he had the broad shoulders and lean hard muscles of a swordsman. He had sun-bronzed fine-grained skin with laugh lines at the corners of lion's eyes that were the color of sunlit amber. His even features and white smile were popular commodities, especially with those of the female persuasion, and the mane of sun-streaked hair that fell to his broad shoulders held glints of pale gold, chestnut and burnished copper.

He was one of the four gryphons of the Earth, revered in ancient India and Persia, an immortal Wyr who came into being at the birth of the world. Time and space had buckled when the Earth was formed. The buckling created dimensional pockets of Other land where magic pooled, time moved differently, modern combustible technologies didn't work and the sun shone with a different light. What came to be known as the Elder Races, the Wyrkind and the Elves, the Light and Dark Fae, the Nightkind, Demonkind, human witches, and all other manner of monstrous creatures, tended to cluster in or near the Other lands.

Most of the Elder creatures came into being either on Earth or in the dimensional pockets of Other land. A few, a very few, came into existence in those crossover points between places, where time and space were fluid and changeable, and at the time of the world's creation, Power was an unformed, immeasurable force.

Rune and his fellow gryphons were just such beings. They were quintessential beings of duality, formed at the cusp between two creatures, on the threshold of changing time and space. Lion and eagle, along with the other ancient Wyr, they learned to shapeshift and walk among humankind, and so they also became Wyr form and man. They had an affinity for the Earth's between places. They could find crossover passages and Other lands that remained hidden from all others, and in early history they were known throughout the Elder Races for being fearless explorers. There would be no others like them. Creation's inchoate time had passed and all things, even the crossover points between places, had become fixed in their definitions.

The past scrolled behind him. The future was the unknown thing that waited ahead of him, smiling its Mona Lisa smile. And the ever-fleeting now was continually born and continually died, but was never anything you could get your hands on and hold on to, as it always pushed you along to some other place.

Yeah, he knew a thing or two about living life on the threshold.

He and Aryal had returned to Cuelebre Tower in New York.

There were seven demesnes of Elder Races that overlaid the human geography of the continental United States. The seat of the Wyrkind demesne was in New York City. The seat of Elven demesne was based in Charleston, South Carolina. The Dark Fae's demesne was centered in Chicago, and the Light Fae's in Los Angeles. The Nightkind, which included all Vampyric forms, controlled the San Francisco Bay Area and the Pacific Northwest, while the human witches, considered part of the Elder Races due to their command of Power, were based in Louisville, Kentucky. Demonkind, like the Wyr and the Vampyres, consisted of several different types that included goblins and Djinn, and their seat was based in Houston.

Upon Rune and Aryal's return, the first thing they did was debrief the Lord of the Wyr, Dragos Cuelebre. A massive dark man with gold eyes, Dragos's Wyr form was a dragon the size of a private jet. He had ruled over the Wyrkind demesne for centuries, with seven immortal Wyr as his sentinels.

Rune was Dragos's First sentinel. Among Rune's other duties, he and the other three gryphons, Bayne, Constantine and Graydon, worked to keep the peace in the demesne. Aryal was the sentinel in charge of investigations, and the gargoyle Grym was head of corporate security for Cuelebre Enterprises.

Dragos had just lost his seventh sentinel, who had not yet been replaced. The Wyr Tiago, thunderbird and longtime warlord sentinel, had walked away from his life and position in the Wyr demesne in order to be with his newfound mate, Niniane.

Dragos was not the most even-tempered at the best of times. At first he had not been pleased with the debriefing. He had not been pleased at all.

"You promised her WHAT?" The dragon's deep roar rattled the windows. They stood in his office. Dragos planted his hands on his hips, his dark machete-edged features sharp with incredulity.

Rune set his mouth in the taut lines of someone struggling to hold on to his own temper and said, "I promised to go to Carling in one week and do a favor of her choosing."

"Un-fucking-believable," the Wyr Lord growled. "Do you have any idea what you gave away?"

"Yes, actually," Rune bit out. "I believe I might have a clue."

"She could ask you to do anything, and now you are bound by the laws of magic to do it. You could be gone for HUNDREDS OF YEARS just trying to complete that one fucking favor." The dragon's hot glare flared into incandescence as he paced. "I've already lost my warlord sentinel, and now we have no idea how long I will have to do without my First. Could you not have come up with something else to bargain? Anything else. Anything at all."

"Apparently not, since I was the one who made the goddamn deal," Rune snapped, as his already strained temper torched.

Dragos fell silent as he swung around to face Rune. It had to be in part, no doubt, from surprise, as Rune was normally the even-keeled one in their relationship. But Dragos was also taking a deep breath before releasing a blast of wrath. The dragon's Power compressed in the room.

Then Aryal, of all people, stepped in to play her version of peacemaker. "What the hell, Dragos?" the harpy said. "It was life-or-death, and Tiago was bleeding out right in front of us. None of us actually had the time to consult our attorneys about the best bargaining terms to use with the Wicked Witch of the West. We brought you a present. Here." She threw a leather pack at Dragos, who lifted a reflexive hand to catch it.

Dragos opened the pack and pulled out two sets of black shackles that radiated a menacing Power. "There's finally a piece of good news," he breathed.

The three Wyr stared at the chains in revulsion. Fashioned by Dragos's old enemy, the late Dark Fae King Urien Lorelle, the chains had the ability to imprison the most Powerful Wyr of them all, Dragos himself.

His outburst of anger derailed, Dragos listened as Rune and Aryal finished telling the story of how Naida Riordan, wife of one of the most powerful figures in the Dark Fae government, had used Urien's old tools in her attempts to kill Niniane and Tiago.

"The shackles prevented Tiago from healing," Rune said. "We nearly lost him while we were figuring how to get them off. That's when I had to bargain with Carling."

The dragon gave him a grim look, thoughts shifting like shadows in his gold eyes.

"All right," Dragos said after a moment. "Use the week to get your affairs in order and delegate your duties. And when you get to San Francisco, try like hell to persuade Carling to let you do something quick."

So Rune spent the week delegating, while Bob and the images in his head kept him company at night, and the sights and the sounds of New York assaulted his senses by day.

Normally he enjoyed New York's energetic hustle and bustle but since returning from Adriyel, the gigantic city steamed in the summer heat, all the smells trapped in a heavy humidity as it emitted a constant harsh, cacophonic noise that scraped like sharp fingernails underneath Rune's skin. It turned him into a feral stranger with a short, unknown fuse so that when his temper exploded, he shocked himself as much as anyone. He felt something he had never felt before in the long uncounted years of his existence: he felt unsafe.

Maybe it wasn't such a bad thing he had to take off for a while. It might give him a chance to regroup, recover his equilibrium. It would be wise to take a break from dealing with Dragos's temper, since his own self-control had become so uncertain. He and Dragos had had a productive relationship that had spanned centuries, and it was based partly on friendship and very heavily on a partnership of reliance on one another's skills, such as Rune's even temper and diplomacy.

But at the moment he seemed to have misplaced all of his not-inconsiderable skills at "managing up." If he continued as he was, he and Dragos could possibly have a serious, very ugly clash, and that wouldn't be good for anyone, least of all himself. There was simply no reason to let things degenerate to that point.

He was supposed to coax Carling into letting him do something for her that was quick, huh? Maybe he could offer to take out her trash or do her dishes. He wondered how well that would go over.

Did the Wicked Witch of the West have a sense of humor? Rune had seen her at inter-demesne affairs over the last couple of centuries. While he might have heard her say something once or twice that seemed laden with a double entendre, or he might have thought on occasion that he'd seen a sparkle lurking at the back of those fabulous dark eyes, it seemed highly doubtful. She seemed too intense for real humor, as if laughter might fracture some kind of critical weapons system inside.

On Thursday, the sixth day, his iPhone pinged. He dragged it out of his jeans pocket and checked it. He had received an email from Duncan Turner at Turner & Braeburn, Attorneys at Law, headquartered in San Francisco.

Who the hell?

Oh riiight, Duncan Turner was Duncan the Vampyre. Duncan had been part of Carling's entourage as she traveled to Adriyel, the Dark Fae land, for Niniane's coronation in her position as Councillor for the Elder tribunal.

The Elder tribunal acted as a sort of United Nations for the Elder Races. It was made up of seven Councillors that represented the seven Elder demesnes in the continental United States, and it had certain legal and judicial powers over inter-demesne affairs. Their main charter was to keep the current balance of Power stable and work to prevent war.

Among other things, the Councillors had the authority to command the attendance of residents of their demesne when they were called to act in their official capacity as representatives of the Elder tribunal. Like jury duty for humans, demesne residents either had to comply or provide proof of their inability to serve.

Rune wondered how many billable hours Duncan had lost for the privilege of attending Carling on the trip to Niniane's coronation in Adriyel. Not only had Duncan proven to be an asset on the trip, he never showed a hint of frustration, impatience or resentment. He had been the ideal travel companion, and while Rune distrusted such exemplary behavior, he had grown to like the Vampyre in spite of it.

Rune clicked the email open and read through it.

> Rune Ainissesthai
> First Sentinel
> Cuelebre Tower
> New York, NY 10001

Dear Rune:

RE: Per verbal contract enacted 23.4.3205, Adriyel date.

As payment for services rendered by Councillor Carling Severan, please present yourself at sundown tomorrow at my office in Suite 7500, 500 Market Street, San Francisco, CA 94105. Further instructions will be given to you at that time.

I hope you have had a good week, and look forward to seeing you in due course.

Best regards,
Duncan Turner
Senior Partner
Turner & Braeburn, Attorneys at Law

Rune rubbed his mouth as he read through the message again. His already grim mood darkened further. Ask Carling if he could do something quick, huh? Take out the trash. Do the dishes.

Bloody hell.

Until he knew what was expected of him, he decided it might be a smart thing to have comfortable accommodations arranged, so he reserved an open-ended stay in a balcony suite at the Fairmont Hotel in San Francisco, opting for the suite's more modest size in favor of the room's view and French doors that opened onto a wrought-iron balcony. Then he said good-bye to his peeps, packed a duffle and fought a nasty short battle with the pride of Wyr-lions that was the Cuelebre Enterprises army of attorneys, for the use of the corporate jet. Despite their vociferous objections, the argument was over the moment he pulled rank. He sent the group of pissed-off cats scrambling to book first-class tickets for their corporate meeting in Brussels.

He could have flown in his gryphon form from New York to San Francisco, but that would mean he would arrive tired and hungry at the law offices of Turner & Braeburn, which did not seem to be the best strategic option when facing an unknown, potentially dangerous task. Besides, as he told the cats, he had some important last-minute things he had to take care of during the flight.

And he did. As soon as the Lear had left the tarmac, he stretched out on a couch with pillows propped at his back and a pile of beef sandwiches at his elbow. He punched a button that opened the shutters that concealed a fifty-two-inch plasma widescreen, settled a wireless keyboard on his upraised knees, a wireless mouse on the back of the couch, and he logged into the World of Warcraft's game *Wrath of the Lich King* via the jet's satellite connection.

After all, he didn't know when he was going to get the chance to play WoW again. And it was damn important to do his bit to save all life on Azeroth while he could. Booyah.

He played WoW, and ate, and napped while the Lear shot westward through the sky, hurtling toward the death of the day. It felt good to be on the move again, albeit in such a leisurely fashion, and Rune's mood lightened until he felt almost cheerful again.

Then the pilot's voice overrode the game on the Lear's sound system. "Sir, we've begun our descent. It should be a smooth one. We'll reach SFO within the half hour, and we're already cleared for landing. San Francisco is currently at a balmy seventy-four degrees and the skies are clear. It looks like we're in for a beautiful sunset."

Rune rolled his eyes at the travelogue, logged out of WoW, stretched and stood. He stepped into the luxuriously appointed bathroom, shaved and took a five-minute shower, dressed again in his favorite jeans, Jerry Garcia T-shirt and steel-toed boots, and went to check out the scenic action in the cockpit.

Pilot and co- were a mated pair of Wyr-ravens. They sat relaxed and chatting, a slender, dark-haired quick-witted couple who straightened in their seats as he appeared. "Dudes," he said in a mild tone, resting one elbow on the back of co-'s chair. "Chill."

"Yes, sir." Alex, the pilot, gave him a quick sidelong smile. Alex was the younger and the more aggressive of the two males. More often than not, his partner Daniel, who was the more laid-back of the pair, was content to play backup. For the longer flights, they tended to switch hats, one flying pilot for the flight out and the other piloting the return trip.

The Lear would be serviced and refueled overnight, and the ravens were headed back to New York first thing in the morning. Rune asked, "What are you guys going to do with your evening—have dinner out, take in a show?"

As they chatted about restaurants and touring Broadway shows, Rune gazed out at the panorama spreading out underneath the plane.

The San Francisco Bay Area was awash in gigantic sweeps of color, the bluish grays of distant landmarks dotted with bright sparks of electric light, all of it crowned with the fiery brilliance of the oncoming cloudless sunset. All five of the Bay Area's major bridges—the Golden Gate Bridge, San Francisco-Oakland Bay Bridge, Richmond-San Rafael Bridge, Hayward-San Mateo Bridge and the Dumbarton Bridge—were etched in perfect miniature in the watercolor distance. The southern San Francisco peninsula sprouted skyscrapers like colossal flowers in some god's back garden. At the other end of the Golden Gate lay the North Bay area, which included Marin, and Sonoma and Napa Counties.

Sometimes there was another land in the distance, sketched in lines of palest transparent blue. One of the Bay Area's Other lands had started appearing on the horizon around a century ago. It seemed to sit due west of the Golden Gate.

The island had first been sighted around the mid-nineteenth century and had caused major consternation and a remapping of shipping lanes. Much research and speculation had gone into the singular phenomenon, sparking ideas such as a Power fault that might be linked to California's earthquake faults, but no one really understood why the island appeared at some times and disappeared at others. Eventually an adventurous soul discovered that the island disappeared once ocean-faring vessels sailed close enough. After that the traffic in the shipping lanes returned to normal.

Soon the island became another Bay Area tourist attraction. Sightseeing cruises increased exponentially whenever the Other land was visible. People began calling it Avalon, the shining land of myth and fable.

But Rune had heard whispers of another name. There was another population in the Bay Area. It was not the population that took cruises, ate in restaurants or went to see touring Broadway shows. It lived in the corners of old abandoned buildings, and hid when night fell and all the predators came out. The crack addicts and the homeless didn't call the land Avalon. They called it Blood Alley.

The island was visible now in the distance, the immense orange-red ball of the setting sun shining through its unearthly silhouette. A small colony of Vampyres reputedly lived on the island. Rune watched it thoughtfully, shifting his stance to take in the change in gravity as the Lear tilted into a wide circle that would bring it into a landing pattern for SFO.

As the seat of the Nightkind demesne, the Bay Area had many Vampyre enclaves, especially in Marin County where an extensive community surrounded the home of Julian Regillus, the official Nightkind King. As far as Rune knew, the street people did not whisper of Julian's community with the same kind of fear as they did the island. Was that because of the island's

•

otherworldly habit of appearing and disappearing, or because of who lived there?

Alex the pilot heaved a sigh and said, "I am required by FAA regulations . . . blah blah . . . seat belt . . . blah . . ."

Rune burst out laughing. "If we wouldn't lose all the shit that's not anchored down in the cabin, I'd be tempted to just pop open a door and hop out."

Daniel shot him a look. "Thank you, sir, for refraining from that action."

"You're welcome." Rune clapped the co- on the shoulder and left the cabin.

Truth was, he wasn't in all that big of a hurry, and they set down soon enough. When they had taxied into position and Daniel opened up the Lear, Rune thanked him and took off. He shapeshifted just outside the jet and, cloaking his Wyr form from scrutiny, he launched into the air and flew into the city.

He was undecided about where to land, since he wasn't familiar enough with the location of 500 Market Street that he could locate it from the air. Finally he chose to set down near the west end of the Golden Gate Park. As he spiraled down toward a paved path, his shadow flickered over a slender furtive figure that stood in front of a sign and shook a can of spray paint in one fist.

Rune landed, changed back into his human form and let his cloak of concealment drop away. He slung his duffle bag onto one shoulder and watched as the figure tagged the sign. The brown creature looked like an anorexic humanoid female, with a skeletal frame and long spidery hands and feet. Her dripping hair had strands of seaweed tangled in it.

She glanced over her shoulder, caught sight of him and scowled. "What are you staring at, ass-wipe?"

He said in a mild tone, "Not a thing, my good woman."

"Keep it that way." She darted to a nearby trash can, tossed away the spray paint can and dashed across the path to dive into a nearby pond. Soon the quiet sound of brokenhearted sobbing came from underneath a weeping willow at the pond's edge.

Rune walked over to the sign. It was one of the myriad signs that were posted throughout the Bay Area's ponds, lakes and rivers that warned tourists: Please Do NOT Feed the Water Haunts.

This particular sign had one word blacked out with spray paint. It now read: Please Do Feed the Water Haunts.

Welcome to the Nightkind demesne, the home of water haunts, night elves, ghouls, trolls and Vampyres. Out of the corner of his eye, he caught sight of several night elves trotting through the park. Unlike real Elves, night elves were typically slender and child-sized creatures, with large eyes and large bald heads and pointed ears, and they schooled together like fish.

He strolled over to the willow tree and cocked his head to look underneath the dripping leaves. The water haunt sat in the water, her bony thin shoulders hunched. She caught sight of him and sobbed harder.

He dug in his duffle bag. The water haunt gave a piteous whimper, her lips trembling, as she tracked his movements with a mud-colored gaze. He pulled out a PowerBar and held it up. The haunt's eyes fixed on it. She wailed as she crept close. He raised a finger. Her wailing sailed upward on a questioning note and hitched to a stop.

He told her, "I'm onto your tricks, young lady. You try to bite me and I'll kick your face in."

The water haunt gave him a crafty grin that had a great many teeth. He indicated the PowerBar and raised his eyebrows. She gave him an eager nod. He tossed her the bar, and she snatched it out of the air. With a whirl and a splash, she dived to the other side of the tree to devour her prize.

He shook his head and checked his watch. He had about a half hour to sunset. Plenty of time to walk west, connect to Market Street, and find out if he needed to hook either a left or a right in order to reach his destination.

Bob started up in his head again as he headed out of the park. Every little thing is going to be all right.

Oh no. Not again. He wanted to at least start out this venture with some semblance of sanity. As he strode down the street, he unzipped a side pocket on his duffle and fished around inside until he nabbed his iPod. He popped in the earbuds and scrolled through his extensive playlists for something else. Anything else. Anything at all.

"Born to be Wild." Yeah, that'd do. He punched play.

Steppenwolf's strong raw voice sang in his ears.

Fire all of your guns at once and explode into space.

It was twilight, one of the world's threshold places, the cross-over time between day and night. The dying sunshine caught in his lion's eyes. They flared with radiance as Rune smiled.

≡ TWO ≡

Market Street in San Francisco slashed diagonally through the city from the Ferry Building at the northeast shore to Twin Peaks in the southwest. The street was one of the city's major thoroughfares and had been compared to the Champs-Élysées in Paris or Fifth Avenue in New York.

Now dusk was approaching on a Friday evening in the heart of the Nightkind demesne. That made Market Street a hip and happening place. The tall skyscraper surroundings provided an effective shield from the last of the day's sunshine. Tourists and shoppers crowded the sidewalks.

A pair of white-skinned, beautiful and elegantly clothed female Vampyres strolled arm in arm toward him. They bent their heads and whispered together as he approached, looking at him sidelong with kohl-lined eyes and pale smiles. When he smiled back, the nearest Vampyre's eyes widened and her ivory skin washed with a delicate blush of color. Rune considered it quite a compliment, coming from the undead.

The crowd grew denser as he approached his destination. It was the thickest just outside the sleek tall skyscraper that was 500 Market Street. Rune studied the throng curiously as he threaded his way to the front doors. The members of the crowd were all human.

One frail-looking woman pushed in front of him pulling a

portable tank in a cart, a thin oxygen tube threaded under her nostrils, and he paused to let her past. As she brushed against him, he caught the scent of serious illness underneath her lilac perfume. The sour, medicinal smell lingered in his nostrils, evoking images of pain and decay, until he turned his head and emitted a polite cough that cleared his lungs. Another pale, thin man was in a wheelchair, accompanied by his wife and a younger man who looked to be his son.

Rune stripped off his earbuds and put away his iPod, then he pushed through the revolving doors and surveyed the main lobby. It was dominated by uniformed security guards, metal detectors, and lines of people that led up to bulletproof glass-plated windows. He rubbed the back of his neck and was about to step outside and check the number on the building again when he heard his name called from the bank of elevators across the lobby. He swiveled back around.

Duncan the Vampyre strode toward him. Dressed in a black Ralph Lauren suit with matching shoes, the male stood around five-foot-eleven. Razor-cut dark hair lay sleek against his well-formed head, and he had pleasant features and intelligent eyes. Duncan gestured to a security guard, who opened a side gate and invited Rune to step through.

"I just arrived, myself," said Duncan. The Vampyre held out his hand.

Rune shook it. The Vampyre's grasp was strong and cool. "I was going to step outside to make sure I had the right address. What is going on here in the lobby?"

Duncan turned back to the elevators. Rune fell into step beside him, shortening his longer stride to accommodate the other male. Duncan told him, "The Bureau of Nightkind Immigration occupies the first three floors of the building. This is where humans apply for visas to become Vampyres—"

Shouting at one of the plateglass windows interrupted him. "Don't tell me it's going to be another four fucking months! My father has stage four cancer—he doesn't have another four months to wait!"

Rune glanced at the man who was shouting then back at Duncan, who gave him a slight wince. They reached the elevator bank where Duncan punched the top button on the panel for the fifty-fifth floor. As they stepped into an elevator, Duncan continued, "Understandably enough, the visa process can get emotional, which is why there is such a strong security presence in the lobby."

Two security guards were walking toward the altercation as the elevator doors closed. Rune said, "Just out of curiosity, what happens to visa applications for people who are terminally ill? Is that guy going to be able to get his father's case expedited?"

"Probably not," said Duncan. "There are always sad cases, and there are too many desperate dying people."

"Dude," said Rune. "Ouch."

The Vampyre glanced at him. "I do not mean to be unsympathetic. But to put this into perspective, the United States received an estimated fourteen million applications for the Diversity Green Card Visa in 2009. The North American Nightkind demesne gets close to ten million visa applications in a year, and our screening process must not only be more rigorous than the federal government's, but we can grant far fewer visas than the 2.5 million visas the United States granted."

"Holy shit," said Rune.

"We're the only demesne that must regulate itself in such a fashion," said Duncan. "The long-lived Elder Races have correspondingly low birthrates. Even for the human witches, nature regulates those who are born with sparks of Power, and not all of those born with the inherent ability choose to study the Power crafts. Vampyrism is a dangerous infectious disease, not just physically but socially. It used to be the purview of the rich, the beautiful, and the Powerful, or anyone who caught a Vampyre's fancy for whatever reason. We can no longer afford to be so capricious. I helped to coauthor the original visa application process in the early 1900s, which goes through updates and improvements every ten years. Each year we also coordinate with the CDC in Atlanta to arrive at a total for the number of applications we are allowed to approve."

"You just took all the fun out of the Vampyre movies," said Rune. "How many applicants could you approve last year?"

"Two thousand."

He whistled between his teeth. "Those numbers are killer."

"Yes," said Duncan. "That is why visa applications are almost never expedited."

"What would it take to get a rush on one?" Rune asked, curious.

Duncan shook his head. "A personal request from Julian or Carling could drop-kick it through, of course, or an edict from the Elder tribunal. Frankly, not much else could do it. And now applicants must not only prove they have sound financial investments and prospects—such as they have the capacity to be gainfully employed—but they must also undergo a psychological evaluation. They must also provide documentation to prove they have a Vampyre willing to host them, or in other words provide stability, discipline and training for the first five years after they're turned. That is when most of the ten million applications hit the trash can. Metaphorically speaking, anyway. Nowadays the application process is online. We have developed a sophisticated software program that automatically rejects applications that have not been filled out properly, or have failed to meet all the initial paperwork requirements."

Rune said, "So what you're actually saying is that in order to become a Vampyre, you have to prove you have money or can make money, and you have to be computer literate, which knocks out a good portion of the country that lives on the wrong side of the growing digital divide. I hate to burst your bubble, but I think you might be headed back to the place where Vampyrism is the purview of the rich, the beautiful and the Powerful."

Duncan laughed. They arrived at the fifty-fifth floor. When the elevator doors opened, they stepped into corporate luxury. Opposite the bank of elevators, Turner & Braeburn, Attorneys at Law was spelled out in gleaming slim gold letters on the dark marble wall.

Duncan led the way in a swift stride down tastefully decorated, busy halls to a corner office. Rune sent a curious glance around as he ambled along behind. The Attorneys at Law were having their version of a busy Friday morning.

"The system isn't perfect," Duncan said. "The bottom line is the Nightkind demesne is trying to avoid letting poor, crazy, blood-sucking immortals loose on the streets to become a burden on the more normal tax-paying society. But here's the kicker."

Duncan paused talking and stopped at open double doors.

With a polite gesture he invited Rune to precede him. Rune strode into an office with a floor space that was a thousand square feet if it was an inch. Metallic shutters had been pulled back from the two walls of windows, and outside the entire Bay Area, including bridges, was ablaze with electric light. The sun had set and all that was left of its memory was a bloodred glow on the ocean's darkening horizon.

Rune swiveled back to face Duncan, who had closed the doors. The Vampyre turned to face him.

Duncan said, "Everything I just told you is the official Nightkind demesne procedure. We're required by federal law to follow it, but it's like the U.S. war on drugs, or worse, the HIV epidemic. How do you really regulate something that is just a living heartbeat, a heated moment, and a blood exchange away?"

"I'm guessing I know the answer to that," Rune said. "You can't."

"Exactly," Duncan replied. "Of course we can't. We can set regulations, issue visas, and work to enforce consequences, but we still have our illegals and crazies, and our non-registereds. Do we possibly know what a Vampyre is doing in your demesne in New York, or the Demonkind demesne in Houston? Of course not, just as you have no idea what individual Wyr might be doing in Chicago. Our police force is effective so we can keep a tight lid on what is visible to the public here in our demesne, but we can only do so much. Also, many of the older Vampyres resent the new restrictions, and they still follow the old ways in regulating their family trees—through secrecy, domination and violence."

"Oh good," said Rune. "All the fun from the Vampyre movies just came back."

Spanned by its famous bridge, the Golden Gate is actually the name of the strait that was discovered in 1769 by Spanish explorers. In 1846, the American military officer John C. Fremont named the passageway "Chrysopylae," or "Golden Gate," before the Californian gold rush. The strait had been compared to ancient Byzantium's Golden Horn.

As Rune looked out, the Golden Gate Bridge towered shining over the darkened waters of the strait. The symbolism of standing before a gateway was not lost on him. He dropped his duffle on the floor near a black Italian leather chair in front of a spotless glass desk that had some serious acreage. He hooked his thumbs into the empty belt loops on his faded jeans and stood at his ease as he regarded the Vampyre.

Duncan did not sit behind the desk, nor did he invite Rune to sit. Instead he moved to the window and looked toward the west. He put his hands in the pockets of his twenty-five-hundred-dollar suit and, for a moment, he went completely still as only Vampyres could. He looked like the airbrushed front cover of a *GQ* magazine.

Here it comes, Rune thought. Mow the lawn for the next thousand years. One single favor, stated in quite a simple sentence. Yeah Dragos, I know quite fucking well what I gave away.

"It's disappeared again," Duncan murmured.

"What?" Rune said.

"The island. It's disappeared again."

Rune looked out the window as well. The residual blood-red sunset glow was all but gone, but his sharp predator's eyes could pick out the details in the night as well as the Vampyre's could. The island had indeed faded from sight.

He shrugged and said, "Okay."

"That is where you are supposed to go," Duncan said.

Rune sighed. "When I got your email, I thought you would be giving me the instructions for this favor."

Duncan turned away from the window to face him. "From what little I understand, any instructions I might give you would not release you from your magical obligation. Your contract is with Carling, and she must order you in person. She is currently at her home on the Other island, and of course time flows differently there. I am merely supposed to verify you made it here by the stated deadline, and to give you directions on how to get there."

"So Carling lives on Blood Alley, huh?" Rune shook his head. Way to build an all-over fearsome reputation, Carling. Much like the feudal Wyr society, in the Nightkind demesne, might often equaled right, and Carling had ruled as Queen for a long time before she gave the crown to Julian. She had abdicated to take advantage of a loophole that had then existed in inter-demesne law, which allowed her to become the Nightkind Councillor for the Elder tribunal. The legal loophole had since been closed. Former demesne rulers were now barred from sitting on the tribunal, but Carling maintained her unique position. She was not just a Councillor on the Elder tribunal. Since Julian was Carling's progeny, he might rule the demesne, but Carling ruled Julian.

Duncan shook his head. "Blood Alley is a very unfortunate label and not at all accurate. The crossover passage and the island were discovered around 1836, and as soon as she had become aware of its existence, Carling laid claim to it. There were a few times when she was Queen that she had to take action against warring Vampyre families. Her response had to be severe enough to quell the upsurge in violence."

"Oh-kay," he muttered. "Been there, done that. I'm sure I've got a T-shirt somewhere to prove it. Why don't you hit me with those directions?"

"You must fly westward for a mile or so and circle around to fly back. As you return toward the Bay, keep the Golden Gate ahead of you, to your right about ten degrees, and fly low over the water. At that point you should feel the crossover passage down below. It follows a fissure in the ocean bed, so you'll have to dive and swim it. For those of us who no longer need to breathe, the swim is not an uncomfortable one. I have an oxygen tank ready for you to use should you need it. The technology is passive enough that it works."

What Duncan referred to was how the concentrated magic in Other lands suppressed certain technologies, especially those that acted on some principle of combustion. Among other things, electricity, guns and other modern weaponry did not work in Other lands, or if they worked, they did so only briefly and with chaotic and destructive consequences, which was why Niniane's friend Cameron had died when she shot Naida Riordan.

Passive technologies, like composting toilets, hypocaust systems, Melitta coffee filters, modern crossbow and compound bow designs, or designs that utilized solar heat worked just fine in Other lands. An oxygen tank was simply a vessel of compressed air that was released through a tube in a slow, controlled fashion. Filling an oxygen tank required a compressor, which would not work in an Other land, but the tank itself would be safe to use throughout the passage until it ran out of its supply.

Rune considered. "How long is the underwater passageway?"

Duncan told him, "I can swim it in just over ten minutes."

"I don't need the tank," said Rune. "I'll be fine." He bent to pick up his duffle. "I could use something watertight to put this in, though. It isn't much, a couple of changes of clothes, toothbrush and razor, Stephen King novel, yadda yadda." Along with an iPod, iPhone, a few more PowerBars, Glock and ammo, knives, a garotte, some throwing stars. Yadda yadda. The Glock, phone and iPod would travel fine as long as he didn't try to use them until he got back.

"We've got something you can use," Duncan said.

Rune took a half turn toward the door and regarded the Vampyre with an expectant expression. Moving along, here. Next phase. Gotta show up for my first day of work on time. I'll be trimming the lawn with a pair of manicure scissors. Trimming the whole island with a pair of manicure scissors? That's a thousand years right there, baby.

Duncan was staring at the tips of his polished shoes and frowning.

Perhaps a human might have seen a man deep in thought. Rune was a predator and far older than the human race. His focus narrowed. He watched how the Vampyre took a deep breath in an old habit he had not needed in over a hundred and twenty years. He noted the miniscule tightening around Duncan's pleasant, dark eyes, and the shift in the near invisible sheen on Duncan's silk tie as he swallowed.

Rune had earned his place as Dragos's First many centuries ago for a host of Powerful reasons. But there were other reasons why Rune was Dragos's First, and they had nothing to do with Power. Rune said in a quiet voice, "You got something you want to tell me, son?"

Duncan's gaze lifted quickly. "I have many things I want to tell you. I find that, for one reason or another, I am constrained."

"Attorney-client privilege?" Rune asked.

"That, and also there are constraints from my maker."

"Who is your maker?" Rune asked, although he was pretty sure he already knew the answer.

"Carling." Duncan gave him a self-conscious lopsided smile that was unexpectedly endearing. "I am her youngest."

Seriously, awww.

"Well, Duncan," Rune said. "Is there anything you want to tell me that you actually can tell me?"

Duncan's smile faded, and in that moment he didn't look young at all. He looked old, grieving, and more than a little frightened.

"Please be careful," Duncan said.

C arling unfolded a well-worn piece of paper and laid it on the polished granite countertop near the stove. She consulted the handwritten instructions that had been prepared for her by a human attendant.

Step one, make sure the wood stove has been lit and the burner is hot. Yes. Did she place the skillet on the burner for step two? She checked the list. No. Step two, spray the skillet with PAM. She did and then she set the skillet on the burner. Now add a few ounces of raw meat to the skillet. Stir with implement. She picked up the implement and considered. What is this thing called again? Ah yes, it is a spatula.

A sunny morning shone outside. The kitchen where Carling worked was a large foreign-feeling stone-walled area, with long wooden tables and granite counters, industrial-sized sinks, and a fireplace that was big enough to roast a pig in. Bright yellow sunshine spilled in from metal-paned windows. The kitchen was a peaceful quiet place without chattering sycophants populating it. She liked it much better now that it was nearly empty.

A small dog whined at Carling's feet. Rhoswen sulked nearby, well away from the spill of sunshine. "I don't understand why you insist on doing this," Rhoswen grumbled. "We have cans of dog food that it loves. Quite good, expensive premium dog food. I checked personally with its vet."

"I do not require you to understand," murmured Carling. She peered at the organic material in the skillet. It had started to sizzle. The red flesh was turning white. "What are we cooking again?"

"Chicken," Rhoswen said. "We are cooking chicken for incomprehensible reasons."

"Yes," Carling said.

She nudged the flesh around in the skillet. This is food. A warm scent filled the air. She sniffed it. Living creatures consider this scent aromatic, appetizing. They salivate, and their stomachs rumble.

The small dog barked.

Yes, and some of them yap.

The chicken must become white all the way through. It is okay if the outside becomes brown. In fact many creatures prefer it that way. With a sense of satisfaction, Carling removed the skillet from the heat. She used the implement to scrape the steaming material onto a plate for a tiny living creature.

She regarded the dog. It regarded her in return. She remembered the details from the vet's report. The dog was a six-pound Orange Sable Pomeranian. It had an exploding puffball double coat of hair that was brown and sable, with a touch of cream in its ludicrous curl of a tail. It had bright button-black eyes and a foxy narrow muzzle with a button-black nose. When she gave it her attention, it stood on its hind legs and twirled. Such happiness and excitement over a thing called breakfast.

She checked the last step on her list of instructions. Wait until the meat is cool enough to consume safely before placing the plate on the floor.

She looked at the steaming material on the plate. She looked back at the dog. It gave her a thrilled canine grin, pink tongue lolling to one side as it hopped on hind legs and pawed at the air. She spoke a word filled with Power. For a moment the air around the chicken shimmered. When she touched a finger to the meat, it was perfectly cool. Ah, that was much better.

A bell tolled on the ocean side of the sprawling stone house.

Both she and Rhoswen lifted their heads to look toward the sound. She told Rhoswen, "Go let the sentinel in."

The younger blonde Vampyre inclined her head and left the kitchen.

Carling twitched aside the hem of her black Egyptian cotton caftan as she crouched to set the plate of chicken in front of the dog. The next bit always puzzled her. She had witnessed many forms of greed over the centuries. But no matter how much the smell of the cooking chicken sent him into frenzy, when she set the plate of food in front of the dog, he always paused first to look at her before he fell on his meal to gobble it down.

Carling was a succubus, a Vampyre who could sense and feed off of emotions from living creatures. The little dog had emotions. They were bright colorful sparks that winked like fireflies. She knew what he felt when he gave her that look.

It was passionate gratitude.

Rhoswen returned after a few minutes. Carling looked up from the dog. He had finished his meal and draped himself across her bare feet. Rhoswen told her, "The Wyr is awaiting an audience with you in the great hall."

Carling nodded. She nudged the sleepy animal off her feet and pushed through the kitchen's double-swing doors before the dog could follow. Ignoring its complaining bark, she walked along the large silent flagstone-floored corridor to the great hall, the only sound a whisper of cloth as her caftan swirled around her ankles.

The house followed the general pattern of a medieval manor, with the kitchen, buttery and pantry off to one side, the two-story great hall with a massive six-foot-tall fireplace and its carved stone overmantel and more private apartments and rooms branching off the other side. Unlike a medieval manor, the great hall and the other oceanside rooms had floor-to-ceiling windows that overlooked the bluff upon which the house sat.

The house was bordered with a waist-high fieldstone wall that followed the furthermost periphery along the edge of the bluff. The land within the walls was cultivated with a dense profusion of flowers, yellow goldenstars, scarlet mariposa lilies, coast sunflowers, stream orchids, seaside daisies and island snapdragons. Climbing roses swarmed up a trellis that framed the front doors, their immense blooms drenched in fragrance.

The island itself was kidney-shaped and over four miles long. The house on the bluff was located in the inner curve of the kidney. A narrow path zigzagged down the side of the bluff to a wide beach where a couple of sailboats were moored. There were several other, smaller houses that dotted the area around the large stone manor house, but currently those stood empty. A redwood forest towered on the farthest end of the island, the gigantic trees thousands of years old, their upper heights fed from the mists that rolled in off the ocean. Shy, secretive winged creatures lived in the uppermost branches of those ancient redwoods. They hid whenever other creatures came near.

Carling felt the Wyr before she stepped into the hall and laid eyes on him. She paused at the kitchen entrance to the hall to absorb the shock of his presence.

He stood hipshot in front of the windows, with the kind of ease that came from someone who had everything going for him and nothing to prove. His back was to her, his hands in the rear pockets of torn faded jeans as he looked out toward the ocean. His hair tumbled damp and tousled to broad shoulders. She caught the smell of brine and the warm virile scent of a healthy Wyr male. Thousands of years ago he had towered over humans, a strange gigantic, fierce god. Even now he stood taller than most men, the long strong lines of his body epitomizing masculine strength and grace.

More than just the impact of the physical, however, was the punch of the aetheric force around him. Even standing at rest, he radiated a ferocious vitality. Energy and Power boiled off of him in a corona of rippling waves that were invisible to most people, but she could see them pouring off of him like heat waves rising from a sun-baked highway in the desert. All of the immortal Wyr that had come into being at the time the earth was formed had this same primal life force. They carried within them sparks of creation's first fire.

Carling took a deep breath, an anachronistic throwback to an ancient time. She took note of her body's involuntary response to the onslaught of Rune's presence, even as his head cocked to one side at the small telltale sound. He turned to face her.

Then there was the other shock to the system as she looked upon the strong, bold clean lines of his face. His facial bone structure had a refinement that was echoed in the frame of his body, a masculine elegance that caught at the eye and tugged at the heart. He had a beautiful mouth, with sensually carved, mobile lips, but his capstone feature was his worldly, knowledgeable lion's gaze.

Those breathtaking eyes were smiling at her now. They pulled her across the room toward him.

"You've got an awesome crib here," said Rune. "Way to be

all-over gothic, Carling. What happens if you sail away from the island?"

"Eventually after you lose sight of the island, you end up sailing back toward land. This is just a small pocket of Other land with only the one underwater crossover point. There is nothing else here but the island and ocean."

"Sweet."

She prowled toward him, this male who radiated like a sun. The Power of his presence prickled along her skin. Each step she took brought her closer to him and made her feel more alive. Compared to his full-blown Technicolor-rich emotions, all the many other creatures she had sensed and fed from were weak and pastel, like watered milk. Rune was a rich and fluid fountain of nourishment like the deepest ruby claret. She felt a ghost of something that must have once been hunger. His blood would taste spectacular, as burning and as intense as the rarest liqueur.

The expression in his eyes changed as she approached. His smile became sharper, deeper, and showed a hint of even white teeth. His emotional palette shifted too, the ruby claret flowing with enticing and inexplicable complexities.

She came toe-to-toe with him. At five-foot-six, she had once been a tall woman. Now she was considered an average height. She had to tilt back her head to look full-bore and unblinking into that lion's gaze. She noted how his breathing deepened and his eyes dilated. What was that emotion she sensed from him? A ghost of elusive memory drifted through the back of her mind. She had felt it once, long ago. It had made her drunken and impetuous, vivid with reckless laughter.

She turned and stalked around him, considering. He pivoted backward in a slow circle that met her pace. He angled his head to match the tilt of hers and came close so that they were nose-to-nose with each other, two predators mature in Power and engaged in a sizing-up showdown.

Unafraid? Yes, he was unafraid, but that was not the emotion she sensed that tugged at her memory. Fascination? Yes, he felt that too, but that was not what she tried so hard to remember.

This gryphon called himself Rune Ainissesthai. Rune for glyph, a sigil that was a stroke on a page, but more than that, rune for mystery, magic. Ainissesthai was old Greek for speaking in riddles. The mysterious magical riddle.

"Rune Ainissesthai," she whispered. "What is the riddle?"

His expression flared with electric light. Oh, I've got your attention now, don't I, Wyr? She smiled. Did you think everyone had forgotten the meaning of your name?

"You know better than to ask a question like that," Rune said. His voice had dropped to a low gravelly murmur that prowled across her skin.

"Rune Ainissesthai," she whispered a second time, and the Power she wielded made the sound of his name reverberate between them like the singing of a Chinese Buddhist bowl. "Why do you come to me?"

"I come to pay my debt," said Rune, and the cry of the eagle echoed in his reply.

"Rune Ainissesthai," she whispered for the third time. "Will you do my bidding for the measure of one favor to pay that debt?"

"You know I will," the gryphon replied, and the growl of the lion was in his voice.

She struck the reverberation between them a single blow with her Power so that it rang like a gong against the stone walls of the great hall, and the magic writ was cast. She smiled. "The bargain has been struck, and answered."

Now he was bound and he truly had no choice but to do her bidding. You are mine, she said silently to his tall strong form. Mine to do with as I wish. For this moment in time, I own you. And what shall I have you do, you easygoing, proud, insouciant alpha male? What task shall you complete before you take your leave from me and go back to your unending life?

What did someone who was dying do with a rare and extravagant gift such as this?

The smile faded from her lips. The predatory impulses in her darkened and grew invisible fangs. Her dark eyes glittered with a carapace like obsidian glass, and the line of her mouth hardened.

She said, "Kneel."

She felt his surprise as her command jolted through him.

But then he did a thing that surprised her in return. He raised his eyebrows, gave her that easygoing insouciant grin of his and said, "Okey-dokey."

With a flourish he went gracefully down on one knee in front of her.

What was this? He was down on the floor, his powerful broad shoulders dipped in subjugation. He even bowed his head. He gave every appearance of submission, and performed flawlessly to the letter of her order, but . . .

Deep in the axis of that fierce remarkable soul, the alpha male still reigned. She circled behind him and stepped close to his broad shoulders to put her lips near his ear. She whispered, "You're not really kneeling inside."

He cocked his head to look at her over one shoulder. His reckless gaze laughed at her. He whispered back, "You didn't order me to do that. It would require an entirely different bargain for me to really kneel to you."

Caught in the unknown riddle, she asked, "What bargain would that require?"

He gave her a slow smile. "You must give me a kiss."

The sleek arch of her eyebrows lifted. "Just a kiss?"

"Just that."

"The bargain is struck," she said.

"And answered," he growled.

Carling put a hand onto his shoulder as she prowled to stand in front of him. Then she slid her hands along the warm sun-bronzed skin of his jaw. She tilted his handsome wild face up to hers and he let her. Then she bent to place her cool lips on his hot carved lips.

Her body moved in the impulse to breathe again, and she allowed it. His masculine Power enveloped her, and it was spiced with sensuality and warmth as it caressed her like a sun-filled breeze.

She lifted her head and stared down at him. She narrowed her eyes. She said, "You're still not really kneeling inside."

Tap, tap, went her bare foot.

He cocked an eyebrow.

"What else did you expect, Carling?" he replied. "That wasn't a real kiss."

≈ THREE ≈

Her eyes narrowed further. "What do you mean, that wasn't a real kiss?"

Rune drew back a few inches to consider her more closely. She had to know, didn't she? She was far too old and sophisticated not to. She had, after all, spent her youth in human-kind's earthy past. She must have taken countless lovers. The lion in him bared its teeth and hissed at the thought.

Sparks of temper had begun to flicker in those long almond-shaped Egyptian eyes of hers. Rune widened his own gaze. He was greedy to suck in every detail of this gorgeous deadly woman. He didn't want to blink and miss a moment.

Somehow Carling managed to make the concepts of beauty and perfection seem mundane. He took in the long glossy dark hair that swung free to her slender waist. It had rich auburn glints in the sun, as though she burned with a deep internal fire. He contemplated the graceful length of her neck, plunging as it did to curvaceous collarbones that spread outward toward shapely shoulders like the wings on a dove. He sensed the ripe fullness of her unbound breasts moving underneath the loose black caftan, and snap, the shutter in his mind took him back to the river when he had stared at those bare round voluptuous globes, striped with white scars and crowned with dark nipples standing erotically erect, and when he had looked at her, he had felt a need so stark it had become a physical pain and a spiritual torment.

For as long as he could remember, Carling had been a singularity. Even though she was always accompanied by a retinue of tall, beautiful and deadly elegant Vampyres as attendants, and even though those attendants often included male companions, she outshone every other star in her constellation as she burned with the intensity of a supernova. Women viewed her as a threat, and males looked at her with avarice, and she taught them all the measure of their own limitations.

Rune's need revved a high-end horsepower engine and took him on a Harley-Davidson ride. He rose to his feet, and her storm-filled imperious gaze lifted with him.

"Perhaps you have forgotten," he said in a gentle voice. "Let me show you."

Then it was his turn to frame the pure slender arc of her jaw between his large callused hands, and she let him. Her honey-colored skin was cool to the touch, and her Power thrummed against his palms. Good night, how did she hold all of it in and not fly apart at the seams?

He stroked her lips with the ball of one thumb. Her skin had a silken texture, the soft plump flesh giving way under the small pressure. His hands were too hardened from fighting and other manual labor. The only way he could truly know the depth of that exquisite softness was to cover it with his mouth.

"If I may," he murmured.

He bent his head toward that incomparable face, giving her plenty of time to react and to tell him no. Then he fought to hide how he shuddered deep inside as he covered her lips with his own, stroking along the unique plush terrain of her mouth, focusing all of his attention on relishing the precious experience.

And she let him.

He took care with her. One should treat the rarest of treasures with respect. He coaxed the tilt of her head into the right angle and adjusted his stance in such a way that he just barely brushed against the front of her body. He laid the length of one of his hands at the juncture where the bottom of her skull curved into the slender flower-stalk of her graceful neck. His fingers were so long they cradled her effortlessly.

He invited her to lean back into his steady supporting hold, leading her into the first steps of an intimate dance. She followed him, shifting just that exquisite amount he coaxed from her and no more, letting her head rest in his hand, which made her spine arch with languorous intent. Holy hell, she would be an intelligent lover, the most ingenious of lovers that understood the intricate nuances of the dance, and when to listen and respond to the tiniest catch of a sigh, and when to let rip-roaring loose with everything one had.

Her flesh warmed beneath his mouth and between his hands, and she took a breath. It was the third breath she had taken since they had met that morning. Each useless, telltale one made him want to growl in triumph.

He dared to take the succulent swell of her lower lip between his teeth and suckle at it, ever so lightly.

Her lips trembled and fell open.

The gryphon inside him roared.

He took his time taking the internal private place of her mouth. He slanted his head sideways and curled his tongue into her. She made a low throaty noise that was so sensual it rocked his soul and shoved him into a paradigm shift. She wound her arms around his neck, leaned full against him and kissed him back.

Rune's control jettisoned off the planet, leaving him behind to snatch at her in amazement. He crushed her to him, his arms around her waist, lifting her off the ground as he speared into her blindly. His heart pounded in massive sledgehammer strokes, and his skin became a thin veneer that cloaked a pillar of flame. He put a hand to her hip and gripped her hard, then ran his hand compulsively up the length of her torso to the weighted fullness of her breast. The plump round mound filled his greedy palm, and she fit, she just fucking fit, like some keystroke password to an unbreakable code. A sound came out of her. It sounded raw with surprise and he swallowed it down. His shaking fingers sought for and found her nipple jutting underneath the cloth.

She kissed him back with the same ferocity. She did, he would swear she did. Her body trembled too, and arched taut with craving.

Then she wrenched her face away. He reared back his head

to look at her in sharp inquiry. Her mouth was swollen, blushed red, and her dark eyes were wide and blank with shock.

In a ragtag shred of sound that was all that remained of his voice, he said, "That was a real kiss."

Her gaze locked on him. Her lips moved, as if she would try to say something. Then he remembered the stupid bargain his damn fool self had offered.

He eased her back down until her bare feet connected with the flagstone floor, and he went down on one knee again to bow in full reverence to the onetime Queen of the Nightkind. She embodied the pinnacle of what a man desired and what he should fear, and she deserved to have the world laid at her feet.

Carling stared. Rune was down on his knee again where she had ordered him, but this time she could sense from his emotions that he meant it. He gave full sincere, gracious homage to her. She could see it clear all the way through him, only instead of humbling that insouciant alpha male, somehow it ennobled him with the courtly aspect of a medieval knight.

Then she understood what the emotion was that she had sensed from him, because he taught her to experience it again for herself.

Desire. He looked on her and felt desire.

As a succubus, Carling had become an expert on all the flavors and nuances of emotion, but it had been so long since anyone had looked on her with desire, so very long since she had felt any form of desire for herself, she felt as though she was experiencing it for the first time. Then a wild upsurge of reaction like rage shook through her, and it was a dark violent storm. When he lifted his head, she slapped him so hard he rocked back on his heels. She intentionally curved her fingers into claws and dug her nails in cruelly, raking him from cheekbone to jaw. Blood sprang from the wounds.

"We're done here," she said through her teeth. "Now leave my home."

He stared at her, his expression turning hard. Deliberately, calmly, he raised one hand to blot the blood that dripped down the side of his face. She saw that the wounds were already closing over.

She could not stand to look at him any longer. She whirled and stormed away. She barely knew where she was going.

Anywhere, away, as the wild upsurge whirled through the cemetery in her head, blowing leaves across gravestones.

He made her feel things she had not felt in a winter's age. How many centuries had it been since she had known desire? It had been so long she had forgotten. She should not feel such things as desire, or yearning, or to look even for the barest moment at the possibility of a branching off in her life toward something hardly seen and deathly beautiful, for it could never be hers.

Desire was not a gift to someone like her. Instead it was a beautiful agony.

"I am a bad woman," she whispered to herself. Two tears slid down her cheeks. There was certain symmetry in that as well.

She was a bad woman at the end of a very long, bad life.

R une stood and wiped the rest of the blood off his face as he watched Carling storm away. Aroused and furious, he breathed hard and fought for control as the predator in him roared to give chase. Tension vibrated through his body and made the world shake.

But we're done here, she said. And no means no.

I gotta hand it to you, Carling, he thought. It's never something mundane with you.

He was free to go, his obligation paid. The favor had been wasted with a spendthrift hand, as if she were a spoiled child who had been given too many toys. His lips curled back from clenched teeth.

In the end, it was not the predator, his common sense or his intelligence, but his pride that won out. He snatched up his duffle. He had left the waterproof container Duncan had given him down on the beach. It was time to move on. He could sneak in a few days of R & R before he headed back to New York. Get his head screwed back on straight before he went home to deal with Dragos again. By God, he had earned that much, at least.

He yanked open the arched double front doors and strode down the path toward the rest of his life. The hot blaze from the yellow morning sun was a welcome blast in his face. The chill bite of the ocean when he swam back to sanity would be even more welcome. There were a lot of fun things to do in San Francisco. He would check into the suite at the Fairmont Hotel, get him some of that five-star treatment and go on the hunt for some scotch and a plate of beef bourguignon as he debated how much time he should take for himself before he got in touch with Dragos again. Maybe the Fairmont had beef bourguignon on their room service menu. Hot food, booze, five-star service and a good game on a plasma TV. Or maybe he could find an old Gamera movie on cable. He loved that giant flying Japanese turtle. Yeah baby. He heard it all calling his name.

"Sentinel, wait!" Rhoswen called behind him. Her urgent call was accompanied by frenzied high-pitched barking. "Damn it, you piece of shit, get back here!"

Excuse the fuck out of me? Incredulous, he tilted his head and pivoted with slow precision.

Rhoswen stood in the shadow at the open front door, well back from the lethal spill of sunshine, while a small puffball with fierce black-button eyes and tiny white teeth hurtled down the path toward him.

Rune's eyebrows rose. If he was not mistaken, that puffball was a Pomeranian. He certainly saw his fair share of them, living as he did in New York.

Let's review.

He looked up at Rhoswen. Vampyre. Then he looked down at the ankle-biter. Pomeranian.

He double-checked. Vampyre. Pomeranian.

He said to Rhoswen, "You have a dog."

"No," she said. The look of loathing she gave the ankle-biter was clear even from a distance. "Carling has a dog. I'm just cursed to look after it sometimes." She hissed at it, "*Come here!*"

It snarled at Rune as it sank its teeth into the hem of his pants leg.

Rune's normal good humor resurfaced and he started to grin. "Carling has a dog," he murmured to himself. "No, Carling has a rude Pomeranian." He raised his voice and said to Rhoswen, "I don't think he can hear you over all the noise he's making."

"The little freak never hears me," Rhoswen said. Frustration vibrated in the Vampyre's beautiful voice. She gave Rune an apologetic smile. "Would you mind terribly bringing him back over here?"

"Not at all," Rune said. He scooped up the ankle-biter in one hand and held it up for a closer inspection.

All four tiny paws scrabbled in the air as it growled at Rune. He noted two of its legs were crooked. Rune said, "What a little Napoleon you are." He strolled back to the doorway. "Why does Carling have a dog?"

"I have no idea," the Vampyre said. "You would have to ask her. Seven months ago we were traveling from a Nightkind function back to Carling's San Francisco town house when she saw this thing by the side of the road. It had been hit by a car. I was going to snap its neck and put it out of its misery, but then Carling cast a healing spell on it and insisted we take it to a vet." Rhoswen looked up at Rune in outrage. "She cooks it chicken."

Rune handed the little Napoleon over to her. Rhoswen clutched the squirming dog to her chest, and her eyes filled with tears.

He frowned. He had never seen Rhoswen as anything but composed. He said, "You're not crying because Carling cooks chicken."

Rhoswen shook her head and buried her face in the dog's fur.

This is the point where you keep your mouth shut and mind your own business, son. This is the point where you turn right around again and walk away. So get your ass moving and roll on down the highway. This is not the point where you lift up your head and realize that you've been noticing for a while now that something is off.

He cocked his head and listened. He heard nothing but the sounds of the wind blowing through trees outside, and the sharp cry of seagulls overhead. When had he ever seen Carling without some kind of entourage streaming behind her like a comet's tail?

He said, "Why are you and Carling the only two people on the island?"

The Vampyre said in a muffled voice, "Because she's dying, and everybody else is afraid."

Midnight stillness spread black ink throughout Rune.

He stepped back inside, shut the door and set his duffle bag against the wall. He said to Rhoswen, "I think you had better tell me everything."

Carling sat in her armchair. It was precisely positioned in front of the window so that the band of morning sunshine fell across the floor just inches from her bare feet.

She looked at the transparent sunshine slanting in the air in front of her. It spilled everywhere, a wealth of light more extravagant than a king's treasure and deadlier than nightshade. She dropped the protective shield of Power she kept wrapped perpetually around her like a cloak. The shield allowed her to walk in the full light of day. Without it, she would burn to death just like any other Vampyre would.

She did not remember the pleasure of basking in the warm sun. She remembered the fact of it, but not the sensation. Had it been anything like basking in the warm glow of a fire? That was how she imagined it was, anyway.

Now all the sun promised her was pain and immolation.

Setting her teeth, she held out a hand and touched the sunshine.

Agony seared her. She saw smoke rise from her skin and smelled her own scorched flesh. A split second was almost more than she could bear. Any longer exposure and her hand would burst into flames. She snatched her hand away and looked at the blisters that had formed along the fingers and the back. The blisters began to heal as she watched.

She braced herself and bathed her other hand in the molten light.

A deep familiar voice swore nearby. Someone grabbed her arm in a powerful grip and shoved her, armchair and all, several feet back from the sunshine. The chair's wooden legs scraped along the floor. She blinked until her vision cleared.

Rune crouched in front of her, the long broad muscles of his shoulders bunched. He held her by the wrists. Shaking with pain, her fingers curled, she tried to pull free but he refused to let her go. Strong as she was, he was stronger. Extreme emotion darkened his gaze, and his handsome face was settled in lines of severity. The skin around his taut mouth whitened as he watched the blisters on her hands fade.

Carling regarded him wearily. After her emotional storm earlier and the twin jolts of agony, she didn't know if she had the energy to face Rune's particular brand of volcanic energy. His presence blasted her hypersensitive nerves.

"Sorry about that," Rune said, his voice controlled and even. His rigid grip on her arms relaxed and became gentle. "I had a knee-jerk reaction when I saw your hand burning. Does it help?"

Her weary look turned speculative. His control was not as reassuring as it might otherwise have been, coupled as it was with the violent upheaval she could sense roiling through his emotions. "What do you mean, does it help? Has someone been talking out of turn? I told you to go. What are you still doing here?"

"Yes, someone has been talking," said Rune. "I know everything, or at least I know everything that Rhoswen knows." He let his hands slip down her arms to clasp her fingers with care. "Come on, tell me. Why were you burning yourself?"

She looked over his broad shoulders toward the daylight, and chose not to struggle for the return of her hands. His were warm and callused, broad-palmed and long-fingered. "Sometimes the pain helps me to fight off an episode."

"Rhoswen called it fading. Is that what it's like?"

"Not really," she said. "It is a disassociation from reality. Sometimes I go into the past. Sometimes I don't know where I go."

Rune eased one of her hands into her lap and released it. He took the long dark fall of her hair and smoothed it behind one of her shoulders.

Her eyelids lowered and she glanced sidelong at his hand. This Wyr had temerity, she would give him that. An impulse to violence flickered through her. She had struck at him once. Maybe she would again. Her gaze lifted to his face. Four pale lines still scored one lean cheek. They would be gone in another half hour or so.

She could see in his eyes that he knew her impulse to violence was there. That did not stop him from reaching higher to tuck a lock of her hair behind her ear, stroking along the delicate shell of flesh. He touched her as he had earlier, as if he thought she was exquisite beyond all words, his expression calm, unafraid. It bewildered her. Why would he do such a thing? Why did his touch cause her to feel such a dark violent pain?

Why was her other hand still resting in his?

"I do not think you are a very sensible man," she murmured.

"No doubt you are correct," he replied. "And I am still here because I have to ask you a question. Why do you have a dog?"

"Rhoswen has asked me that many times," she said. "I don't know why. He was hurt badly when we found him. He was down to almost half his body weight, so the vet thought he had been a stray for a while, and then he had been hit by a car. Even though he is so tiny, he has a ferocious spark of a spirit. He was broken all over and he just wouldn't die." She shrugged. "And I brought him home."

Rune's gaze was too keen as he inspected her face. What did he think he saw in her? "And now you cook him chicken," he said.

"He's so happy to eat," she said. She looked down. Her hand was still in Rune's. He was rubbing her healed fingers with his thumb. "Dancing fit-to-be-tied happy."

"I must say, he's got a point there," said Rune with a lop-sided smile.

"I've been trying to remember what it's like to be hungry," Carling said. "I cook the chicken, and I smell it and I say to myself, this is food." She whispered, "I think I'm trying to remember what it is like to be alive before I die."

Her words ghosted through the silence in the room.

Rune was still crouching at her feet like a great lion. His presence was more intense than a fire's. He had not only warmed her through, she felt nourished and revitalized. He raised her fingers to his lips and kissed them. "I would far rather try to find a way to keep you alive before you die," he said.

She stirred. "Rune," she said.

His fierce gaze captured and held hers. "You threw away that favor I owed you."

"I did worse than that," she said. She touched his cheek with a finger. "And I may do worse again."

He rolled his eyes. What a remarkably handsome man he was. "So what," he said. "I kissed you and you slapped me. What an utter heroine you are."

"You have got to be joking," she said.

"Utter. Heroine."

She leaned forward, so she could better stare him down. "You wear the most god-awful clothes. Look at you, with your jeans torn out at the knees. Who would want to wear a T-shirt like that, with a hairy man in spectacles on it? It's ridiculous."

"Don't be knocking my Jerry Garcia threads," Rune said. His strong-boned features were creased in a sharp, catlike smile. "You're one to talk, the way you run around in those Egyptian caftans without a single stitch of clothing on underneath. Lady, I've been watching you and I can tell."

"You've been watching me ever since I walked out of the river," she whispered. "I could tell."

"I haven't been able to look away," he whispered back, "because you are stunning. In fact, you can go ahead and slap me again if you want. Let's get it over with, because I think I'm going to have to kiss you again, and it is so fucking worth it."

The desire was back. It roared out of him, or out of her. She wasn't sure, she couldn't tell. He leaned forward, and she sat back sharply and put a restraining hand against the hard broad muscles of his chest. "Rune," she said again, her voice cold and clear. "Stop."

His eyes narrowed. "Why? You were totally with me in that kiss."

"And you're a fool." She shoved him hard. It sent him sprawling back several feet, in the full spill of the morning sunshine. He propped himself back on his hands and looked at her in assessment, a great powerful beauty of a man, with rich suntanned skin stretched over a long, sinuous gracefully muscled body. It hurt to look at him.

She stood and stepped right up to the edge of the sunshine, and his lazy smile vanished. He sprang to his feet faster than she had ever seen him move, and he put his body between her and the sunlight.

"Look at us," she said. Her face and eyes were hard. She gestured at them both, at him standing bathed in the light and her in the shadow. "This is why. And one of us is dying."

"I take it back," Rune said. "You're not an utter heroine. You're a drama queen." He smacked her in the shoulders with the flat of his hands and knocked her back a step. She stared at him in shock as he stepped from the sunlight into the shadow. "Well, would you look at that. It's a perfectly permeable line. You can cross it too when you've got yourself shielded."

"How dare you?" she hissed.

"People always forget I have this side to me. I don't know why. You might be surprised at what I would dare," Rune said. He advanced on her, his expression blazing. "What did you think? Were you just going to sit out here on your lonesome island and pass away?"

He looked furious, magnificent. The sight of him clawed at her. She blurred with her deadly speed and struck at him, and she was shocked anew as he knocked the blow away. Holy gods, he was fast.

"I've got news for you, princess," he snarled. "It's time for you to wake the fuck up and do something about saving your own life."

"Do you think I have not tried?" she shouted. Rage blinded her. She struck at him again, and this time managed to hit him in the chest. "You impudent son of a bitch. I have been researching this for almost two centuries. I have dosed myself with my own healing potions, and they've worked for a while but now they don't. I don't know *WHAT ELSE TO DO.*"

She spun away and drove herself forward, wild to get away from him.

He sucked in a breath and lunged to snatch her against his chest.

She froze as she realized what she had done. She had almost plunged unshielded into the full light of day.

She stared at the line she had nearly crossed. Rune wrapped his arms around her from behind and held her so tight she felt his heartbeat thudding against the skin between her shoulder blades. They were both breathing heavily.

"That was remarkably idiotic of me," she said. She had to clear her throat before she could get the words out. "Thankfully I am not often this stupid or I wouldn't have survived for so long."

She recast the shield spell and Power shimmered over her skin.

He must have felt her cast the spell, but he made no move to let her go. Instead he laid his head on her shoulder.

He said in her hair, "I still owe you a favor."

She sighed. "You don't owe me a thing," she said. "You are perfectly free, as nature intended you to be."

"Then forget about the damn favor," said Rune. "I'm still going to stay. We're going to find a way to make this better, because Carling, I am not ready for you to go gentle into that good night."

She held herself tense as she considered his words. Could she summon the energy and interest to live when she had grown accustomed to the thought of dying? What could Rune do that she hadn't already done? She was a sorceress at the top of her game, but no matter how old or accomplished she was, he was still a creature that was far older. He might well know of things or think of options she hadn't tried.

The tension flowed out of her body, and she rested back against him in tacit acceptance.

"I have not gone gently anywhere," Carling said as she turned her head to put her cheek against his. "I don't know why death should be any different."

═ FOUR ═

Rune held still as he savored the feel of Carling's pliant body in his arms, her cool cheek pressed against his.

She tingled along all of his senses. The weight of her curved body rested in his arms, and her skin felt unbelievably soft against his own weather-beaten cheek. The spiced fragrance she wore plucked at his imagination with images of distant places, and underneath that, she carried the delicious, sexy scent of an aroused woman. The clever dangerous volatility of her mind roused him to razor-sharp alertness, and the smoky hint of her Power brushed along his like a sleek black cat winding around his ankles. It made his claws itch to come out. He wanted to take the delicate lobe of her ear between his teeth and suckle at it. He wanted to claw at the walls.

He knew he had to curb this fascination he had developed for her. In fact, as soon as he had an opening in his hectic schedule, he planned to get right on that. There were so many reasons for him to do so it made him tired just to think of listing them all. Carling's little gesture between light and shadow might have pissed him off, but that symbolism also held all the weight of the complex differences between them in terms of race, lifestyle and political allegiance.

He also knew he had not been wrong. He could still feel the sensuous length of her arms as they had wound around his neck earlier. She had kissed him back and she had liked it too much. That was the reason for the shock he had seen in her eyes, and it had everything to do with why she had slapped him.

And she was dying. Everything inside him shouted in outraged denial against it. It didn't seem possible. All the evidence pointed to her being in perfect health. Her energy was too vibrant, too vital.

Not only that, she had been a fact of his existence for far too long. At first she had been a vague rumor he had heard about a desert tribal queen in North Sahara. Then she had become a reputation, as she rose in rank within the Vampyre communities of the ancient Mediterranean. During these last few centuries in North America, as various Powers in the Elder Races carved out their political niches and geographic boundaries, she had become a reality in power-brokering inter-demesne relations.

He sensed her intention as she began to move. He let her go before she had a chance to think he held her for even a moment too long.

His mind sharpened into crystalline lines of logic as he turned to the issue at hand. He said, "I would like to know what steps you've taken and what research you've done. There's no point in going over ground you've already covered."

"Of course," Carling said. She frowned as she considered him. Then she apparently came to some decision. She told him, "Come with me."

He fell into step beside her. She led him a different way through the house. Rhoswen had disappeared with the dog, perhaps to rest. While Vampyres could and often did remain awake throughout the day, sometimes for days at a time, it was typically as much a strain on them as staying up all night was for most humans.

Carling led him out the back through a bright sun-drenched vegetable garden, where overripe tomatoes, green peppers and cucumbers spilled to the ground. She took him down a short path to a stone cottage nestled in a copse of eucalyptus and palm trees. He could feel the Power in the building as they drew close. It was saturated with a sense of her feminine presence.

She stopped at the arched wooden door, took hold of the

door handle, and spoke a word. There was the small sound of a metallic click. She pushed the door open.

She said, "I have another office in my town house in the city, but I prefer to work on magic or Power-related issues here, where I can better control the consequences of any unforeseen events and there aren't so many other people around." She gestured in invitation.

He stepped inside and looked around with acute interest. The cottage was bigger than he had first thought. It looked clean and airy with polished oak floors. The main room and short hallway were painted a mellow sage green, with cream trim. Two armchairs were pulled in front of a fireplace, and there was also a wooden table and benches, clean bare countertops, a wood stove, a sink and cabinets.

Carling strode down a short hallway, and he followed her past a small modern-looking blue-tiled bathroom and two other rooms, one painted a warm orange and the other a rich gold. Both rooms held tall wooden bookshelves that were filled with books. Rune caught a glimpse of one shelf that was comprised of cubbyholes that looked to be filled with scrolls of papyrus. He was quite sure he was looking at one of the rarest collections of magic lore in the world, amassed, no doubt, over many centuries of patient research and effort.

Carling stepped into a third room where a mahogany desk and leather chair were placed strategically near French-style doors. The room's neutral tones brought the eye immediately to the small private walled courtyard, where a brilliant profusion of flowering plants burgeoned just on the other side of the doors. The rest of the room was filled with file cabinets and what appeared to be a large old wooden wardrobe carved with symbols that seemed to shimmer. The front doors had a metal lock that was tarnished with age.

When he looked at the carved wardrobe, something crept along the edges of his mind. It was a dark oily perversion of a feeling. His lip lifted in an instinctive snarl.

Carling slammed her fist into the wood as she walked past and said, "Shut up."

The whispering stopped abruptly.

Well, now that was just too much to pass up without comment. He didn't even try. He said, "What's in the wardrobe?"

She glanced at him. "Books that don't behave."

Misbehaving books? Not bothering to hide his skepticism, he said, "Uh-huh."

She gave him a narrow-eyed look and went back to the wardrobe to unlock it with another Power-filled word. Then she opened the doors wide, stepped to one side and gestured with a snappy flip of her fingers. "See for yourself."

The interior was filled with shelves, and what certainly did appear to be books. Rune stepped closer, angling his head in order to read the spines. There weren't any titles printed on the spines. These books were hand-stitched and very old.

That one—was that . . . ? The whispering started again, very low, at the edge of his consciousness. He reached out and Carling grabbed him by the wrist. After the first hard squeeze, she pushed him away gently.

"These should only be handled with gloves," she said. "Their magic is too dark and invasive."

"You make them sound infectious," he said. He glanced at her. "That one is not made of leather."

"Well," she said, "it is a certain kind of leather."

His eyebrows plummeted in a fierce frown and his nostrils pinched in distaste. "Your magic doesn't feel black like this."

"That's because it isn't." She shut and locked the doors again. "I've made my fair share of mistakes over the centuries, but I'm glad to say turning to Powers that black hasn't been one of them. They demand too high a level of sacrifice. They eat everything you give them and then they take your soul as well."

"Then why do you keep these?"

The look Carling gave him at that had turned quizzical. She walked to her desk. "Do you not study the tools your enemies use?"

He folded his arms across his chest and frowned. "Yes, but generally those tools are not . . . infectious."

"Where would treatment methods for the Ebola virus be if it were not studied? This is no different and, believe me, I take precautions. Thankfully the need to consult those resources is rare, which is why they sometimes get restless. Things that are made with black magic are hungry and they are never satisfied."

"You talk about them as though they're sentient." He glared at the cabinet, the hackles raised at the back of his neck.

"I think they are, at least semi-sentient. Something lingers of their creators, along with something of the souls of the victims that were sacrificed in their creation." She sat at the desk and opened the lowest drawer, which was unlocked. He could see it contained files labeled in a neat hand. She pulled out a few notebooks and closed the drawer. "This is the distillation of the last few centuries of work I've done on trying to find a way to halt the progression of Vampyrism."

He regarded her with a keen gaze. "And halting the progression of the disease is more preferable than finding a cure, because a cure would make you human again?"

"Theoretically. Unfortunately too much of this is still theoretical, because there really is no known cure. And there are serious issues and questions should a 'cure' ever be found." She handed the notebooks to him.

He opened the top notebook to look at the first page. It was written in the same neat hand that had created the file labels. "I would want to know how a cure would be tested," he remarked. "And where, and on whom."

She shrugged. "Perhaps a big medical facility with a focus on research might take it on, like Johns Hopkins University. There might be enough Vampyres who are unhappy enough that they would be willing to take some risks, but there has been no code of ethics developed for clinical trials because there's nothing that has been successfully developed enough to test."

"What are the other issues that need considering?" he asked.

She regarded him for a moment, as if collecting her thoughts. Then she said, "What are the consequences of a potential cure? Could a 'cured' Vampyre be turned again, and if so, what would be the results? Or would it be irreversible for a Vampyre, like Vampyrism is now for humans? Would a Vampyre simply revert back to being human? What would be the state of their health when they reverted? Would they become as they were before? Some Vampyres were terminally ill from other diseases before they were turned. Or would there be other complications such as, for example, advanced or accelerated aging, or a compromised immune system? And would those complications increase in severity according to the age of the Vampyre involved?"

He shook his head. "In those scenarios, the cure would quite literally kill you."

"Yes." Carling gathered her long dark hair together and twisted it into a long rope that she wound into a knot. She pinned the knot into place with two pencils from the desk, her movements fast and economical.

Rune's gaze lingered on the heavy sable-colored twist of hair lying on Carling's elegant neck. He wanted to see her pin her hair up again, and he fought a sudden puerile urge to pluck out the pencils. Her hair would spill down that hourglass back, the silken ends splashing like midnight water against the womanly swell of her trim, shapely ass. She would give him that quick annoyed look of hers, or maybe she would be angrier. Maybe she would try to slap him again, and he would catch her wrist and yank her to him . . .

Arousal sank sharpened claws into him and dug in deep. His body hardened and he turned away to hide it.

Walking over to the French doors, he opened the top notebook and flipped through it then took a quick look at the others. There were perhaps two hundred and fifty pages, all told, which was concise, given the amount of time and effort she had put into the research. She had called it a "distillation," which would have meant at some point she had gone through it all and stripped out everything extraneous.

He went back to the first notebook and read a few lines. He tapped a finger on the page and murmured, "This is not light reading."

"I could summarize verbally for you," said Carling. "But I don't recommend it."

He didn't want to listen to any verbal summary before he'd had a chance to look at the details of her research and come to his own conclusions, but he was curious about her reasoning, so he asked, "Why not?"

She gave him a bitter smile. "I no longer trust my mind and neither should you."

The pain in her dark eyes was terrible. He noted the stiff way she held herself and knew better than to offer a physical gesture of comfort. He took a deep breath and let it out slow and easy. "Fair enough," he said after a moment. "Do you want me to read it here?"

"It doesn't matter," she said. Her gaze flickered and fell away. She looked out the window at the small courtyard. "We have the island to ourselves. You may read wherever you are comfortable."

"All right." He willed her to let her rigid spine relax, for the pain to ease away. More to distract her than from any real sense of hunger, he said, "Got any more of that chicken you cook for the dog?"

Rune was just too . . . something.

In the kitchen, Carling shoved several large pieces of cooking flesh around in the skillet and glared at them. For the second time that day, the warm scent and sizzling sounds of browning chicken filled the air.

He was too what? What were the words that should go next?

She glanced over her shoulder at him. Just by sitting at the massive country-style table in the industrial-sized kitchen, he made the room and furniture look almost normal. With those long legs and wide shoulders, that lean torso and his typical quick strong, confident stride, he dominated every room he entered.

He was definitely too large. Check.

His head was bent over the first notebook. He rested his forehead on the heel of one hand as he read. His shoulder-long hair had dried from his morning swim. The careless tousled length made her want to get her hairbrush and smooth the tangles out. His tanned, chiseled features were intent. The sharp high blades of his cheekbones were balanced by the strong straight nose, a strong lean chin that had something of a stubborn bent to it, and that elegant cut mouth of his that was so wise in sensuality.

Well, he was obviously too handsome. He was the rock star of the Wyr, famed throughout not only the Elder Races but also the human society for his good looks, so all right, goddammit, check.

Fine lines framed the corners of his eyes and that sinful mouth. She thought of how those lips felt as they hardened over hers, how he had speared into her with the hot thrust of his tongue. She let her eyes drift shut as arousal pierced her body with an intensity that brought along with it a new wave of shock. Just the memory of that one kiss shook her to her foundations.

Yes okay, he was far too sexy and charismatic for his or anybody else's own good, so check. Carling had always found it ludicrous, even infuriating, how so many otherwise sensible and intelligent-seeming females apparently lost their minds whenever they came near him, and no matter how he affected her, she was *by gods not ever* going to become one of the vacuous hordes. She would jump off the nearest cliff first.

She sighed. Actually that would be a pretty meaningless gesture. Even though she was now at the end stages of the disease, it would still take more than just a simple dive off a cliff to kill her.

The cooking chicken snapped and popped, and a splatter of grease hit her cheek. The sting was negligible compared to the searing agony of the sun, but it was enough to catch her attention. Her eyes flew open. The small burn had already healed by the time she wiped the spot of oil away with her thumb. She poked at the chicken with the . . . the implement—spatula, damn it!—and flipped the pieces so the other side could brown.

Back to Rune.

He was too quiet. He moved with a cat's sinuous predatory grace. Added to that, he was fast enough to make her heart freeze if it hadn't already stopped beating. She pulled her bottom lip between her teeth and sucked on it as she thought.

Could she take him in an outright fight? She was faster and stronger than most. She could take her progeny Julian, the official King of the Nightkind, and that was a claim not many creatures could make. She had turned Julian during the height of the Roman Empire, and he was quite an old, Powerful Vampyre in his own right. But she didn't think she could take Rune without a serious struggle and investing in a considerable expenditure of magic.

She sucked harder on her lower lip. He was here as an ally with the intention of helping her. There was no reason whatsoever to think things would come to that. But just in case, she should do a little research on what might be the right spells to use in battling a gryphon. It never hurt to be prepared, and it never hurt to fight dirty if the situation called for it. The best way to take any of the really ancient, Powerful creatures was through the element of surprise.

There was the quiet sound of a page turning, the only sound in the kitchen aside from the cooking meat, and the infinitesimal sound of Rune's calm unhurried breathing. The page had turned ten times since he had started, and she knew very well what kind of dense material he was reading.

She had learned the laws of logic from Aristotle himself. She had studied each scientist who had furthered the development of the scientific method. Those notebooks Rune read held some of her finest thinking. They contained historical fact, rare accounts of oral history and snippets of information from everything she could possibly think of to get her hands on that might fuel her research.

She had acquired fabulous wealth over the course of her life. She owned various properties scattered throughout the world in places such as New York, London, the French Riviera, Morocco and Egypt's Alexandria. She owned irreplaceable historical artifacts, and diamonds and sapphires the size of duck's eggs, but her finest treasure was currently spread out on the table in front of him.

A page turned. Now he was on page eleven and he had not yet asked a single question for clarification. So he was far too clever as well. A clever male was a dangerous one, and all that much harder to surprise. She would do well to remember it.

She sliced into the largest piece of chicken and checked the middle. The meat was white all the way through and crispy dark on the outside. He was the type of creature who would enjoy that. She piled all the pieces onto a plate and removed the skillet from the stove.

She glanced over her shoulder. Rune had sat back in his chair. He lounged with his long legs stretched out, watching her with his full attention. Which was, one-on-one, in the quiet solitude of the sunlit kitchen, quite a considerable force of nature. He drew on her like a magnet. She picked up the plate of steaming meat. She looked at it and back at him, and she spoke a word and the meat cooled. Then she walked over to set the plate in front of him.

She had a bizarre experience as she approached him. It

started first with this thought: what an exotic thing it was to place a cooked meal in front of a waiting hungry male. No doubt it was something millions of women did daily, but throughout the several thousand years of her existence, she had never before been one of them.

Rune gave her a slow smile, his gaze very male and lit with appreciation, and it stirred something inside. What was that? Distracted, she poked at herself, like poking at a sore tooth. That was another strange thing for her to be feeling, what was it?

Pleasure.

He smiled at her as she placed the meal in front of him, and she felt pleasure.

The muscles in the pit of her stomach tightened, like a snake coiling to strike. She opened her mouth, to say what, she didn't know. Something scathing, a suitable put-down, something *by gods* not vacuous, or she would have to throw herself over the nearest cliff just on principle alone—

Rune's smile had deepened and it carried a hint of puzzlement. "What did you do just now?" he asked. "It was a spell of some sort. I could feel it but I didn't understand it."

Confused, the snake in the pit of her stomach fumbled and lost the ability to strike. She blinked and glanced at the stove. What had she done? She said, "I cooled the meat."

Rune's eyes danced and his lean tanned features lit with laughter. "You . . . cooled the meat for me?"

"Rasputin cannot eat the chicken when it is too hot," she said, frowning at him. "It seemed logical that you would not be able to either."

"Of course. How remarkably—thoughtful of you." He put a hand over his mouth to cover an explosive cough. "You named the ankle-biter Rasputin?"

The sense of his amusement was intoxicating, like champagne must be for humans. She regretted never having had the opportunity to drink champagne when she was human. She had been a Vampyre for a very long time before she had first heard of the drink.

She raised an eyebrow. "Your attempt to hide your amusement is futile. And Rasputin seemed an appropriate name, since he is apparently so hard to kill."

She had met the original Grigori Rasputin once, as she had

traveled through Russia to consult with a certain hermitic and irascible witch. She had found Rasputin to be an odd, intense man. He had been undeniably human and very likely insane, but anyone who could survive reputedly being stabbed, poisoned, shot multiple times, mutilated, and badly beaten before finally drowning, deserved a certain amount of respect.

"And," murmured Rune, "the ankle-biter's more than a bit rabid."

Now both her eyebrows rose. "I do not find him so."

"Of course not," Rune told her, his tone cheerful. "You rescued him, you're female and you cook him chicken. That makes him yours, heart and soul."

Her mouth tightened. "He's a ridiculous creature."

"He's a dog," he said, his wide shoulders lifting in a shrug. "That's what they do."

She crossed her arms under her breasts. Only later did she recognize it for a defensive gesture. "I did not ask for his devotion."

Rune's gaze darkened into an expression she didn't understand, so she had no words for it. He said gently, "You know, there isn't anything wrong with simply being kind for kindness's sake, or other creatures responding to it."

This conversation had not only turned uncomfortable, it was unnecessary. She looked away from his penetrating gaze. "Do you require anything else that will help you read?" she asked, her tone frosted with ice.

"No," he replied. His tone was as easy and relaxed as the rest of him. "Not a thing. Thank you for the chicken."

"Fine." She turned to go but found herself unable to step across the doorway.

Being kind for kindness's sake.

Now the tightening was in her chest. She pressed a hand to her breastbone, bewildered. She no longer knew her own body. It was betraying her in a thousand inexplicable ways whenever she was around this male.

She forced herself to say, "Thank you for staying and trying to help me."

Twenty feet away, he took a breath. He replied quietly, "You're more than welcome, Carling. It's my pleasure to do what I can for you."

Those words. He gave them to her so easily, like a gift. They were far more gracious than she deserved. She fled before her body could betray her in some other way.

As soon as Carling's tantalizing and distracting presence left the kitchen, Rune was able to hit his stride with the text.

He also ate every scrap of the cold meat she had cooked for him, and good gods, it was pretty awful. Somehow she had managed to wreck the simple task of browning chicken in a skillet. The outside was charred black, and the inside oozed juice that was still pink. If he had been human, he would have been concerned about salmonella poisoning. As it was, Rune wasn't a picky eater and had eaten some terrible meals in his time. His tastes had changed when he had first learned to shapeshift and socialize with other species, but he was actually not averse to eating raw meat when necessary, and he had endured any number of campsite disasters.

He started to chuckle again when he thought of her cooling the meat for him the way she did for the dog. Then he remembered how she had held herself when he had spoken of kindness, averting her face and eyes, and his laughter faded.

Both Wyr and Vampyre societies could be brutal ones. Sometimes conflict could only be settled violently. All of the sentinels were enforcers of Wyr law, but as Dragos's First, Rune was the ultimate enforcer. If Dragos was ever actually not in a position to do so, it was Rune's responsibility to hunt and take down even the other sentinels if they ever went renegade. The other sentinels were his friends, partners and comrades in arms. He was glad it had never come to that, but he never forgot the responsibility of his position.

For all of that, Rune was really an easygoing male most of the time, and quick to both laughter and affection. He was that rarest of creatures, a man's man who had no problem admitting he enjoyed chick flicks and women's fashion. They brought out things in women he adored, from the spiraling of emotions to mysterious heights and depths, to the flowering of wonder-filled feminine pleasure as a woman tried on new outfits and she discovered for the first time in the mirror that she was, in actual fact, beautiful.

From what he had seen, Carling was not quick to either laughter or affection. She did not inspire thoughts of comfort or cuddles. Had she once possessed those qualities, or had her experience of life really been that harsh and unyielding? He frowned. The scars covering her body told their own tale.

When he tried to imagine her giggling with a girlfriend, it bent his head. Rhoswen clearly worshipped her, and it was obvious Duncan felt something for her too, but as far as he could tell, those relationships were not on any kind of in-depth, equal footing. He suspected most women felt threatened by her, as well they should. Life had fashioned Carling into a sleek, lethal weapon, the double-edged kind that would cut off the hand of anyone who dared to wield it if they should try to grasp hold unwisely.

Taking that kind of weapon would take a hard, firm hand, from one who knew how and when to hold on with a strong grip, and when to let go and let the weapon free to cut where it would. No one mastered such a weapon. If one were lucky, one might gain respect, trust, alliance, an agreement to work together.

Carling was so shielded, and she had built up her personal arsenal over such a long period of time, he doubted if anything would change her at this late date. In that realization, at last he found the conceptual frame he needed in order to curb his fascination for her. There was simply nowhere for his fascination to go, and nothing for it to latch on to in any long-term way. She was brilliant, gorgeous, deadly and even quirky, but she would not allow someone to get too close, not even a dog.

Fair enough. Sometimes pinnacles were so narrow and elevated, there was only room for one at the top. If she managed to live for so long with such isolation, she must like her own company. As far as he was concerned, he was happy to help her out if he could, and he would be happy to move on when it was over. And it would be over somehow. They would either find a way for her to survive, or they wouldn't. As Duncan pointed out, people die all the time. Sometimes old, long-lived creatures died too.

Those thoughts produced a clench in his gut, but he ignored it. One way or another, this stop on the island was just an odd blip in his road, and he would do well to keep that thought firmly at the forefront of his mind. His real life waited for him back in New York, where he had good friends and any number of people who loved him.

He read until late afternoon, when he went on the hunt for something to drink. There were two chains at the kitchen well. One was attached to an empty bucket. Curiously he hauled on the other one and brought up a stash of Corona in a metal basket. The bottles of beer were quite chilled from resting at the bottom of the well. Score one for the thirsty Wyr.

He grabbed a couple and lowered the rest back into the well then went back to his reading. Scientific journals were more Dragos's schtick, not his. Carling's research was undeniably difficult reading. Whenever he reached a chemical or magical equation, he simply memorized the formulas without trying to decipher or understand them at this point. But he had thought he would find slogging through Carling's notes to be a mind-numbing chore, and that wasn't so. The process she had gone through pulled him in, almost in spite of himself.

Many creatures, human and otherwise, approached matters of magic in different ways. Throughout history, magic had been shrouded in mysticism, and sometimes outright religion, and many of those religious or mystical practices were still in use. Others practiced magic as a matter of folk tradition, much like the herbalist lore in indigenous societies that had been passed down by word of mouth for generations.

Given her roots in early Egypt, he guessed that Carling would have originally learned her magic from the standpoint of religion. By the nineteenth century, Vampyrism was, in large part, no longer viewed as a mystical curse but as a disease, and her approach to solving the issue was correspondingly scientific.

Her analyses were cool and precise. Upon learning the symptoms of the end stages of the disease and the challenges she would be facing, her attitude was unflinching. How humans lived with the knowledge of their own mortality was beyond him. He tried to imagine what it would be like to learn he was mortal, that his time was measured and must come to an inevitable end, and he simply couldn't. If he was ever killed, he would go into his death with astonishment and incomprehension. Among all the other reactions she elicited from him, Rune had to admit to a certain grudging admiration for Carling's courage.

But each research path she took came to a dead end. Her attempts to isolate the infection that caused the disease failed.

So what was wrong? What logic path or experiment had she not considered? He could see nothing among the elegant lattice of thought laid out so meticulously on the pages, and yet something niggled. What was it that bothered him? He wasn't going to try duplicating any of her processes. He didn't have the ability to replicate any of the experiments she had chronicled. She was the scientist, the clear expert in this field. He took it as a matter of faith she had been as meticulous in her experiments as she was in her handwriting. If something failed, it failed.

So it was something else that bothered him. Was it a premise or a conclusion?

The light was fading in the kitchen when he finally admitted he needed a break. He pushed away from the table and stretched his stiff neck and shoulders. He had almost a hundred pages left to read, but he had reached a point where he was no longer absorbing the information. Some fresh air might help clear his head, and his body needed to move.

He went outside and walked through the gardens, around the house toward the cliff. It was nearing sunset, and the shadows thrown by the foliage were elongated. The twists and angles of the shadowed tree limbs cut exaggerated dark paths across the lawn.

He walked along the waist-high stone wall that bordered the edge of the cliff, and he looked out over the water. The sun was an enormous blazing orange ball. It seemed to grow larger as it neared the horizon. Like Carling, the island was wrapped in its own strange, solitary existence. This piece of Other land gave the perfect illusion that nothing else existed except for it, the cobalt ocean and the limitless sky. He took in deep breaths of the salted air and pretended he was up there, high in the air, flying over the water until all sight of land disappeared.

Then he felt something ripple, like a breeze fluttering

against his skin, and everything shivered and changed. He blinked hard and stared around him, as he tried to figure out what was different.

The flaming sun still lowered in the west, an Icarus who flew too high and died his daily death. The ocean was still cobalt blue, darkening as the daylight faded. He turned. Cliff, wall, garden, shadows, great sprawling, crazy-gothic house . . .

. . . and beyond the house, far in the east, were electric lights, like a spray of stars that had committed mortal sins and had fallen from heaven. They lay strewn in a smoldering carpet on a distant, barely visible land.

Wow, so that's what it looked like on this side, when the veil between this land and the Bay Area thinned. He strolled eastward along the wall as he soaked up the strange sight. The illusion of land was immense, sketched in transparent lines across the entire east. Through it the ocean was clearly visible. The double horizons were dizzying.

"Sentinel?" Rhoswen's sharp call came from the direction of the kitchen door, the eastern side at the back of the house. "Sentinel!"

The Vampyre sounded upset, even urgent. He broke into a jog. By the time he rounded the corner, he was at a flat-out run.

Rhoswen stood in the doorway, Rasputin tucked under one arm. The powder puff with teeth broke into a frenzied barking when he appeared. Out of patience for the dog's histrionics, Rune bent, bared his teeth and growled a deep-throated warning. *"Behave."*

Rhoswen stared at him. Rasputin froze, his frenzy stopped in midbark. The whites of his eyes showed around shiny black irises. He looked like a startled stuffed animal.

"That's better," Rune muttered grimly. He patted the little dog on the head. "Good boy." He straightened. "Now, what's wrong?"

"I just woke up a few minutes ago," Rhoswen said. Her hair was mussed, and she had a crisscross of pillow lines on one cheek. "I went to check on Carling. I thought you should know—she's faded again."

Rune grew grimmer. He said, "Show me."

≡ FIVE ≡

Rhoswen strode quickly through the house. Rune kept effortless pace beside her, his long legs eating up the distance.

The oral histories in Carling's research stated that the mysterious episodes increased in frequency and intensity the closer a Vampyre came to the end. He wasn't sure yet what "the end" was, or what happened once a Vampyre reached it. It was possible Carling herself didn't know, or at least she hadn't at the point in her research when he had taken a break from reading.

Carling's text was chronological in nature, and one of the things she was meticulous about was recording the date and time of each event or discovery. She did not leap ahead or fall behind. Whenever she made reference to something earlier in her notes, she did so in a kind of shorthand by simply noting the date/time. It was a simple enough method of cross-referencing short of using a software program for footnotes, although it slowed his progress down as he had to flip back and forth through the entries to get the full gist of things.

Rune asked Rhoswen, "How often are these episodes occurring?"

"Almost daily," she said in a strangled voice. "It's why I hate so very much leaving her alone. What if she goes into an episode when she's cooking for the damn dog, or when she has taken off the spell that protects her from the sun? She sits so close to the edge of shadow when she does that. What if she has an episode and then the angle of the sun changes?"

He swore under his breath. Daily episodes weren't a good sign. In one of Carling's oral histories, one Vampyre had reached such a point and he was gone in a matter of weeks. Had he simply collapsed into dust? Usually mortal creatures struggled with death. Their hearts went into arrhythmia and their breathing became labored. If Vampyres were killed by the sun, they burst into flames first and expired in horrible agony. When they were killed in other ways, they disintegrated into dust.

He and Rhoswen reached a flight of stairs and took them three at a time. Rasputin rode silently under Rhoswen's arm, his small foxy head swiveling to track Rune's movements.

Rune said, "From here on out, we don't leave her alone. Agreed?"

She nodded. "Agreed. Sentinel, maybe I haven't seemed very welcoming since you arrived, but I want you to know— I'm glad you're here."

Rhoswen didn't seem very welcoming at the best of times, but he shouldn't get snarky on her just when she appeared in need of a moment.

Instead, he said, "Don't sweat it. Just stop calling me Sentinel, would you? It makes me feel like some kind of flea and tick repellent."

The Vampyre darted a quick startled glance at him. He winked at her, and she coughed out an uncertain laugh. At the top of the stairs, Rune put a hand on her arm. When she stopped, he gave her a steady look that had nothing of humor in it.

"We should be prepared for the possibility that Carling won't survive," he said. Saying it aloud made his muscles clench, but he forced himself to speak calmly. "But I promise you, we're going to do our damnedest to see that she does."

Rhoswen's mouth shook. "Thank you."

He nodded and let go of her arm. She turned and led the way down the second-story hall, toward a pair of carved wooden doors at the hallway's end. Rhoswen started to open one door, and sunlight—what looked like sunlight—spilled through the widening gap from the room beyond.

Rune didn't pause to think. He grabbed Rhoswen's shoulder in a hard grip and yanked her back, away from the light.

She stumbled and clutched the dog close as she looked around wild-eyed. "What is it? What happened?"

He said, his voiced edged, "I'm sorry. Look, it's a knee-jerk reaction. That looks like sunlight, but it can't be because the sun is setting and the house is almost dark. What is it?"

"What are you talking about?" Rhoswen stared at him. "What light?"

He took a deep breath. Let it out again. He gestured toward the half-open door. "There is light spilling out of that room, a very bright, strong yellow light like sunlight in the middle of the day. Are you telling me you don't see it?"

"No I don't," Rhoswen said. Now the whites of her eyes were showing too, just like the dog's. She looked nothing like her usual sleek composed self. She looked disheveled, frightened and very young. "It's quite dark, actually. I just figured since you're Wyr, you would have good eyesight and you'd be okay with that."

"Oh-kay," said Rune. He pursed his lips in a soundless whistle. "Let's go carefully here."

He stepped toward the door and pushed it wider open slowly, watching to make sure that none of the light he saw—or thought he saw—spilled directly onto Rhoswen. The hallway brightened further as the door opened. It still looked like sunlight to him, and it felt saturated with magic.

He drew a line through the air with a finger. "This is where the light that I see ends. I want you to cross that with just the tip of your finger."

Now she looked at him as if she suspected he was crazy, but she did as he asked and extended her forefinger until it crossed the demarcation he had shown her. They both stared at her finger, which remained unburned.

"Do you still see the light?" Rhoswen asked.

"As plain as day," he told her. "But at least it doesn't appear you are in any danger of burning from it. We should still go carefully." He gazed at her as he considered. "Do you have Power or magic ability?"

She shook her head. "I have only what every Vampyre has, which is enough for telepathy or making a crossover to an

Other land. It's a by-product of the virus. When I was human, I was a complete dead-head."

A dead-head, when used the way Rhoswen meant it, referred to someone who had no Power or magic ability whatsoever. It did not refer to a Grateful Dead fan. If Rhoswen didn't have much magical ability, then she didn't have many magical defenses. Rune shook his head. "Right. Well, magic is spilling out of that room, just like sunlight, and I'm not inclined to trust any of it. I want you to stay here."

The Vampyre's chin firmed. "Carling might need me."

He refrained from rolling his eyes. It wasn't his responsibility if Rhoswen chose to risk her life, and who knew, maybe she was right and Carling *would* need her. He said, "Fine, but I'm going in first."

Rhoswen stayed behind him as he stepped into the doorway, into both magic and light. The soles of his boots landed on something shifting and pliable. He looked down. That looked like sand. It felt like sand.

If it walked, talked and quacked like a duck, if it tasted like a duck when he caught and ate it . . .

He took another step, and another. The barest outline of a shadowed room surrounded him. Superimposed upon the room was a brighter, hotter reality. He looked up and squinted into a pale blue, cloudless sky that held a burning yellow-white sun.

"Sentinel?" Rhoswen called him again. This time she sounded panicked. "Rune! *You're fading.*"

He could just see her. She was a pale, insubstantial ghost-like sketch, as was the rest of the room. He called back, "I'm here. Can you hear me?"

"Barely," she shouted. She sounded far away. "You're disappearing right in front of me. What's happening?"

"I don't know," he shouted back. "I'm going to look around and see what I can find out. I don't know how long I'll be."

"I'd much rather you didn't," she called. "I would like for you to come back now, please."

But the mystery that lay spread out all around him was too compelling to ignore. Ahead of him was desert, and greenery, and the blinding glint of sunshine on distant water. Behind him was Rhoswen, the doorway and the island.

Son of a bitch, this kinda felt like a crossover to an Other land. Crossovers were the dimensional passageways that lay between Earth and Other lands. They had been formed when the Earth had been formed, when time and space had buckled. Crossover passageways followed physical faults in the landscape. The crossover passage that led to the island was part of a fissure at the ocean's bed. He had never before heard of one existing in a manmade structure, such as in a second-story bedroom in a house.

But this also felt different somehow than a normal crossover. He fumbled for a way to describe it to himself, to understand what he was sensing. It felt . . . bent, as if it turned a corner that other crossover passages didn't. And if this was a crossover point, why didn't Rhoswen sense it and cross over as well? Was it because of her lack of Power? Carling had a hell of a lot of Power. He would have thought she would have noticed by now if there was a dimensional passageway in the middle of her bedroom and considered it worthy of some mention. If it was a crossover passage, where did it cross over to? Or was he caught in some kind of elaborate illusion?

And where, in all of this mystery, was Carling?

He rubbed the back of his neck. He had always thought he was more of a Cheshire Cat than an Alice, but this really was curiouser and curiouser.

There was only one way to try to understand it.

He strode forward, into the full light of a scorching desert day.

At first he heard nothing but the vast, lonely howl of the wind as it sang its eternal song. Then the harsh, wordless cry of a bird sounded overhead. Heat hammered down and sand blasted him in the face. He paused to pick three landmarks to triangulate his position so he could return to this point if it really was a crossover passageway and the area ended up being his only route back to the house.

He put at his twelve o'clock a sere, squat bluff that rose above the rest of the landscape. That put the silvery glimmer of water at ten o'clock, a little too close to the bluff for the best triangulation, but it would have to do. He looked over his right shoulder, and saw nothing but desert dunes. He picked the tallest dune, at five o'clock. The dune would be useless for long-term navigation, of course, since the wind and the dunes would shift over time, but hopefully it would do for his purposes. He didn't plan on staying . . . wherever here was . . . for very long.

Then like discarding a suit of clothes, he let his human facade fall away as he shifted into his Wyr form. He stretched massive wings out and crouched, his lion's tail lashing, and he leaped into the air to fly through the brutal heat toward the bluff. Usually when he flew in an urban area, he cloaked himself to avoid complications with air traffic control systems, but this scene looked rural enough that he didn't bother.

His flight gave him a bird's-eye view of the land. The watery shimmer became a great, winding river bordered on either side with lush green vegetation and gold fields of grain that came to an abrupt end at a bordering desert.

Realization battered him. Hells bells. Unless he was very badly mistaken, that had to be the Nile. He had flown the length of the Nile several times in years gone past. He had seen it in all three stages of its ancient flood cycle, before the Aswan Dam in 1970 brought all seasonal flooding to an end. With the fields ripe with rich barley and wheat, this looked like *Shemu*, the Season of the Harvest, which fell roughly between the months of what would be May and September on a modern calendar.

He banked and flew in a wide circle as he scoured the landscape. With his eagle-sharp eyes, he could see for miles.

He saw no power lines, no satellite dishes, no motored boats on the river, no vehicles, nor any paved or gravel roads. No modern irrigation techniques or machinery. No plumes of smoke from distant refineries. No airplanes.

Simple dwellings made of mud-baked bricks dotted the riverbanks. A plume of dust rose from a group of brown-skinned men traveling on horseback along the western bank. They were over a mile away. From what Rune could see, they wore *shentis*, or loincloths, and were armed with copper-headed spears and wooden shields.

Okay, he was still looking for something to make sense here.

He inclined his eagle's head to study the land below him.

He saw a tiny upright figure, staring directly up at him with eyes shaded, about five hundred yards away from a cluster of eight buildings. A bundle of grain and a knife lay on the ground at the figure's feet.

And here he was with no Rand McNally atlas or GPS system. Not only did Rune like chick flicks and women's fashions, but he also knew how to stop and ask for directions when he was lost. Plus he was secure in his masculinity. He might be one of the world's only four gryphons, but he figured if you added those qualities up with all the rest, it made him unique as all shit.

Keeping the figure in sight, he slowed into a spiraling descent.

It was either a child or a small adult. Well okay, if he suspended all disbelief and just went on empirical evidence (which was patently impossible, but he was really trying to go with the flow here), any adults he might encounter would also be small, at least smaller than those in the twenty-first century.

The figure wore a *shenti* as well, and nothing else. The grubby scrap of cloth was wrapped around narrow hips. Child or adult, every line in the figure's posture shouted amazement, but at least it wasn't running away in a panic. So far, so good.

Rune shapeshifted as he landed about twenty yards away. He paused to give the other figure time to react. He was betting it was a female child. She appeared frozen in shock. Her skin was darkened from the sun into a rich nut brown. She had a light delicate bone structure, dirty feet, and a small rounded belly under a narrow rib cage.

The child's tangled dark hair had rich auburn glints in the sun, as if she was lit with a deep, internal fire. Her hand fell to her side, and he saw that she had long, lustrous almond-shaped dark eyes that glittered with sharp intelligence.

Recognition kicked him in the teeth. Her immature features already showed the promise of a spectacular bone structure. Her mouth hung open, the childish curve of lips hinting at the sensual beauty that was to come.

Holy shit.

"Hello darling," he whispered, staring.

She was a breathtaking impossibility. He couldn't be looking at the child Carling had once been, but somehow he was.

Was he caught in her memories? How could that be? It all felt so real, it couldn't be an illusion. Could it?

The girl said something in a shaky, high voice, the liquid-sounding words alien and unintelligible.

For a few moments his frozen brain refused to respond. Then, like flexing an unused muscle, his mind made sense of what she had said to him. She had spoken in a long-dead language.

"Are you Atum?"

Atum, to the ancient Egyptians, was the god of creation, the being from which all other deities came. Rune shook his head and fumbled to find the words and the concepts for a reply that this version of Carling might understand.

"No," he said, trying with all his might to project comfort and reassurance into his voice. Whether this was reality or illusion could be discovered later. At this point it didn't matter—gods, he just hoped the child Carling didn't bolt and run from him. "I am something different."

The girl pointed with a shaky hand. "But I saw you come out of the water."

Rune turned to look where she pointed. The river wound out of sight. Atum, according to the myth, rose out of a primordial watery abyss that circled the world. When Rune had changed into his Wyr form and launched into the air, from a distance it must have appeared that he had come out of the water.

He repeated, gently, "I am not a god. I am something else."

He did not expect her to believe him. She had just seen him fly in his gryphon form. To her, how could he be anything else? The early religions were filled with such things, as the Wyr shape-shifted and began to interact with humankind. Egypt's pantheon of gods was especially filled with human/animal forms.

He was useless at human things, but if he had to guess, he would place this Carling at under ten years of age. Was this really what she had been like as a child, or was this a projection of her mind? Was this who she thought she had once been? Simple wonder made her intelligent eyes shine. She was so delicate, the sight of her caught at the back of his throat. She was the merest infant. She had the whole of a very long, strange, and what must have been an often difficult life ahead of her. This Carling couldn't possibly understand any of that.

Moving slowly and easily, he crouched into a squat so he didn't tower over her. She shivered when he moved but still she did not break and run. Such a brave baby. He cleared his throat. "What's your name, darling?"

Darling. He used the English word. He knew of no direct equivalent in the ancient Egyptian language.

In a classic childish gesture of self-consciousness, she lifted one of her narrow shoulders toward her ear as she gave him a small smile. "Khepri," she whispered.

Rune tumbled head over heels in love. He laughed a little breathlessly, feeling like a mule had just kicked him in the chest. "Khepri," he repeated. If he remembered right, the word meant morning sun. "It's a beautiful name." He pointed in the direction of the cluster of small buildings near the river's edge. "Does your family live there?"

She nodded. Curiosity overcame her wonder, and she dared to sidle a few steps closer. "What is your name?"

His breath caught. He willed her to trust him and come closer. "I am called Rune."

He watched her mouth form the strange word as she tried it out silently. She would have been a quick child and would have rarely needed to be told something twice. He wondered when she would have taken on the more anglicized name of Carling, and what the reasons had been behind the change.

He gestured toward the bundle of grain and the knife. "You are harvesting."

She looked at the bundle and heaved an aggrieved sigh. "It is hard work. I would rather fish."

He grinned. "Where does your village take its grain?"

She pointed north, downriver. "Ineb Hedj," she told him. She added, proudly, "It is a very great place."

Ineb Hedj. The White Walls. The city had been named for the dam that surrounded it and successfully kept the Nile at bay, one of the first of its kind in human history. Established around 3,000 BCE and sitting twelve miles from the Mediterranean coast, the city had a long, illustrious history. Eventually it would be called Memphis. At one point it had been the largest city in the world. Khepri was right, it was a very great place.

He heard the rhythmic strike of hoofbeats in the distance, and remembered the men on horseback that he had glimpsed earlier when he was airborne. If Khepri's village was able to get grain into Ineb Hedj, the city could not be more than a day's walk away. Probably the riders came from the city.

He smiled. Everything about this child enchanted him, from the way she pulled at her lower lip with thumb and forefinger to how she stood with one dirty foot balanced on top of the other. How had she come from such a poor, obscure beginning to become one of the most Powerful rulers in the Elder Races?

He asked, "Have you been to Ineb Hedj?"

She shook her head. "I am not allowed."

"That will change some day," he said.

Khepri looked in the direction of the hoofbeats. She asked, "Do you hear that?"

"Yes," he said.

"Something is happening." She looked excited and disturbed all over again.

The village must be far enough from the city for the men on horseback to be an event. He frowned and straightened to look north. Khepri moved closer to stand by his side.

Villagers emerged from the huts as the riders appeared. No one noticed Rune or looked in their direction. They were all staring at the approaching riders. Rune set his jaw. He did not like the look of how the riders held their spears, or their aggressive speed.

He put a hand on Khepri's shoulder. She felt so fragile underneath his fingers, her bones as light and slender as a bird's. She gave him a frowning look.

"Listen, darling," he said. He kept his tone quiet and easy. "I think we should step into the field and hide in the grain, just until we know what those men want."

Or at least that's what he tried to say to her. Even as the words came out of his mouth, the solid feel of her shoulder melted from underneath his touch. He made an instinctive attempt to grab hold of her. His fingers clenched in an empty fist. Khepri stared at his fist and reached for it with small brown fingers that had gone transparent. Her hand passed through his. Her face tilted up. They stared at each other.

Rune sent a swift glance around. The outline of a room had appeared, sketched over the hot desert afternoon. A vertical line of curtain slashed through the riders who had lifted their spears. The rider in the lead took aim and threw his spear at the nearest villager, a slender middle-aged male. The spear's copper head emerged from the man's back in an explosion of liquid crimson.

Ah, hell no.

He glanced down at Khepri and saw her lips move on another word. He recognized it even though he couldn't hear her. Papa. She opened her mouth wide to scream.

No, dammit. Whatever was really happening—memory, illusion or reality—he did not want to leave the child this way, not now, not yet. He tried to lunge in front of her so she couldn't see anything else the riders did. He tried to scoop her up and run away with her, but she passed through his arms, as insubstantial as a ghost.

Khepri and the rest of the desert scene faded from sight. He sensed again a kind of passage, that peculiar bent, going-around-a-corner feeling, but no matter how his mind tried to grasp hold of the concept, it slid away.

Then he stood sweating in a large cool, darkened bedroom. A king-sized four-poster bed dominated one wall. A sitting area with armchairs, footstools and side tables was set up on the other side of the room, in front of a comfortable-looking, well-used fireplace.

Carling sat in one of the armchairs, an open book resting on one of the chair's arms. Rasputin had leaped onto her lap and was licking at her cheeks. Rhoswen knelt on the floor beside her, gripping her by the hand and saying her name. With a grimace, Carling nudged the dog away from her face. Rasputin switched to licking her hand as he wagged his tail frantically. Carling caught sight of Rune. She looked at him, at the dog and at Rhoswen as though she had never seen any of them before.

She said, "Something's happened."

Carling struggled against a feeling of disorientation. She had been trying to read a rather mangled history of the Dark Ages, finding the author alternatively amusing and irritating. The last thing she remembered was putting down her book as she looked at the late-afternoon sunshine, and now her bedroom was in near-complete darkness. Despite her best effort to stave it off, apparently she had faded again.

Distress weighted the air. Rasputin was always disturbed whenever she had an episode. How the dog sensed what was happening, she didn't have a clue. She gave up trying to calm him and simply clamped her hand down on the back of the dog's neck to contain his frantic wriggling body in one spot.

There was never any ambiguity about Rhoswen's upset either. When Carling faded, it invariably threw the other Vampyre into a panic, which was why Carling had put off telling her about the episodes she'd had on the trip to Adriyel.

While Rhoswen's panic was tiring, it wasn't anything new. Carling's attention switched to the source of the sharp, fierce emotions in the room. Rune flared against her mind's eye like an aggressive, violent infrared volcano. He was breathing heavily, and he smelled of sharp male sweat and exertion. What had happened to him?

As she stared, he seemed to collect himself. He walked over to her with every appearance of calm, but of course she knew better.

"All right," Rune said. "What's happened?"

"I don't know," she said. She frowned as she tried to reach for the elusive feeling, but it had already melted away. "Something did," she insisted. "Something shifted."

Rhoswen started a tearful babble. Carling was so weary of dealing with the younger Vampyre's self-involvement she simply covered her eyes with one hand.

Rune snapped sharply, "Rhoswen, stop it."

Rhoswen's babble cut off in midsentence. She looked at Rune in affronted astonishment.

He told her, his voice hard, "Nobody needs that kind of excess right now. If you cannot add to the situation, get out."

Carling's eyebrows rose behind her hand. She was almost inclined to laugh.

Rhoswen's reply sounded strangled. "I'll—feed the dog his supper and take him out."

Carling touched Rhoswen's hand and told her, "Thank you."

Rhoswen sniffed and nodded. She scooped Rasputin off Carling's lap and left with her head lowered.

Rune waited until the younger Vampyre was gone. Then he began to pace around the room. He kept his movements controlled in a slow prowl, as though he would give the appearance of relaxation, but the hot corona of violence that surrounded him all but obliterated her ability to see or sense anything else in the room.

He asked in an even voice, "The episodes aren't painful, are they? Are you in any discomfort?"

"No," she said. "I'm just tired."

She was more than just tired. She was mortally exhausted. Not even the remarkable vitality of Rune's powerful emotions could energize her this time. She couldn't remember the last time she had slept, or even just rested enough to become refreshed. It was all part of the progression of the disease: one lost the ability to take in physical nourishment and began to feed off emotions, and after a few centuries, one became unable to sleep and the episodes increased. She wrapped her arms around herself and huddled in one corner of the armchair.

Rune gave her a sharp, searching glance. He stopped at one of the side tables to light an oil lamp. It flooded the sitting area with soft light. He glanced at a windup clock on the fireplace mantel and continued on his prowl. "Rhoswen woke up earlier and came to check on you. The sun had not yet set, so you may have slipped into the fade at any time from late afternoon to early evening. It's almost midnight now. Is that a typical length of time for one of these episodes?"

"They vary," she murmured. "I recently had one that lasted a couple of days. It sounds like this one only lasted hours."

"All right." He stopped in front of the large windows and looked out. He went still, then muttered to himself, "Interesting."

She regarded him wearily. As fascinating as she found him, right now she wanted nothing more than for him to go away and leave her alone. "What?"

He looked back at her. "Your windows face the east."

She lifted one shoulder in a shrug. She caught how his attention diverted to the small movement. A strange expression crossed his lean tanned features, and a sharp emotion like pain pierced him.

She told him, "I like to look at the morning sun."

"Khepri," he whispered.

Icy shock rippled over her skin as she heard him utter a word that no one had spoken to her in millennia. "*What* did you just say?"

He walked to the other armchair and leaned his folded arms across its high back as he watched her with unswerving intensity. "The San Francisco Bay was visible earlier," Rune said. "Now it isn't. I was outside when it appeared just before sunset, which sounds very close to the time when you might have faded. Is that a coincidence?" He paused to give her a chance to respond. She said nothing. "Not?"

She admitted reluctantly, "Maybe not."

He straightened and folded his arms across his chest. He did not look pleased. "It appears we have a lot to discuss."

"We sure as hell do," said Carling.

═ SIX ═

She glared at him. "How did you know to say that . . . sword?" She felt so exposed and off balance she could not even admit out loud that Khepri was a name, much less confess that it had been her name, so long ago she had literally been a different creature. She could not imagine how Rune, of all people, would have heard of it.

Rune made an impatient gesture with one hand. "I'll get to that in a minute. Why didn't you say anything about a connection between what was happening to you and what was happening to the island?"

"Because I don't understand why it's happening," she snapped. "I'm not even sure there is a connection."

He snapped back, "Don't lie to me. I said I would help you, but I cannot do that if you do not come clean about everything you think is happening."

"I didn't ask you to stay," she said, her tone clipped.

His anger detonated. The force of it was like an invisible air bag inflating, pushing her back into her seat. "Do you really want to go there? Because based on what I've read so far, you've done great working on your own all this time. I'm sure you're going to turn things around any second now before you *fucking die* in as soon as a couple of *fucking weeks*."

She let her head fall back against the chair. "Fine. There

may be a connection. The island started to become visible when I began to have the episodes." She discovered she was breathing hard and forced herself to stop. She told him, "But I can't figure out what would link the two things together, so I still don't understand why it happens."

"May be a connection. May be a connection?" Bloody hell. A chill rippled down his spine. If Carling's episodes were so Powerful they affected the land around her, what else might she be affecting? What could her episodes do to the world around her when she wasn't in an Other land? He ran an impatient, long-fingered hand through his tousled hair. "Did you have any episodes on the trip to Adriyel?"

"A few," she admitted reluctantly.

His sharp gaze stabbed her. "I don't remember any anomalies occurring in the landscape, and I sure as hell didn't . . . well, I didn't sense anything remotely like what happened here today."

She shrugged and shook her head. "We can't even be sure there is a correlation. *If* there is, Adriyel is still one of the largest Other lands in the Northern Hemisphere, with several crossover passages not only to Earth but also to Other lands. I think it would take something of unimaginable size and scope to affect it. This island is one of the smallest known Other lands with just the one crossover passage. And as far as you're concerned, you were never around when I went into a fade. I was close to one when Niniane was kidnapped and Tiago injured, but focusing on healing Tiago helped me to stave it off for a time. By the time it hit, I was back in our encampment 'resting.' I had another one earlier at the hotel, but I don't think you had arrived in Chicago yet."

His jaw tightened. "I've got about a hundred pages left to read of your research. Is any of this in your notes?"

Her gaze fell from his. She said, "No."

After a moment he said between his teeth, "Much as I would like to, we're not going to waste time on having a conversation about why the hell not."

She said stiffly, "There was no point in writing it down. It's neither scientific nor productive to state this thing seems to happen, and at the same time this other, apparently unrelated event also seems to happen, and I don't understand any of it."

He looked incredulous. "Out of all of what is going on, being scientific is what matters the most to you?"

Her brief flare of anger faded. She rubbed her face. She said with a sigh, "It matters that I leave behind the best work that I can, so hopefully someone can move forward with the research. Then maybe they can find a cure or some way to halt the progression of the disease in a way that I haven't been able to. It will not do anybody any good to leave behind fruitless speculation that contains, in the end, more desperation than sense."

Silence spread through the room. It was filled with such tension, her muscles clenched. Rune pushed off the back of the chair and came around. She watched him warily as he scooped up one of the ottomans, placed it in front of her and sat down on it. Her expression chilled as he reached for her hand, but she allowed it. For the moment.

He looked down at her fingers, and she did too. They appeared so slender and delicate in his much larger, square-palmed hand. Appearances were deceiving. She had lost count of the number of creatures she had killed with her bare hands.

Rune's anger and aggression had vanished. She wished she could find a way to keep the sight of his lean, handsome face from hurting what was left of her tired, useless heart. The emotion was just another thing she didn't understand about herself, and she didn't know how to make it stop. She wished she had the ability to make the most of this fleeting time because it would be gone all too soon. She wanted to regard Rune's male beauty in a way it deserved, with simple pleasure.

When Rune spoke next, his voice had gentled. "You have become too used to the thought of dying."

She did not bother to dignify that with a verbal response. Instead she lifted an eyebrow.

He told her, "I know, but take what I say seriously, Carling. I think the mind-set may lead to some sloppy thinking. You no longer have the luxury of centuries or even years ahead of you for research. You can't afford to be passive or silent about things right now just because they don't make sense to you."

She regarded him for a moment. Then she shocked them both, as she lifted her free hand and laid it against his warm, lean cheek. He froze, his gaze startled.

"I think you're a good man," she said. As old as she was,

she had met far too few of those over the years. As a woman of Power, she had tended to attract men of ambition. Not that ambition was necessarily a bad thing, but it tended to skew ethics and perspectives. In the end there had never been anyone secure enough in his own power to not feel threatened by hers, nor anyone who was more interested in her than in meeting his own agenda. And there had never been anyone strong enough to make her believe in him beyond all else. She smiled at Rune. "I appreciate that you want to help me, and I am happy to try to fight for my life. But I'm afraid you may be tilting at windmills here."

He gave her a crooked smile in return, his cheek moving under her palm. "Earlier I was pretty convinced I was Alice in Wonderland. Come to think of it, I faded out of sight on a few people, so I was actually the Cheshire Cat as well. I don't think channeling Don Quixote should pose any problems."

Amused, she said, "You're not making any sense."

A dimple appeared beside his mobile, sensual mouth. "That is only because you don't know what I'm talking about."

"I'll give you one thing," she told him. "That was actually a very Cheshire Cat thing to say."

"Now we're getting ahead of ourselves," he told her. She started to let her hand fall away from his cheek. He caught it and pressed a kiss to her palm. He let go of both of her hands before she could react. Confused, warmed and somehow disappointed when he released her, she laced her hands together and held them stiffly in her lap. He said, "I'll catch up on reading the rest of the research on my own. For now, I want you to tell me everything, even if it is conjecture or if you don't understand it."

She frowned. "You say we should not waste time, but I don't see how—"

He overrode what she was about to say, his gaze stern. "You have to start trusting me a little bit. Not a lot. Not, I think, outside your comfort zone. But I am actually a very good investigator, and I'm quite experienced at deciding for myself what information might or might not be useful." Then the sternness melted from his eyes. He gave her a coaxing smile. "And I can be so terribly charming while I do it. You'll see. It'll be fun."

Her mouth shut with an audible click of her teeth. "Oh for heaven's sake, all right."

"Good, we're making progress." His expression as he regarded her was filled with such lazy, caressing warmth, she wanted to bask in it all night. He looked at her as if she were the only thing in the world that mattered. It was heady, exotic, dangerous, completely irrelevant stuff. She straightened her spine as she tried to drag her recalcitrant self back into line. "First, I want you to tell me what you experience when you have an episode."

"Episode episode episode," she said with sudden venom. "Gods, how I've grown to hate that word."

"Oh-kay," said Rune. He switched gears with apparent ease. "We'll have to start calling it something else. You suffer from an extreme case of attention deficit disorder."

She glared at him and grumbled, "Whatever."

He suggested, "You kept the light on when you left the house."

No. He wasn't funny. She would not dignify that either. Somewhere in the middle of her glare, she started to smile. "Don't be ridiculous."

"You fed the bats in your belfry? You went crazier than a shit-house rat."

"What?" Laughter burbled out of her. It felt strange, ebullient and light. She could not remember the last time she had laughed out loud, or why.

"I know, they're too long to say in the middle of a sentence," he said with a grin. "I'm brainstorming here. You were just showing your Vegas, baby."

"You know, the word 'episode' doesn't seem so bad anymore," she said, still laughing. "I think we should stick with simple English."

"All right," Rune said. His warm gaze lingered on her, the expression in them caressing. "Tell me about when you cracked out."

Cracked . . . She tried to glare at him again but she had lost the ability. The laughter had swept it away, along with her exhaustion and the lingering weight of discouragement.

Then she sobered as she thought back to earlier that day, and Rune put a hand on her knee. Maybe he did it to offer comfort or encouragement. He seemed to like touching her. He did it so often. The weight of his hand was warm through the caftan, his long callused fingers cupping the joint of her knee. She decided she liked the feeling of his hand on her knee too. She allowed it to remain where it was. For now.

"I was reading," she said. "I put the book down and looked outside at the fading sunlight. Then I felt my Power flare. That's what I call it, anyway."

He murmured, "You said it happens whenever you go into a fade."

"Yes. I never experienced menopause, but I wonder sometimes if hot flashes might be a little like that. It's a good warning sign. If I can respond quickly enough, I can sometimes stave off an episode."

"Why do you suppose pain helps?"

"I'm not sure. The shock of it seems to snap me back into sync, at least for a while." She looked at him and bit her lip. "All right, I'll confess. Maybe I didn't want to tell you about the Power flares, or how the island seems to appear and disappear when it happens, because I didn't want you to change your mind and leave. I don't honestly know how safe it is to be around me when it happens. That is why everybody else has left, except for Rhoswen."

"Can they sense what is happening?" Rhoswen couldn't, but he didn't know how much of a yardstick she might be for this. Not only did she have relatively little Power or magic, she was also young.

"No one has ever admitted to it." Carling closed her eyes. "It frightens them."

"Well, good riddance to them." His hand tightened on her. His gaze remained rock-steady. "But I'm not going to leave. I'm just glad you're telling me now. Go on."

That look in his eyes pulled on her more powerfully than anything else she could remember. It made promises she had never heard before, things like he was unafraid and would stand by her, that she could rely on him no matter what.

It said she was worth fighting for.

She did not know if she believed that, but something burned at the back of her eyes at the thought that he might. She put her hands over his, her fingers squeezing tightly. "So my Power flared and I disassociated from reality. Do you remember how I said sometimes I go into the past, and sometimes I don't know where I go?"

He nodded. His stance and expression didn't change, but somehow his attention sharpened.

She said, "Today I went into the past. I keep cycling through early memories. I don't know why. Maybe it's because they held such defining moments for me. Maybe there isn't a reason and it just happens."

He murmured, "Tell me about that early memory."

"Does it matter?" She cocked her head, studying him as much as he studied her.

"I don't know yet."

"Fair enough." She shrugged. "I went back to when I was a child. I lived in a small village on the Nile. It was a very simple, primitive, poor life. We lived and breathed the cycles of the river. We fished and dried what we caught, and we planted and harvested grain. We were a day's walk from Memphis. Of course it wasn't called Memphis then."

Rune whispered, "Ineb Hedj."

"Yes." Surprised, she gave him a smile. Sometimes it was an unutterable comfort to talk to other creatures at least as old as she was. So many things that had happened to her had occurred so long ago they had disappeared from history itself. They had become distant to her, like words on a page, a story that had happened to someone else, but this time she let herself drift back in actual memory as she said, "That day was quite eventful. I met a god and my life changed forever."

Rune appeared frozen. His hand was rigid as stone. Only his lips moved as he repeated, "You met a god."

"I was helping to harvest barley when I saw a giant winged lion flying overhead," she murmured. "He shone copper and gold in the pale morning light. He was so beautiful I felt as if my soul left my body as I watched him, and he had the head of an eagle. . . ." Her gaze widened on Rune. "Of course," she whispered. "Of course he was a gryphon."

His eyes were too full of the things he was feeling, a wildness and joy when she mentioned flight, and a certain sense of tragedy she couldn't begin to comprehend. Bewildered, she watched his throat move as he swallowed. He said, "It was me, Carling."

She stared at him. "How can you know that for sure? It happened thousands of years ago. You were the most amazing thing I had ever seen. I had *never* imagined anything like you, but to you, I was just another human child. I had to have been so forgettable."

"Khepri," he said. His voice was soft. "You were never at any time in your life forgettable."

The sadness in his expression wrenched at her. She leaned toward him, touching his arm. "What is it, what's wrong?"

"Never mind that now," he said. "This is your story. It's important you tell it."

"All right." She frowned but continued, "I don't remember much else about our encounter. I remember the color of your hair. It shone golden in the sun, like the lion. You were very large and strange, and we talked for a while, but I was pretty much in shock and I didn't retain any of what we said to each other. Then you left."

He looked down at their hands. "Do you remember how I left?"

"No," she said. "Did you take flight again? I wish I'd remembered that."

He shook his head but remained silent. He rubbed his thumb lightly against the edge of her kneecap and appeared to be concentrating on the small movement.

"Well," she said after a moment. "That same day soldiers from the city harvested our village for slaves. They took the young, the healthy and the pretty, and they killed anyone who tried to stop them. I saw them kill my father. It was terrible, of course. I was maybe seven years old. But I've had a long time to get over it, and the brutal fact is, I might have lived and died a very short life in the river mud if I hadn't somehow been taken out of it. I never forgot seeing you flying overhead though."

He nodded, his head bent. After a moment he asked, "What made you change your name?"

She gave an impatient shrug. "I took my freedom and I took control of my life, and then I took control of my identity as well. I wanted a more modern name, something that was wholly my own creation. Carling wasn't that far off from Khepri, so it made the transition easy. One day it was time to bury that little slave girl. It actually was a bit of a relief."

His mouth tightened. "I wish I could have stayed to help you and your family."

She frowned. What had she said? He looked like he was in pain. "As I said, it happened a very long time ago."

He stood with such abruptness she sat back sharply. He met her gaze for one burning moment then his eyes slid away. "Sure it did," he said. His voice had grown hoarse. "I'm going to take a break and stretch my legs. Let's pick this up again in ten."

"If that's what you need," she said slowly.

He gave her a curt nod and strode out of the room.

She looked at the empty ottoman where Rune had sat and tapped her fingers on the arm of the chair. The intensity of his turmoil was a hot, sharp weight that lingered in the room for several minutes after he had disappeared.

It was obvious something was terribly wrong, but for the life of her she couldn't figure out what.

Rune tried to breathe as he made his way through the darkened house. A hot, invisible boulder crushed his chest. The adult Carling had looked at him with the same pleasure and wonder that the child Khepri had. Her face was even lovelier when it was washed clean of all cynicism and calculation, stripped of the distance she held between herself and the rest of the world.

How could he look at her wonderful expression and tell her he had not met her in Egypt thousands of years in the past, but here just a few hours ago? What the hell had happened? Had it been an elaborate illusion her mind had created? How could he watch the most pleasure he had ever seen in her turn to horror as she realized how terribly her mind and magic—the two things she took the most pride in—had betrayed her?

He couldn't. She was facing the end of her life with such courage and a very real, if acerbic dignity and grace, and instead of facing it with her, he was running away like a craven coward. He felt self-disgust and disappointment, but he could also not make himself turn around and face her. Not yet. Not until he'd had a chance to react to what had happened, and he had cleared his head enough so he could be there for her, to add to the situation, as he had told Rhoswen, and not drag on Carling's already overstrained resources.

A light shone at the cracks of the kitchen doors. He found

Rhoswen sitting at the table, her forehead propped in one hand as she watched Rasputin eat his dinner on the floor near the stove. Rhoswen looked up at his entrance.

"I have to think and I need some air," Rune told her. "Are you up to staying with Carling until I get back?"

Rhoswen wiped her cheek. "Of course."

He paused. The Vampyre's face was streaked from crying. He reined in his impulse to move, to get lost out in the night and take flight. He asked reluctantly, "Are you all right?"

A small spark lightened her dull eyes. She nodded. "I'm sorry about earlier," she said. "It won't happen again."

"As far as I'm concerned, you're standing head and shoulders above all the rest," Rune told her. He sent a pointed glance around the empty kitchen.

Rhoswen chuckled a little. "To be fair, some people would be here if they could."

"Like Duncan?"

She nodded.

He frowned as another thought occurred to him. There were no humans on the island. There was also no refrigeration. He asked, "How are you doing for sustenance?"

"We have plenty of bloodwine. I won't need fresh blood for a couple of weeks."

Bloodwine was exactly as the word sounded, blood that had been mixed with wine and bottled. Rune wasn't exactly sure how it was made. All he knew was that the process involved a low-level alchemy and it required a wine with a high alcoholic content.

Bloodwine did not have the capacity to mature over time as some wines could. At best, it might have a shelf life of two years, and it didn't have the nutritive quality of fresh blood, but a Vampyre could survive on bloodwine for months at a time, and it could be used to supplement a fresh blood supply during lean times. Invented sometime in the mid-eleventh century, it was credited for how European Vampyres managed to survive the Black Death in the fourteenth century, when up to sixty percent of the human population had been killed.

Rune's frown deepened. As a succubus, Carling could take sustenance from the emotions from living creatures, but she'd had only Rhoswen and Rasputin on the island for company. He said, "What about Carling?"

Rhoswen's eyes filled. She said, "I've been trying to convince her to go back to San Francisco, but she won't budge."

"You mean she was starving herself," Rune growled. Eager to burn off the weight of the strange crushing sadness, his temper flashed quick and hot.

"We've not been alone for more than a few days, and she's been looking much better since you've arrived," Rhoswen said. Rasputin finished his meal, and Rhoswen went to scoop the dog up. Rasputin tried to run away from her, but she was too fast for him. He gave her a leery look, his paws paddling at the air. She told the dog, "You're such a little freak."

Rune nearly turned back to confront Carling, but if he did that, he knew he would also have to confront the speculative look she gave him as he left with such abruptness. Carling had given up by the time he had arrived, but he had already known that, and it was in the past. If she tried to give up again, he would kick her ass and make sure it hurt.

Besides, he wasn't ready to talk to her. He had too much to think about first, and he simply didn't know what he could or should say.

"I'm going to take a flight," he said. "See if I can clear my head. I'll be back soon."

"Okay," Rhoswen said. She and Rasputin watched him leave.

Take a flight. Clear his head.

Yeah, like that had done him any good over the last couple of weeks.

Still, a body had to try.

As a Vampyre, Carling didn't feel the cold like a normal human. That did not mean she couldn't feel the lack of warmth. The spell of protection that allowed her to walk in the middle of a sunlit day was a great triumph, but at times the victory rang hollow because she would never again know the warm comfort of the sun on her skin.

She craved warmth and light. Every house she owned had fireplaces in most of the rooms. Rune's presence finally faded from the bedroom, leaving it feeling slightly damp, dark and empty. She crouched at the hearth to lay wood for a fire. She stacked plenty of wood. She wanted a big, cheerful bright blaze.

She lit it, and hugged her knees as she watched the small new flames lick at the wood. With a sigh of relief, she let the protection spell fall away so that she could bask in the building warmth of the fire.

What had caused Rune such inner turmoil? She stood abruptly, impatient with herself. It was useless to speculate. She couldn't know what disturbed him until he chose to tell her. Waiting for him to return made her feel helpless, and she abhorred feeling helpless.

She moved to her large east-facing windows and opened them. A restless breeze blew into the room and ruffled her hair as she looked out at a gigantic full moon. A witch's moon. It would appear to decrease in size as it moved away from the horizon, but for now it hung impossibly huge over the ivory-tipped black ocean, its color rich champagne. The brightest jewel in the night sky, it hung as though from the pendant of a goddess's necklace, the spray of stars surrounding it the filigree within which the jewel had been set.

Ever since she had claimed the island, she had sketched the positions of the night stars throughout the seasons. It was an idle, useless hobby. She had never been able to determine if the stars were actually the same ones as seen from Earth. Their positions were too different in relation to each other. There would never be any satellite telescope to capture and compare deep-space imagery with that of Earth's.

Perhaps they were different stars altogether. Carling tended to think not, but ultimately it didn't matter. Here, the stars were nothing more than a mystery and ornamentation. No weight of historical belief hung on their configuration. There were no myths attached to any constellations. There was nowhere to navigate to by their positions. No matter where one sailed, one always came back to the island. This little bubble of dimensional reality was nothing more than a seed pearl strung beside the goddess's pendant moon.

This had been a good place to retreat to when the rest of the world grew to be too much, a good place to find at least a measure of solitude and quiet whenever she could find time to attend to her research and studies.

She supposed it had been as much a home as anywhere else had been, and it had been far better than most. She had made peace with the shy winged creatures that lived at the top of the redwoods. She set wards around the forest and refused to let anyone hunt them. In return, presents were sometimes left on her window ledge, a black iridescent feather, a perfect sea-shell, or a gold-veined rock, or sometimes a handful of tart red berries on a leaf, and once, there had been a string of strangely carved wooden beads.

The place had not changed, but what peace she had managed to find here had fled, and she missed it. She missed it badly.

All that it had taken to wreck it was the presence of one insouciant Wyr, a strange and ancient creature who, at his heart, was a compassionate man.

She caught movement out of the corner of her eye and her attention shifted.

Rune strode out in the champagne and ivory night. As she watched, he turned toward the cliff and started to run. With each powerful thrust of his long legs, he kicked to an astonishing speed, his vigorous wide-shouldered body moving faster and faster as he approached land's end. Then he sprang like the great cat he was, landed in a crouch on top of the stone wall at the edge of the cliff, and leaped into the air, his arms spread wide, his athletic body thrown into a perfect diver's pose.

As he soared into the air, he changed. Enormous wings flared into existence. Moonlight glimmered on his broad-muscled back as his body turned feline. Colossal paws tipped the columns of his four legs. The strong length of his neck and head became the pure sharp arc of an eagle's, with a wicked, razor-hooked beak that had to be as long as her forearm and a great fierce raptor's gaze. In the full light of the desert day, he had shone hot with color, copper and gold. In the light of the witch's moon, his colors were darker and sharper, bronze tipped with the palest silvery edge.

Humans were not meant to bear the weight of immortality. Each Vampyre had to find her own way of coping with great age or eventually go mad. In the end, the best way to survive the endless onslaught of event as it turned into memory was to compartmentalize. Carling had countless closed doors in the corridors in her mind, doors that were shut against all the grinding relentlessness of the past. Those closed doors had, inevitably, become barriers to other things as well.

As Rune took flight, all the many thousands of doors in all the corridors in her mind opened and opened and opened, until she stood in solitude, utterly naked, and felt as she had as a child.

Rune was one of the oldest mysteries of the earth. His existence predated language itself. She watched him soar against the starry backdrop of the champagne moon, and just as the long-ago child Khepri had, she felt her soul leave her body all over again.

When ten minutes became longer than a half hour, she stopped waiting and became busy with other things.

The books screamed as she burned them. The screeching sound they made clawed at the inside of her skull.

She was braced for it. She had made Rhoswen swear to not leave the main house. That had been a fierce argument she hadn't seen coming, and really, she had grown too tired of how everything had become such a struggle. That was going to have to change.

Then she had spelled a circle of protection in her cottage with salt around the fireplace. She stuffed her ears with wax softened with myrrh and smudged with sweetgrass and white sage, and she wore leather gloves that were also spelled so that no magic, dark or light, could cling to them.

The task was still a noxious, exhausting business, and one that she had put off doing for far too long. It was just as well she did not need to breathe. The fumes from the fire were toxic. She was soot-streaked and cranky by the time the book-burning was over.

Rune had made an excellent point. She had to think with a robustness that would help her fight to live. She must also act as if she were about to die. The black magic books were too dangerous to leave without a guardian, and she didn't trust anyone else enough to keep them without eventually giving in to the temptation to use them.

If she did nothing, sooner or later their magic would eat

through the bindings she had carved into the cabinet. Either that or some damn fool would find a way to get to them. There was always some damn fool who thought he was strong enough to handle using black magic without letting it suck him in. Hubris, cruelty, greed and stupidity. They were the reasons why black magic had survived for so long. Dark Powers dined on those qualities as though they were the finest hors d'oeuvres.

She had built the fire with cedar for more purification, and she stoked it with Power so it burned unnaturally hot and fast. When the last of the books had crumbled to ash, she stripped off her caftan and the gloves and threw them into the fire as well. Then she took the pitchers of water she had set out under the witch's moon. She poured one pitcher of the moon-filled water over the ashes, so they were purified three times over, by salt, and fire, and water.

Finally done, she took the other two pitchers into the cottage's bathroom. She washed away the soot from her hair and body with handfuls of soft soap she had made for just such an occasion, with eucalyptus, frankincense and lavender. She emerged from the bathroom wearing a clean cotton caftan and smelling rather pungent, but at least her skin was clear of any hint of lingering dark magic.

After checking the soggy ashes one last time, she left the cottage open so that it could air out and walked back to the main house.

The night had almost passed. Predawn was lightening the sky in the east. In the kitchen, she found Rasputin sound asleep on a cushion and Rhoswen drinking bloodwine. There was no sign of Rune, but then she hadn't expected any. He would have known better than to interrupt her as she burned the books, but if he had returned, he would have been waiting just outside the cottage.

She left the kitchen door open as well. Cool, fresh air wafted into the house as she sat at the table. A sleepy Rasputin roused and puttered over to lie across her bare feet. She picked him up, and he curled on her lap with a grunt, tucking his narrow nose under his fluffy tail.

Then she smiled at Rhoswen and said, "You have given me more than I have ever had the right to ask, and far more than

I ever expected. Thank you for your devotion, and for everything you've done. I need you to do one more thing."

"Of course," Rhoswen said.

"I need you to take Rasputin and go back to San Francisco. I know you don't like to take care of him, so I want you to hire someone out of the household account. Make sure they pass all the required security checks, they get along with the rest of the staff, and they are available to stay in the town house. Then you are going to figure out what you want to do with the rest of your life."

"No," Rhoswen said. Tears sprang to her eyes.

"You should take your time," Carling said quietly. "I know what a big lifestyle change this will be for you. I have told Duncan to set up an account with plenty of money. He should have it ready by now."

"I won't go."

"Yes you will," Carling said. She kept her eyes and voice gentle and yet adamant. "It's past time, Rhoswen. You have not been happy for quite a while, and I have been selfish and let you stay with me for too long."

"But I can't go," Rhoswen said. "I love you."

"I love you too," said Carling, and she was surprised to find that she meant it. "But you have used me as an excuse to avoid living your own life, and I never gave you permission to try to curtail what I do or to control how I choose to do it. And I never promised that you could be with me for everything. I have some things I need to face on my own right now, and so do you."

"Please, don't make me leave," said Rhoswen. "I swear I can change. I'll look after the damn dog for you. You just said you needed me to hire somebody anyway."

"No, Rhoswen," said Carling. "That would not be the right thing for you, and I have been selfish for long enough. I'm sorry."

"You can't do this to me," said Rhoswen. "You can't just discard me like this, not after everything I've done for you."

"I am not discarding you," Carling said. She kept her voice even with an effort. Why did this have to be as much of a struggle as everything else had become with Rhoswen? "I am setting you up well and giving you plenty of time to adjust."

The next half hour was as difficult as she knew it would be, but eventually it had to end because she wouldn't budge no matter what Rhoswen said or how she pleaded.

Finally Carling's patience came to an end. Her voice, edged with command, cut through the last of Rhoswen's protests as she said, "That's enough." She sent Rhoswen, along with the dog, off to bed.

The younger Vampyre fled, and Carling sagged in relief as the atmosphere in the kitchen lightened considerably. Then she opened a bottle of cabernet sauvignon and poured herself a glass. She could no longer tolerate blood or bloodwine, and Vampyres remained unaffected by alcohol, but she could at least enjoy the taste. She sipped a glass and listened as the birds outside started to bellow with early-morning exuberance.

Then they fell abruptly silent, and she heard a giant rush of wings. Her spirit leaped at the sound. Moving with deliberation, she set her glass of wine on the table and stood to face the open door.

Moments later, Rune filled the open doorway with his long rangy body and hot sunlike presence. At some point he had shaved and changed into a black T-shirt that molded to his long muscled torso and another pair of faded jeans that were torn out at the knees. His hair was windswept, and he smelled like healthy male and the ocean's salty air. His lion's eyes met hers with a shock of connection she felt to her bare toes.

She remarked to no one in particular, "I notice that ten minutes was over quite some time ago."

From several feet away, she heard his heart kick into a faster rhythm, fueling the fierce energy of his body in hard, powerful strokes. Rune said, "Apparently I needed more than ten minutes."

She raised an imperious eyebrow. "Have you been sulking about something?"

"No," he said. "I have been thinking."

"That took you the rest of the night?"

The sun-bronzed muscles in his biceps bunched as he crossed his arms. He tilted his head as he regarded her. "Thinking," said Rune in a deliberately even tone of voice, "requires a great deal of thought."

"Well, that certainly is very Cheshire Cat–like of you. Along with your apparent knack for disappearing at times that are inconvenient for everyone else but yourself." She tried out a scowl. It seemed to be an appropriate expression for such a morning.

"Are you trying to pick a fight?" he asked. He gave her a sharp smile that showed the edge of his white teeth. "If so, cool."

"I don't know. I haven't decided yet," she said.

He prowled into the kitchen. "Make up your mind. I like a good fight."

She began to tap a bare foot, and his gaze dropped to track the movement. His face went still as he focused on the moment with a predatory laziness, like a lounging cat that was too comfortable to pounce but was liable to change its mind at any minute. She said, "You left when we were in the middle of a conversation."

His smile vanished. "I'm well aware of when I left."

"It was a conversation that interested me," she informed him.

His mouth drew into that hard unhappy line from earlier. "It was a conversation that interested me as well, I promise you."

"I am particularly interested in all the things that were left unsaid," she said. "Why you were so upset, and why you had to leave so abruptly. You were also upset when I woke up. I had forgotten that until after you left. You were full of aggression, like you wanted to fight someone then too. I would like to know why that was, and who put you in that state."

"I have things I need to say to you," Rune said. "They won't be easy to say and they won't be easy to hear."

"All right." She gave him a curt nod and muttered a line from *Macbeth*. "'Then 'twere well it were done quickly.'"

⇒ SEVEN ⇐

She turned away from him, toward her seat, and her gaze fell on the cool stove.

She said, "You have not eaten in quite some time. You must be hungry." She had witnessed just how much Wyr tended to eat at several inter-demesne functions, and again on the trip to Adriyel. They could put away horrendous amounts of food, especially those who were athletic. "Do you require sustenance?"

"I'm fine, thanks," he replied. "I went hunting when I was out."

She whirled in dismay. If anyone could break through the wards she had set around the redwoods, he could. "Not in the forest?"

His expression changed. He said quickly, "No, not in the forest. I felt your wards and left the area alone. I went fishing."

She relaxed and took her seat at the end of the table, closest to the open door. After a hesitation, he sat at her right. She regarded her half-empty wineglass as Rune leaned his elbows on the table. She sent him a quick sidelong glance. He was staring at the table's scarred surface, his gaze as turbulent and moody as the storm-swept sea.

She had seen him in many moods, she realized—sharply predatory, laughing, angry, dangerously intent. This quiet contemplation of his added another dimension to those strong, handsome features. She wanted to ask what he was thinking, what had put the sharp lines between his brows, why he held that elegant mouth of his in such a straight, severe line. Reluctantly she realized just how fascinated she had become with him. What would she do, if they discovered a way to halt the progression of her disease, and then he simply went away, back to his life in New York? How strange, that she had so quickly become accustomed to his presence. She would . . . miss him when he left.

She let her gaze fall to the tabletop as well, disturbed by the direction of her own thoughts and the intensity of her own reactions to him.

Rune began to speak. "I was outside yesterday evening when Rhoswen called me," he said. "It was close to sunset and you had faded again. We went up to your room, so I could see for myself."

None of that was news. They had already been in her room when she had come out of it. But it was apparent he had to take his own path toward whatever was the difficult part he had to say to her, so she curbed her impatience and simply nodded.

He ran his thumb along a knife mark on the table. "When we got upstairs, I saw sunlight spilling out of your bedroom doors."

Wait. Whatever she thought he had been about to say, that wasn't it. She sat forward, her sharpened gaze returning to his downturned face.

Rune continued, "Rhoswen didn't see it. We checked to make sure that the sunlight I saw—or thought I saw—wouldn't burn her. It didn't, so we stepped into your room. I went somewhere else. Rhoswen didn't."

He went on with his tale, his tone expressionless and his words precise. By the time he finished, she was gripping her hands together so tightly the tendons were distended white ridges against the rest of her honey-colored skin. He put his hand over hers. His broad palm and longer fingers covered both of hers effortlessly. He held on to her with a hard, reassuring grip.

He had thought about not telling her, as he flew over the ocean throughout the windswept night and tried to figure out what he should do. In the end, he couldn't keep silent. He refused to keep from this proud woman information she had a right to hear, no matter how hard it might be to tell her. And in the end, he needed her expertise in helping him analyze what had happened. But it was unspeakable to watch her suffer and not be able to prevent it.

She was whispering. He leaned closer to catch what she said. ". . . doesn't make any sense. None of it does."

"Why not?" he said. "State your reasons out loud."

She looked up. Her eyes had dampened but their intelligence was sharp and clear. "My Power has built up markedly over the last several years," she said. "I have so much sometimes it feels like I'm drowning in it. It flares up each time I'm about to go into a fade. But I simply do not have the *kind* of Power to create what you're describing. My magic is based on skill and education. It is an entirely different thing from the kind of Power that you have. And I don't have either the knowledge or the spells it would take to build something that huge or elaborate."

"How do you see the kind of Power I have?" he asked, curious.

"Wyr have attributes. You can practice with them and refine them, and you can bring them to a high level of expertise, but they are an intrinsic part of you."

"Your Power is an intrinsic part of you, and you study and practice to refine it," he pointed out.

"Yes, I know. How can I explain this better?" She frowned at him. "Okay, here is an example. Tiago is a thunderbird, a creature of storm and lightning. He can call a storm or a lightning bolt without words or spells. It's a characteristic, a part of who he is, yes?"

"Of course," he said.

She told him, "I might be able to call lightning, but I would have to study it first in order to do so. I would need a specific spell, and time enough to recite it. You can shapeshift. It's part of who you are. I can't shapeshift. I don't have the attribute, and I don't have a spell for it. It's all Power and it's all magic, and yes it can all get better with practice and refinement, but the two things stem from very different places. Dragos has studied sorcery, or spell magic. He can use both spell magic and his attributes of Wyr magic. That's one of the many things that make him so dangerous. You see?"

He nodded, playing with her fingers as he listened. He was

pleased to note that as her intellect took over, the pain in her eyes eased. It had not gone away, but it was better.

She said, "I can't do what Dragos does and access both types of magic, of course, because I am not Wyr. I can only practice spell magic, and I cannot even come close to creating the kind of reality you described. The best illusions I could create would be suggestions, sleights of hand, things you would see out of the corner of your eye that might attract you or make you want to turn away. Or I could build on something that already existed."

He stirred. "What do you mean?"

"Take my cottage. I could make it seem derelict and abandoned. The illusion would dissipate the moment you decided to walk up to it and explore. Or I could send a dream to you, but it really would be a dream, and any number of things might interrupt or change it. For example, you could disbelieve what was happening. People break out of dreams all the time. Or your alarm might go off and wake you up."

He frowned. "The way you describe it, anything you could do would take a great deal of work to set up."

"It does take a lot of work, yes." She pulled one of her hands out from underneath his to gesture. "It couldn't just happen when you're talking about spell magic. That would be like saying the Power flare could enter a computer code on a security door, and then walk into a bank vault, pick the right safe-deposit box, choose the right key off a key ring and insert it into the box's lock, pick the right file out of a pile in the box, put it all back in place and go to a notary public to get the papers in the file notarized. There are too many sophisticated steps that would need to be taken, including some high-level interaction with the person you wished to practice the illusion on."

He took her glass of wine and drank the contents. She reached for the nearby open bottle, refilled the glass and offered it to him. He said, "So what you are saying is that what happened had to be a different kind of magic."

Her brow cleared. "Yes," she said. "Maybe it was still some kind of an illusion or shared hallucination, but it wasn't any kind of spell magic my mind could have accidentally produced because I—how did you so poetically put it?— cracked out."

He gave a ghost of a chuckle. "All right, now we're getting somewhere," he said. He drank half the wine and nudged the glass over to her.

She picked up the glass and drank, then regarded him over the rim curiously. "How did it feel?"

He shrugged. "It didn't feel like an illusion. It felt as real as you and me sitting here. When I walked onto the sand, it felt like a kind of crossover passage only . . ."

She leaned forward as his voice trailed away. "Only what?"

His frowning gaze met hers. "Only it was bent somehow."

She waited but he didn't offer more. She said, "I don't understand."

He shook his head, a sharp, impatient gesture. "I don't either. But if it was a crossover, why could I walk it and not Rhoswen? She can make other crossovers. And if it was a crossover, how could it just appear and disappear? All the other passages I've seen are a fixed part of the landscape."

Carling's forehead wrinkled again the way it did when she was perplexed. "You both can make other crossovers. So it stands to reason, if you could make this one and she couldn't, it had to do with the differences between you."

"You mean I could make the crossover because of my Wyr attributes."

"Yes, although I don't know exactly what those are, other than you turn into a truly stunning gryphon."

He refused to let the compliment sidetrack him, even as the eagle part of his nature preened. He held out his hand for the wineglass, and she gave it to him. He drank from the place where her lips had rested. He thought she was too preoccupied to notice.

"Let's just say I have an affinity for crossover passages and between places," he said.

"Do you?" she breathed. "I wonder what would have happened if you had been holding Rhoswen's hand."

Even though Rhoswen could traverse normal crossovers, her inability to follow Rune earlier was akin to how dead-heads, or people with no Power, were unable to cross over to Other lands on their own. They needed to be brought over by someone with enough Power to make the crossing, and the only way to do that was through physical touch. When someone with no Power walked the path of a crossover, they simply followed the ravine or break in the landscape where the crossover was located, just as Rhoswen had walked into Carling's bedroom instead of stepping into the desert scene with Rune.

He considered Carling's question then shook his head. "It might be a good thing we weren't. We probably wouldn't have been touching when the scene disappeared—or I disappeared from the scene—and then what would have happened to her? Would she have come out of it too, or would she have been trapped there, like dead-heads are trapped in Other lands if they don't have someone to bring them back?"

They exchanged a sober look.

"So, what do we know?" Carling said. "If what happened was an illusion, it could not have come from my spell magic."

"Somehow it still has to be an integral part of you," Rune said. "The scene was a very intimate and important part of your past."

She bowed her head and the curve of her mouth turned unhappy, but she gave a reluctant nod.

Rune remembered the conversation he had had with Rhoswen. He said, "You may not be Wyr, but you are like Dragos in that you also have another kind of magic. Vampyre magic. Rhoswen said that a by-product of the virus was a certain amount of Power, at least enough for telepathy and crossovers, but the virus itself is also magic in nature. There are all the famous attributes that come from Vampyrism, like longevity, strength and speed."

Her head came up. She gave him a puzzled look. "Yes, of course, along with all the famous limitations like the need to drink blood, inability to eat solid foods, and vulnerability to sunlight, but I've never heard of this kind of thing happening to any of the other Vampyres who reached the end stages of the disease."

"How would you know?" he said. "The oral histories state that other Vampyres experienced some kind of episodes. You're experiencing episodes too, along with all the other symptoms you've categorized. It seems clear they must be connected to Vampyrism. Whatever actually happened yesterday—whether it was an illusion, shared hallucination or some kind of alternate reality—it was an interaction of me coming into contact with what was happening to you, and that has never happened before. Apparently I could connect with your event because of my Wyr attributes. What I went through had a very real, if strange, crossover experience. That's the information we have right now."

Carling shook her head slowly. "We also know that neither one of us was in control. I had no idea how dangerous this could be for you. I don't have a choice; I'm going through this whether I like it or not. But you do have a choice, and you need to protect yourself."

"We don't know enough," he said. "And we need to learn more. What I need to do is go back into the next episode, if I can, and see what else I can discover. Carling, your life depends on us figuring this out."

"I know." She met his gaze. "But I don't want you getting hurt."

He gave her a slight smile. "And I don't want you dying. We'll just have to look out for each other as best we can. When you have another episode, I'm going to try to engage again. Agreed?"

She straightened her spine and nodded. "Agreed."

She looked at the table. Rune had laced his fingers through one of hers while they talked. They had passed the wine back and forth with their free hands.

She murmured, "What do you suppose it means?"

She did not question his overtures any longer. Along with the rest of the list she had made earlier, it was clear Rune was too affectionate. Reaching out to touch or hug her seemed to come as easily as breathing to him. She was convinced that, like his penchant for flirting, it meant nothing. No doubt he did as much with everyone around him.

However, gestures of physical affection had never come easily to her. She meant to question how she had let him hold her hand without a shred of protest, but Rune's response was ambiguous enough that he could have taken her meaning another way.

"It means," he said as his fingers tightened on hers, "that I'll be very interested to see what happens next."

· · ·

The morning had brightened as they talked. The air turned heavy and yellow as the sun rose high overhead. Carling reclaimed her hand and went to stand at the open door. She supposed the temperature must have warmed as well. A steady brisk breeze blew from the ocean, smelling of brine and change. Things unresolved, things not understood. It was irritating to think of dying in the face of so much mystery. Could irritation become enough motivation to stay alive? Perhaps curiosity? She sighed, rubbed her face, and wished she could experience the restoration of sleep again.

Rune moved up behind her. She could feel the heat of his body along the length of her back, a siren's call of warmth and strength. He said, "Rhoswen didn't stay with you."

She turned her head slightly. "Why, was she supposed to?"

"We thought it would be best if one of us did, in case you slipped into an episode."

So that was why Rhoswen had argued with her so fiercely. She set her jaw. "I sent her to bed," she said. "She and Rasputin go back to San Francisco tonight." She turned to stab him with an angry gaze. "I can send you away too."

His eyelids dropped down, veiling the flare of ferocity in his gaze. "Can you now," he said. His voice dropped to a quiet low rumble in his chest, like the warning rumble of an earthquake deep in the earth before it rattled to the surface with a roar that toppled skyscrapers.

"Do not ever again make decisions for me, or about me, without my knowledge," she said between her teeth. "I am not senile. I am not suffering from dementia. *I will not tolerate it*, do you understand?"

His gaze lifted. He studied her tense face, and the anger that had taken over his own expression broke apart. "I'm sorry, Carling. It wasn't meant like that. We just didn't want you to go into a fade by yourself, especially if the situation might become dangerous because then you wouldn't be able to defend yourself. And you weren't available at the time for us to consult with you."

She searched his face and saw nothing but sincerity. After

a moment her rigid stance relaxed somewhat. She gave him a curt nod and turned back to the open door, her arms wrapped around herself tightly.

Then he moved, to do what, she didn't know, but she propelled herself forward, because she couldn't stand it if he touched her right then with another one of his affectionate gestures. One of these days she thought he might touch her one too many times, and she would shatter like a piece of overstrained porcelain. "You have reading to do," she said shortly. "And I have a mess to clean up."

She walked fast down the sun-filled path to her work cottage, stood in the open doorway, and took stock of last night's work. The air was tinged with a hint of soot and the lingering echo of dark magic, but the sun and the wind would help to take care of that. Herbs, empty pitchers, and her jar of sea salt littered the work table, and the fireplace was full of soggy ash. The circle of sea salt she had cast still lay strewn on the floor, its former pure white turned dingy.

She had better start with the salt or she would track it all through the cottage. She went to the closet and pulled out a broom. Rune's hot sunlike presence filled the open doorway. She gritted her teeth and gripped the broom handle hard. One wrong word or move from him and, swear to gods, she was going to smack him over the head with the broom.

"You've been busy," he said, his tone mild. "Do you mind if I read in here?"

She struggled with herself then said, "Not as long as you're quiet."

"I promise," he said gently. "I'll be as good as gold."

His voice seemed to brush along her skin in a featherlight caress. She bristled against the sensation and said, "Shut up."

He laughed, a quiet husky chuckle that filled all the cold, dark corners of the room with warmth and sounded like it belonged between silken sheets. She gave him a glare and then attacked the floor with the broom.

He was as good as his word. If he hadn't been, she really would have smacked him. He pulled one of the armchairs over to the open doorway and the morning sun. Then he settled himself, one ankle propped on the jeans-covered knee of his other leg, and he opened her journal. She glanced at him. His tousled hair was crowned in bright gold, his lean spare face turning still with concentration.

Her greedy soul drank down the sight. Then she forced herself to turn away. She set to work, and gradually, as she cleaned and Rune read, a fragile calm stole into the cottage and into her mind. When she finally had the room spotless and all her supplies put away, she set several branches of dried white sage in the empty fireplace. The sage would dispel any lingering darkness that might cling to the stones.

As the morning evaporated into afternoon, the edges of her vision began to flicker with the telltale sign that her Power was building again, and she knew she was headed into another fade soon. She would not accept the feelings that tightened her stomach and dried out her mouth. She refused to feel trapped, and she would not let fear rule her. With Rune present, they had an opportunity to learn more together than she had been able to in the last two centuries combined.

The best thing to do was to keep busy until it happened. She went into her office to frown at the empty cabinet where she had stored the books of black magic.

She sucked on her lower lip as she regarded it. It was a fine, well-constructed cabinet built of cedar. She had carved the surface herself with spells of protection and binding. The work had taken days, and she hated the thought of destroying it. But the books had been stored in the cabinet for too long. She could feel their lingering malice. It had soaked into the wood.

Reluctantly she came to the only conclusion she could. She could try to purify the cabinet, but that would be time-consuming and she was never going to trust storing delicate things in it. In the end, there was only one way to be absolutely sure all of the dark energies were well and truly dissipated. The cabinet would have to be destroyed as well.

She heaved a sigh, retrieved a hammer and screwdriver from the small toolbox in the office closet, and began to dismantle the cabinet by striking at the joints.

Rune appeared soon after the first hammer blow. She had grown so sensitized to his energy, she knew without bothering to look the moment he stepped into the room.

"So that's what the mess in the other room was about," he said. "You decided to get rid of the misbehaving books."

"It was past time."

He sent her a thoughtful glance but refrained from commenting. Instead, he said, "I take it the cabinet is contaminated."

"Yes. It's best to be on the safe side and burn it." She positioned the tip of the screwdriver at the juncture of a panel, struck it with the hammer, and levered the pieces of wood apart. They came apart with a sharp crack.

He came up beside her, standing too close. He asked, "May I help?"

How like a male. Pull out some tools and start banging on something, and they flocked in from miles around. She pushed her hair out of her face with the back of one hand and scowled at him. "I am perfectly capable of breaking it down myself."

"Of course you are," he told her, smiling. "That's not what I said. I said may I help?"

She shrugged irritably and stepped back. Rune studied the cabinet for a moment then grasped the sides. She said, "I could tear it apart with my bare hands too if I wanted, hotshot, but I don't want my office walls scratched."

"Have some faith," Rune said.

"Fine." She threw up her hands. The fragile calm she had achieved blew into tatters. She wanted the broom again. She might still smack him before the day got much older. "If you scratch my walls, you're going to repaint the office yourself."

He gave her an amused glance over one wide shoulder. "You're in a mood." The muscles in his wide, powerful back tensed, and he pushed out with controlled force. The cabinet split apart at the joints. He made quick work of dismantling it without, she noticed, scratching the walls once. Then he bent to stack the pieces together. "Do you have any twine?"

She went over to the open toolbox that sat on the floor just outside the closet. She set the hammer and screwdriver in the box, found a ball of twine and threw it at him hard.

It whistled through the air with such speed a human couldn't have seen it, but he reached out and plucked it from the air with a lazy-seeming gesture. Of course he did. He bound the cedar pieces together swiftly, pulled out a pocketknife, cut the twine and pocketed the knife again. Without looking up, he flung the ball of twine back at her. Hard.

She flinched back a step but caught it. She glared at the ball and slam-dunked it into the toolbox, and suddenly Rune was right in front of her. Too close. Of course. He was always too close, and he stepped forward, closer still, until their bodies brushed together.

She looked up, her gaze narrowed. "You're in my space."

"I know I am." He brought his amused, sensual face down to hers. In a murmur so quiet it came out as a throaty purr, he asked, "Would you like to tell me what might coax you out of your mood? I would be happy to oblige you with just about anything."

She stared up at him, her eyes widening. Desire roared back between them, both his and hers. It flared low in her belly and weighted her limbs so that she wanted to lie down. Her imagination supplied her with the molten image of him lying on top of her, his nude muscled body flexing, that beautiful wild face of his sharp with sex and need.

Her body insisted it needed to suck in some air. She fought and lost a battle with control, and took a breath, all of her senses thrumming with his hot vivid presence. The light brush of his hard chest against her nipples ignited sensations that were so long dormant, they should have remained dead and buried.

This was a wicked madness. He caused her to feel too much. It had gone beyond a dangerous, useless distraction and was fast approaching obsession. She couldn't cope with all of it, both his emotions and hers. Coping with simple hope and fear were hard enough.

She tore her gaze away from his compelling face. Her hands shot out. She fisted them in his black T-shirt. "Did you finish reading?"

His sensual amusement faded. "Yes, just before I came in here."

She concentrated her gaze on her fists as they rested against the hard plate of his breastbone. "And?"

He cupped her shoulders. "And, I don't know. Your work is brilliant, but then you knew that. Something bothers me, and I haven't been able to pinpoint what it is. It's like trying to say that word that's sitting on the tip of your tongue. You know the word is there and you've used it many times before, but you can't quite think to say it."

"Try harder."

His fingers tightened. "What's wrong?"

She tried to smile. It came out all twisted and wrong. "I'm starting to feel my Vegas again."

He took a deep breath and pulled her into his arms. "That's okay," he said. His voice was as rock-steady as his gaze had been earlier. His cheek came down on the top of her head. "We knew it was coming. We'll go through it together and we'll learn more."

She forced the words out. "That's what I've been telling myself."

Damn him, he stroked her hair, and then there were more feelings, traitorous feelings accompanied by weakening thoughts.

What would it hurt if she relaxed her rigid spine just once, just for a little bit? She tried it and found herself leaning against him. He guided her head so that it rested in the hollow of his shoulder. Her head seemed to fit there so flawlessly, the realization felt like it bruised her. Strength coursed through his long massive body, an inexhaustible well of Power that surrounded her with warmth. He wrapped his arms around her and somehow her arms found their way around his waist, and then they held on to each other tight.

Her eyes prickled again. They filled with burning liquid and spilled over. It had been so long since she had cried it took her several moments to identify the wetness.

He had done this to her. He opened doors in her that never should have been opened again. He was a sirocco that blasted through the topography of her mind and soul until they shifted like desert sands, and he forced her to confront feelings she had thought she would never feel again, wonder and desire, hope and fear.

Then he taught her how to feel new things, things that were so fresh and fragile and crushable, she was afraid they might break her. Fight to live, he said to her, and it was such a hard thing to do, because she couldn't rouse herself to care enough to fight without also feeling afraid. Before he came, she thought she would only lose her life. She had distanced herself so she could witness her own end with detachment. Now she felt like she might lose something else just as valuable: her understanding of who she was.

She whispered, "Sometimes I think I hate you."

He rubbed his cheek in her hair. "Why is that, darling?"

Her lips parted. Hadn't he called her that once, so very long ago . . . or at least what seemed to her so very long ago? Only she hadn't known what the word meant or understood what he was saying. She had thought he was a strange and beautiful god, calling her by a sacred name . . .

Rune cradled her close as he felt his T-shirt grow wet. He could smell a trace of frankincense in her hair, along with the clean fresh scent of lavender. Underneath that was her lush womanly fragrance, and she was so utterly perfect that bewilderment and outrage roared through him again at the thought of her dying.

Wait. His breath hissed. There it was, the word on the tip of his tongue, only it wasn't a word but a concept. A premise, not a conclusion.

He buried his face in the slender crook of her neck, crushing her to him. She stirred and murmured either a protest or a question. He muttered, "Hold on just a minute."

He wrapped his Power around her and opened his Wyr senses wide, and inhaled Carling's fragrance again.

Wyr, especially the older and more Powerful Wyr, could sense disease in a way that animals could. They could taste when food was tainted, which made them extremely difficult to poison. They could smell when injuries became infected, or when illness was exuded in a person's sweat glands.

Carling's research had taken the path of modern medicine. She had followed closely the research done by Louis Pasteur and Emile Roux. She had chronicled how she had corresponded with the two doctors in the 1880s, asking detailed questions about their development of a vaccine for rabies. In turn the two scientists had studied Vampyrism with fascination.

Vampyrism had all the characteristics of a blood-borne pathogen. It was found in blood and certain other bodily fluids and had a 98.9 percent infection rate when a direct blood exchange had occurred. It could not be transmitted through air, and intact skin acted as an effective barrier. The conviction that

Vampyrism was an infectious disease had become so well-entrenched in modern thought, it was no longer questioned. Now in the twenty-first century, virtually all medical and scientific research on Vampyrism was based on that premise.

But every instinct Rune had was telling him Carling's energy was robust. She did not smell diseased. He thought of the woman he had passed just outside the Bureau of Nightkind Immigration. That woman's sickness had been evident. The taint had lingered on her skin underneath the scent of lilacs.

Carling smelled sexy and feminine with the tantalizing sultriness of her own Power, and the faint metallic tinge that all Vampyres shared.

In fact, to Rune she smelled perfectly healthy.

"I've got it, I figured out what bothers me," he said. He straightened and pulled her away as he talked. Her arms fell loose to her sides. "What if everything you tried didn't work because Vampyrism is not a disease?"

Grinning, he looked down into that haunting, beautiful face of hers that had grown on him like an addiction. Her expression was blank, those long almond-shaped eyes of hers fixed on something only she could see.

His stomach clenched. He guided her over to her office chair and nudged her to sit. She went without a protest, as passive as a doll.

A ripple went through the office. Then the scene changed. He relaxed and let it take him.

It was time to hit Vegas again, baby.

═ EIGHT ═

He didn't walk a path this time, but the shift in energies felt just like a crossover again, a crossover that somehow turned, was bent in some fundamental way. It was like taking a flight of stairs that doubled back on itself, or turning a corner and discovering a different landscape than expected. He tried to hold on to the feeling so he could examine it more closely. He had the sense of almost grasping it, but then the feeling flowed past him and was gone.

Carling's office faded, and a hot, humid evening enfolded him. Disoriented, he stood still and soaked in impressions.

Somewhere nearby there was the hoarse rhythmic bellow of bullfrogs. He looked up. The shadowed, spiked tops of palm groves dotted the edges of the night sky, which was brilliant with stars in a way that modern cities with their light pollution never saw anymore.

He stood in the shadows of a columned building built of granite blocks, close by other, larger buildings. Indirect torchlight flickered in various places. The air was pungent with the fetid smell of the nearby river, and the lingering odor of rich food. He smelled yeasty things, beer and bread, along with spiced fish and meat. The evening must still be fairly young.

He also smelled people, and he heard raised voices. A man, shouting in rage. A lighter, younger feminine voice, spilling out a desperate-sounding patter of rapid words. Too accustomed to modern languages, his mind felt rusty as it tried to switch gears and make sense of what he heard.

There was no mistaking the meaty sound of a blow, and a sharp pained cry that was cut short. Nor the sound of a whip as it sliced through air.

A whip.

Fucking hell.

Moving on panic and instinct, Rune lunged forward. He slammed into a wall and sprang off it, and hurtled up wide carved stairs, following the projection of echo back to its source.

Come on. Kick up the speed, goddamn it. He moved faster than he could ever remember moving in his life, but the flat wicked slice of the whip tore through the air in a second stroke, and the sound flayed him alive.

He exploded into a large, luxurious room. Arranged for a seduction, it had become the scene of a torture. Metal braziers lit the space with an abundance of flickering light. The room was open on three sides to a simple balcony and the night air, and framed with gauze hangings that kept out the river insects. There was artfully arranged bedding, untouched. A low table held a feast of meat, fish, spiced vegetables, beer, bread and honey.

A girl child sprawled on the floor, her narrow honey-colored back split and bleeding with whip lashes. A dark man stood over her. He wore a *shenti*, tooled sandals, and a collar made of beaten copper, and he had a close-clipped beard and a gaze glittering with fury. The man pulled back his arm and shook out his whip.

Rational thought vaporized in an internal nuclear explosion. What was left was a murderous beast. Claws sprang out. The gravelly roar that burst out of his chest split the night with the force of a rocket launcher.

The beast leaped. With a single swipe of his paw, he nearly split the man into four pieces. The whip fell discarded. The man was dead before he hit the floor.

The killing had happened too soon to assuage the beast's rage. He roared again, scooped up the corpse and flung it. Blood sprayed through the air. The corpse hit the wall. Bones cracked audibly upon impact. The broken body left a wet smear of crimson as it slid down along the wall.

Utter stillness filled the night. Even the bullfrogs and night insects fell silent in the presence of an apex predator. It seemed the whole world held its breath.

Except for the whimpering gasps at the feet of the beast.

He looked down, breathing hard. The girl child cowered into the floor, digging at it with the nails of both hands as if she would tear the stones open and disappear if she could. She wore the shreds of some filmy garment, along with a necklace made of copper and lapis lazuli, and bracelets of carved bone. Her delicate rib cage shuddered, the skin of her back torn and bleeding.

Whimper-gasp.

The beast became Rune again. "Poor baby," he whispered. He bent down to touch her shoulder.

She cried out and cringed, and his beast resurfaced just enough to claw at him from the inside. He came around to kneel at her head. She was older than the seven-year-old he had met, but not by much, maybe by five or six years. Her emerging beauty had been carefully emphasized, those long eyes lined in kohl and green malachite, and her shapely mouth painted with red ochre. The malachite and kohl streaked her tear-stained face, and the red paint was smeared. Underneath the extravagant wreckage of color, the normal honeyed warmth of her skin was pallid with shock.

His stomach roiled. It did no good to tell himself that this was a much more primitive time and that girls were often married by the time they were twelve. She still looked like the victim of child porn. For a few scorching moments his sanity slipped. He did not know what he would have done if the smell of sex had been in the room.

She was in too much of a panic. At a loss, he hesitated then he did the only thing he could think of to do. He lay down on his stomach beside her and put his head on the floor, face toward her, so he was down at her level. Then he began to talk in a quiet, soothing patter of noise.

"Khepri, my name is Rune. We met once a few years ago. Do you remember me? I remember you very well. I was flying overhead when I saw you watching me, so I came down to talk to you. You had been working to harvest grain from the field."

Did the blind panic in her young face ease just a little, or was that his imagination? Her shaking lips struggled to form a word. She whispered, "A-Atum."

Rune's eyes grew damp. "Yes," he murmured as softly as he could. "You thought I was Atum, and I told you I wasn't. Do you remember that?"

Her overbright gaze focused on him. She gave him a jerky nod.

Dimly he was aware of other people running into the room. The beast was still roused and tracked their movements with cold precision. If they had come an inch too close, they would have died, but they stopped at the edge of the room. After exclaiming to each other, they prostrated themselves on the floor.

That was well enough. To them he was, after all, a god, and this time he did not try to deny it.

He smiled at Khepri. "Please, darling, don't be afraid of me. The man who was hurting you can't hurt you any longer."

She lifted her head. Her gaze tracked left toward the shredded corpse that lay in a crumpled heap by the wall. He shifted to hold his hand as a shield between her and the sight, not quite touching her cheek. She whispered, "Is he dead?"

This was no modern sheltered child. He knew she had already seen death before. He said, "Yes. He injured you. It made me very angry, and I killed him."

She took a deep, shuddering breath and let it out. Ferocity flashed in her eyes. For a moment she looked as feral as a tiger cub. "Good."

Just like that, he fell head over heels in love with the child all over again. "May I help you now?"

The spark of ferocity vanished. Her lips trembled and her eyes swam with tears as she nodded again.

At that the beast threatened to take over again. He rose up on his hands and knees, and gathered her carefully in his arms, working to make sure he didn't touch the wounds on her back. He carried her over to the bedding and eased her onto it so that she was lying facedown. Then he looked at the humans who remained prostrate before him. There were four, a woman, two men with spears, and another, older man. Judging by the ornamentation of his clothing, the older man was the most powerful of those present.

Rune restrained the urge to kick them. He said, "Get up."

The humans peered at him, saw that he was talking to them and cautiously eased upright. They remained on their knees and stole glances at the bloody corpse and at each other. He said to the older man. "I want hot water, medicine and bandages, along with something clean for her to wear. Be quick."

"Yes, my lord." The man hissed at the woman, who backed out of the room. A moment later, Rune heard her running footsteps on the stairs.

He settled beside Khepri. She moved her head closer to put her cheek against his knee, and he stroked her hair as he struggled with his self-control. He said to her, "Beer would help with the pain. Would you like some?"

She nodded. He gestured to the older man, who sprang to his feet to bring two full goblets to him, the rich, heavy liquid shivering in his unsteady grip. Rune took one goblet, ignored the other, and helped Khepri to drink while the man knelt at his feet and awaited further commands. The beer would have a strong alcoholic content, but she had probably been drinking it since she was two or three. It was a wheat beer, and no doubt the grain had gotten a little moldy. That meant there would be tetracycline in the liquid, which was good. It would help to stave off any infection from the lash marks. He encouraged her to finish the goblet.

When the hectic brightness of her eyes began to glaze over, he said to the man, "Are you a priest?"

"Yes, my lord."

He was unsurprised. Ancient Memphis had a surfeit of temples and necropoleis. He said, "Do you have authority?"

The man bowed his head. "Yes, my lord."

"You will listen to me now and do as I say."

"I live to serve you." The man dared to look up, the fanatical light of devotion in his dark eyes.

Rune's lip curled. What the fuck ever. He thought for a moment, choosing and discarding things to say. There was so much that would simply make no sense to this man. Finally he said, "What happened here tonight is an abomination to me."

The man said quickly, "My lord, I promise you, the slave was not being disciplined without reason. She failed in her duty to please another god who was here—"

Another god?

Rune's eyes flared in quick, jealous reaction. He looked around, taking in again the feast that had been so carefully laid out, the scene of seduction that had not been enacted. The man cowered before him. Khepri's fingers stole behind her head to touch his hand, and he realized belatedly that he had started growling.

He made himself stop. He took a deep breath then another, analyzing the many scents in the room, and he realized what panic and rage had not let him realize before: another Wyr had recently been in the room.

Gently, he curled his hand around Khepri's fingers, as he leaned over the priest. "Look at me." The priest looked up, eyes wide, and Rune bared his teeth in a show of naked aggression. "A god chooses to do what he will. *How dare you place the responsibility of that onto the shoulders of a mere girl?*"

The priest fell forward to prostrate himself again. "My lord, I am sorry! We did not know we transgressed. Forgive us!"

"This is my decree," Rune said. "You will take this slave and treat her as your most favored daughter. You will educate her as well as any man, and protect her, and see she has the best life you can give her. *You* will do this, and no other. If you fail in the slightest to do this one thing, I will find you. I will pull out your entrails, and leave you to watch them bake in the noonday sun. Do you understand me?"

As the priest babbled his agreement, the woman returned, carrying medicines and a pile of linens under one arm. She was followed by two other women bearing urns of steaming water. They hesitated at the doorway, their eyes wide, until Rune gestured them forward impatiently.

"Tend to her," he said to them.

Whispering to each other, the women did as he ordered. He watched them. When he saw for himself how carefully they treated Khepri, he began to ease himself away.

Her small hand clenched on his and anchored him in place. He bent over her, and smoothed the hair from her forehead. She watched him with a mute entreaty. He did not understand what she wanted. Perhaps she didn't either, and she only clung to the one person who had made her world safe again.

He said to her, "I am not sure when or how, but I can promise you one thing, darling. We will see each other again. Would that be all right with you?"

She nodded, her smudged face half hidden by the slippery dark silk of hair. On impulse he bent forward and pressed his lips to her forehead. Her fingers tightened on his hand, and then she let him go.

He stood and stretched his spine as he looked around. Gods. The scene was so intense, so real, he had completely fallen into it.

Could it be an illusion or a hallucination? Could it be something else, something more real? Could he somehow be affecting things in the past? He felt the impulse to laugh, to shove the idea aside. Then he looked at the whip marks that were still bleeding on Khepri's back and lost the impulse.

When he turned away, the priest was watching him with close attention. Rune stared at the man, his gaze brooding. In the Bible's Old Testament, Gideon laid out a fleece to ask for evidence of God's will.

Rune shrugged. He might not be a Christian and he did not depend upon the gods' will, but asking for evidence seemed like a hell of a good idea. He turned his back to Khepri and her attendants, dug into his jeans and pulled out his pocket-knife. It was a thoroughly modern, sturdy Swiss Army knife. He wondered how it would hold up for roughly forty-five hundred years.

He asked the priest, "What is your name?"

"Akil, my lord."

"Who is your king, Akil?"

The whites of the priest's eyes showed. It was clear he could not imagine why a god would not know such a thing, but he answered readily enough, "Djoser."

Rune relaxed. He knew a little about Djoser, not least of which the man's architect Imhotep had built one of the biggest, most famous ancient structures known to men. He held the knife up to the priest and pulled out all of its blades, watching as Akil's eyes grew round with wonder.

"This is my gift to you," he said. "Do not show this to Khepri or to anyone else. Do not write of it or leave any record of its existence. As proof of your devotion, I want you to bury it at the entrance of Djoser's temple in Saqqara." Saqqara was the giant necropolis, or city of the dead, that served as a burial ground for Ineb Hedj and later on for Memphis. "It might be a very long time before I can return for it, but I will."

He closed the knife again and held it out. Akil took it with reverence. "I will, my lord. You can be sure of it."

Yeah well, Rune thought. We'll see about that.

Carling's gaze focused on the interior of her office.

She was sitting in her desk chair. The cedar cabinet lay dismantled in a bundle against one wall. The slant of the sun had shifted from afternoon to early evening. The sunlight poured through the window in lethal bars of burning gold. She shuddered and looked away.

The room echoed with the emotional aftermath of aggression and violence. Rune prowled the office with the intensity of a caged animal. His face was set, his eyes roiling with the restless flicker of rapid thought. His long athletic strides made the roomy office seem stifling and too small. He shifted the heavy bundle of cedar to check underneath it. Then he moved to search alongside the floors beside the filing cabinets, and the space between the desk and the wall.

She cleared her throat and asked in a rusty-sounding voice, "What on earth are you doing?"

He swung around, his gaze flaring. He sprang to crouch at her feet. "How are you?"

"I'm fine," she told him. It was a ridiculous thing to say, given everything that was going on. "You looked like you lost something."

"I was looking for my pocketknife. I had it in this room and now I can't find it anywhere." He searched her face with a peculiar intensity that felt like a physical touch. "Do you remember seeing it anywhere?"

She scowled. "Of course I remember seeing it. I watched you cut the twine with it. Why do you ask?"

"It's been an eventful afternoon," he said.

"That doesn't really answer my question," she said.

"I don't have any answers," he told her. He gripped the arms of her chair. "I'm busy grappling with too many questions of my own. Do you remember going into a fade?"

"That's right," she murmured. "Of course I did." She fell

silent as she studied him. She thought of the memory she had gone back to when she had slipped into the fade, back and back, to one of the most painful, traumatic and pivotal times of her early life. She had been kept pristine, her virginity intact, saved and trained until she could be given as a gift at a strategic time to an important personage.

Then an immense, dark and terrifying god had touched down to earth to regard white-walled Ineb Hedj and its people with a passing curiosity. In the end, he had been indifferent to the city, its devout priests and religion, and uninterested in her as a gift. He had left, and she had been punished for it.

Then, with a crystalline clarity that the many intervening centuries had not dimmed, she remembered the whistle of the whip as it snaked through the air and plunged her into the most savage, transcendent pain, turning her world raw with the screams she did not have the breath to cry out.

And into that raw place an enormous golden monster had erupted, roaring with an agony as if he had been the one who was whipped, bringing with him both death and salvation.

The world rattled. Carling's mouth opened. She tried to form words.

"God, you're shaking like a leaf," Rune muttered. "Talk to me."

"I'm trying," she gritted. She grabbed his strong, tanned wrists. He seemed to be the only thing that wasn't shaking, that held steady. Their eyes met. "I s-see you went back a second time."

He turned his hands to grip her wrists as well. "Yes. Can you tell me what happened to you? There was another Wyr involved, or at least there had been before I got there. Do you know who it was?"

The other Wyr had been Tiago, of all people, who had never remembered what had happened, because to him the whole incident had been unimportant. He had never known what the consequences of his indifference and departure had meant for her.

She shook her head. She had been angry and resentful at Tiago for so long, but for once, she meant what she said as she told Rune, "It doesn't matter. It was just a curious Wyr who looked around briefly and then left again. The priests wanted him to stay, of course, which was why they gave me to him, but he wasn't interested."

Something unpredictable and razor-edged prowled in his lion's eyes. "So he didn't come back."

"No," she said. "At least not while I lived in the city."

"Okay." Rune seemed to relax only slightly. "Does . . . what happened . . . feel as real to you as the first time when I appeared?"

The world started to rattle again. She nodded.

His hands tightened on her wrists as he whispered, "It does to me too. Carling, I need to have a look at your back."

She stared at him. "Why?"

The handsome, clean lines of his face were rigid with an emotion that rioted through the heavy afternoon air. "I need to look at your scars. It's important."

With a bewildered shrug, she leaned forward and bent her head. She held the caftan in place over her breasts and allowed him to ease the loose cotton material away from her neck. With a featherlight touch he pulled her hair to one side. He handled her as gently as if she were spun glass, and his big body was so near as he knelt in front of her, that she let herself lean a few inches farther to rest her cheek on his wide shoulder. He caressed the nape of her neck as he slid the caftan down her back.

She felt the breath leave him hard. His fingers were unsteady against her bare skin. She lifted her head to stare at the clean, spare lines of his profile. She was so close she could see the fine lines deepen at the corners of his eyes, and sense the shift in his throat muscles as he swallowed hard.

"What is it?" she asked.

She craned her neck to look over her shoulder. She could just see the ends of the long, white sinuous scars that crossed her spine like two snakes winding around a staff. She had lived with those scars for thousands of years. She knew them like she knew the back of her hand. She would never forget the night they happened, or how Rune had broken into the room to stop a third one from falling on her . . .

She stiffened. No. That hadn't happened thousands of years ago. That had happened just minutes ago, this afternoon. What had happened before Rune took action? What had really occurred to her, four and a half thousand years ago?

"Something else happened before you showed up," she whispered. "I don't remember. I don't remember what originally happened to me."

Before Rune had burst into the room, the priest had stood over her in a rage. He had shaken out the whip. He would have struck her again, except that Rune had killed him with one savage blow.

Rune looked at her, his eyes darkened. He said in a low voice, "All I know is that a couple of weeks ago you went swimming in the Adriyel River and when you walked out, you didn't have just two whip marks on your back. Your whole body was striped with scars."

She remembered it well. She walked nude out of the water while Niniane and Rune waited on the riverbank. Rune had stared at her with such a fire in his eyes they had glittered like yellow diamonds. His handsome face had become a carved mask, and every muscle in his body had stood in etched relief against the long masculine frame of his bones, as if he had been created by a classical sculptor.

She said, "You're *changing* me?"

"I think what we are doing together must somehow be changing something," he said. "Because I swear to all the gods, Carling, your back was not like this before."

She stared at him in horror.

She had compared him to a sirocco. She'd had no idea how accurate that was. A sirocco was a hurricane that came out of the Sahara. In Egypt the hot desert wind was called *Khamsin*. It could reach speeds of up to eighty-five miles an hour. She remembered the howl of the wind at night. It was an immense, unearthly, inhuman sound. It stripped flesh off of bones, literally reshaped the land.

First she thought she would lose her life. Then she became afraid she would lose everything else. Her Power, her sanity. Her dignity.

She had not known there could be anything more to lose, that bits of her past might slough away like flesh peeling from the bones. The change was vaster and more Powerful than anything she had ever experienced, and she had never felt the difference.

She had not known she might be in danger of losing her self.

≈ NINE ≈

"Get away from me." She shoved him back and leaped out of her chair.

He sprang upright and stepped forward, hand outstretched. He said, "Not while you're in a panic."

She spun behind the chair, picked it up and flung it at him. She shouted, "Get the fuck out!"

With a swipe of his arm, he knocked it to one side. Determination stamped his features. "Think a minute, Carling. You've just had an episode. Another won't occur for at least another several hours, perhaps even a day or more. We have time to discuss this and figure out what it means—"

She stared at him in incredulity. She could not remember the last time someone disobeyed a direct order of hers.

"Fine, goddamn you," she hissed, "I'll get out."

She made it to the doorway before she felt his hand come down on her shoulder. It was too much. She knocked him away and spat out a Power-filled word that iced the air.

Rune froze in midmotion, his arm still stretched toward her. Then his Power surged in response, hot like a solar flare, and even though she had put enough force behind the spell to throw half the Vampyres in San Francisco into stasis, she knew it wasn't going to be strong enough to hold him for long.

She never did get around to researching what spells would be effective against gryphons. She might regret that some day.

Fury pulsed from him like the outward rolling blast of a thermonuclear explosion. Slowly he began to move.

She fell back a step, staring. Then she turned and ran.

At first she headed for the house. Then she thought of Rhoswen's stifling, resentful devotion, Rasputin's frantic adoration, and she switched directions, racing along the path far faster than a human could ever hope to run, along the path that followed the cliff toward the other end of the island and the redwood forest. The evening sunshine slanted bars of light everywhere, transforming the idyllic scene into a deadly luminous prison.

When she was young, she had been taught that she was composed of many parts, her souls, her heart, her shadow, name and spirit.

How many pieces of yourself could you survive losing? When she had been just a child, she had lost her family and her freedom, and then she had lost her name. Just a few short years later, she had lost her breath and her heart had stopped beating. Then she lost almost everyone around her, not once but many times. With each decision she made that was based on Power, expediency, politics, survival and war, she lost pieces of her souls throughout the centuries. Her spirit felt gossamer-thin, in tatters.

She looked at the ground. Her attenuated, nimble shadow fled before her, as if trying to escape the nightmarish haunt she had become.

What if her shadow was the only real thing that was left of her? Had she, in the end, become nothing more than just the exercise of Power, the will to survive? If she removed the spell of protection, she would erupt into flames, but unlike the phoenix, she would not undergo a rebirth. Like a struck match, she would simply flare out of existence.

She could do it. She could go out, not gently into that good night but in a brilliant sunlit blaze, with no one around to witness. Her death might be solitary, as so very much of her life had been, but it would be her choice, her decision. *Hers*. She would own it, like she had claimed ownership of her life.

A cloud passed over the sun, so dense it eclipsed her shadow. She looked up.

It was no cloud but a great gold and bronze gryphon, soaring overhead. She could not imagine the kind of strength it must take to keep that heavy, muscled body of his aloft, and yet he made his flight seem so effortless.

Her fists clenched. He was a rampant impossibility, an enormous freak of nature.

He was such a *stubborn ass*.

She sucked in a lungful of air and screamed wordlessly at him. A harsh wrathful eagle's cry sounded in reply.

The whole damn island wasn't big enough for both of them. Okay fine. She already swore she was going to do it, and anyway, she was perfectly capable of being the one to leave if he wouldn't do so. She took a sharp left, picked up speed, and sprinted at full strength over the edge of the cliff.

The wind whistled in her ears. As she fell, she was already making plans. She would swim back to San Francisco. Julian wouldn't like her return. They had reached an understanding, she and the Nightkind King, when she had come to the island to die. But Julian would have to adjust, and Rhoswen was perfectly capable of making the crossing with the dog on her own.

Carling rolled in the air to dive headfirst and watched the foaming white-capped water rush toward her. She reached out to it with both arms, anticipating the cold shock of the plunge into water with grim satisfaction.

Hard claws jerked her upward with gut-wrenching force just before she hit. *Son of a bitch.* Her head snapped back. As the universe wheeled, she caught a glimpse of the gigantic lion paws that curled to grip her by the shoulder and thigh. The edge of tremendous bronze wings hammered down on either side of her.

She shouted at Rune, "You did not just do that!"

His deep voice sounded overhead. "How is that disbelief working out for you?"

The need to do violence caused her fists to shake. He swooped up with her to the top of the cliff and dumped her on the ground. With a twist of her hips, she flipped onto her back and drove her fist upward as hard as she could. Before she could get the blow to full extension, he knocked her hands aside and pinned her by driving his claws deep into the ground on either side of her arms.

He imprisoned the rest of her body by the simple expediency of lying down on top of her. It felt like she had a Hummer parked on her chest. While she might have the strength to shift a Hummer—she didn't know, she'd never tried—she sure as hell didn't have the strength to do it without any kind of leverage.

Outrage steam-whistled. Not in thousands of years had anyone dared to try to lay a hand (or paw, as it were) on her without her permission. She felt like she was about to blow a gasket. "*YOU BASTARD!* Let go of me!"

"Shut the fuck up." His growl vibrated through her body to rumble in the earth beneath her.

Sunlight blinded her as she glared up at him, turning him into a towering blur overhead. She scrambled mentally for a spell and sucked in a breath—

—and the towering blur plummeted toward her. It resolved into an immense, sleek eagle's head the length of her arm, with a long wicked hook of a beak that snapped at her. Rune tilted his head to stare at her with a blazing fierce eye the size of a headlamp. He roared, "*DON'T YOU DARE!*"

It was like having an F-16 bomber take off in her face. Her hair blew away from her face.

The spell died on her lips as she stared at the enraged gryphon. She had never seen him so close in his Wyr form before. His sheer magnificent size and regal barbarity were overwhelming.

She refused to get swept away by such bizarre perfection. She said in a cold, precise voice, "I would dare."

His head lifted. She felt him struggling with his own anger. Then he said, "Will you at least calm down enough so we can talk about what happened? You are one righteous hellcat when you decide to get going, do you know that? Way to throw an all-over hissy fit, Carling."

She ground her teeth. How dare he lecture her? "If you ever try to do anything to restrict my movements again, you'll find out I know how to hold a grudge too," she said between her teeth. "In fact, I have a real talent for it."

"I'm sure you do," he said. "Goddammit."

In a startlingly humanlike gesture of exasperation, he shook his head and shifted his body off of her. He did not deign to glance down as he carefully pulled his claws out of the sod and shifted his paws to one side. She watched as he did it. Those retractable claws were curved like scimitars and sharp enough to pierce steel. He settled on the ground beside her and looked out over the water, a predatory leviathan wearing a ferocious frown.

She didn't move. She looked up at him again, at that broad, strong feline chest to the long, graceful, strong column of his neck, and she lost whatever she had been about to say. Even though they were no longer touching, the great, heavy sprawling length of his body radiated warmth that began to sink into her bones.

Time passed and as she calmed, her perspective shifted. His severe, silent contemplation of the ocean and sky suddenly made her feel impetuous and oddly young. Or perhaps it was not so very odd. To him, she *was* young. What an amazing thought. When he wore his T-shirt and ragged jeans in his human form, and he made wisecracks in modern slang, he lived much more in the moment than she did. The weight of passing years did not press on him. He had no mortality.

In the process of scooping her out of a dead fall and pinning her down, Rune had not given her so much as the equivalent of a paper cut. She remembered how he had gently kissed her forehead before he had left her child-self, and burning tears filled her eyes again.

"I gave you permission to go back," she whispered. "I didn't give you permission to change me."

The gryphon bowed his head, and somehow that giant fierce eagle managed to look humble and chagrined. "I heard the whip," he confessed in a quiet, pained voice. "And I heard you cry out, and I couldn't think. All I knew was I couldn't let that lash fall on you again."

The tears spilled over, sliding down her temples to soak into her hair. She glanced at his immense paws again. She hadn't seen him kill the priest who had been whipping her, but she had seen the priest's body afterward. The broken corpse had been in ribbons, its bones split apart. She reached out to touch one paw. "Okay," she said unsteadily. "Okay. But I don't remember what happened to me before you did that."

He sighed and lifted up his mammoth wings to resettle them more comfortably into place along the sleek arch of his muscled back. Only then did he lift his head enough to look at her. "I don't believe I have the Power to change you," he said, still in that quiet, careful voice. "Not *you*, not your soul or spirit, or your *ba*, if you will. We don't yet know what the rest of it means."

She gave in to impulse and rolled over to sink her fingers into the fur at his breast. The fur was as thick and soft as it looked. Underneath, his hot skin was a tight cloak over muscles that were so massive they were as much of a shock to feel as they were to look at. She ran her hand upward through the fur, reaching the place where it gave way to a luxuriant burst of soft, small feathers. The feathers lengthened and darkened until they lay in a sleek bronze cap over his neck and head.

He began to purr as she petted him. The sound rumbled through her body. She raked her fingernails gently through the thick fur and soft profusion of feathers. He lay naturally in the position known in heraldry as the *lion couchant*, relaxed but alert as Carling studied him.

How could he not believe he had the Power to change her? What thrummed under her fingertips was indescribable. She realized how much of Rune's personality came from his cat-like sense of play. In his gryphon form, he revealed something much more ancient and unknowable.

How could he exist as two creatures melded into one? He said he had an affinity for crossovers and between places. She had nodded and thought she understood. Now as she stared at him, she didn't think she had understood anything.

The Power of the between places roared in his body. By its very definition it was a transformative force filled with tension and dynamic movement. Yet instead of the tension tearing him apart, he contained it, the transformative force held steady as a rock by his immortal spirit, and the Power *that* required was unimaginable to her. It seemed the very definition of impossibility.

A mysterious, magical riddle.

With that realization, she had an epiphany.

"The mystery is written in your form," she said. "Your body is the rune."

His massive head tilted. He regarded her with a gaze made tranquil by the bright sun and the limitless sky.

She said in wonder, "You are the riddle."

"Of course I am," said the gryphon.

She rolled onto her knees and, since he appeared willing to indulge her scrutiny, she continued with her exploration of his fabulous body. It brought such simple pleasure, she found it soothing. She ran her hands along the huge graceful arc of one wing. His primary feathers were the darkest bronze. They held glints of gold in the sun. She stroked along the vane of one feather. It was as long as her torso.

"Do you ever lose these?" she asked. The feather felt so strong, it might have been made out of metal.

"Sometimes," Rune said. "Not often."

"Next time you lose one, think of me at the Festival of the Masque or at Christmas," she told him. The Elder Races celebrated the seven primal powers at winter solstice with an annual event called the Masque of the Gods. While the Masque was traditionally a dance, it was also a time to exchange gifts, much like Christmas or Hanukkah.

He craned his neck to give her a skeptical look. "And give you something of mine you can spell during one of your shit fits?"

She looked at him with wide eyes. "I would never use a gift to spell someone."

His incredible lion-colored eyes narrowed. The gryphon said, "I think your pants are on fire."

She burst out laughing. She conceded, "Perhaps they might be a little singed around the hem." Part of her was in shock that she could laugh at all, or that they had achieved such a strong turnaround of feeling in such a short amount of time.

She settled the feather gently back into place, and Rune shimmered and changed into the form of a man. He sat cross-legged on the ground, and her hands rested on his wide shoulder. He was the same creature. That incredible Power still roared under her fingertips. His tanned skin radiated heat. All the colors of his Wyr form streaked through his hair.

She wasn't ready to stop touching him just because he had decided it was time to change forms. She fussed at his tousled shoulder-length hair, running her fingers through the length to smooth out the tangles.

"Don't you ever comb this mess?" she grumbled. It was gorgeous. She refused to say that. It was bad enough she'd already slipped and called his gryphon form stunning. "Or wear jeans that don't have holes in them?"

"I'll buy new jeans when I get back to the city, just for you." He turned his face into her hands and closed his eyes. She bit her lips and let her hands flow around him, her fingers framing those warm, lean features that were so handsome they made her chest ache.

"I'm scared," she said. The words fell out of her mouth, and more tumbled out after. "Before I wasn't letting myself feel anything. I'd gotten to a place where I accepted what was happening, and I was ready for it to be over with, but now I'm feeling everything again. I'm feeling too much, and I'm really, really scared."

His arms came around her as she talked. He pulled her down and around, until she sat sprawled across his lap. Her head remembered the perfect fit in the hollow of his neck and shoulder, and she burrowed back into that place. He held her with his whole body, one hand cupping her head. She felt strange, surrounded by his strength. She felt breakable, and somehow cherished. One of her arms crept around his neck, and she found herself clinging to him.

"It's all right," he said, and for a moment she thought he was uttering stupid platitudes. "It's all right to be scared. This is scary stuff."

"I'd rather face monsters," she muttered. She buried her face in the warm skin at his neck and inhaled his clean masculine scent. "Monsters are easy. This isn't easy."

"No, it isn't," he whispered. He rocked her a little.

There they were again, the strange new feelings he prompted in her, the sense of all her doors and barriers opening inside. Even though her caftan kept her covered down to her ankles, she felt naked and exposed. "I don't know how to cope with the thought of my memories changing," she breathed. "Even when I've lost everything and everyone, I always knew I could rely on myself. Now I don't even have that. I don't know what to rely on."

"Rely on me," said Rune. He pressed his lips to the fragile skin at her temple. "Listen to me. I am not sorry I saved you from that whipping or tried to make a horrible situation better for you, but I am profoundly sorry I did it without thinking through the real consequences of what might happen. Still, I do not believe that *you*—you at your essence—have changed. And you know that things *must* change if you are to survive, correct?"

She nodded.

"You could try to surrender to the experience and let change happen."

"Change or die?" she said.

"Yes. Change or die."

"You might have noticed, I don't do surrender very well," she told him in a dry voice.

"No, I don't either." He sighed and was silent a moment. Then he asked, "Did you choose to become a Vampyre, or were you turned against your will?"

She shivered. She did not know this person huddled against Rune's chest. She said, "I chose it. In fact, I heard rumors and went in search of it."

She felt him nod. He told her, "You embraced a change once that was so profound, it altered the definition of your existence. You can do it again if you have to."

"I was a lot younger then," she muttered.

His chest moved in a quiet chuckle. "Now you have experience to help guide you. Think back to that time and how you embraced the change. I have faith in you. I know you can do it."

She soaked in his humor as she rested against his body's support. When had his every move become important to her? How had she let that happen? She asked, "Why do you have that kind of faith in me? What did I do to deserve it?"

His chuckle turned into an outright laugh, the husky sound vibrating against her cheek. "Oh, I don't know," he said. "Perhaps it has something to do with the fact that when everyone around you had a lifespan of perhaps forty years if they were lucky, you outlived them all by over four and a half thousand. You survived the rise and decline of the Egyptian, the Roman and the Islamic Empires. The gods only know what you did for shits and giggles during the Crusades or the Spanish Inquisition. And you were one of the principal architects for how the Elder Races demesnes interact and coexist with the U.S. government."

"You did all of that too," she muttered. She plucked one of her long hairs off his black T-shirt. "The Spanish Inquisition, shits and giggles and whatever."

He captured her hand and brought it to his mouth to kiss her fingers. He said, "Yes, but there is a fundamental difference between us. I only did what was already in my nature, and lived. *You were human.* You not only transcended your nature, you found ways to excel through some of the most misogynistic times in human history. It is incomprehensible to me how you can have such a sense of pride, but no real sense of self-worth."

"Well," she said with a frown. "I don't think people like me very much."

She hadn't meant it as a joke, so she was startled when Rune clutched her tight and guffawed. He leaned back to look at her with dancing eyes. The impact of his handsome face laughing full bore into hers was a sucker punch she hadn't seen coming. She struggled to find some sense of inner equilibrium and failed utterly. The sight of him filled her to the brim, and all she could do was cling to him and stare.

Rune told her, "You know the real reason why I snatched you up when you went over the cliff? I knew you were about to swim the ocean. I was just saving Tokyo, baby."

She shrugged with a blank expression. "I have no idea what you're talking about."

His expectant expression turned to disappointment. He said, "I just called you Godzilla?"

She rolled her eyes. "Of course you did. Your reference to Tokyo made it so obvious. No doubt I should have picked up on it immediately, just as I should have known the identity of the hairy man with spectacles on that awful T-shirt of yours."

"Clearly, this is a teasing session that has not gotten off on the right foot," he said. "You've got to start watching old monster movies on TV. Oh, and football. Otherwise we're going to run out of things to talk about."

She raised an eyebrow. "I'll be sure to get right on that."

"Actually," he confided with an intimate smile, "I was more afraid you would melt when you hit the water."

She pointed at him. "I got that one. You think I don't know people have nicknamed me the Wicked Witch of the West?"

He grinned and kissed the tip of her finger. "And a very accomplished lady she was too, if a bit combative."

"You're ridiculous." Somehow her hand slipped, and she stroked his face. She felt like she could spend forever like this, resting against his long sprawling body, talking and laughing in the lazy, late afternoon. She might not be able to feel the warmth of the sun directly on her skin, but she could feel how it warmed Rune's, and the heat from his body sank into hers.

The laughter in Rune's face died away, and was replaced with an expression that was edged and raw. His gaze darkened and fell below hers, his mouth level and unsmiling. Realization pulsed. He was watching her with such hunger it was a palpable force. She licked her lips and saw in the flicker deep in his eyes that he tracked the movement.

He was going to kiss her, and she wanted it. Gods, she wanted it, full-bodied and openmouthed, both of them tearing into each other like there was no tomorrow, because there really might not be a tomorrow, and all they had was here and now.

This was such a fleeting treasure, this sense of ephemeral beauty, this gorgeous, impossible ache that came when the passions of the spirit turned flesh. This was what it meant to be alive and to be human, to cup the abundant, champagne light of a goddess's pendant in one's hands but never be allowed to grasp hold of it.

She took a breath and trembled.

He turned his head and looked away, and the light flowed out of her empty hands. The muscles in his lean jaw flexed. He said, "Are you ready to get serious again?"

She let her hand fall from his lean cheek. Disappointment tasted like ashes. She had done that to him. First she had struck him so hard and cruelly, she had drawn blood. Then she had knocked him away with such violence, she sent him sprawling to the ground. She had spelled and threatened him too, whereas he had shown her nothing but generosity and kindness.

An accomplished lady, she was, if a bit combative.

Really, it was for the best. She had no time for inconvenient attraction, or the luxury to explore strange new feelings or indulge in lazy sun-filled afternoons. If something didn't happen to change the normal course of events, soon she would have no time at all.

"Of course," she said, her voice toneless. She pushed off of his lap. She told herself she was not further disappointed when he let her go.

He stood and held a hand out to her. She took it, and he lifted her to her feet. The wind and their struggle had tangled her waist-length hair. She gathered it up impatiently, wound it into a messy knot and tucked the end into the knot itself to anchor it away from her face. Rune watched her, his hands resting on lean hips, his expression inscrutable.

"Do you remember the conversation we had just as you were fading?" Rune asked.

The question knocked her out of her preoccupation. She focused, thinking back. Oh yes. *Sometimes I think I hate you*, she'd said. She'd forgotten to add that to her list of things she'd done to him. She had to hand it to herself. She had quite a bag of tricks, and none of them were charms. She rubbed her forehead. "Look, I'm sorry about what I—"

He interrupted, his tone impatient. "Do you remember what I said? Because I don't think you do. I think you were already gone."

She shook her head, her mind a blank.

He watched her expression closely. "I told you I figured out what was bothering me. I said, what if Vampyrism is not a disease? What if it's something else?"

"Something else?" Her eyes widened.

"Your research chronicles the history beautifully," Rune said. "Reading through it, I got to watch it all happen in fast-forward. But you were immersed in it. You lived it all at a much slower pace. You were part of the scientific discussion in the nineteenth century with brilliant scientists who were engaged in cutting-edge medicine. It all made so much sense at the time that now virtually everybody accepts the premise to be true. Vampyrism has so many characteristics of a blood-borne pathogen, but Carling, to me you seem perfectly healthy."

"How can that be?" She struggled to absorb what he was saying. He kept taking hold of the ground and yanking it out from underneath her, like a magician yanking away a tablecloth set for dinner. "Are you sure?"

"I'm sure," he told her. "At least I'm sure of what I sense. Wyr have highly developed instincts and senses—and the older the Wyr, the more sensitive they are. The older Wyr can smell sickness and infections, tainted food, and many poisons undetectable to others. To me, you do not carry any scent of disease. You have the characteristic tinge to your scent that all Vampyres have, but I do not register that as an unhealthy scent."

"If you're right," she said, staring at him. "Everything I've done—or anybody else has done in the last hundred and thirty years—has been based on a false premise."

"Yes," he said.

Not a disease. If he was right, no wonder her research kept stalling. All the vaccines she had tried to create, all her experiments, had been wasted effort. She coughed out an angry laugh. She whispered, "All that time."

She had lived for so long, she had forgotten what a precious commodity time was until now, when it had nearly run out. She turned to walk back toward the cottage.

He fell into step beside her. "I've had several more hours to process this than you have," he told her. "And I still don't know what to make of it. I did think about all the physicians you listed that you worked with. Were any of them Wyr?"

She shook her head, frowning. "No. In fact I don't know of any Wyr pathologists who have made Vampyrism their subject of research. Humans and Nightkind are the ones who study the subject in any real, serious way. We're the ones with the vested interest."

He nodded. The day had melted into early evening. The slant of the sun picked up the gold glints in his hair. "There's a chance even a Wyr physician wouldn't have caught this, especially if he or she were a younger Wyr with less developed experience or senses, because Vampyrism *does* have so many characteristics of a blood-borne pathogen. I had to get right up to the subject and consider it in depth, read about all your blind alleys and dead ends and get puzzled as to the why of it—and then also come into very close contact with you repeatedly before it ever occurred to me."

"God, the implications," she muttered.

"So what do we have?" Rune asked.

She said bitterly, "We're back to square one and we're running out of time."

"No," he said. He threw her a chiding look. "You're still

reacting. If you wiped out all the research, you would be wiping out all the realizations that came from it, including this one. A negative answer is still an answer."

"Fine." She gritted her teeth, and forced herself to think beyond feeling poleaxed. "If the research didn't exist, logic would still have us deducing that Vampyrism is a disease."

"So we're not back to square one." They reached her cottage, and he held the door for her and let her precede him. "We've reached some other square where no one has ever been before. Now we've got to figure out what to do next."

She sat at the table and put her head in her hands. Immortal Wyr, interacting with aged Vampyre, made for one shaken cocktail. On the rocks.

Rune leaned against the table beside her. Naturally. The other chair was too far away on the other side of the table, and apparently he couldn't be bothered to retrieve it. She was already expecting it when he placed his hand on her shoulder, expecting and looking forward to his touch.

"There is one thing about square one," he said.

"What's that?" Somehow she found herself leaning into his grip. She struggled with herself, gave up, and rested her cheek against the back of his hand.

He squeezed her lightly. "If this was a crime and I was investigating, I would be headed back to the beginning and the scene where it happened. Maybe there's missed evidence. Maybe the information has been put together incorrectly. The crime scene needs to be reprocessed, and we need a second opinion." He pulled at the knot resting at the nape of her neck, and her hair came loose and slid down her back.

She pushed at his thigh. "Stop that."

"But I don't want to." He gathered up a long silken lock and began to twirl it around his fingers.

She lifted her head and gave him a sour look. "What are you, the emotional equivalent of a five-year-old?"

He gave her a slow lazy smile and rubbed the end of her hair against his well-cut lips. It was such a blatantly sexual thing to do, she felt her knees weaken and knew it was a good thing she was already sitting down.

So flirting with her was okay but kissing her wasn't?

Confused, angered and more than a little aroused, she

glared at him and snatched her hair out of his hands, and he chuckled. She gathered her hair and twisted it into a knot again. She tucked the ends into itself.

"Back to the beginning," she said. "Do you mean back to Egypt, when I was turned?"

He shrugged, considering her. "Maybe that too. But we're talking in more general terms, so I think we should consider the origins of Vampyrism itself. It was not always part of human history. Where did it come from? If we can answer that, then we may be able to define it in such a way that we can find a way to counteract what is happening to you."

She dug the heels of her hands into her eyes. "The beginning is a legend. Vampyrism is also called the serpent's kiss, did you know that?"

"I've heard that before," he said. "I thought the term was because of the fangs Vampyres get that descend when they're hungry."

Listening to his rich, deep voice with her eyes closed evoked more erotic images, of him murmuring velvet words against her bare skin in the dark of a desert night. She stiffened and brought her flattened hands down on the table with a stinging slap, as she forced her mind to stay on topic. "There is that," she said. "But it has been called the serpent's kiss for a very long time."

He frowned. "Was it called that in your youth?"

"Yes. Once, it was believed the bite was a necessary part of a ritual for changing someone. Now we know there's very little possibility of Vampyre bites themselves causing the change, otherwise they would infect everyone they fed upon. To successfully spread the pathogen you need a blood exchange, and Vampyres don't need to drink the blood of those they change, only offer their own. The human can either drink the Vampyre's blood or let it flow into a cut. As long as the Vampyre's blood flows fresh, and the integrity of the human's skin is compromised, in most cases that's all that's needed to initiate the change. Anything added to that is just . . ." She lifted a hand in a fill-in-the-blank kind of gesture.

"Personal choice," he said. "Superstition. Religion. Fetish."

"Sometimes all of the above," she said. She had already reached the point where she had stopped taking physical nourishment by the time she had turned Rhoswen and Duncan. She frowned as well as she thought back to the time when she had changed.

Those early memories were not pleasant to revisit. As soon as she had learned there was the possibility of *changing* and becoming immortal, it had driven her beyond all reason. She had needed to discover if the stories told around her campfires had any merit to them, whereas she had learned long since then that myth and legend were too often an impenetrable tangle, the stories saying far more about the people who told them than imparting any real truths about the world they lived in.

Rune stayed silent as if he sensed she needed the time to think. She sighed.

Then, because he was waiting, she said, "It started for me when I heard stories. You know the kind of thing, those tall tales told across the flicker of firelight late at night. I guess I heard something one too many times, about a stranger wandering into an encampment full of hunger and a burning gaze that mesmerized, or a caravan found with everyone dead and covered with bite marks. About a rare, strange people who avoided the sun and lived forever. About a dark miracle called the serpent's kiss that could transform someone into a god. I began to ask the storytellers where they had heard their tale. I moved across the desert, following each thread back as far as I could. I lost the trail of most stories but was able to follow one to its beginning, and of course that was all I needed."

"What did you find?" Rune asked. He watched her with close fascination.

She gave him a wry smile. "A Vampyre, of course. She was a hermit living in a corner of a huge cavern, with the remains of a settlement nearby. She talked of a serpent goddess who had once lived in the cavern and honored her with the kiss of life that was also death."

"Serpent goddess," Rune repeated. His eyes narrowed.

She nodded. "The settlement had been filled with worshippers of this serpent goddess. According to the woman, the settlement had gradually died out when the goddess had left. Either all the humans had been killed or they ran away, and the Vampyres had abandoned the place, all except for this last priestess who had stayed, hoping her goddess would return."

Rune thought of Rhoswen, existing on the bloodwine. But bloodwine hadn't been invented that long ago. He asked, "How did she survive by herself?"

Carling shrugged. "As best I could guess, she lived off the blood of rats and other small desert mammals. Animal blood doesn't have the same nutritive value for us as human blood, so she had to have been malnourished. I took everything she said with a healthy dose of skepticism, because she was quite mad. I might have dismissed her stories completely except for the things my people found in the settlement itself, like the empty sarcophagi in the houses, and the strange carvings on the cavern walls depicting a huge, part-serpent, part-human creature. Then the woman showed me how her fangs descended when she hungered, and how she burned in the sun, and I was hooked. In retrospect I had to be more than a little crazy myself to let her bite me, let alone consent to a blood exchange, but I was still young, and the young are always crazy."

Rune's eyebrows rose. "Could you draw what the carvings of the creature looked like?"

"Not from memory, not after so long," Carling said. She watched his wide shoulders sag. Then she smiled. "So I guess it's probably a good thing I drew lots of sketches at the time."

His gaze lit with a fiery expression that spread to his face. "You didn't. Did you? Where are they now?"

She nodded toward the hall. "In the other room."

"They're *here*?" He smiled. "You're a wicked tease. I like that about you."

She smiled back. "I'm learning it from an expert."

His smile widened. "Come on. Don't just sit there."

He grabbed her by the hand and yanked her out of her seat before she realized what he meant to do. Laughing, she led the way down the short hall to the part of her library that held the oldest scrolls. There, back in one corner of the room, she went to her knees to look along the row of cubbyholes that held scrolls of papyrus so old they had to be spelled in order to keep them from disintegrating.

Rune watched Carling kneel on the floor and run her fingers along the bottom row of cubbyholes. He found every aspect of her scholarship fascinating, from her scientific research to the neat notations she had made on the labels over each cubbyhole. More than fascinating, he found it endearingly nerdy, refreshingly efficient and sexy as hell.

He rubbed his mouth. Of course he found everything about her as sexy as hell.

She murmured something to herself and pulled out a scroll. "Here it is. We have to be careful. I haven't bothered to renew the protection spells on these in a long time. It looks like the humidity is starting to get to them."

He knelt in front of her. "I'm just amazed so many of these have lasted as long as they have. It must be your penchant for keeping your libraries and workshops in quiet, out-of-the-way places."

"I'm sure that has helped."

He gently took hold of the corners of the scroll she indicated, watching as she eased it open with slender fingers.

Then he stared down at the faded lines that had been drawn in some unknown ink, at a face and form he had not seen in a very, very long time. It had four short muscular legs with powerful, gripping claws and an elongated, serpentine body. Its tail wound in coils, and its neck rose up from the two legs into a cobra-like hood that framed a distinctly humanlike, female face.

"Hello, Python," he said softly. "You crazy old whack-job, you."

≡ TEN ≡

It was Carling's turn to stare at him. "This is someone real?"

He corrected her. "This *was* someone real. Our paths crossed a couple of times. She disappeared a very long time ago. Last I heard, she was rumored to have died. She was one of the between creatures."

"What do you mean?"

Rune released the ancient sketch, letting it curl back into a scroll. "There are a few creatures who came to form, not on Earth or in Other lands but in a between place, like in a cross-over passage," he explained.

In her crouch, the angle of Carling's eyes and cheekbones were pronounced, giving her a feline look. The urge to pounce on her pulsed through him like a drug, but he held himself in check, just barely.

She asked, "Like you?"

"Yes. Python was another one." He stood, the urge still clawing through his system and making him antsy. "She was one of those strange, hard-to-categorize creatures. She wasn't Wyr. As far as I know, she never developed a human form, so in modern terms I suppose we would have classified her as Demonkind."

Carling picked up the scroll and stood as well. "I sketched the cavern walls several times and after I transitioned, I tried to find out as much as I could about her. But there were so many Egyptian gods and goddesses, and the truth was often so mangled it was impossible to pinpoint their origins. Many of them were just folktales. I was never convinced she actually existed outside of the priestess's imagination and in the end I gave up searching for her." She studied Rune's face curiously. "What was she like?"

He shook his head. "Being around her was like tripping on a bad dose of LSD. Not that I would know what that was like." He offered her a bland smile. Carling gave a ghost of a laugh, and he paused to savor the quiet, husky sound before continuing. "She was filled with as many riddles and psychoses as the Sphinx. In fact, I wouldn't be surprised if someone told me the legend of the Sphinx was modeled after her. She was always getting her tenses . . ."

Rune's voice trailed away, Carling waited, watching his arrested expression. She prompted, "What?"

He came back from where he had gone with an internal click that brought his sharp, focused gaze in contact with hers. "She was always getting her tenses mixed up," he said. "The past, the present and the future."

"Getting her tenses mixed up?" Carling sucked in a breath. Her hand quested out, and he gripped it with his. She whispered, "What if the beginning of Vampyrism really did start with her? She might have suffered from the same kinds of episodes."

"Don't get your hopes up too high," he murmured gently. "Her brain might have just been on permanent scramble, and anyway, she's most likely gone now."

She nodded, although he wasn't sure how much she was actually paying attention. "We need to try to find out what happened to her."

"Yes," he said. She withdrew her hand and he stepped back, allowing her the space to move. She strode back to the cottage's main room and he followed, watching the graceful sway of Carling's hips moving in front of him as he explored the strange terrain they found themselves in. "About that second opinion I mentioned. There's someone I would like to consult on all this, if you don't mind."

Carling set the scroll on the table and collected a few things from a nearby shelf, a couple of candlesticks, along with an empty marble mortar and pestle. She opened the scroll again and anchored it flat by using the pieces. Then she settled in her chair to study the ancient drawing in the encroaching shadows of early evening as curiously as if someone else had sketched it.

"I don't mind, if you think it will help," she said. "As long as whoever it is can be discreet."

"She's a pathologist and a medusa," Rune said. He settled into his former position, leaning back against the table beside her. "So she has a certain point of view that I think might be useful."

That caught Carling's attention. She looked up. "Are you talking about that ME in Chicago that conducted the autopsies on Niniane's attackers?"

"That's the one," Rune said. "Dr. Seremela Telemar."

"I read her autopsy reports. She was quite competent." Her mind went back to earlier in the afternoon when she had come out of the fade and she remembered something. She said, "Why were you looking for your pocketknife?"

He leaned back on his hands and kicked a foot. He said, "I lost it."

She told him, "I distinctly remember you cutting the twine and then putting it back in your pocket."

"I didn't lose it then," he said. "When I was caught in your memory, I gave it to the priest Akil."

She breathed, "I never knew."

"You weren't supposed to. I told him to keep it a secret from everyone." He regarded her with a gaze that had turned brooding. "I see two possibilities here. The first possibility is that what happened was self-contained and we changed just your reality—which, believe me, is earthshaking enough all on its own."

She stretched her hands out on the table, on either side of the scroll. "Tell me about it," she muttered. "Theoretically it could happen. Some spells work on the power of belief, especially illusions. You can kill someone that way, if they believe in something strongly enough."

He gave her a thoughtful look but refrained from pursuing that train of thought. "So if you believed what happened was real, that could potentially have the power to physically change you, correct?" he asked. She nodded. He said, "Maybe it would have the power to change me too. I cannot shake the conviction that this has all felt very real when I've gone through it. It's important to remember this does happen to both of us. It's just that, for me, the events are occurring in a more linear fashion."

"You haven't experienced anything physically traumatic in one of the episodes either, like I have," she murmured.

"Then there's the second possibility," he said. "And there's no point in dancing around it. We might have changed the actual past, and the key to finding that out is to see if we've influenced something outside of ourselves."

She searched his face. "You think you might have actually gone back in time?"

"I don't know," he said. "The crossover passages and Other lands have already shown us that time slips. Theoretically, time is also supposed to slow down the faster one travels. Time isn't a completely uniform phenomenon, and we know the universe must self-correct so that paradoxes cannot happen. Maybe we're experiencing a slippage so far out of sync, I'm experiencing it as a trip back to the past."

Paradoxes cannot happen. The universe self-corrects. It flexes, like a breathing entity, absorbing and adjusting to anomalies. It had an automatic built-in defense mechanism. It was generally believed that no one could topple history, not even the gods. If the universe could not accommodate an event, it could not happen. Rivers of events would shift only so much to accommodate change.

"You seem remarkably calm about it all," she said. She wasn't calm. Maybe she hadn't been calm since he had showed up on her doorstep. You should be careful who you invite into your home . . .

He gave her a small smile. "I'm just being clinical right now."

"You're good at it." He really was an excellent investigator. She sat back in her seat and looked up at the ceiling. "And at the moment, I'm not."

He said gently, "I know it's scary. Thank the gods all I've done so far is stop to talk to a child one afternoon, and prevent someone from beating you much worse than he already had. If I had done more, the repercussions could be much worse."

He didn't realize the profound effect he had on her.

She closed her eyes. She thought of all the many times she

had looked up at the sky, hoping against hope to see the impossible happen again, and see the strange winged lion-god fly back into her life. All of the nights she had looked at the stars, wishing upon wish to see him one more time. Whether those times had happened in history or they had happened all in her mind, they had in fact happened.

And they hadn't before he had come to the island and met her child-self. If she and Rune were actually changing the past, something else had occurred, something other than what she now remembered, something similar enough that the flow of time had flexed to accommodate the difference.

Had she once looked at the stars in some original past, and wished for something else so passionately? It was almost impossible to imagine wishing for anything as much as she had wished to see him, one more time.

She murmured, "The knife."

There was a pause. He said, "Yes, the knife. I told Akil to bury it in a distinctive place, somewhere that I knew would survive the test of time."

"So aside from consulting with Dr. Telemar, we need to find out if the knife is where Akil was supposed to put it."

"Yes," Rune said. Something was in his voice. She couldn't identify it. She brought her head up to look at him. He was studying her, his brows contracted. He said, "Suspend disbelief for a moment. Forget about asking why or how. What happened after I left? I made Akil swear to look after you."

"He did," she assured him. Or at least she thought he did. Then she did as Rune asked, and pushed all the consideration of that aside. "He gave me a new name and adopted me, just as you told him to. He gave me the best of everything he had, including the finest education, just like he promised you he would. I think he even grew to love me in his own way. At least he cherished me, if for no other reason than his god had."

If they were really changing the past, none of that would have happened without Rune's intervention. One way or another, it seemed she could not escape her early life being shaped by the Wyr. Something else would have occurred, something similar enough that the universe accepted the altered timeline as true. Perhaps what Rune had really given her was a kinder, gentler beginning, at least as much as he was able. Now that her panic had receded she found that she could be grateful for that.

"He gave you a new name? What did he name you?"

She whispered, "What do you think? None of us understood you at the time, none of us. We only knew that a god had touched our lives, found something of favor in me, and pronounced his decree. None of us really comprehended the things that you said."

Rune frowned at her. He looked so puzzled, that despite all the uncertainty she faced, she had to smile. "You called me 'darling,' " she said. "Remember? And we thought a god had called me something sacred."

"Carling," he breathed.

"What else?" she said.

Of all the shifts that might have occurred, this was not one Rune had seen coming, the possibility that the universe might flex and accommodate the intrusion of his presence into her past to such a profound and intimate extent. Before she had been the one to choose her own name, and while he had been saddened to hear of the demise of Khepri, he had understood it. Now he felt like he had stolen something precious from her, albeit unknowingly, and it sickened him. He sat frozen while Carling looked down at the table. She stroked her hands along the surface of the scroll as if to smooth out a tablecloth, smiling a strange smile that was glasslike in its fragility.

Carling had always had a poise that lay along her skin like a second spell of protection and made her look bulletproof, but now she looked more vulnerable than he had ever seen her. She looked tired, at a loss, even sad. The heavy mass of her hair lay against the graceful nape of her neck in an untidy knot. A few individual strands had escaped. They shone with ruby glints in the early-evening light.

His chest ached again. He rubbed his breastbone. When he spoke, his voice had filled with gravel. "No wonder you hate me sometimes."

Her head tilted toward him but she didn't look up. She kept smoothing the invisible tablecloth with those long slender fingers. "I don't hate you," she said. "I'm afraid of you. I wasn't afraid of you before, but I am now. Change is hard, Rune."

She didn't know, he realized. Of course she didn't. How could she? The sickened feeling increased to the point of actual nausea. He couldn't look at her as he forced himself to speak. "You chose your own name. Before. I'm so profoundly sorry I disrupted that."

He sensed rather than saw her quick, sharp look, the inhuman stillness of her rigid body. Then she moved and said softly, "We thought you called me something sacred, but I chose to take it as my name, Rune. I remember that distinctly. You didn't take away the fact that I made that choice, or that I chose to keep it for all these years."

At that he was able to breathe again. He touched the smooth skin on the back of her hand. He found every excuse to touch her. He couldn't stop himself. Before she looked at him with outrage, bewilderment, and now she seemed to welcome it. Or so he told himself.

They sat in silence, absorbing what had happened. After a few moments, he shook his head and growled, "I still want to fight something."

She nodded as if to herself. "Now there's a logical reaction," she murmured. "Why didn't I think of that?"

He wanted to fight something and win, so he could show her there was nothing to be afraid of anymore, that everything would be all right. But he was no longer certain of that himself. She was right, monsters were easy. "You know I can't leave you now, don't you? No matter how you might demand it of me. I just can't."

Her lovely eyes flashed up to his. She sighed. "I don't want you to leave," she admitted. "That was my fear talking earlier. Even though what is happening is strange and frightening, it's got to be better than coming to a standstill and waiting to die. We might actually find something in all of this mess that will save my life." She turned her hand over and curled her fingers around his. "Because I do want to live, if for no other reason than to solve this mystery and discover what else life can be. Maybe it will become so strange, it will be interesting."

"Living is always interesting," he said. "You just got bored."

He loved watching her laugh. Every time she laughed, she looked surprised. She said, "I guess I did."

He nodded, looking at the pearl-hued ovals of her finger-nails. With a brutal honesty, Rune acknowledged where he was because he couldn't afford to do anything else.

He had a thing for her. He had it bad and it gnawed in his gut, a craving he had not yet found a way to satisfy.

Wyr, when they mated, did so for life. There was a line beyond which an irrevocable change occurred. No one fully understood where that line was drawn because, he believed, it was different for everyone. Mating, for a Wyr, came from a complex combination of choice, sex, instinct, actions and emotion.

He did not think mating could happen unless something deep and fundamental within a Wyr invited it in. He had witnessed firsthand both Dragos and Tiago as they had experienced the throes of mating. He had talked to each male at some point as they had gone through the experience, and he had, in fact, tried his best to get Tiago to reverse course, which had nearly cost him not only Tiago's friendship, but Niniane's as well. Neither Dragos nor Tiago had chosen to back away when they realized what was happening. Instead they seemed to embrace their fate. More, they did everything in their power to make it happen.

Rune had acknowledged the presence of a few other potential mates throughout his life. There had been a couple of rare women who had a combination of personality traits that caused him to look at them in speculation and think to himself, you might just be perfect. In the end he had not pursued any of them.

He wondered now what would have happened if he had. Perhaps nothing. They might have been terrific lovers for a time and become a good memory. He had not wanted to take a mate and had chosen not to risk it.

He believed he was all right for now. A dangerous fascination did not turn into mating all on its own. Carling's own barriers would help with that.

He had been wrong about her. Maybe she wasn't a giggling girlfriend type, and maybe she didn't allow very many people to get too close, but she wasn't alone on a pinnacle and completely closed off. She cared, sometimes very deeply, sometimes, he thought, more than she knew, which was why Duncan had been grieving when Rune had talked to him. It was also why Carling had tolerated Rhoswen's excessive devotion for so long, and why she insisted on healing and keeping Rasputin, even though it was not easy or convenient for her to do so. He wondered if she realized the real reason she cooked Rasputin chicken. It wasn't to remind herself of the details of physical appetite. It was to remind herself of love.

That being said, the invisible line she had drawn between them still stood. They were still too different from each other, their lives too far apart. He could come up to the line and then choose to go no further.

A mating Wyr gave his life to his mate. Such an extreme gift called for an extraordinary kind of devotion or loyalty in return, especially from those who were not Wyr, for they could always choose to walk away while the Wyr who had mated to them never would. Although Rune had been concerned at first when Tiago had bonded with Niniane, he had come to admit, Niniane had the kind of capacity for devotion Tiago needed. Rune did not believe he could throw himself one-sided into mating with someone. He simply was not impetuous to the point of being suicidal.

But what a spectacular lover Carling would make. The thought caused his groin to tighten. Rapid-fire images bulleted through his brain, images of her curved luscious body writhing under his, her head thrown back, gorgeous eyes glittering with desire and pleasure as he pistoned into her. She would be a truly haunting lover. He wanted her mouth on his skin, her hands on his body. He wanted it more than he had wanted anything before. He broke into a sweat just thinking about it.

He regarded her, his lids dropping to hide whatever expression might be in his eyes. The way to satisfy a craving was to indulge it. To gorge on what one craved, taking and taking it, until the blaze of desire finally melted into satiation. That was how he could work Carling out of his system once and for all.

As fascinated as he had been with her these last few weeks, he hadn't made the decision to actually pursue her.

Not until just now.

And she would want him to. He had already seen the kernels of passion in her, like a banked fire that had been abandoned but had not yet gone out, and he had tasted it on her lips. Earlier on the cliff, he had watched as desire warred with other emotions on her expression. He had chosen not to push, but not any longer.

By the time he was done with her, by all the gods, she would want him.

Carling watched in bemusement as Rune's face and body grew tight and sharp-edged. His heart rate increased, a flush of color darkened his lean cheeks and an intensity of emotion exploded out of him.

What was that feeling? It was the same kind of feeling that had poured out of both Tiago and Niniane whenever they were together, a driving force that had impelled them into a new, uncertain future. Carling had known the feeling before as well, so very long ago. . . .

Hunger. Rune looked at her and felt hunger.

She stilled and opened her mouth, just as he launched off the table to pace throughout the room, his restless movements filled with a tight, liquid, urgent grace.

"We need to come up with a plan and it should be a fast one," he said. "We have to go to San Francisco to call Seremela. Maybe she'll be able to fly out for a consultation."

Carling nodded slowly. She had been angry and shaken earlier, and ready to do anything that would let her escape from Rune. Now, with a cooler head, she thought of Julian again. Julian considered her deteriorating state too dangerously unpredictable. Even though she had originally agreed to stay on the island, now there really wasn't any other option.

Rune continued. "And we need to discover whether or not the knife is where I told Akil to put it without expending any time or energy on it ourselves."

Carling stirred. "I can see that it gets done. A Djinn owes me two favors. He's very old and Powerful. I'm sure if anyone can retrieve your knife quickly, Khalil can, and there's certainly no reason any longer for me to save those favors for a rainy day."

"A Djinn." He barked out a laugh. "Is this the same Djinn that kidnapped Niniane and threw Tiago into a frenzy?"

"The very same," she told him.

He swiveled to look at her. A strange angry feeling gnawed

at his insides. "What did you do for him that got you three favors?"

Her expression shuttered. "That is not my story to tell."

"It had to have been a hell of a thing to get a Demonkind that Powerful indebted to you." He said roughly, "You had to have given him something rare and precious, something no one else could have given him. And he had to have wanted it very badly."

Carling raised her perfect brows. She said, "All of that is true."

He felt goaded by her impenetrability, by what clawed at him from within. He started to growl.

Her eyes widened in surprise. "Are you *growling* at me?" Her face hardened. "Whatever the hell is going on with you, I suggest you think twice about it."

Instead of stopping, he actually bared his teeth at her. Bared his teeth. He turned her chair while she was still in it, moving so fast she made a muffled sound of surprise. He slapped his hands onto the table on either side of her, pinning her in her seat. "What did you do for him?"

She looked from one side to the other at his corded arms trapping her in place. The angle of her slim eyebrows turned wicked. "Remember what I said earlier? Do not try to restrict my movements."

"Damn it, Carling," he hissed. He leaned down close so that she came nose-to-nose with his angry face. "Now is not the time to cop an attitude with me."

"Pause that." She flicked his chin with a forefinger, hard. "Who's copping an attitude here?"

His expression turned murderous. "Your life is riding on what happens next, and maybe mine is too. You know how capricious and malicious the Demonkind can be."

"I know exactly what the Demonkind can be. Khalil and I have known each other for a very long time."

"What did you give him that got you three favors?"

"That's none of your business!"

"Like hell," he bit out.

She glared at him, her dark eyes snapping. "He's the one who came to me. He asked me for help, and he offered me three favors. He has no reason to resent me, and now he can't renege, and that's all you need to know." She thrust her face even closer so that the tips of their noses touched. "Now get out of my face, Wyr."

The low, rough sound he emitted at that was infuriating, fascinating. Wait. Was he still growling? Or was he *purring*? His eyes drifted half closed. He gave her a heavy-lidded, sleepy, sensual, entirely disingenuous look.

"Make me," he said. "Witch."

The force of feeling that punched out of him was stronger than anything she could remember sensing before from anyone, the molten sirocco that reformed her world.

Violence. Rage.

Not simple hunger. A voracious, ravening urgency.

It clawed all common sense from her bones.

She growled back, shoved him away, and then she launched out of her chair to body slam him.

Surprise bowled him over more than anything else. He fell back onto the floor with a force that would have knocked the breath out of anyone human, and she came right along with him. Still growling, she landed on her knees straddling his body and planted her hands on either side of his head. Her loose caftan rode up to her bare thighs, and her hair came loose and spilled all over them in an extravagant waterfall of midnight silk.

He stared up at her, transfixed, all the rage knocked out of him.

He was such a beautiful man. He was far more beautiful than he had any right to be, and then he started to laugh and his handsome face creased with vivid recklessness. Her legs tightened until she gripped his long, lean torso with her calves, and there was so much Power that coursed through the massive muscled body between her legs, it caused a railroad spike of need to slam into her body from the long-dormant nerve endings at the apex of her legs.

As old and disciplined as she was, as solitary as she had been, out of choice as much as anything, it was all too much for a woman to take. She made a muffled sound and reached for him with both greedy hands.

He surged into a sitting position even as she sank her fists into his tangled hair. His arms came around her waist. Her legs were still on either side of him, and he yanked her down onto his pelvis so that the empty part of her that ached so desperately slammed onto the hard swollen length of his erection. He jammed his open mouth over hers.

Then they were together, locked in the same place of extremity, shoving their tongues into each other. Nothing about it was gentle or civilized. She jerked at his hair, pulling it with enough force it had to have hurt. He hissed against her lips. He pulled her lower torso closer as he ground upward onto her, hard, with his hips.

She was locked rigid into place, her need so severe that when she tried to pry her fingers out of his hair, she couldn't. All of her plotting, all of her fine thinking, was vaporized until what was left came out of her in a thin, shaking animal whine.

His lungs worked like bellows. Heat blazed out of him. The rough vibrating rumble in his chest turned into a raw groan. He ran one hand up her spine to grip the back of her head, supporting her head and shoulders on his arm. With his other arm, he clenched her hips firmly against him. She took the hint and wrapped her legs around his waist as he rose up on his knees. He bent over to place her on the floor and then he came down with her, until there it was, what she had envisioned for what had seemed like forever, as she lay down with weighted limbs and his heavy body settled full on her.

Then she was able to loosen her grip in his hair only enough to hook her fingers into his T-shirt. She tore the cotton down his back, baring a wide expanse of muscle that flexed as she dug her fingers into him. He dragged his mouth away from hers with a shaken gasp. She had no idea what he said, but it seemed like it was in the form of a question.

"I hate your clothes," she muttered.

He flattened his hand on her breastbone just under her throat and held her down as he reared back to stare at her. He was so roused, a luscious flush of blood darkening his tanned skin, those lion's eyes glittering brilliant with desire, his face taut.

"I hate your stupid clothes too," he said. He took the neckline of the caftan and ripped it wider, baring her breasts.

The door to the cottage opened, and a chilly rush of wind entered the room. Rhoswen stood in the doorway, clutching the dog under her arm. Rasputin erupted into a frenzy of snarling and barking. Moving almost quicker than sight, Rune lunged forward to cover Carling. She turned her face into his chest, not from any modesty but from the need to continue touching him in any way that she could.

He cupped the back of her head, shielding her face from scrutiny, and growled again, and this time there was no mistaking that low menacing sound. The heavy bones in his broad chest seemed wrong, as though he might have flowed into a partial shapeshift. She thought of Tiago's monstrous partial shift when he had come after Niniane, both at the hotel and later when Niniane had been kidnapped, and need pulsed through her again. Carling closed her eyes and opened her mouth on Rune's skin. She drank down his feral emotion like wine.

In her precise, Shakespearean-trained voice that was frigid with bitterness, Rhoswen said, "Apparently this was not the best time to say good-bye."

═ ELEVEN ═

Carling coughed out an incredulous laugh that had nothing to do with amusement. The snarl that came out of Rune sounded infuriated, guttural. *"Get the hell out and SHUT THAT GODDAMN DOOR."*

There was a frozen moment, filled only with Rasputin's frenzied barking. Carling closed her eyes and leaned into Rune's hot body, and his arms tightened on her in a hard, possessive hold. Then Rhoswen slammed the door, the sharp wooden report echoing through the shadowed cottage.

A corner of Carling's mind worked hard to process what just happened. The rest of her was shaking with the aftermath of the firestorm that had swept through her. She felt like a drug addict coming down off a high. Rune knelt on one knee as he held her. His heartbeat thundered in her ear. His T-shirt hung in shreds off his tightly bunched biceps, and his body vibrated with such tension he felt poised to attack something.

Then he released the tension on a sigh, and she felt his body flow back into its normal lines. He stroked her hair, threading his fingers through the loose, tangled strands. He said roughly, "You all right?"

She gave him a jerky nod. It was almost a complete lie. Need still pulsed low in her pelvis, a sharp, empty pain that was shocking in its intensity. She didn't recognize herself in the untamed creature that had launched at Rune.

He said, "I'll be damned if I apologize for any of that."

She stirred and managed to find her voice. "What would you apologize for?"

"Throwing my own shit fit. Yelling at Rhoswen."

"I'll make a pact with you," she whispered. "If you don't apologize, I won't either."

"It's a deal." He kissed her temple. Then, after a pause, he said, "She interrupted us deliberately, you know."

"I know." Carling sighed. Rhoswen hadn't been caught by surprise. She would have heard them before she ever reached the cottage door. "She was completely inappropriate."

Rhoswen had achieved her objective, however; she had destroyed the raw out-of-control moment Carling and Rune had been engaged in.

Rune settled his weight back on his heels as he released her. Full night had descended, and the only illumination in the cottage came from the moon that had risen. Even though it had begun to wane, it held tremendous Power, spilling through the windows and limning the edges of their bodies with a delicate lattice of silver. For a long moment she sat still and let him look at her, the fluted wings of her collarbones, the full ripe globes of her bare breasts with their plump jutting nipples and the shadowed indentation of her narrow rib cage underneath.

He crouched over her like the giant cat that he was, looking as if he were about to pounce, unblinking intensity in his moon-silvered gaze, his wide shoulders bowed as he leaned on one fist he had planted on the floor beside her hip. An aftershock of urgency rolled out of him and into her, but their earlier frenzy had splintered with such a crash, it left her feeling slightly sick.

She looked down to pull her ruined caftan up her torso, and he helped her to find edges of the material to knot together to cover her temporarily, his long-fingered hands so gentle that the alien, traitorous tears filled her eyes again.

For so long she had treated her own body like a weapon, and yet he treated it like it was a temple. It made her feel ludicrously fragile, as though she might shatter into pieces without his high regard, and she wrapped her arms around herself.

"We need to get to the city," he said quietly. "And get a move on all the things we talked about."

Wariness touched her. Reluctant to start the whole ridiculous argument again, she just nodded and kept her tone noncommittal. "Yes."

He watched her closely. "I was jealous."

She froze, and her eyes widened. "You were—what?"

He leaned over to whisper in her ear, his warm breath caressing her cheek. "You heard me. I said I was jealous. I am not apologizing. I am explaining."

Then as she turned her head to stare at him, he did pounce. His hands snaked up to grip her by the head as he brought his mouth down to hers. He hovered there, deliberately brushing his taut lips against hers as he breathed, "I was jealous of the Demonkind, your Djinn, whom you've known for so goddamn long and bargained with every appearance of goddamn amicability, who needed you and you were there for him in such a meaningful, Powerful way he bargained away *three goddamn favors*, and you don't have to say anything because I already know how stupid that sounds. So I acted like an ass. A stupid, crazy, illogical, senseless, rampantly jealous ass."

She gripped his wrists and started to shake again. "Rune."

"And I was jealous," said the gryphon, speaking from the back of his throat as he made his words into a burning caress, "because I want you so bad, it's messing with my thinking. It's a hook in my gut I can't pull out. I've wanted you ever since that evening on the Adriyel River. I dream about taking you. And in my dream, you take me too. Just like what nearly happened here on the floor."

Her unsteadiness increased, until her mouth trembled under his. His wrists felt iron-hard and rock-steady under her shaking fingers. "That's enough now, stop. We—we need to go."

"All right," he murmured easily. "I just wanted us to be clear about what almost happened here. This was not a fluke. I am going to come after you again."

She sucked in air. She whispered, "This—thing between us—"

"This isn't a 'thing.'" He pressed a quick kiss onto her mouth. "It's attraction."

She shook all over. "It's totally inappropriate."

"I know."

"It can't last. It's got nowhere to go."

"I get that." He bit her lower lip and held her with such careful tension she wanted to claw the last of his clothes off of him. "But think about how good it will be until it ends. Because it will happen, Carling."

Will happen, he said. Not could happen. Because he was going to come after her again, sometime, somewhere, and the thought of him on the prowl made her groan. Then his hands opened and he let her go. Just like that.

Just like that? Her hands clung to his wrists as his hands fell from her head; she found herself leaning forward, reaching for his mouth with hers as he pulled away, her gaze falling along the clean lines of his face that was shadowed gray and black, and limned with the faintest touch of shining silver, as if he were gilded with the moon's eldritch blessings that were just barely visible to the naked eye.

"Rune," she murmured again, and the previous shock in her voice turned throaty.

"Darling Carling," he said very low. He paused and shuddered, and something like pain caused his face to spasm. "Just fucking say it."

Desire is vulnerability. But they were all alone, just them and the moonlight, and the moon never told the secrets of what she saw. So Carling took hold of every scrap of her courage and said it.

"I want you too."

The moon opened wide its invisible sails and soared through the starred sky over the island's redwood forest.

It was already night again. Carling struggled against a sense of disorientation. When she had lost the ability to sleep, time had increased in velocity. Meditation helped but only to a certain extent. There were no longer any breaks in her experience, just the relentless cascade of events, until she felt like she was being shoved into the future by a gigantic unseen force, faster and faster until she approached the speed of light.

She walked into the trees. Far overhead the moonlight filtering through branches was a study in ivory and black. At ground level the forest was so shadowed, only her sharp Vampyric vision allowed her to pick her way along the path. She paused to listen to the tiny night sounds. Once there would have been total silence when she walked through this wood, but the creatures that lived here had long since grown accustomed to her presence.

Rune agreed to wait for her on the beach. He wanted to come with her, but she needed to be alone to do this one last thing before she left the island. He said he would give her a half hour. If she had not returned by then, he was going to assume she had gone into a fade and come looking for her. Carling didn't argue with him. There was nothing here that would hurt her, but even so she didn't like the idea of sitting helpless and unaware, alone in the forest.

She tucked her research journals into a worn leather bag, along with the papyrus sketches and a few other odds and ends from the cottage, and she gave it to Rune to take with him. When he had left, she dug through a cupboard for another clean, intact caftan, which she donned after throwing the ruined one away. So he hated her caftans, did he? She snorted. How many had she ruined in the last couple of days? There was a reason she wore them so much. They were easy on, easy off. She tended to be very hard on clothing, especially when she was engaged in matters of magic.

After dressing, she came to the forest to find her usual spot, a dark squat stone that was so old that time had melted its rough edges smooth. It made for a good seat. She settled herself on its cool, hard surface and waited.

It was one of her favorite places in the world. The ferns and orchids that thrived under the towering redwoods provided a scene of generosity and extravagance to someone from her old desert roots. This place had its own kind of Power, green ancient dreams filled with an endless parade of sunlit days and moon-traveled nights, and the wild crash of sea-blown storms.

She listened until she felt a faint nudge against her awareness. It was not so much a sound that was distinguishable from any other of the small noises in the night, but more of a presence that touched the edge of her Power with shy delicate fingers, and she knew she was no longer alone.

"I came to tell you," she said in a quiet voice to the winged creatures she never quite saw full-on in daylight. "I have to leave now. I will try to come back. I wish I could say I will return but I don't know if I will be able to, so I left as many protections for you as I could." She had worked with Duncan, and had left legal safeguards and magical wards in place, but neither laws nor magic were immune to time. Things arrived on this earth and they passed from it; still, at least she knew she had tried her best.

It was one more obligation she had released. She could come to like this growing sense of freedom, all except for the dying bit. Then without her conscious permission a truth slipped out of her mouth, the words winging into the darkness like freed dragonflies.

She whispered, eyes stinging, "I will miss you."

For so long, she had felt all but dead, more intellect than emotion. Now after so many arid centuries, her soul was undergoing a renaissance of feeling. But rebirth, like change, was hard, and the well of tears she had discovered seemed to be inexhaustible.

Something rustled, then other tiny noises joined it, and she heard wings in truth overhead. As she looked up, a length of softness touched her cheek. She reached up to grasp it.

It was a feather, like the one left as a present for her on her windowsill. She couldn't see it in the shadows, but she knew the feather would be an iridescent black. Then more softness touched her, on the face, the neck, her hands, as the forest creatures flew overhead and showered her with feathers spiraling down, like the gentle nourishment of midnight rain.

She wiped her eyes and straightened her spine. Her past had become as uncertain as her future. Time had become a crucible burning everything away. There could be no greater or profound crisis.

But this much she could know. In both versions of her past she had been born into poverty and taken as a slave. And in both versions she had reached for immortality and had become a Queen.

I didn't change you, Rune had said. *Not you, not your soul or spirit.*

She finally understood what he meant.

"I know who I am again," she whispered.

And I will take ownership of this new life as well, for however long I may have it.

. . .

Rune slung Carling's bag on one shoulder, collected his duffle bag from the main house, and went down the bluff to wait for Carling on the beach. A briny breeze blew off the water. The cool wet air felt good on his tight, overheated skin. He stripped off his ruined T-shirt and dropped it on the ground by the bags and the waterproof container he'd left on the beach when he arrived. Then he rotated his shoulders to work out the tension that strung his muscles as tight as piano wire.

He felt antsy, just barely over the county line from the land of irrationality. He didn't like being apart from her. Didn't she realize how vulnerable she was when she went into a fade? The thought of her caught on a busy city street made him just about break into a sweat. She was one of the most dangerous of the Nightkind or of any of the Elder Races, but now at times she was also one of the most defenseless. It would be such a simple matter to slip a stiletto between her ribs as she stood still and unresisting, her mind locked in another time.

And if being in proximity to one of her episodes could affect him the way it did, who or what else might be affected by it? What other creatures or Powers might be able to slip into her mind or the past, or whatever the fuck was actually happening, to encounter that brave, fierce, painfully fragile tiger cub that was Carling's child-self?

Do you not study the tools your enemies use? She had said it in passing, and that one question had hinted at a hidden vista of magical tensions and Power plays. He thought of the dark Powers she had talked about, those hungry forces that ate the souls of both victims and black magic practitioners alike. He pictured something coiling around the young Carling like black smoke, and then he did break into a sweat.

He also lost all interest in keeping his promise. As he turned to go search for her, he caught sight of Rhoswen coming down the bluff path. Rhoswen was dressed in a wet suit, her pale hair pinned back in the usual tight chignon, and she carried a bundle in her arms. She had a pair of diver's swim fins, a dark waterproof bag, and Rasputin's silent, motionless form. Her cold bitter gaze raked down the length of his body and ran over the bags on the ground, and paused on Carling's worn leather bag.

"Carling's leaving?" she asked.

"We're going to the city to research a few things," he said.

Even as Rune started to ask about Rasputin's odd stillness, she tossed her armful, Rasputin and all, to the ground. He lunged forward to snatch up the dog before Rasputin hit the sand. He said, "The hell's the matter with you?"

The Vampyre curled a lip at him. "Relax, Wyr. The little shit's in a stasis spell. He wouldn't have felt a thing."

Rune studied the dog he held in his hands. Rasputin's body was lax and warm under thick, luxuriant fur. He wasn't breathing, but Rune could feel his life force, glowing like a firefly underneath his fingers. An unfamiliar metallic collar at his throat thrummed with magic. Gently Rune manipulated one of his legs. The flesh was pliable under his fingers, and the delicate muscle and bone flexed easily. The dog might not have felt the initial impact, but the stasis spell would not have prevented him from being injured in the fall.

"How long can he stay this way?" he asked.

"For as long as a day or so, until the collar wears down and has to recharge. It's the same spell Carling used to hold Tiago in stasis when he was bleeding to death. The dog doesn't know a thing. He's perfectly fine, more's the pity."

He noticed the leg he was flexing was one of Rasputin's crooked ones. He bent to place the dog carefully on the sand.

Then he pivoted on one heel and sprang at Rhoswen with a snarl. Shock flared across her face. She tried to leap back, but he was far too fast for her to evade.

He locked one hand around her slim neck, lifted her off of the ground and shook her hard. Her body snapped back and forth. Her eyes flared red, her mouth opened wide and fangs sprang out. So did her claws. She raked at his forearm, gouging deep furrows until his blood splattered over the sand.

He ignored it as he yanked the Vampyre close. He said into her distorted face, "Grow the fuck up, you petulant bitch."

Her claws dug deeper. He felt the scrape as she hit bone. Rhoswen hissed, "I gave her everything."

"Oh, you did not," he said, exasperated. He slammed her into the ground with such force he could hear as well as feel something snap in her body. A strangled cry broke out of her. Her back arched as she tried to flip out of his hold. "Shut up.

You'll heal. Which is more than I can say for Rasputin if he'd broken his neck when you dropped him."

"Come on," she gasped. She clawed at his arm again. "You don't care about that horrible little creep any more than I do."

"I understand him better than you think. He's an alpha dog. There's not a thing wrong with him that some obedience training wouldn't fix." He bent over her. "I also don't go around killing or maiming just because things haven't gone my way. You got handed a pink slip. Get over it."

"She threw me away like garbage." Tears glittered in the Vampyre's red gaze.

"Did she, now. Did she, really." He rolled his eyes. "She's been remarkably patient with you, considering. Interrupting us at the cottage? Slamming the door on us like a goddamn teenager? You would have been happy just now if you had hurt her dog."

Rhoswen didn't say anything, but he could see the truth in her eyes. She had wanted to hurt Carling and had, in all seriousness, hoped Rasputin would get injured.

"You know," he said. "Dragos would have filleted you by now, if you had acted out around him the way you have acted around Carling."

Rhoswen looked at him with loathing. She spat out, "She only got rid of me when you came along."

"Were you her lover? Did she cheat on you?" He paused. Rhoswen glared at him but remained silent. He said, "I'm gonna take a wild guess and say that's a no. Did she really have to get rid of her servant just because I came along? Wait, here it comes again: no."

"She needed me. She didn't have anybody else. You changed all that."

Okay, that was getting a little too unbalanced for him. He said, "I can see there's no talking sense to you. Here's what we're going to do."

He shifted his hold on her, grabbing her by the arm and the leg. She tried to escape again, bucking her body hard, but he held her easily as he stood up. Then he threw her down the beach and walked after her as she tumbled head over heels on the sand.

Rhoswen caught herself and came up on her hands and

knees. As he approached, the Vampyre watched with an animalistic cunning, all trace of humanity gone from her distorted features.

He had faced them so many times before, Powerful children who rampaged like drunken godlings, profligate with their gifts as they brutalized more vulnerable creatures in fits of sullenness. He had no patience for it. He squatted down in front of her, leaned his healing forearm on one knee and regarded her calmly. Gradually the snarl faded from her expression, to be replaced with a flicker of fear.

She knew better than to try to attack him, even though he could see how badly she wanted to. He said, "You've been good to Carling in the past, so even though I am tempted, I will not kill you. You are going to leave now, and maybe someday you'll realize that life is not all about you. Then again, maybe you won't. I don't really give a shit either way. But what you will do is stay the hell away from both Carling and that dog, because if you don't, I will tear the limbs from your body and burn them on a pyre while you watch. Vampyres can live for a very long time that way."

She whispered, "You wouldn't."

He raised his eyebrows. "I have."

The fear in her face grew. He saw that he had shaken her at last. He really didn't know why people always forgot he had this side to him.

"I can't even say good-bye?" She didn't even try to pull the pitiful card or to appeal to his better nature; she just asked it in a flat, matter-of-fact voice as her red, fascinated gaze clung to his.

"No," he said. "Not after the shit you've pulled. I don't trust you now. If I see you again, I will kill you. No excuses, no conversations, no second chances. Do we understand each other?"

She held his gaze as she raised her fingers to her mouth and licked away his blood. "We understand each other quite well, I think," said Rhoswen.

He stood, hands on his hips and watched the Vampyre dive into the ocean. She did not resurface. After several minutes of waiting to make sure, he scooped up the dog, tucked him in the crook of his elbow and went in search of Carling. He met her on the path to the forest.

Carling studied Rune curiously as she walked toward him. She was growing almost used to the mélange of unfamiliar emotions that started rioting the moment she laid eyes on him. He was shirtless, dressed only in jeans, boots and the bright silver cascade of moonlight, and his powerful body moved with liquid feline grace. His chest was heavy with the muscles of a swordsman, a light sprinkling of hair arrowing down the long taut abdomen.

She had no racing pulse for him to detect, and she put her hands behind her back to hide how much they started to shake as he grew close. Then she caught the rich iron scent of blood, his blood, and she noticed Rasputin's small form in his arms and suddenly she was running toward them.

As she reached him, he said in a calm voice, "Don't worry. Everything's all right."

She touched Rasputin and scanned both dog and collar magically even as she searched Rune with her gaze. The dog was fine, the collar working as it should. She tried not to be affected by the play of shadows along Rune's bare torso but found it to be impossible. He had no softness anywhere, not even an ounce of extra padding that civilization gave to so many creatures. He was all ridges and hollows, and the thick flex of hard-used muscle underneath the flow of skin. Even though he was standing relaxed beside her, his breathing slow and unhurried, the force of his presence punched the air.

Then she found the marks. The long scores ran the length of his forearm. They were faint in the moonlight and fading fast. She touched them and ran her fingertips lightly along his skin. They were claw marks, made by a hand very similar in size to hers.

Rage locked up her body. She said, "Rhoswen did this."

"It's nothing," he said.

"This is not 'nothing,'" she murmured. The wounds had gone deep, maybe to the bone. The heavy scent of blood lingered in the air. The scent was as intoxicating as she had imagined his blood would taste. She saw that he had bled on his jeans. "Did she taste you?"

A long-fingered hand came under her chin. He eased her face up. His head was bent over hers, his expression mild, the lean features peaceful, those lion's eyes clear. "You're smoking around the edges, darling," he said gently. She was, too. He could sense in his mind's eye the fury spreading through her aura.

"Did she taste you?"

He went immobile, staring, his expression arrested. Then his beautiful carved mouth lifted at the corners, just a little. He said, "She tasted the blood on her fingers."

Carling's long dark eyes flashed ruby red in the light of the silver moon.

Rune caught her by the arm as she started toward the house. "She's gone. I've already drop-kicked her on her way."

Carling struggled to take in what he said. The rage was an overriding force with a life all its own. It bucked against her attempt to control it. "What did she do?"

"She was indulging in petty vengefulness," Rune told her. He raised his hand to turn her face back to him. His smile had disappeared. He looked serious. "I've warned her to stay away, so if you see her, don't trust her, Carling."

"I won't," she said.

He slid his fingers in the heavy hair at her nape and bent his head. She was already lifting her face to him as he gave her a soft, lingering kiss. All the passion from the cottage was still there, still burning hot, underneath the gentle, leisurely caress. His enjoyment of the kiss for its own sake allowed her to relax and enjoy it too. None of the distant memories of her previous sexual experiences held this dimension. The pleasures of sex had seemed perfunctory, and the few lovers she had taken too self-involved, so much so that she had grown bored and stopped taking lovers altogether. Intrigued by the foreign concept of sexual affection, she moved her lips experimentally under his. The serrated edge of her rage eased into a smooth murmuring pleasure. She found herself leaning toward him, tilting her face further.

He slid his free arm around her and pulled her against his body, keeping the kiss easy. She spread her flattened hands across the broad expanse of his chest, and the feeling of his naked skin under her palms was so erotic, she almost sank to her knees.

As hot as her rage had flashed, this flashed hotter. She felt like she had been starving for an eternity, trapped in a black, sense-deprivation oubliette for so long she was only just beginning to realize how much her soul had been screaming. She broke into a spasm of uncontrollable shivering and found herself holding on to him tightly. A sound came out of her and she was shocked anew, for it was nothing she could remember ever hearing herself make before, a raw, shaken groan.

"Shh," he whispered. He rubbed her back soothingly as he kissed the corner of her mouth, her cheek, her temple. He hugged her hard against him. He was so much taller, and so stable in his strength she could imagine him standing in just such a relaxed stance as mountains fell down around him. "We'll get there, darling. And it will be better than anything. I promise."

It was such a gentle, nurturing moment and so completely devastating. She turned her face away from his caressing mouth when she wanted nothing more than to lean against him and soak up everything, his scent and his presence, his easy confident affection, that silent roar of Power that continually filled him, that eternal, elemental column of creation's flame.

All that time she had worked in the acquisition of Power. All that time she had been ruled by ambition. All those centuries that she had lived in such a vast yet fleeting journey, and here he was holding everything she had reached for, not striving, not continually learning to be better, not fighting to acquire any of it. He just was, the mysterious, magical rune, the riddle of a creature that nature decreed should not be able to exist, and yet he did.

She stiffened her spine, bracing herself against the moment. She tried to stiffen her knees and stand on her own, and after a moment she managed to do it. She fought to stop the cascading emotion, to reassert her control, and somehow she found a way to do it.

Then she happened to look down.

Rune was still cuddling her dog in the crook of his arm.

The wild feeling surged back, higher and more devastating than before, and she—the woman who had bargained with demons and stared down monsters, who had counseled pharaohs and created kings, who had once looked into dust-filled shadows of her empty, partially constructed tomb and said no, I will not go there—she broke down and fled.

Rune's body went into a clench as he looked after Carling's slender, escaping figure, his eyes narrowed. He took in deep draughts of the cool night air, fighting his instinct to give chase. After a few moments, he followed at a slower pace.

His battle was hard-won, because all of his instincts were roaring to go after her. He wanted to drag her to the ground, tear off that god-awful wretched caftan and spear into her naked body. He wanted to watch her face as she climaxed with him inside of her; he wanted to climax as he watched her beautiful face. He felt immense, full up to bursting and hard as a rock. His erection strained against the zipper of his jeans, and he had nearly come from just the touch of her hands sliding across his chest, from that broken needy little groan Carling—*Carling*—had made against his mouth.

And the way her eyes had turned that pretty, scary ruby red when he had been hurt was just fucking adorable. He wished he'd seen her fangs descend too. They probably didn't do that anymore, since she no longer fed on physical nourishment.

But it was kind of a major clue when a lady ran away from a bloke.

That said something, it did. That was a signpost that read: approach with caution. Falling rock up ahead. Handle with care. You've come so far with her, much further than you ever thought you'd get. Don't fucking blow it now, son.

That signpost was one of the busiest he had ever laid eyes on. It had a hell of a lot of text. He figured pausing to read all of that was a good thing.

He hitched Rasputin up higher on his chest and stroked the dog's soft fur. This was probably the quietest Rune would ever see him.

"I've eaten critters that were so much bigger and badass than you are," he said to the dog. Then he listened to the silence. He sighed and patted Rasputin's warm little body, and strode forward to meet Carling on the beach.

She was standing at the edge of the shore, holding herself by the elbows and looking over the water. She had packed all the bags in the waterproof container. She looked so beautiful, lonely and defensive, Rune's heart melted and his cock grew hard, and hells bells, if that wasn't enough to confuse a bloke, he didn't know what was.

He weighed his options and decided to stop just a few feet away, not too far but not close enough to spook her either.

Then he turned to look over the water too as he tried to figure out if he had any other options available. Further action on his part seemed undesirable at the moment, because he wasn't at all sure what might make Carling run away again.

So he stood and waited, and he tried to hide how greedy he was as he breathed deep to catch snatches of her scent on the wind. And he wanted with all of his might to go put his arms around her and hold her, just fucking hold her, just rest his head on her shapely, slender shoulder and feel her arms slide around his waist as she hugged him, but that goddamn signpost was busily ticker-taping more text. Now it read: not yet, son. You can't go there yet. So he petted the dog, and did nothing.

Finally Carling turned. She gave Rune a confused glance. She didn't feel capable of figuring him out at the moment. The clean lines of his profile, with the bold cheekbones, strong nose and lean jaw, were clearly outlined against the churning foam of the sea. He looked so patient and calm, so completely at odds with the tumultuous mess that was churning inside of her. He looked as if he was prepared to stand there and wait forever for whatever it was he wanted.

Instead of facing him, she turned to face inland. She looked up at the dark sprawl of her crazy-gothic house and wondered if she would ever see it again. She felt a pang and let it go, and it was another release.

She glanced back at Rune. "Ready?" she asked.

She watched him take a deep breath and nod. "Yep," he said. He turned to her. "You?"

After all Rhoswen's melodrama, all the internal crash of Carling's turmoil, and it came to this. Yep. She suddenly found herself smiling and nodded.

He strolled over, and there it was. There was the snapshot she wanted to take of him and keep forever, that easygoing way he had of moving his big body, the intent expression in his eyes as he looked at her that was so much at odds with the deceptive sleepiness on his handsome face, and she realized that sleepy, relaxed look of his was when he was on the prowl and at his most dangerous.

She whispered, "You don't fool me."

He gave her his slow, famous, heart-stopping, rock star smile. "You think too much. Where do you want your dog?"

She took Rasputin, wrapped him in Rune's ruined T-shirt, and tucked him gently into the waterproof container. Rune rubbed the back of his neck and winced as he watched. She said, "You know, he's perfectly safe traveling this way."

"I get it," he said. "He doesn't need to breathe right now. It just looks disturbing."

"Short of a little scuba mask, I couldn't think of any way to get him through the passageway." She stroked the dog's soft ear. "And this way he isn't distressed by the journey. It's like taking a nap on a car ride. He just goes to sleep and wakes up somewhere else."

Rune's face softened. "You love him."

She kept her head down as she secured the fastening. "I don't know. I suppose."

"You totally love him. He's your widdle snookums."

She snorted a laugh. "Yeah, I guess he is."

"Who kept him when you and Rhoswen traveled to Adriyel?" Rune took the container by its strap and slung it over one shoulder.

"My household staff looks after him when I travel. I don't think it's fair to ask that of them all the time, though, which is why I had asked Rhoswen to hire someone to look after him. I think we should drop him off at the town house for now, though, when we get back to the city."

"I agree. It will free us up to do whatever needs to be done." He held his free hand out to her. She hesitated only a moment. Then she put her hand in his and they walked into the ocean together.

The water was cold enough it would have sent an unprotected human into hypothermia within minutes. Rune found it just as refreshing as he thought he would. Better than a cold shower. He estimated the crossover passage that ran along a fissure on the ocean floor to be at a depth of around six hundred feet. It was very dark, but the crossover blazed clearly ahead in his mind's eye.

He mulled the experience over as they swam the passage. It was utterly familiar. Underwater or on land, he had crossed over passageways like this countless times before. And it was almost exactly like the crossover experience he had had during

Carling's episodes, except for that bent feeling, that sense of turning a corner.

Or maybe it was more like folding a piece of paper. For such a dramatic event, the image was rather boring and prosaic. But still there was something to it, an intuitive fit that appealed to him. The two portions of the folded paper existed side by side so close they touched. One portion of the paper was the present. When he crossed to Carling's past, he was traveling around that tiny, tight fold to stand on the other side.

Only the analogy broke down almost immediately, because there would have to be a countless number of potential folds in the paper to account for every moment in time. But still there was something to the concept of traveling around a bend that was so impossibly small and tight it took up absolutely no space at all. It made sense to him in a way, because . . .

. . . because the concept felt like it might be a direction he could actually follow.

If he hadn't already been doing so, he would have held his breath.

That feeling could very well be an illusion. He had nothing at all to base it on. He could just as well take a flying leap off a strange cliff into absolute darkness; it felt that dangerous. But he would be very interested to take that feeling into Carling's next episode.

He realized he was starting to believe that he really was interacting with the past, the actual past, not just what had happened to Carling in her own mind. He was looking forward to finding out what that damn Djinn discovered when Carling set him on the task of finding Rune's knife.

Either Carling sensed he was deep in thought, or she was preoccupied with thoughts of her own, for they made the trip in almost complete silence. After following the underwater fissure and completing the passage, they kicked upward. On the other side, daylight rippled along the water's surface. Rune's lungs had begun to burn by the time they broke the surface on a pale, chill fog-enshrouded day.

They treaded water as they gathered their bearings. Rune asked, "How do other Vampyres make that crossing safely when you never know what time it is going to be on the other side? Rhoswen's face, hands and part of her feet were exposed."

Carling shoved her soaking hair out of her eyes. She started to swim, and Rune kicked along beside her. "They can take precautions and dress so they are completely covered before they make the swim," Carling said. "There is also an underwater tunnel here, and a cave on the other side. When they are coming up from the passageway, they have plenty of time to see whether or not it's daylight. Then they can stay underwater and swim to either the tunnel or the cave. On this side, the tunnel is part of an old city sewage system."

"I've heard stories about old secret tunnels under San Francisco," Rune said. "There're supposed to be Vampyre and opium hangouts."

"Most people think the stories are an urban legend, but they're real. They're not safe and it's not just because of Vampyres and drug addicts—dangerous creatures live in those tunnels."

"Coolio," said Rune. "Sounds like a fun vacation spot."

Carling shook her head. He was irrepressible. She said, "The particular tunnel I'm talking about is straightforward enough. It leads up to a street-level building with the windows blocked out. Most of the Vampyres don't take the chance that something might happen in the water and leave them floating exposed to the surface, so they take extra precautions and wrap up from head to toe anyway."

"I would too." Rune rolled in the water. "You know, it's a nice day for a swim and all, but if you're game, I can get us to shore a lot quicker."

She looked at him questioningly. "I'm game."

He kicked around so that his back was to her. "Put your arms around my neck."

He almost groaned aloud from pleasure as she slipped her cool arms around his neck and her curved body brushed against him. He handed her the container's strap. She said, "Taking off from the water must be strenuous."

"It's not the smoothest way to get in the air," he said. "So hold on tight."

Her arms tightened, which pressed her breasts against his back, and his cock stiffened again despite the cold swim. He shook his head hard so that drops flew. Then he kicked into a swim, moving faster and harder as he changed into his Wyr form. He waited until he felt her find her place on his back, her arms still tight around his eagle's neck as she gripped him with her knees. Then with a massive heave, he lunged up out of the water as his giant wings unfurled and hammered down several times hard and fast.

He had not exaggerated. It was not the smoothest way for a gryphon to take to the air. He basically had to claw his massive body out of the water through sheer strength and speed, but within moments he had them airborne. Carling laughed as he worked into a steep ascent and the tall ghostly lines of the Golden Gate Bridge appeared in the fog ahead of them. He smiled to hear her laughter. She sounded so carefree and full of glee, so unlike the intense, dark-spirited woman who had met him in her great hall just a few days ago.

Then he banked and wheeled into a turn, and they flew toward the city.

⇒ TWELVE ⇒

Carling could not remember the last time she had felt such intense joy. In his gryphon form, Rune's muscular feline back was so broad she couldn't get a stable enough grip with her legs. She pulled the strap of the container higher on her shoulder, kept a tight hold on his neck as she hitched forward until she was perched more securely on his front shoulders and could grip the base of his neck between her knees. Only then did she open the container to take Rasputin out and cuddle him in the crook of her arm, though she wouldn't remove the stasis collar until they were safely on land. She looked back at the powerful flex of Rune's gigantic bronze wings beating steadily on either side.

"You all right back there?" Rune asked.

His deep voice was a clarion bell that thrummed between her legs. "I'm perfect," said Carling. "I was just getting into a more secure position."

"Don't worry, darling Carling," he said. "I won't let you fall."

Darling Carling. She found herself grinning. What a truly awful endearment. Only he could pull off something so ridiculous, with that gentle, caressing, teasing note in his deep voice that invited her to laugh along with him at the silliness of it. With his voice alone he made extravagant, intimate promises. Promises that said he spoke only to her this way, her and no other. She didn't believe it for a moment, although she confessed to herself, in her secret heart of hearts, it was rather nice to pretend.

When would he come after her again? When would she turn around and see that look of intent in his eyes that he masked so cleverly behind a sleepy expression? Her smile disappeared as arousal flared all over again, and her own predatory impulses stirred, like the lazy stretch of an animal that had long been asleep.

What would he do if she came after him? She liked that thought, them stalking each other, one moving forward, the other pulling back until that last pounce. One way or another they would become lovers. It was another promise from him, of a pleasure that already was so surprising it caught at her soul. She had thought that the days of her taking a lover were long over. How gorgeous, that she could be surprised.

They were soaking wet, and the chill wind was slicing. Although she craved warmth, the bitter cold did not hurt her. Even though Rune's body roared with heat and effort, the cold might be uncomfortable for him.

She stroked the back of his sleek powerful neck and whispered a spell. A ripple of Power washed over them both, and then suddenly they were both dry.

"Mmm." Rune started to purr. "That felt good."

"I thought you might be getting cold," she told him.

"I wasn't, but I like it when you practice magic on me," he said throatily.

She snorted. He was clearly in a playful mood. Her amusement died as she remembered the dark, calculating way she had planned to research ways to attack him. It seemed to make sense at the time, but now the thought of throwing an offensive spell to hurt him made her feel queasy. Even if, for some reason, Rune became her enemy, she didn't think she could do that to him, not anymore.

Once she would have done anything to survive. Whatever it took. Living was the supreme priority. Now even though time had become more precious than ever before as it ran out, she finally discovered there were other things that were more important than survival.

They were damp again quickly from flying through the

thick fog. The city was shrouded and indistinct, until suddenly they were upon it.

Then Carling felt something shimmer into place around them. She stiffened but almost immediately realized that the sensation, whatever it was, came from Rune. It felt strange, warm and intimate, as if he had somehow expanded his aura to wrap it around her.

"What is that?" she asked. "What are you doing?"

"I'm cloaking us," Rune replied. "I should have done it as soon as I took to the air, but I was distracted. SFO's air traffic control is probably having a conniption right now."

She raised a hand and looked at it. She could still see herself but she was blurred as if she were looking through an antique window. She studied Rune. He was blurred as well, but perfectly visible. "Are you sure it's working properly?"

He chuckled. "Yes, I'm sure."

"I can still see us," she said.

"That's because we're both inside the cloak. Other people can't see us, which is the main point."

"Uh-huh," she said, squinting skeptically at her hand again. "It's a nifty trick, if you're not pulling my leg."

"Oh ye of little faith," murmured the gryphon. "Where is your town house?"

Carling looked down at the ground as she gave him directions. They were just flying over the Presidio at the northern tip of San Francisco. Originally a Spanish fort, it had been a military installation for almost two hundred years. Now it was a public park. Wreathed in the mist that had rolled off the ocean, the aged, well-tended trees looked vaporous, the ground indistinct underneath.

She sighed. "I would say we should just stay at my town house, except I'm almost certain someone on the staff is a spy and I would rather Julian not be apprised of our every move. He's not going to be happy as it is when I call to tell him I've come back to the city. We had decided my condition was too dangerous for me to be around very many people right now."

"Fuck Julian," said Rune. "I don't care if he's happy or not."

Carling sighed heavily again. "I've handled him many times before when he's chosen to be unpleasant, and I will handle him again if I have to, but we have more important things to focus on than clashing with Julian right now."

Rune paused for a moment. He continued in a softer, more serious voice. "You're right, of course. We don't have to rub your presence in Julian's face. Since I didn't know what to expect when I got here, I arranged to have a suite available at the Fairmont Hotel for whenever I might need it. After we drop Rasputin off, we can go there. No doubt there'll be spies there too but it won't be the same as it happening in the intimacy of your own home."

"I'm sure you're right," she muttered. "I don't care where we go."

"Then the hotel it is," said Rune. He climbed steeply in the air, soaring over the tops of buildings, and plummeted to the street corner near her house. The town houses were luxurious, and Carling's home was mere blocks from Market Street. He realized her house would be an easy walk to the Turner and Braeburn offices, and the Bureau of Nightkind Immigration. That seemed too convenient to be a coincidence.

He landed lightly on his feet and after Carling had slid to the pavement, he shimmered into a shapeshift. Only then did he relax the cloaking around them. "See?" he said. "No one saw us."

She looked around and laughed. Traffic was all around but by some trick of chance, there weren't any vehicles passing by them at the moment, and the nearest pedestrians were a half a block away and walking in the other direction from them. The fog was not terribly heavy, but it did give everything a sense of space and privacy that might not otherwise have been present in the full light of sunshine. "No one saw us, my dear genius gryphon, because there's no one around to pay attention."

He looked around, his eyes narrowed. "All right, I can see that you'll take some convincing. Here, give me that." He took the container from her.

She strode down the street with Rasputin in her arms, and Rune fell back a few steps so he could watch her. She moved with her characteristic imperiousness. She was barefoot and bedraggled, her hair a tangled mess down her back, her awful caftan a ragtag, crumpled mess. And there was no doubt in his mind—there could be no doubt in the mind of anyone who saw her—that she was royalty. Goddamn, that was smoking hot.

She led him up the steps of an elegant four-story Mediterranean Revival home. Loosely based on Italian palazzo architecture, the facade was simple, an elegant pale ochre, with arched black wrought-iron windows. She took hold of the doorknob, spoke a Power-filled word, and Rune heard the small click as the lock turned. Hell of a handy trick, that. She never had to worry about losing a key and locking herself out.

Rune followed her into a spacious front hall, with gleaming oak floors and a simple antique hall table that was so beautifully constructed, Sotheby's would have drooled over it. A vase filled with fresh lilies provided the only adornment. Carling gestured to a doorway on the right. "Make yourself at home," she told Rune as she strode down the hall. "I'll be right back."

"Okey-dokey," he said. He strolled into a room that was as elegant as everything else he had seen of her home. She had continued with the Mediterranean theme in the interior decor. The room had textured walls, thirteenth-century Florentine tapestries and artwork, and leather burgundy furniture. Way to be all-over classy, Carling.

As he opened up the container to pull out his duffle and Carling's leather bag, he heard the sound of rapid footsteps approaching. They were much heavier than Carling's soft, almost imperceptible tread, no doubt belonging to a male. "Councillor!" Yep, it was a male. "What a surprise! What may I do for you? Would you like for me to wake the others?"

"There's no need to bother them, Rufio," Carling said. "I'm not staying."

"The others" must be Vampyres, as it was fairly standard practice in Vampyre households to have a human or two on staff to attend to daytime affairs.

Carling was continuing. "I have dismissed Rhoswen. She is no longer acting on my behalf, nor is she to be trusted. She may come by for her things, so you are to have everything packed and waiting for her, but do not allow her access to any part of the house unsupervised, is that understood? I want to know if she becomes a problem for you. If she does, or you feel threatened in any way, let me know and I will take care of her."

"Yes, ma'am."

Startlement-R-Us. Was there something else in the male's voice, something like relief, or was that Rune's imagination? He wished he could see the human so he could get a take on the other male's expression, although anyone Carling had on staff would have the ability to be discreet.

"Two more things before I go. First, the staff needs to look after Rasputin for the time being while I attend to some unexpected business. Rhoswen was to have hired someone to look after him, but I had to let her go before that happened. Have Abelard look for someone. He should have a list of prospects prepared for me by the end of the week. Is that clear?"

"Yes, ma'am. And what is the second thing?"

"Pack some clothes and things for me, and send it to the Fairmont Hotel."

"Yes, ma'am. Right away. Has the little man eaten recently?"

Little man. Rune grinned. He might grow to like this Rufio guy.

"He's due for his evening meal. What is the date and time here?"

Given that the Other land was not in sync with the time in San Francisco, it was not as odd a question as it might otherwise have sounded. Rufio informed her that it was late Monday morning. Rune had left on Friday evening, so the time slippage hadn't been all that bad.

"Excellent. Give him a late breakfast, and he'll be on track for the next evening meal. Don't take the stasis collar off of him until we are gone. There's no need to go through all his drama while I leave the house."

"We? My apologies, Councillor. I did not realize we had a guest to attend to."

"We don't. Wyr sentinel Rune Ainissesthai is with me, and he and I are just leaving."

"Very good, ma'am. I'll have some of your things sent to the Fairmont within the hour."

Rune rolled his eyes. He knew just what those things would be too. The forecast called for more wretched caftans with a ten percent chance of classic black Chanel scattered throughout. Shoes, optional. Makeup, nonexistent.

"Feed Rasputin first, Rufio," Carling said.

"Yes, ma'am. Of course. Will there be anything else?"

"No, that will be all, thank you."

Rune walked out of the room, their two bags in his hand, and he met Carling as she returned. He looked over Carling's shoulder at the tall, wide-shouldered man who cuddled Rasputin at the opposite end of the hall and stared back, his face alive with curiosity. Rufio was perhaps a fit forty years old and well groomed.

Of course he had to be a good-looking male, didn't he? Rune wasn't so sure he would like the other man after all. He found his lip curling and instead of suggesting Carling take her time and at least have a hot shower before they left, he growled, "Ready to go?"

She looked at him in surprise, but whether that was for his tone of voice or his question, he didn't know. "Of course." He walked with her out the front door. When they were outside, she turned to face him. "What is wrong?"

As soon as the door was shut behind them, he began to feel better. "Nothing," he said. "Nothing at all. Why don't I change again? I can fly us to the Fairmont more quickly than a taxi could take us."

She frowned. She was certain something had been wrong. In the hall he had flared with aggression, but whatever had set him off, the aggression was gone now. She put it out of her mind and shrugged. "Fine, if that's what you want to do."

Secretly she was thrilled. She couldn't wait to fly with him again. She schooled her face to hide her excitement as they stepped down to the sidewalk, he handed her his duffle and her leather bag, and shimmered into the change. Just before he shifted, he cloaked them again. She felt the ripple of it settle over them both like a warm blanket. As she leaped onto his back, he pointed out, "And still, nobody has seen us."

Amused, she tapped the back of his sleek eagle's head. "Pay attention. There's nobody around."

"You want more proof? I'll just have to show you more proof." He crouched and launched.

The power in his spring was even more incredible as he took off from land. Her spirits launched with him, in a straight-up trajectory toward exhilaration. After a steep climb, he wheeled to head in the direction of the hotel.

The Fairmont Hotel was one of the premiere luxury hotels

in San Francisco. It sat atop Nob Hill and looked over the city and the Bay, and it had hundreds of rooms and suites, three restaurants and lounges, ballrooms, multimedia rooms for business conferences, shops and a spa. It was not far from Carling's house, so in just a few minutes they landed on the hotel's spacious manicured grounds, and Rune waited until Carling slid off his back before he changed into his human form.

Carling watched in fascination as he rippled through the change again. She had seen him change a few times now, and she still could not quite grasp what happened. This time the blur of his change was made even more indistinct by the cloaking . . . spell? no, that didn't seem quite right, as it didn't involve an incantation . . . that he kept wrapped around them. Then he was in his human form again, with his broad bare chest, horrible blood-streaked jeans and all.

He stepped close to put an arm around her and she leaned into him. "By the way, how are you feeling?" he asked. "Any hint of an approaching fade?"

She shook her head. "I'm fine."

"Good." He squeezed her shoulders. "Check this out; here's your proof. We've landed, you're here in public, I'm half dressed, and nobody's noticed. Now Councillor, you've got to admit, that's just not right."

Her eyebrows shot up and she laughed. She took a quick look around. The fog blew vaporous tendrils of white along the streets. She could hear and see people and traffic in the distance, but by some trick of chance, once more nobody happened to be nearby. "That's sheer luck," she said. "Nobody has noticed us because again, nobody is paying attention. I'm not convinced."

"All right," he said. "Come with me. Just remember to be quiet now. The cloaking only works on the visual, not on the auditory senses."

He took the bags from her again and slung them onto one shoulder, kept his other arm around her, and walked with her to the flagged, well-lit portico at the front of the hotel. She stayed silent, watching the street that was busy with honking traffic and pedestrians as Rune steered them down the sidewalk. This time they came closer to other people, and not one person glanced their way.

Even with the fog, the late morning was too bright for any of the more photosensitive of the Nightkind, and there wasn't a Vampyre in sight. All of the people they passed were human.

Are you convinced now? Rune asked telepathically.

She smiled to herself. She liked walking down the street with him. She liked moving together and basking in the warmth of his Power as it wrapped around her. She liked his clean, masculine scent. And maybe she liked teasing him a little too. *I might be a bit more convinced than I was. But you know, San Franciscans are used to some pretty odd sights, nudist parades, the Vampyre Exotica ball. It could just be we're boring.*

Never, he said, his arm tightening on her shoulders. *We're never boring. Let's step inside.*

They had to pause to wait for someone else to walk through the front doors, and then they slipped in after, Rune urging Carling to go in front of him.

The lobby was massive, filled with gold brocade furniture, towering plants in huge floor pots, marble-veined columns that supported a two-story-high ceiling, patterned marble floors polished to a high gleam and rich cream lights. It was also quite busy, filled with people dressed in designer and shabby chic clothes, and sleek, tailored business suits. The lobby was filled with random noise, from the street traffic outside to conversations and sudden trills of laughter, and the unpredictable ping of cell phone ringtones. After the relative peace and quiet of the windswept island, civilization was jarring.

Rune guided Carling adroitly to one side near a wall, where there was a quiet clear space out of the way of traffic. He set their bags down and stood with his arms crossed. He told her, *Feel free to commence praising at any time.*

She chuckled under her breath. The lobby traffic wasn't all human. A couple of Light Fae were checking in at the desk, tall slender figures with their signature pale blond hair and elegantly pointed ears. The Light Fae would have the ability to sense magic, but they were busy with their own affairs and never noticed Carling and Rune. Nobody looked their way. She had to admit, she was impressed.

Not that she was going to commence praising on cue. The eagle in him was perfectly capable of preening his own feathers. She grumbled, *Okay, I'll concede you might have something here.*

He murmured, *At last, success.*

But what's the catch?

He squinted at her. *There is no catch. Nobody can see us. You could tear off all your clothes, jump up and down, and wave your arms, if you like. Nobody can see a thing we do.*

There's always a catch, she said. *And I'm not talking about the auditory. There's always a drawback or some kind of limitation to matters of magic and Power.*

You're just a glass-half-empty kind of girl, aren't you? He cocked his head in exasperation.

Girl, she said, mulling over the word.

Very much a girl. Rune swiveled and paced in a circle around her. She turned her head to track him. His Power changed and tightened on her. It was a heavy, sultry feeling as vivid as a physical caress. He moved behind her, so close his hard chest pressed against her shoulder blades, and his hands came over hers and curled on her slender wrists. His hands were corded with strength, broad along the back and long in the fingers. They were heavily calloused from sword work and other physical labor. He stroked those long, clever fingers of his up her arms lightly. *A spiky, beautiful girl. The most beautiful girl I've ever seen.*

The tiny friction of his touch raised goose bumps along her bare skin, and she shuddered. *I bet you say that to all the spiky, beautiful girls.*

Never. I've never said it before. He spoke with such conviction she was actually tempted to believe him. He took her shoulders and pulled her back against him. Then he bent to put his lips against her ear and said in a whisper against the delicate shell of flesh, "There is one catch to the cloaking. Anyone with Power can look and see a shimmer where we're standing. I'm told it looks like a heat haze rising off asphalt. But that happens only if they're looking in the right direction at the right time, and are paying attention enough to question what they see. And nobody is looking at us."

The Light Fae finished checking in and headed for the stairs. She watched them climb upward and disappear. Rune's whisper was the barest thread of throaty sound. His breath tickled along her sensitive skin, and she shuddered harder as her knees weakened. She found herself leaning back against him. She breathed, "What are you doing?"

He felt it again, the sense that here was some keystroke password to an unbreakable code. He put his lips against her neck and mouthed, "What do you think I'm doing? I said I was going to come after you again."

"Yes, but here? *Now?*" She tried to turn around, but his hands tightened and held her in place.

"What can I say, I'm an opportunist," he murmured. "And you're making me crazy. I loved the feeling of your legs gripping me tight when you knocked me down at the cottage. I love the fact that you could knock me down. I love your strength and confidence." He realized the depth of truth in that statement. Back on the island it had hurt him to see her so profoundly shaken, and he would do just about anything he could to avoid seeing that happen to her again. He whispered, "Look at the couple that just walked in the door. They don't have a clue we're standing here. Or the doorman over there, standing just outside. He can't see a thing as I do this."

Unable to resist, Rune's hand slid around and he cupped her full, round breast.

Even though he had given her plenty of warning, acute shock still bolted through her, washing her from head to toe. She made a small, strangled sound and suddenly Rune's other hand was clapped tight over her mouth.

"Shh," he whispered. His breathing had roughened. "We can't make any noise."

She gripped his forearms tightly, shaking, as she watched the couple, a man and a woman, walk by obliviously. The heat from Rune's hand on her breast burned through the thin barrier of the cotton caftan. He stroked along the firm, weighted flesh until her plump nipple jutted between his first and second fingers. Then he pinched her gently, and the sensation speared right down to the juncture at the top of her legs.

She jerked in his arms and sucked in a useless, frantic breath. Her fingers dug into the muscled flesh of his forearms.

And she did not push away either the caressing hand at her breast or the hand that covered her mouth.

His mouth felt taut against her skin, at the sensitive spot where her neck met her shoulder. "Tell me to stop," he breathed. Because he could not stop himself. The compulsion he felt kept driving him toward her. Dimly he was aware of warning bells going off somewhere, but they were far off in the distance, cloaked by a sensual haze that covered everything in his head.

Her head fell back against his collarbone. She gazed blindly at the ceiling and mouthed the word soundlessly against his broad palm. Stop?

He massaged her breast, rolling her nipple between his fingers, and good fucking hell, once again he almost came in his jeans. The luscious heavy weight of her breast filled his palm just right, and her nipple was a delicacy his mouth watered to taste, but the by-God real ass-kicker was how she shivered in his arms and held on to him like he was the last stable thing on earth, how her gorgeous, healthy scent bloomed with feminine arousal. That was his scent. That was for *him*.

And she breathed for him, in ragged, telltale gasps.

"You need to say that word again," he whispered roughly against her neck. "Because I'm feeling a little thick right now and I'm not processing too clearly. And this time you need to say it like you mean it."

The gears in Carling's head ground as she tried to understand what he said. Word. He wanted a word from her. What was it?

Girl. No, that wasn't it.

Out of the corner of her eye she caught sight of a teenage boy slouching through the hotel's front doors, wearing ripped designer clothes and goth makeup, and carrying an iPad under one skinny arm. He glared at the world as if it owed him an explanation. Yeah, good luck with that one, kid.

Then Rune opened his hot mouth on the sensitive skin of her neck and suckled at her, and she lost the ability to get any word out. He grazed her lightly with his teeth as he let go of her nipple. His infernally clever fingers moved to the front of her caftan.

All of her caftans were hand-stitched, of varying designs. Some were simply fashioned to pull over the head, and others were fastened down the front with a row of small buttons carved of either bone or wood. None of them contained zippers, as she used them so often for work and metal could sometimes interact or interfere with magic.

This caftan was fastened in the front with a row of buttons. As he suckled at her neck, Rune slipped one of the buttons free of its hole. His hand was clamped so tightly on her mouth she couldn't turn her head. She tried to track his movements by just moving her eyes.

The buttons ran close together. He unbuttoned another and slipped his hand inside to cup her breast again. They both hissed as his calloused palm came in contact with her heavy, naked, sensitive flesh. Every muscle in his body felt ridged with tension. When he pushed his lean hips against the rounded curve of her ass, she could feel the long thick ridge of his erection. She could sense the blood hurtling through his body like a stealth bomber, and his jagged breathing sawed against her skin. He massaged her breast and scraped the tip of her nipple with his fingernail.

Every pulse point on her body screamed in response, the sexual need ratcheting higher. Normally so cool, she was shocked all over again when she broke into a sweat and her sex moistened in a liquid gush. The sense of urgency, of possible exposure, was agonizing.

Stop. Stop. Stop.

She started shaking her head. Somehow she found a paltry scatter of words. *I—I don't think—I can't—*

Can't what, beautiful girl? Can't relax and enjoy this? It's wicked but not bad. It's just a little naughty fun and even if it doesn't feel like it, it's perfectly private. Rune whispered temptation in her head with as much wily wisdom as the snake in the Garden of Eden. He pinched her harder, and she strangled a squeal as her back arched. *You're safe, trust me. I would never let anyone see you like this. God, your breast feels like it was made for my hand. Such a perfect, perfect fit.*

She was going to push him away. She was, any minute now, but then he pulled his hand out of the caftan, which left her blinking in disappointment.

She twisted to face him, her arms going around his neck even as his mouth came down on hers. He kissed her, hard and hungrily, and she let her eyes fall closed as she kissed him back. His heart pounded. She loved the sensation of his blood coursing throughout his long, powerful frame.

He turned them and pushed her back against the wall, covering her with his body, and fresh shock detonated as he ran a hand down her torso between them to unfasten the two buttons of her caftan that were over her groin. Before she quite knew what happened, he had slipped his hand inside and slid his fingers into the moist silken tangle of private hair.

He was touching her. Right there in the hotel lobby. He was touching her. The pleasure of it had her so crazed it escaped in a high, thin, nearly inaudible scream as she clutched his hand against her. He swallowed the sound as he fucked her mouth with his tongue.

And nobody noticed. Nobody saw. The indifferent world wheeled on its clockwork way around them.

Shh, darling, Rune said. His mental voice sounded as ragged as she felt. His big body bowed over her, lungs working like bellows. He was so hot, the feel of his body burned through the caftan. *Holy gods, I'm finding religion here. You feel like heaven on earth, you're so soft and wet and silky. What I wouldn't give to be able to taste you right now.*

She let go of his hand and gripped one of his rock-hard thighs as she sank the other fist in his hair, and somehow she managed to find her telepathic voice again. *Okay okay okay. This has been really amusing—*

Amusing. More like apocalyptic.

—but I don't think I can take any—any more of this—

Even as she stuttered, he found the small stiffened bud of her clitoris and stroked it with a forefinger.

The climax sucker punched her, a left hook that came out of nowhere and clipped her on the jaw. All the strength ran out of her body and her legs turned to rubber, and she went down for the count.

She slid to her knees and he came down with her. He cupped her between the legs and kept a firm steady pressure on the tiny throbbing pulse of her pleasure, bracing his weight on one forearm against the wall as he bowed over her. He was panting as if he were running in a full-out sprint, his Power a fiery cascade around them. He pulled his mouth from hers to sink his teeth into her neck as she shuddered through the throes of the climax. He was swearing steadily in her head, and the jagged curses sounded like poetry.

Then the cataclysm racking her mind and body eased. They both held still, breathing heavily.

Rune asked, *Are you all right? I didn't push things too far, did I?* Even his mental voice seemed hoarse, as though he had been shouting.

She had to think about it. She had witnessed many things, always holding herself separate from the sexual excesses of history, but she had never seen or heard of anything like what she had just experienced. It was not just the exoticism of the act itself. It was the exoticism of *him*, that playful, affectionate, dangerous on-the-edge man.

Just a little bit of naughty fun, and perfectly private. You're safe, trust me.

A ghost of a chuckle escaped her. He poisoned her with affection and compassion, and he taught her what it meant to play again. He gave her hope and tore down her past, all with a fierce laugh in those remarkable eyes. He had already taken her soul on an impossible moonlit flight. She might as well give him her shredded, useless heart too, since she hadn't been using it all these years.

She whispered, "I'm okay, you lunatic. But I really cannot go any further out here . . ."

He was already shaking his head. "I don't think I could hold on to the cloaking and take you at the same time," he growled. "And I will not risk exposing either of us like that."

Because she was safe, and she really could trust him. She really could.

She hiccupped in a silent sob, a physical reaction as involuntary and shocking as the climax had been.

He smoothed the tangled hair away from her face. *Are you sure you're all right, darling?* he asked again, sounding concerned.

His handsome features were blurred like the memory of a dream, and the giant invisible force that had been propelling her forward these last several years, faster and faster, shoved her into a realization and then she really was moving at the speed of light.

What was this feeling? She had sensed it before in so many others. She felt shards of it, for dogs and other creatures, nations and ideals, and old lovers who had been gone for so many, many years. She had always felt those shards were pieces of something that was bigger than anything she would ever be able to understand, until just now, as they coalesced and made a whole.

Love. This feeling was love.

She sat back on her heels, dragged the back of one hand across her face then leaned forward to kiss him. *Stop worrying*, she told him gently. *I'm fine.*

He frowned and rubbed her back. *Okay. Here, let me help you.*

She buttoned her caftan unsteadily as he finger-combed her hair into some semblance of order. He tried to twist it into a knot at the nape of her neck and tuck it in on itself the way that she did, but he didn't have the knack and it fell down her back again. *Damn. You'll have to let me know how you do that.*

She gathered it up swiftly again and tucked it into place. *Or maybe I'll just cut it. It's been a long time since I've had it short.*

Really? He helped her to her feet. A short haircut would show off the gorgeous bones of her face, but that long extravagant fall of dark hair cascading to her hips was flagrantly feminine and outrageously beautiful. *Could you grow it back if you cut it?*

How did he do that? How did he manage to tuck that crazy out-of-control passion out of the way and act almost as if nothing had happened? She could barely stand on her feet, and even though she had climaxed, her body still felt empty and aching and unfulfilled.

Or maybe she was the only one who had experienced the crazy out-of-control passion, just as she was the only who had realized she had fallen in love. Falling in love was such a lonely business.

They had achieved an understanding back at the island cottage. They had made a pact, and she was very aware she had agreed to it. This was supposed to be a love affair with a built-in expiration date. Clearly he had been in control the entire time.

Well, he had discovered too many of her secrets already. He could not have this one as well. She would keep her epiphanies and realizations to herself.

She realized he had asked her a question and answered absently. *My hair and fingernails stopped growing when I stopped taking in physical nourishment. If and when I cut it, it'll be gone for good.*

That would be tragic. Your hair is one of the wonders of the world. She smiled with pleasure at the compliment in spite of herself. He bent to pick up their bags. He asked, *Are you ready?*

She assumed a composed expression, twitched the skirt of her caftan to make sure it fell into place, and told him, *Yes.*

She felt his Power flex in a kind of release, and the shimmering cloak fell away. They strode toward the hotel's front desk.

Gradually all the noise in the lobby died away. As far as everyone else was concerned, they had apparently appeared out of nowhere. Carling knew what they must look like, half dressed and disheveled, like shipwreck survivors. Rune was still shirtless, and her feet were bare. Sooner or later someone would recognize one or the other of them. Eventually somebody would call the paparazzi and all possibility of discretion would go to hell. After this kind of entrance, and especially after stopping at home, she really needed to make a point of calling Julian sooner rather than later.

None of it meant a thing to her. She certainly didn't care what she looked like, and it was clear Rune didn't either. She glanced sideways and down at his long legs keeping pace with hers. What struck her most was how she and Rune moved together, hip-to-hip in a smooth, ground-eating stride. They must look like they were a couple. She ignored the pang she felt at that. Feelings were so often an inconvenience to the rest of one's life.

She focused on the front desk. A man in a charcoal gray suit rushed over to join a uniformed employee standing at attention in front of a computer. As they approached, the man stared, his face filled with wonder.

"Good morning, I'm Harry Rowling, one of the assistant managers," he said in a hushed whisper. "Councillor Severan, what an unexpected honor."

She nodded a greeting and watched as he turned his attention to Rune. The man went white and started to babble. "Sir, ah—Sentinel Ainissesthai . . . what a pleasure, I mean it's an honor to have you here as well—"

Well yes, of course the rock star of the Wyr did not have just female fans. She would not let herself sigh, although she indulged in a pointed glance at Rune.

She went still and stared like the hotel manager.

Rune glittered everywhere with a barely restrained tension. His face was a loaded weapon, the bones standing out in stark relief, and his eyes were lambent with a dangerous, unpredictable light. One hand was clenched in a white-knuckled grip on the straps of their bags, the other fist pressed against his thigh. He breathed with such measured evenness, she found herself taking a step back.

Perhaps his control had not come as easily for him as she had thought. She started to smile.

Rune's voice was soft as he said to the man, "I would like the key to my suite, please."

"C-certainly, uh, would you like for me to check for any messages?"

"Later." Rune glanced at Carling, who was staring at him in fascination. Rune turned his attention back to the man and waited a moment. Nothing happened. The man stood frozen like a rabbit in front of a wolf. He raised his eyebrows. "The key?"

Rowling started. "Of course! Sorry! Yes, the key!" He whirled to the uniformed employee and hissed between his teeth, "Get the key!"

They scrambled and fumbled, and within moments the key was offered to him. He held the hand that had caressed Carling's—*Carling's*—most private place clenched against his side, the fingers curled against his palm, and even then he could still catch the faint lingering scent of her arousal.

He wanted to lick his fingers. He wanted to punch the hotel employees for standing too close. It was a good thing they were just humans with weak human senses, or he might have. He felt like he was going crazy, and he did not dare look at her or the insane beast that bucked so wildly against his control might slip loose.

He took the key gently with his other hand. The assistant

manager started to bleat something. Rune said in an iron-hard voice, "That will be all for now."

Much nodding and more bleating. He pivoted away in the middle of it, grabbed Carling's hand and stalked to the elevator. She came along, choosing for whatever reason to be acquiescent.

They rode up to the suite in silence, and strode down the hall. His pulse picked up speed as they reached the door. He had too much blood in his body. It roared through his veins, and his skin could barely contain it. He felt like he was speeding down a winding mountain road with his car in overdrive, just barely holding the tires onto the pavement, with his brakes liable to fail at any moment. He swiped the keycard and held the door open for her, still not trusting himself to glance at her.

Then he was stepping in, and throwing the security bolt, and setting aside their two bags. He ran a shaking hand through his tangled hair, and only then did he dare to look at Carling's face.

She was already watching him. Her long, dark, gorgeous eyes held an emotion he hadn't seen in them before. It had something to do with shadows and gentleness, and an odd, quizzical understanding.

Then she smiled that subtle, mysterious Mona Lisa smile of hers that tilted the corners of her lush mouth and caused the tiny lines at the corners of her eyes to crease, where that bastard mortality had stroked her velvet skin with skeletal fingers and carved his mark on her before she had kicked him in the balls.

And Rune's brakes failed. He lunged at her and took her over the mountain cliff with him.

⇒ THIRTEEN ⇐

I don't have to stay in love with you, Carling thought as she smiled at Rune. Falling in love is just a passing realization. Merely the by-product of some brain-cooking heat shared with a world-class, five-star sexy male. Passion is a choice, and staying in love is a decision. I can walk away from you like I have had to walk away from virtually everything and everyone else, because only one thing holds true over time.

Nothing ever lasts and everything always changes. . . .

As if he could hear her thoughts, Rune's handsome, wild face hardened. Then suddenly he blurred as he moved so *fast*, and he tackled her to the floor, and hell's siren bells, she did not know how she had ever thought he had handled her with such delicate care, because he tore her caftan off of her body with such savagery she cried out, a sharp wordless sound that was cut off as he slammed his mouth down onto hers.

And she found herself shocked all over again at her own naiveté. She had thought that what had happened before in the lobby was apocalyptic, but it didn't hold a candle to what erupted inside of her now.

Rune drove his tongue into her mouth, as he yanked at the fastening of his jeans. Naked at last and pinned with his body weight, she widened her legs and arched up to him. She raked fingernails down his broad back, scoring him as he rubbed the broad head of his erection at her slick entrance. The rich, burning liqueur scent of his blood filled the air. It smelled so intoxicating her mouth tingled, almost as if her fangs would descend.

She wanted to bite him. She wanted to *bite*. She growled, confused at the predatory impulses that had been dormant for so long, and he growled back as he grabbed hold of her hips and surged inside.

His penis was huge and his abrupt invasion of her body was so outrageous, she screamed into his mouth. Her feral response shuddered through him. When he would have pulled back to look at her, to check to see if she was all right, she sank her fists into his hair and held him to her, kissing him with such ferocity he lost track of everything except for the overwhelming need to drive into her.

He had to hand it to her, with a bow and flourish. It really was never anything mundane with her.

He withdrew, the slide liquid smooth and torturously tight, and he slammed into her again, into that lush velvet sheath, and he couldn't get far enough inside so he ground against her pelvis, pushing harder. She bucked underneath him as another climax skyrocketed through her.

He felt her inner muscles start to spasm as she groaned into his mouth, and it was so fucking *perfect* and somehow so much more than what he had imagined, he was already climaxing as well, climaxing too soon even as he pulled out to slam back in again. He snarled in frustration against her lips, a raw guttural sound as animalistic as everything else they had done to each other, as he spilled into the clenched, welcoming bowl of her body.

Then silence sprinkled around them like the drift of winter snowfall, as they gripped each other with shaking limbs and tried to come back from the alien place they had just taken each other. Rune pulled his mouth away to press his cheek against hers, his eyes closed. Carling stared at the ceiling blindly. There was no making sense of what had just happened. It was as far outside of sensible as a person could go.

Say something. Her mouth worked.

"That was classy," Carling said.

He reared his head back, his expression arrested.

Rune said, "Just wait until you see what I can do with the fancy stuff, like a bed."

Their eyes met. She quirked an eyebrow at him. His sexy mouth twitched. Then they both exploded. He hugged her tight and rolled around the floor with her, laughing.

Listen to us, she thought. We sound drunk. We sound like crazy people. She clung to his neck and wrapped her legs around his hips, and her emotions careened on a ride that was some kind of mash-up between a spook house and a roller coaster.

Underneath Rune's amusement, he studied himself with sharp attention. The hook was still in his gut, still yanking him forward to a strange, undefined place. He was not sated. His body screamed that he was dying of starvation, that he had not had nearly enough, that he needed to take her again and again, until she had given everything she had to him, until he had spilled everything he had into her, until he had given her everything he was. Even though he was still hard, he fought a vicious battle for control and forced himself to pull out. He hissed as his cock came free of her body.

For a moment he balanced on the knife edge between a passionate affair and mating. He clenched his arms around her and shook with the conflicting forces inside of him. He felt like he had slammed into some kind of crisis and he was being torn apart inside. Then somehow he managed to yank himself back from that final place.

I cannot mate with you, Rune thought as he kissed her temple and cradled her delicious, addicting body against his. I like you so terribly much, so much more than I ever thought I would, and I am even growing to love you, but I cannot throw my life away on something that cannot last, that has nowhere to go.

She sighed and leaned her face against him, and he steeled his still racing heart.

I cannot, darling, because you would never need me as much as I would need you. Your desire is beyond lovely, but it isn't enough. I need to be needed. And I cannot become a supplicant to that kind of inequity and hope to survive.

. . .

Several minutes later, Rune let go of her to tuck himself back in his jeans and stand. Unself-conscious in her nudity, Carling curled like a cat on the floor and watched him. He prowled into a bedroom and returned with a complimentary hotel robe, which he handed to her. She sat, dragged it on and belted it.

Rune watched her with a moody expression but kept prowling restlessly around the room. She studied him thoughtfully. It was an interesting reaction to . . . well, to what she thought of as mind-blowing sex.

If she recalled right, and it had in fact been quite a long while, most men yawned, rolled over and went to sleep. Or they ran away. But what had just happened—both here on the floor and before, in the lobby—was beyond anything she had ever known. Since Rune was neither running away nor sleeping, she wasn't actually sure she had done things right. She knew at the most mundane of times she got a bit too fierce for most people, and nothing of what had just happened between her and Rune could be called mundane.

And then something had happened to him, something profound and disturbing. His laughter had died away, and a strange conflict had raged through him. He was a man of intense emotion anyway, and both the intensity and the emotion were increasing, along with the flare-ups of aggression. Sometimes he looked at her and felt torn, and for the first time in a long time she regretted that age had turned her into a succubus, because no woman wanted to know her lover felt such things when he looked at her.

Maybe she should ask him what was wrong. Maybe she should tell him to go away.

Maybe the wisest thing she could do was wait, to see if he would tell her what he was feeling in his own time.

She rubbed her forehead and turned away to hide any sign of what she was thinking. Insecurity was vulnerability, even more so than desire, and the moon was no longer complicit in hiding her secrets. Unkind daylight exposed everything it touched, and the shy mist outside was burning away in the sun's immolating light.

She looked around to take stock of her immediate life. "So much to do," she muttered. "So little time."

Didn't that have a wicked ring of truth to it.

Outside the living room was a filigreed wrought-iron terrace, the city's skyline clearly visible against a bright blue sky. The suite was elegantly decorated in muted gold and cream, offset with a blue couch. While the furniture was modern, the claw-foot design to the legs and the brocade cloth gave it a hint of old-world charm. A vase of fresh-cut flowers adorned a nearby dining table.

While pretty, the suite did not have the most durable of design themes. The angle of her mouth twisted as she remembered how she, her entourage and Tiago had trashed the Regent Hotel in Chicago. Perhaps the Fairmont would fare better.

She picked up the shreds of her caftan. There wasn't even enough intact material to tie together in a temporary covering like the last one. She sighed, tossed it aside, and went to the couch where Rune had tossed their bags.

Rune stopped pacing. Sensing his scrutiny that was as intense as a physical touch, she kept her face averted. She hadn't thought to stuff any clothes into her leather bag along with the journals, sketches and other items. She should have at least grabbed a change of clothes when she was at home, and now she had no personal servant to think of such matters. At least she'd had the forethought to tell them to send over some of her things. She pulled out Rune's duffle.

"I have nothing to wear until Rufio sends my clothes over," she said. "Literally nothing. We have things to do. We have phone calls to make, a medusa to consult, and I have a Djinn to summon, and God only knows what else we'll have to do after that or where we'll have to go."

She jerked open his duffle bag and started to rummage through the contents. She pulled out a Ziploc bag filled with several green packets. She peered through the plastic. Wrigley's chewing gum, spearmint flavored. She tossed the bag of gum onto the couch, reached into the duffle and dug out a book. Stephen King's *Christine*. She threw that on the couch as well. What did he have in this bag that made it weigh so much?

Suddenly the wide expanse of his bare chest was in front of

her. She tried not to notice or care, but with one thing and another, she hadn't had enough time to give that bare chest the kind of close, leisurely attention she really wanted to. She kept her head lowered as her gaze wandered over the broad expanse of his muscled pectorals. His suntanned skin was a warn inviting brown, his darker flat nipples surrounded with the crisp hair that sprinkled the rest of his chest and arrowed down that long, ripped torso to disappear into the top of his zipped but still unfastened jeans. She swallowed hard and closed her eyes. She knew how warm his body was, and she was beginning to crave it like she craved the vivid warmth of a fire.

Rune rubbed her shoulders. He said soothingly, "Don't worry, your horrible caftans will be here soon."

"I am not worried, I am grumpy," she announced. "Quit calling my caftans horrible."

"I call them as I see them, baby," he said. "Just as you did with the hairy man with spectacles."

"If I never saw that T-shirt again, it would be too soon," she told him.

"I see you understand exactly how I feel about those caftans."

She glared at him. Was that amusement in his face? She dug into the duffle and pulled out a Glock. Ah, there began to be some explanation for the duffle bag's weight. He must have half a dozen guns tossed in there, along with a couple of grenades, an assortment of cannonballs, and maybe a rocket launcher or two. She tossed the Glock onto the couch. She knew he had to have clothes stuffed somewhere in that duffle. She had to get to them sooner or later. She pulled out a pair of knives, rolled her eyes and tossed them after the Glock. "There's got to be something in here I can put on, at least temporarily."

"You can have anything you find in that bag that you take a fancy to," he told her. "Including the hairy bespectacled T-shirt. But I only brought a few changes of clothing with me, and those are pretty much shot."

"Figures," she said in disgust. She dropped the duffle bag.

Rune said, "I was going to call the concierge and order some new things for myself. Why don't you take a nice hot shower while I order some clothes for you that you might actually enjoy for a change?"

She raised her eyebrows. Standing under a hot cascade of

water and washing her tangled, sandy hair sounded like bliss, but she had the suspicion he was managing her for reasons of his own. He had some kind of agenda. Her mouth pursed. "Do you want me out of the room?"

He said immediately, "Only so that I can order the kind of clothes for you that I would like without it turning into an argument."

She regarded him warily. "You won't order anything hairy or bespectacled?"

He burst out laughing, cupped her cheeks and kissed her, savoring the feel of her lips moving in response to his. At first she had kissed him awkwardly, as if she was unfamiliar with using her mouth in a gesture of affection, but she was a quick study and now she leaned into him and kissed him back with such sultry sensuous promise, he nearly dragged her back down to the floor to take her again. He only just barely managed to pull back.

He said huskily, "I promise. Nothing hairy or bespectacled."

She had to admit, she was beginning to be intrigued by what he might buy for her. It would no doubt be horrible, like those clunky steel-toed boots he wore.

Surrender to the experience and change, *hmm*? She bit back a smile. Well, why the hell not? What difference did it make if she tried on new clothes? The thought of buying her clothes seemed to bring him a great deal of pleasure, and she found she enjoyed bringing him pleasure. Besides, who would care, if she died two weeks from now?

"All right," she said. "You may order me something, if you like. If I don't care for it, I can always wear my own clothes."

"Of course," he said. "What size do you wear?" He ran his hands down her sides to explore her narrow waist. "I'm guessing a size eight. Your shoe size?"

Then she did smile. "Six and a half, narrow. I don't need to hear how you got so accurate at guessing women's sizes. I can guess."

"None of them meant a thing to me, darling," he told her, his husky voice turning even deeper.

Hunger pulsed again, along with the urge to bite him. She managed to articulate, "I'm going to take that shower."

"Have fun," he told her. That dazed look on her face was so goddamn sexy. If they weren't facing such serious issues, he would have offered to join her. He had gobbled her down and now he wanted to savor. The thought of standing under the spray of hot water with her and soaping those luscious curves he had barely had a chance to enjoy, let alone taste, made his groin tighten until he was in actual pain. But she was right, they had so much to do and so little time in which to do it. He gritted his teeth, took a step back and let her go.

Then because he was being so damn good, he gave himself a good-boy cookie and watched her beautifully rounded ass sway gently as she walked away from him. She looked like heaven and moved like sin. She stopped to swipe up one of the knives she had dropped on the couch, and his eyebrows shot up. He wondered what that was about. What an incomprehensible, crazy-hot wicked witch. She was like reading a murder mystery novel, all cliff-hangers and smoking guns, only she was so much more fun.

The suite had two bedrooms. She disappeared into the nearest one, and he forced himself to get relevant.

His first phone call should go toward the issue that would take the longest to accomplish. He used switchboard services to connect to the Illinois Cook County morgue then went through a long series of voice prompts until he reached the Medical Examiner's Office of Paranormal Affairs. He had been prepared to leave a voicemail message, so he was pleasantly surprised when Seremela picked up and said, "Dr. Telemar speaking. Make it brief, or I'll get bored and hang up on you."

"Seremela," Rune said. "How are you doing?"

The medusa's voice warmed with surprised pleasure. "Rune! How nice to hear from you. I'm doing fine, thank you. Things have calmed down considerably around here. My office hasn't seen a single dead body since the last time we talked. How are you? How was your trip to Adriyel?"

He smiled. That was her polite way of saying things had calmed down ever since Tiago and Niniane had left Chicago. "I'm doing well, thanks. Adriyel was eventful, but at least the coronation took place, and the last I heard, Niniane and Tiago were fine. Listen, I'm afraid I've got to cut right to the chase. I'm involved in an issue in San Francisco that's turned urgent, and I was hoping you would be available for a consult."

"That sounds intriguing," Seremela said. "And you already know my workload here is less than hectic. What's the issue?"

"I can't tell you over the phone," he said. "The consult would have to be in person. But you would be compensated handsomely for your time, and of course for all your travel expenses." He would see to that personally. He waited a short time for her to process the request. Then he said, "I need you here quickly, Seremela. This is life or death."

The sound of his own words punched him in the face. Fuck, it really was life or death. Carling's life, Carling's death. He broke into a cold sweat.

Don't panic, son. Get things done.

The pleasure in Seremela's voice turned somber. "Of course," she said, so immediately he could have kissed her. "I'll be glad to help in any way I can. I'll book the first flight I can get."

He rubbed the back of his neck. "I'll charter something for you instead. It'll get you here more quickly."

"Guess I'd better hang up so I can go home and pack a bag," Seremela said. "I'll head straight for . . . O'Hare?"

"That'll do. Give me a cell phone number so I can get in touch with you in transit if I have to." She rattled off a series of digits, and he jotted them down. "Seremela. I'm going to owe you a big one. Thank you."

"Forget about it, you're welcome. Now get me that flight."

She hung up, and Rune dialed Tucker, the Wyr-badger in Chicago who was on retainer to handle such local needs on short notice. A taciturn, rather unfriendly individual, Tucker worked well in isolation outside of the Wyr demesne. Rune didn't bother to explain that he was acting outside of the Wyr demesne's interests. He wasn't sure Tucker would get the distinction, or care anyway.

The Wyr-badger listened as Rune explained what he needed. Then Tucker said, "What you're really saying is you want me to get snakes on a plane."

Rune coughed out a laugh. Tucker was so often surly, his odd, rare humor usually came as a surprise. "You are not at all PC, my friend."

"That's why I live all by myself."

"I need this as fast as possible."

"I'm on it." Tucker hung up.

Rune moved on to other things. He called the concierge desk to request a personal shopper. He got connected with pleasing alacrity to a woman named Gia. He was in the process of explaining to her exactly what he wanted her to acquire when the call-waiting on the phone beeped. He switched the line over.

Tucker said, "Flight is chartered. A plane will be waiting for Dr. Telemar when she reaches the airport. The good doctor will be with you by evening."

"Awesome." The clench in his gut eased a bit.

"Just so you know, the company we use is wicked booked right now. I had to get them to bump a couple of other contracts to get a plane. This is going to cost you."

"Cost is irrelevant," Rune said. He switched back to the shopper, finished his order and hung up.

What did Carling want with that knife?

He ran his hands through his hair, and a knock sounded on the door. He strode over to answer it. A slender young woman with a sleek blonde pageboy, wearing a hotel uniform, stood smiling in the hall. When she caught sight of him, her smile died and her eyes went very wide. She looked poleaxed. She said, "Oh. My. God."

"Sorry about that," Rune said. "I should have put on a shirt."

"Not on my account," breathed the young woman. Her gaze fell as if under the weight of gravity and remained riveted on the trim waistline of his jeans.

"What can I do for you?" Rune said, impatient.

"Whatever you want," she told him in a strangled whisper. Then her gaze flew up to his, as her cheeks turned a bright scarlet. "Ohmigod, I'm so sorry. Don't tell anyone I said that, okay? I could lose my job."

"I won't." He smiled at her, in spite of himself. "What I meant to ask is, why are you here?"

"The assistant manager, Mr. Rowling, sent me up to warn you and Councillor Severan that several members of the press have arrived. He's downstairs dealing with them now. He wanted you to know that if you would like some privacy when you need to leave the hotel, just call down and he'll arrange for you and the Councillor to have access to one of the service entrances."

"Thank him for us." He emphasized the "us" and watched her face fall. "We'll call ahead if we need to." Although he had no intention of needing to. It was one of the reasons why he had booked a suite with a balcony. He immediately had his own private entrance. Given the limited space, takeoffs and landings called for some finesse, but it was well within his ability.

"Yes, sir."

He closed the door and turned around to face the interior of the suite. Two bedrooms, two baths. He didn't need to wait for Carling to finish before he took his shower.

But he was still curious about why she took that knife.

He raised his voice and called, "How are you doing in there?"

"I'll be out in a few minutes," Carling called.

She had found the bedroom she had picked as elegantly decorated as the living room. There was another vase of fresh-cut flowers, the bed was made with French linens and another pair of French doors opened onto the wrought-iron balcony. The marble bathroom was large and as luxurious as the rest of the suite.

Carling stared at her reflection in the bathroom. She was halfway through cutting off her hair. She had luxuriated in the hot shower, soaping herself all over with the complimentary soaps and shampoo. Then she had toweled off, and considered the long wet tangled mess that hung down her back, and her without a brush. So she had reached for the knife.

She could only achieve a ragged cut without hair scissors, so she considered the teenage boy with the choppy hair style and tried to mimic that effect. She left just enough length so it could be restyled with more finesse at a later time. She finished quickly then fluffed the damp silky locks and considered the effect.

A stranger in the mirror looked back at her. The short ragged hair emphasized the stranger's high cheekbones, full lips and narrow jaw, and turned her long dark eyes huge. After wearing the heavy waist-long length for so long, her head and neck felt so weightless it was dizzying.

It would do for now. She suffered yet another pang when she

looked at the large pile of hair on the marble floor, but the sense of freedom was a much stronger lure. She smiled, shrugged on the hotel bathrobe and walked into the living room.

Rune stared at her, stunned. "Oh bloody hell, you didn't," he muttered. He rubbed the back of his neck. "You look magnificent, but all that gorgeous hair."

"It's a season of change," she said. And none of that hair was going to mean a blasted thing to her if she was dead, so she might as well enjoy the feeling of freedom while she could. "Who was at the door?"

"A hotel employee. The paparazzi have started to flock."

"Of course they have." She regarded him. "You haven't showered yet."

"I've been busy." Rune grabbed a leather kit out of the duffle bag and gave Carling a quick kiss on the cheek. "Bloody fucking gorgeous, but fucking hell. I'm going to miss that hair. I'll be five minutes. Wait to call the Djinn until I'm done, okay?"

Warmed in a way that had nothing to do with the physical, Carling touched his jaw in a brief caress. "All right."

When he had left, she picked up her shredded caftan and looked around the living room for a wastebasket. She found one tucked discreetly under a table. When she pulled it out to stuff the caftan in it, she found a wadded-up piece of cloth already in the bin. Curiously, she pulled the cloth out and shook it open.

It was Rune's T-shirt with the picture of the hairy man. What was his name again? Jerry Garcia. Rune had thrown his favorite shirt away when she wasn't looking. He had to have done it just now, when she had been in the bathroom.

How about that.

She let the caftan fall into the wastebasket and pressed her hand to her mouth. She closed her eyes and put her face in the shirt. It was saturated with his masculine scent. She took several deep breaths. The worn cotton material was soft against her cheeks. Then she gently folded the shirt and tucked it into the bottom of her leather bag.

Rune was as good as his word. When he rejoined her, she had opened the balcony doors and was looking over San Francisco's distinctive skyline.

He had forsaken the bloodstained jeans in favor of slipping

on the other pair, dirty though they were, although he had elected to remain shirtless and shoeless for the moment. The sprinkle of hair on his chest was several shades darker than his tanned skin and still damp. His wet hair lay sleek against his strong, well-formed skull, and just a whiff of his clean, masculine scent was enough to make the backs of her knees tremble.

She struggled between pride and desire. But really, how much would she miss her pride in a few weeks when she was dead?

Even with that thought, it was still remarkably hard to do what she wanted. She jerked forward and hit an unreasoning wall of fear. She had to shove her way through it to reach Rune's side. His arms were already going around her as she put her head on his shoulder and leaned against his chest.

That was what she wanted. Just that one thing, his arms around her while she rested her head on his chest, and reaching for it had been one of the hardest things she had ever done.

Rune put his cheek against the top of her head. The rough haircut had done startling things, like lend a hint of piquant charm to her face. The odd flash of fear in her eyes as she came toward him tore up his gut, somewhere deep inside where that fucking hook was embedded.

I'm so scared, she had said to him, back on the island. He could not imagine what it must be like to face the possibility of one's death. The thought of facing Carling's death . . . He couldn't process the thought. His mind whited out.

"Rune," she murmured.

He realized he had clamped around her with bone-bruising force, and he made himself ease up. He cleared his throat and said roughly, "Sorry."

"Are you all right?"

He didn't answer her directly, mostly because he didn't know if he was all right. "You need to call the Djinn. We need to get him looking for the knife."

"Yes, of course we do." She straightened and ran a hand through her short hair, making it spike all over.

She looked so rumpled and it was so unexpectedly adorable, Rune breathed between gritted teeth and pivoted sharply away. His hands shook. He felt like an addict looking to mainline his next fix. He was so busy fighting emotions that bucked like an untrained stallion that he missed the next thing that Carling whispered, although he felt her Power shoot out like an elegant, laser-focused spear.

A moment shivered. It held the trembling tension of a droplet of sweat about to fall from the Titan Atlas as he strained to hold up the world.

Then Rune sensed a maelstrom of energy streaming toward them from some undefined, faraway place. It tore through the open balcony doors and filled the suite with such a chaotic roar of Power, for a moment the walls of the massive hundred-and-ten-year-old hotel felt as thin, fragile and transparent as newspaper. Then the walls settled into place around them, and the Power coalesced into a defined point.

This was a very old, Powerful Djinn. This one was a prince among his people. Rune's lips peeled back from his teeth in an instinctive snarl. He took a wider stance and braced himself against the cyclone's presence.

The figure of a man formed in the room. Long raven-black hair whipped around an elegant, spare, pale inhuman face. Narrowed crystalline diamond eyes showed through the strands. The rest of his body solidified. He was easily as tall as Rune, with a lean graceful frame that matched his face. The male wore a simple black tunic and trousers, and a fierce regal pride. He gained form and substance.

The Djinn ignored Rune as if Rune didn't exist. All of his attention focused on Carling.

Rune loathed the slippery-assed son of a bitch on sight.

Because, see, the thing about the Djinn, the really irritating thing about the Djinn, is that they could dematerialize at will at any time, so you could almost never get a good solid physical blow landed on one. And even if you did manage to get in a good crack, they were spirits of air that assumed the form of physical bodies like wearing a suit of disposable clothes, so you could almost never really hurt them. To battle the Djinn, you had to engage them in a Power struggle.

Rune knew very well how to fight Djinn, but it just didn't have the same visceral satisfaction as planting a fist right in the kisser, the way he wanted to plant his knuckles in that handsome, too-perfect, regal, aloof face.

Carling turned to stare at Rune. Her expression was incredulous. She said, "Are you *growling* again?"

Rune glared at her. Her adorable goddamn hair was standing up all over the place, and she was wrapped in that goddamn hotel bathrobe like she might have just gotten out of bed after having sex. Somehow the modern setting—the hotel, the skyline, the fluffy robe—made her makeup-free face look naked. He snarled, "Why didn't you wait to call him until we had gotten some goddamn clothes?"

Her mouth dropped open. *"But you said—"*

Seeing Carling flummoxed was a rare sight. It made her look even more adorable. He might have enjoyed the sight, if he hadn't been possessed by a trumpeting, untrained stallion. He put his hands on his hips and roared, *"FORGET WHAT I SAID."*

The Djinn crossed his arms and raised a sleek black brow, looking so supercilious Rune started across the room toward him.

Suddenly Carling was there in front of him, impeding his path. She slapped her hands against his chest. He kept plowing forward, pushing against her strength, and her bare feet slid across the carpet. She said between her teeth, "I do not know why we are indulging in a fit of psychosis right now, but so help me, I will throw your crackbrained ass out the window if you don't *stop right there*."

The Djinn stared at them both. He smiled. He said, "I have seen this behavior in Wyr before."

Glaring at him over Carling's head, Rune spat words like they were bullets. "I want to know why you gave away three favors. And what Carling did for you."

"Do you?" said the Djinn in a languorous drawl as he opened his diamond eyes wide. "Or you'll do what?"

≈ FOURTEEN ≈

Rune hissed like a cat. He looked so feral and malevolent, Carling was jolted. She didn't understand what was going on with him, but the aggression had flared in him again so hot it seemed to drive him with as much ruthlessness as a slave master's whip. It finally sank in. He was really dangerous in that moment.

Even though his hands had changed, the fingers lengthening and tipped with killing claws, he gripped her shoulders with the same exquisite care as he always did. She was not at all concerned for herself. She knew she was quite safe with him, but she got a searing mental image of Rune and Khalil engaged in battle. If that happened, they would both sustain serious damage.

She cast around for ways to derail the situation. She didn't see many options. She leaned her forehead against Rune's chest and muttered to him in a low voice, "Rune, listen to me. This is not okay, and you're beginning to alarm me. Don't make me put a spell on you."

His chest moved. He had taken a deep breath. His arms came around her. *You can put any spell on me you want*, he whispered in her head.

Aaaaagh, the idiot. She nearly did throw him out the window at that. She didn't know how, in one moment, she could feel such a strong sense of connection with him, and then in the next feel like she was looking at some alien creature from one of those monster movies he said he loved. If there was ever a time he should not be flirting, it would be now.

What had he called himself? A stupid, crazy, illogical, senseless, rampantly jealous ass. Damn right, he was a stupid ass. . . .

Wait, that wasn't the relevant part she should remember.

Rampantly jealous. That was the relevant part.

If she had decided to stay in love with him, she might have felt a little pleased about that. She folded her lips tight and drop-kicked the ridiculous pleasure out of her head.

She said, "Khalil?"

"Yes, my dear Carling," purred the Djinn in a velvet voice that positively oozed sex and sin. "You know I'll do anything I can for you. Anywhere. Anytime."

Rune erupted into growling again.

She threw her arms around Rune's lean waist and locked on to him by gripping her wrists with both hands. He tried to pry her away, but short of hurting her, he couldn't break her hold. They engaged in a careful, wholly undignified struggle. Carling hissed in the Djinn's head, *Have you gone insane too?*

Wyr are so fun to tease when they get like this, said Khalil.

If you tease him any more, I will hurt you. She said aloud, "I'm done with this nonsense. Khalil, tell him what he wants to know or I will."

Khalil's bright, malicious smile faded into a scowl. Then something darker came into the Djinn's crystalline gaze, a raw haunt of memory. Khalil said, "Many years ago, my daughter Phaedra was kidnapped and tortured. Carling agreed to help me rescue her. It was not easy. Carling earned those three favors."

Rune stilled as the Djinn's words sank in, and Carling's tight-locked grip cautiously loosened. "Your daughter," he said. Children were rare in the Elder Races, and both prized and protected. The crazed, bucking stallion in Rune's head calmed enough to let in a sliver of rationality. "Did she survive?"

"She's alive." Now the Djinn's expression was like stone. It was clear he would not be speaking further on the subject.

Rune listened, both to what was said and what was not

said. It had been a difficult rescue, and if such a Powerful Djinn required help, it had also been a dangerous one. And even though the kidnapping had occurred many years ago, from Khalil's terse reply it was clear that his daughter had sustained lasting damage of some sort.

Carling patted Rune's back impatiently. She asked, "All right now?"

He rubbed the back of his neck and muttered, "Yeah."

She let him go and stepped back, and Khalil focused his attention on her. The Djinn asked, "Why have you summoned me?"

"I have a task for you to complete as quickly as you can," she told him. Khalil inclined his head. "We need for you to retrieve an object, if it exists."

If the Djinn thought a go-fetch task was a waste of a valuable favor, he didn't show it. "What do you wish for me to retrieve?"

"It's a Swiss Army knife," Rune said. "Specifically it's a Wenger New Ranger 70 Handyman knife, black handle, about this long." He demonstrated by holding his forefingers at the appropriate distance apart. "We need to find out if it is buried under the entrance stones of Djoser's funeral temple in Saqqara."

Khalil's strange diamond eyes dropped to Rune's hands. He said slowly, "That funerary complex has stood for thousands of years."

Carling's smile twisted. "I did not say the task would be easy or would make sense to you. And the knife may not be there. We need to know if it is, and we need to know as quickly as possible. The answer is important, Khalil. Do not make a mistake."

The Djinn's regal aloof expression had given way to open speculation. He said to Carling, "This will complete the second of the three favors I have owed you for so many years."

"Yes," she said.

Khalil inclined his head, all mockery gone. Rune thought he caught a hint of relief in the Djinn's face before Khalil became the cyclone and disappeared.

Carling looked at Rune, and her mouth pursed. Tap, tap went her foot.

No doubt he should apologize. He knew he wasn't acting rationally, or normally. His struggle to contain his mating urges was taking its toll, not only on him but on everyone around him. That fine line he was trying not to cross was beginning to cut him, but he could not leave her. Not yet. Even if she had all the help she needed, he wouldn't be able to leave. He needed however much time they could have together before their separate lives pulled them apart. And he could not confess to his struggle either. He would not place the burden of that on her, not while she had so much else to cope with. He was not Rhoswen, some self-involved unbalanced child.

He cast about for something sane to say. He came up empty. So he said instead, "That went well, don't you think?"

She stared then smacked him in the chest, hard, with the back of her hand.

Now that the other male was gone, Rune was able to relax enough to indulge his catlike sense of play. He said, his voice rough and throaty, "I like your penchant for violence."

A slightly crazed expression came into her eyes. She hit him again, harder.

He knew he deserved it. But it was so much fun, he couldn't make himself stop. Goddamn, he loved it. He might as well admit it: he loved her. He gave her a sleepy, innocent smile. "What'd I do?"

She pivoted away and appeared to be searching for something. She looked at all the doors. Then she came to some kind of decision, marched to the bathroom and slammed the door behind her. He could hear the distinct snick of the lock being turned.

Rune angled his jaw out and rubbed his eyes. Yeah, that went well.

Carling flipped down the toilet seat lid and sat down. She leaned over to put her elbows on her knees, her face in her hands. She didn't try to think. She didn't want to think. There was too much to think about, too much to feel, and the cacophony in her head was making her demented. She just wanted a little damn privacy.

Breathe in. Breathe out. Slow and even.

Breathing for her might be good for nothing else, but it was a good meditation exercise. It could help one achieve a Zen-like calm. Which Carling needed very much, instead of rampaging around her head and seething about what a *jackass* somebody was, and what the hell was the matter with Rhoswen, anyway? You would think she was a consumptive eighteen-year-old diva again, treading the boards again in that deplorable, shabby Shakespearean acting company during the California Gold Rush, instead of being a hundred-seventy-year-old woman. . . .

How had she gone so wrong with Rhoswen? What had she done, or not done? What could she have done differently? Had she become so reliant on sensing emotions from living creatures that she never bothered to try to see what lay behind Rhoswen's smooth facade? She dug the heels of her hands into her eyes.

Stop. Breathe in.

Rhoswen was not a problem Carling had to fix right now. Later—if Carling had a later—she would decide if something needed to be done about the younger Vampyre. Indulging in pettiness and vengeful behavior because her feelings were hurt did not necessarily mean Rhoswen had gone off some kind of deep end. But if it came to it and Rhoswen had, as Rhoswen's maker, it was Carling's responsibility to put her down.

And by the way, here was the great big pile of hair Carling had left on the bathroom floor. She nudged the silken pile with a bare toe. Normally she would never walk away for so long from such an abundance of personal matter available that anyone might steal and use to cast a spell on her. Her usual meticulous care was slipping, and that was yet one more vulnerability. She could ill afford acquiring any more of those. . . .

Breathe out, damn it.

"Oh, fuck Zen," she muttered. "I'll get enlightened when I die."

She shoved off the toilet, wrapped the huge pile of hair into a towel, unlocked the bathroom door and strode out.

In the meantime, Rufio personally hand delivered two large Gucci suitcases to the suite. Rune took the luggage from the other man without inviting him in. He kicked the door shut, put the suitcases in the bedroom Carling had chosen and moved on to his next task. While Carling took some alone time, he sat on the couch, dug out his iPod and set it on the coffee table nearby for easy access. Then he turned on his iPhone to go through his messages.

Email? Uh-uh. He didn't even try to go there. He was just checking his voicemail messages. There were sixty-three. Fifty-four of those messages were from females. He hit delete without listening to those. Eight of the messages were from the other sentinels. They went like this:

Bayne: "So, how's it going out there working on Team Whack-Job? She got you doing crazy shit yet?"

Crazy shit. Rune snorted. *The likes of which you could never have seen coming.*

Graydon: "Where are those files you wanted me to look at? I can never figure out the new system on the shared drive, and you promised you'd show me. Call me back when you can."

No, son. You can figure it out on your own. I have faith in you.

Constantine: "Dude, it's Friday night, and all the chicks are starting to pile up flowers and teddy bears and candles and shit in front of your door. They're talking all hushed and tragic, like you might have died, or something. So I'm gonna take a few of them out, you know, just to console them. That set of twins. Thought you'd like to know."

Rune knew the twins Con was talking about. *Take 'em, horn dog.*

Graydon: "Just calling back to tell you never mind. I gave up and went to IT, and they showed me how to get the files. Hope you're having a good weekend."

And there it is. You figured it out. I knew you could.

Aryal: "You suck."

Apparently Aryal had just discovered the pile of work he had left on her desk. His grin turned evil. *Yeah, I know I do.*

Grym: "FYI, I closed the investigation on the incident in Prague. It was an accident, pure and simple, not industrial sabotage. No need to call me back. Just thought you'd like to know."

Good job, buddy.

Aryal: "You SUCK ASS."

Rune's grin turned into a chuckle.

Bayne: "Duuuuuude. You're listening to these messages

and avoiding us, aren't you? Because with Tiago quitting and now you out of commission, you gotta know how much this hurts."

Quit your bitching. You'll live.

The final voicemail message was from Dragos. It was, as Dragos's messages tended to be, simple and to the point, and devoid of any pleasantries. The dragon growled, "Call me as soon as you can."

Rune's smile died away and he sighed. Dragos rarely bothered to pick up the phone, let alone leave a message. It almost never meant anything good. He checked the time stamp on the message, which read Saturday 11:03 A.M. Whatever the issue was, it'd had the chance to ferment for a few days already. At least Dragos hadn't left a second message, so Rune could hope they hadn't yet reached Defcon One.

He shook his head and pinched his nose. He just realized he hadn't heard the news in three days. He located the TV remote and turned the channel with the mute on to CNN. No scenes of a cataclysm sprang immediately to view.

He was just debating whether or not he should return Dragos's phone call or possibly wait for a less pressured time when Carling stepped out of the bedroom. She hadn't yet opened her suitcases. She was still wearing the hotel bathrobe and carrying a towel. He watched her walk out onto the balcony. She snapped out the towel and her hair fell. A bright flash filled the air as it caught fire. His hand, still holding the iPhone, lowered to his side. Within an instant, the blaze crumbled to gray dust that blew away on the wind.

Vampyre hair. Huh.

He asked, "Are you speaking to me yet?"

She gave him a grim look. "I haven't decided."

Fair enough. Women needed time for these kinds of things. Someone knocked on the suite door again. He answered it.

A stylish brunette woman stood in the hall, along with a pair of bellhops and two clothes racks on wheels. The woman had several packages at her feet. When she caught sight of Rune, her artfully made-up eyes widened, and she smiled.

For the first time in his very long life, Rune was tired of all the relentless female attention. He bit it back and said courteously, "Let me guess. Gia, right?"

"That's right."

"You work fast." He stood back, holding the door wide.

"You did say it was urgent," Gia said. Her smile widened into a grin. "And prorating the tip according to how fast I got things here turned it into a real emergency." The brunette stepped across the threshold, gesturing to the bellhops to follow. "Luckily it's a Monday. I got most of what you wanted, but I'll have to go pick up a few items, like the jewelry, in person. I hope that's all right."

"Of course it is." Rune pivoted backward on one heel, considering the space in the suite. He noted how Carling's tight expression had faded into a feminine curiosity, but he thought it best not to smile. He told the shopper, "You'd better put everything in one of the bedrooms." Since he had already set Carling's luggage in one bedroom, he pointed to the second one.

"Certainly." Gia gave Carling a friendly nod as she headed in that direction, bellhops and clothes racks in tow. Rune strolled along behind and stood in the doorway, watching as Gia directed the bellhops to put the racks on opposite sides of the room. Carling joined him, her arms folded. She wore an expression he wasn't sure he could read. It looked like a combination of lingering anger, curiosity and perhaps the beginning of amusement.

Carling murmured, "This seems excessive. I was expecting one or two outfits."

He gave her a sidelong smile. "I wanted you to have plenty of choices to try out."

The shopper said, "It's very simple: men's clothing is on the rack to the right, women's on the left. When you've had a chance to go through everything, if there's anything you need returned, just give me a call. In the meantime, I'll go out and pick up the jewelry and other things."

"Jewelry is not necessary," Carling said.

Gia's smooth stride hitched. Rune said to the shopper, "Pay no attention to anything this woman says. You are shopping for me, not her. She has no fashion sense or any normal feminine instincts. Jewelry is always necessary."

Gia gave him a wide-eyed smile over her shoulder.

"Excuse me?" Carling said ominously.

He wasn't altogether sure, but he thought her real anger

might have dissipated. There was a glint lurking in the back of her eyes. How could he have ever thought she had no sense of humor? She was brimming with a kind of guerilla warfare humor that slid along the shadows of a conversation and took aim at the unwary. It delighted him so much he had to swoop in to kiss her sour, puckered mouth. "Don't sulk," he told her. "It doesn't become someone of your age."

She rolled her eyes even as, he was delighted to note, she kissed him back. "Oh, the age thing? You just had to go there, didn't you?"

"Just teasing, darling," Rune said. "I've seen you at those inter-demesne functions. You wear classic black Chanel with frightening aplomb. When you're not wearing those catastrophic muumuus."

"Catastrophic *muumuus*?" She began to tap her bare foot again. God, he loved that slender arched, imperious foot. It was so pretty, so tempestuous. He looked at her bare toenails.

"I forgot something," Rune murmured to Gia. "Pick up half a dozen shades of nail polish when you go out, will you?"

Gia gave him a sidelong, conspiratorial smile. "I took the liberty of ordering a few bottles in different shades when I placed your Guerlain order."

"Perfect," he said. "Did you get some Christian Louboutin boots?"

"Did I get some boots," Gia said. She held up a Saks package that she placed on the bed.

"Outstanding," said Rune.

"Let me take a wild guess," Carling said. "You brought boots, jeans and a T-shirt."

Gia gave her a wide-eyed look. "Well . . . yes, that's one of the outfits I brought."

Carling strode into the room. "Fine," said Carling. "I said I would try something new, and I will. Hand it all over."

Rune watched in fascination as suddenly Gia and the bellhops revolved around Carling. She redefined every social space she walked into. Goddamn, he thought, I don't love you a little. I might actually love you a lot.

Gia searched through the rack of women's clothes, pulled out a pair of jeans and handed them to Carling along with the Saks package containing the boots. "7 For All Mankind skinny jeans, ankle-cut to show off the boots," Gia explained. "And here's an asymmetrical silk crepe de chine flared tank top by Behnaz Sarafpour that I thought would go really well with the outfit."

"Outstanding," Carling said crisply. She muttered in Rune's head, *Whatever the hell any of that meant. You know I'm only doing this to humor you, don't you?* He covered his mouth to muffle a laugh as she continued aloud, "Lingerie?"

Gia handed her an assortment of silken underwear. Carling swept out of the room with her arms full. She gave Rune a look from under lowered brows as she passed. Then she disappeared into the bedroom she had claimed. A moment later he heard the bathroom door close.

Rune stood aside as Gia and the bellhops came out of the bedroom, and he signed the invoice the shopper gave him, then dug his wallet out of the duffle to tip all of them. Gia tore off his copy of the invoice and scribbled on it. "I'll go out now to pick up the rest of the things," the shopper said. "Here's my cell number. Call me any time, if you need anything." He took the paper she offered. Gia held on to it for a moment, and met his eyes. "Anything at all."

"Got it," said Rune, with a dry smile. "But I am quite sure after you run your errands, you will have gotten us everything we need."

"Yeah, I figured," said Gia. "But you can't blame a girl for trying."

Carling could blame a girl for trying. She was paying attention, and of course she could hear the conversation in the living room perfectly from the bathroom. She might have been tempted to go out and kick a girl's ass for hitting on a man who was, to all appearances, with another woman, except she had already shrugged out of the bathrobe, and she was tired of being other people's karma. That girl didn't need Carling's involvement. She would crash someday on a rocky shore of her own making, because that's what people did, Carling included.

Carling had something much better to do. She looked at the pile of things she had brought in with her and prepared to be entertained.

First, the lingerie.

Oh. Oh my.

Black silk, French-cut knickers that slid over her thighs as light as a lover's whisper. A matching silk camisole that framed her breasts and emphasized her narrow waist.

Carling swallowed, staring at the beautiful feminine body in the mirror. The lingerie gave her a sexy look in an entirely classy way. She turned away from the sight and picked up the jeans. Here's where she could start to chuckle.

But as she slid her legs into the jeans, the denim felt butter-soft and pliable. As she secured the fastening at her waist, they molded to her like a custom-made leather sheath molding to a hand-forged Spanish steel blade. She twisted, squatted, and lifted each leg sideways, and the butter-soft jeans moved with her easily, like a second skin.

Damn. She might actually love these jeans.

She turned to the black T-shirt with an entirely new respect. She slipped it on, and it flowed over her body, loose yet feminine, with a simple flared shape, a lacy scooped neck, and cut-out shoulder straps.

By the time Carling opened the box containing the boots, she had turned quite thoughtful. And the boots did not disappoint. They were Italian-made, calf-length black suede with wraparound straps and buckles at ankles and the arches. The heels were nearly four inches in height, and the soles were fire-engine red.

She stood straight and stared down her legs at the boots. She felt very tall, with every curve on her body exposed. She looked in the mirror. A flirtatious, fashionable, feminine, young-looking, big-eyed stranger looked back.

The woman in the mirror looked . . . Fun?

That couldn't be right. Carling had never been fun in her life.

She shook her head. "I don't know who the hell you are," she told the woman in the mirror. "But you look mighty cute."

Rune called out, "What did you say?"

"I'm not sure about this," she said as she walked out of the bathroom. "It's been very amusing, but—"

Rune was already in the bedroom, clad in black.

Carling jerked to a stop so abruptly she nearly fell off her boots.

He was standing in profile by the bed, in the process of buttoning up what looked to be a hand-stitched shirt that molded to his powerful, lean muscled torso. Clothes hangers and tags littered the top of the nearby dresser. The black highlighted his bronzed skin, and the rich coppery and gold highlights in his hair. The chic cut to the linen trousers emphasized his long, graceful legs. A matching suit jacket hung off the bedroom doorknob. No matter how deplorably he dressed, nothing could disguise the fact that he was already elegantly made and handsome, but these clothes lent him an air of sophisticated severity that came so far out of left field she felt sucker punched all over again.

Her mouth worked. It might be time to say something again. Was it her turn in the conversation? She couldn't remember.

"Uh," she said.

"What's wrong, darling? Are the boots not comfortable?" Rune asked. He turned toward her, frowning, and his eyes widened. "Well, I knew it had to be good," he murmured. "The reality is so much better than I imagined."

"You, um," she said.

"I, what?" He bent to pick up something at his feet. It was another shopping bag.

"You didn't dress the way you usually do."

"I wanted to look nice for you." He walked toward her, his big swordsman's body flowing like a panther's.

He had thrown away his T-shirt and dressed up for her. Her voice came out all husky and wrong, as she accused, "You said you were going to buy yourself new jeans."

"I did that too," Rune said. He stopped in front of her and let his gaze travel down the length of her body. A quiet smile touched the corners of his well-cut mouth.

Before she knew it, she heard herself ask, "What do you think?"

"I love it," he said. "But the important question is, what do *you* think? Do the boots fit? Is the outfit comfortable?"

"It is, actually." She scratched her fingers through her strange, short hair. "I'm just surprised. This isn't what I was expecting."

His gaze searched hers. "Do you like it?"

She looked down at herself as well. "I do. I'm not sure it's me though."

"It can be you if you want it to be," said the tempter from the Garden of Eden. "Sometimes, you know, as a mood thing." He held up a finger. "Wait, don't make up your mind yet. We're not done."

She pursed her lips. "What do you mean, we're not done?"

His eyes smiled into hers. "Humor me for a while longer. Please? It won't hurt. It's just for fun. And this time it's not even wicked or bad," said the voice of original sin. "And you might even like it as well."

Fun. There was that word again, that incomprehensible, three-letter word. His eyes were so warm and inviting, as warm as his body, and more compelling than any fire. It was so easy to indulge him when he coaxed, she found herself smiling back. "Whatever. Just, fine."

"Thank you, Carling," he murmured. He kissed her lightly and took her by the hand, and she found herself going back into the bathroom with him. He coaxed her into sitting on the counter. Then he dumped the contents of the shopping bag onto the counter beside her. She looked down at a pile of Guerlain cosmetics and burst out laughing.

Rune opened up a palette of eye color and held it up to her face, considering. He nodded and set it aside.

"You've got to be joking," she said.

Next he opened a blusher compact, held it up to her face, and considered again. He squinted an eye, shrugged then set the blusher aside.

"Rune," Carling said, staring at him. She had no words to describe the incredulity she felt.

"What?" He gave her that sleepy, dangerous smile. "You said you'd humor me," he said. "So humor me."

Carling said, "But I have phone calls to make."

"Seremela is on her way, the Djinn is working on his task, and any phone calls that need to be made can wait fifteen minutes." As she struggled to find some argument, Rune raised an eyebrow. "Am I right?"

She heaved a put-upon sigh, because really, sometimes there was just no other way to communicate something.

"I know," he soothed as he opened a packet containing a

sable brush. "High-heeled boots, jeans and now this. It's all so very hard to take."

"You have no idea," she muttered.

"Hush. Now close your eyes."

Then, because humoring him for fifteen minutes would be much faster than arguing with him, she did just that. After all, it wasn't as if she had never worn makeup before. She had worn makeup countless times. During the Roman Empire, she'd had a *cosmetae* just for the purpose of putting on her cosmetics. She had worn her face and hair powdered in the Rococo style, in mid-eighteenth-century France. She had grown to find the canvass of her own face so utterly boring she had walked away from all of it long ago.

But for Rune to take such a ludicrous notion into his head, to do this here, now. It turned something that had become old, cynical and eventually tedious into something utterly strange, erotic and somehow touching.

She gripped the edge of the counter with both hands in the effort to hold still as he made love to her face. He stroked brushes over her sensitive skin. He prompted her to tilt her head with a featherlight touch of fingers and barely audible murmur. She felt the heat of his body burn against the outside of her knee as he leaned his hip against her leg. She smelled the scent of his arousal as she listened to the sound of his unhurried breathing and the light shift of cloth against skin when he moved.

It was clear that he had no agenda of seducing her into sex, and none of it felt like objectification. He merely enjoyed her, and it was such a new experience it threw her back to that first new experience, that terrifying time when she was made up with kohl, green malachite and red ochre so that she could seduce a god. How strange, that something that happened so long ago could still have the power to fill her eyes with tears.

Or maybe that was just Rune, reawakening her soul.

And she let him.

"Purse your lips," Rune murmured.

She did, and he kissed her mouth with soft lipstick. She opened her eyes the merest sliver to look at his quiet, intent face. The light from over the bathroom mirror shone in his eyes and filled them with light. He put a forefinger under her chin to hold her in place as he studied her.

"Okay," he said. "I'm done."

She opened her eyes. They stared at each other. His gaze dilated, fixed totally on her. He wiped the edge of her lower lip with the corner of his thumb, and breathed, " 'She walks in beauty, like the night Of cloudless climes and starry skies, And all that's best of dark and bright Meets in her aspect and her eyes.' Darling, you have always been gorgeous but now you are now officially the shit."

One corner of her mouth trembled, and lifted. "You really think so?"

"I know so," he said, and his voice was lower, rougher than it had been before. He pulled her off the counter and turned her to face the mirror, and once again, she stared at herself. She ignored her own features to concentrate on the deft delicacy with which he had enlarged her eyes, emphasized the high cheekbones, and brightened her full mouth. He had not put a single brush stroke wrong. She looked bright and beautiful, and she glowed like a cherished woman.

Cherished.

She leaned back against his chest. He put his arms around her. Their eyes met again in the mirror, that elegant dangerous Rune and the strange new woman, and the impact of the connection was as raw as when Paris and Helen first looked into each others' eyes and brought a world of gods and men to war.

Or maybe that was just the cyclone that roared into the bathroom to coalesce into the tall figure of a haughty prince.

Carling and Rune both turned as one to look at Khalil.

The Djinn held out his hand. On the broad white palm lay a black, half-crushed length. Time had corroded it so badly it was barely recognizable as a knife.

⇒ FIFTEEN ⇐

Rune stood like stone, his body clenched.

Carling reached out slowly to pick up the knife and closed her fist around it. She looked up at Khalil's strange diamond-like gaze. The Djinn was watching her, head cocked, his expression filled with curiosity.

However, he did not ask for an explanation. Instead, he said, "This completes the second of the three favors I have owed you."

"Yes, of course," she said. "Thank you, Khalil."

He inclined his head. Something else flickered across his spare features, and in a rare gesture, he touched her fingers. Then he disappeared in a whirlwind of Power.

Carling turned to Rune. He was staring at her fist, the skin around his mouth white. A vein in his temple throbbed visibly.

She could not remember her original past, but in this past they had created together, she remembered the first time she had laid eyes on him as a mature Vampyre. She almost didn't recognize him, it had been so long since he had killed the priest and changed her life. But then there was something about the way he moved, and the way he smiled that wild white smile of his that drove females crazy with desire.

She had watched it all with a cold, expressionless face and an aged heart that had grown so cynical it no longer believed in anything except that things always change. And then on the island, she had demanded he kneel, and he had kissed her and she was dying, and *he still had not remembered her*, and so she struck at him with all the rage and pain she had inside—

Her past may have changed and yet it was all deeper and truer than it had been before. She could even see how she must have lived her life before he had ever come into it, like shadows of reality, another Carling, much like the sketch of the island outline as it lay over the Bay's horizon. It was so strange, how all the pieces fit seamlessly together.

Now she realized there was a problem with choosing not to stay in love with him. How could she hope to recover from such feelings or set them aside, when he was standing right in front of her, embodying everything that had slipped past her barriers and caused her to fall in love with him in the first place?

He was everything she could have wished for in a life partner and far more than she had ever hoped to find, with his compassion and caring, his intellect that was so well seasoned in nuance and strategy, his ruthlessness tempered with reason, mischievous wit and a warrior's strength that was so indomitable, she could lean on him when she felt weak and he could match her when they went head-to-head.

As she had told him, she was not good at surrender. Something inside of her was too fierce to bend easily or often, too well entrenched in the habit of rule. But she found she had to bow to her own feelings on this and surrender to the experience of loving him, because it was simply impossible to do anything else.

She reached up and stroked his temple. He was clearly suffering for some reason, and it hurt her to see it. She said gently, "We knew this was possible."

"Yes." He took her hand, pressed her fingers against his mouth and closed his eyes. He wasn't sure what hit him the hardest.

He had actually changed history. He thought of the priest he had killed and he realized that wasn't what shook him so badly. Every time he had to kill, he changed the course of the future. He had accepted that responsibility a very long time ago.

No, what really shook him to his foundation was the thought of how many times Carling had slipped into the fade either alone or with only Rhoswen, or other Vampyres and humans to guard her. The doorway to her past had stood wide open many times for any dark creature or spirit of Power with the capacity to slip through. She had once mentioned that she had enemies. Any person with her Power and at her level of position would.

What if something had already slipped through and was stalking her in the past? Her episodes seemed to be some kind of conduit for him. When they stopped, the passageway closed and he came back to the present. What if something else found a way to stay back in the past?

The tiger-cub Carling would make such a delectable morsel for some dark vengeful thing to devour.

What if she simply disappeared?

Could the universe flex in such a way to accept Carling's death, and absorb all that that might change? Might he turn around one day to discover that she had vanished like she had never existed? If that happened, no one would know she was gone—no one except perhaps him, since he still remembered how cruelly Carling had been whipped in the first timeline.

Or maybe, if she died and the past was changed to that profound extent, he would not remember her either. He might become oblivious Rune, living out his life in New York. He would never see her walking naked out of the glimmering river, the droplets of water sparkling like diamonds on her nude body. He would never give her that first sizzling kiss, or hear her rusty, surprised laugh, or take her on the floor with such savage need she would scream into his mouth and claw at him as she took him too.

Gods have mercy.

"We've got to stop these episodes from happening," she said, so clearly her thoughts had run along a similar vein to all the possible consequences of what they had done.

"Yes," he said hoarsely. "But before we do, Carling, I've got to go back again one more time."

"Why?"

He opened his eyes to find her looking at him as if he were a madman. He didn't blame her. He felt like a madman. "If I can get through to your past, something else might be able to get through too. The younger Carling doesn't know to protect herself. She has to be warned."

A prickling chill ran down her spine. Her mind raced as she tried to find fault with his logic, but she couldn't.

What a dangerous game we are playing, you and I, she thought as she stared at his tense face. We are meddling in the past and with each other, and I think I barely have an understanding of all the things we may have set in motion.

She set her jaw. "All right," she said. "You go back, one more time to see if you can warn me. If I'm too young to understand, you'll have to go back again until I'm not. But you can't change anything else, do you hear me? If you see something happening that makes you uncomfortable, *walk away*."

"I might change you again just by talking to you," he said.

You've already changed me in the most profound way possible, she thought, and the change has nothing to do with traveling in time.

"I accept that risk," she said. "And I take responsibility for it."

"You may not remember that." A muscle ticked in his jaw. "You may not remember any of this."

Her expression held steady. In his imagination, he could see her wearing that same expression as she sent thousands of men to die in battle. "If it comes to it," she said, "then we will have to accept that too."

Rune tossed back a hotel-sized bottle of Glenlivet and moodily spun his iPhone in circles on the coffee table as he watched CNN on mute in the suite living room. Closed captioning ran underneath scenes of Egypt's famous pyramids, telling the tale of a sudden earthquake that cracked the foundation of Djoser's temple at the one true gate to the funeral complex. Accompanying scenes showed the gaping hole that ran into the earth. The dust still hung over the site, and the surrounding ancient structure was reduced to rubble. Rune thought of all the warning tales of Djinn offering favors, and the horror short story "The Monkey's Paw" by W. W. Jacobs. Be careful what you wish for, because the consequences can be a freak-out bitch. Fuck, yeah.

The knife sat on the coffee table in front of him, beside the cell phone. He picked it up and played with it, trying to pry

open the various blades. The straight blade snapped off, but
he got the pliers out partially.

He told himself he wasn't surprised. He had been telling
himself that since the Djinn dropped the knife off, and it was
even true in a way. Then he looked at the scenes on CNN and
the knife in his hands, and he felt his own kind of internal
earthquake again.

He unscrewed another hotel bottle of liquor, a pretty blue
bottle of SKYY vodka this time, and drank it down. He listened absently as Carling made the phone calls she needed to
make from the bedroom. First she called Duncan to tell him a
truncated version of recent events. She refrained from men-
tioning any of the more dangerous details and just simply said
that she and Rune were following up on research leads on a
possible cure. She also told Duncan she had let Rhoswen go,
and while Rhoswen could still have access to the account Carling had set up for her, she was no longer authorized to act on
Carling's behalf.

Then Carling called Julian.

That was the phone call Rune had been waiting to overhear. He stopped playing with the knife as he pictured Julian
Regillus on the other end of the phone line. Julian had been
turned at the height of the Roman Empire. Serving under the
Emperor Hadrian, he had been a distinguished general in a
military culture that had once been described as quite like the
Marines "but much nastier." The Vampyre's Power had a
sharp potency that was characteristic of all aged Vampyres.
There was nothing pretty or soft about him. His scarred six-
foot-tall frame was packed with the heavy muscles of a man
who had spent his life at war. He had short black hair with a
sprinkle of salt at the temples and a face that carried forceful-
ness like a bullet, coupled with the kind of sharp intelligence
needed to pull the trigger.

Rune thought of the times he had seen Carling and Julian
together. Their relationship had been a matter of idle speculation over the years. Rune thought they had probably been lovers once, perhaps as long ago as when Carling had turned
Julian, but that was a guess based purely on the intimacy that
was often created between Vampyre and progeny, not based
on any evidence he had seen. Whether or not they had been

lovers, any embers from that pairing had died out long ago. Now Carling and Julian treated each other with the cool courtesy of business associates.

Rune force-fed that thought to the insane creature that tried to take over his head again, and this time he managed to keep the creature contained. He was glad he didn't have to face Julian at that moment, because if the other male had actually been present, Rune didn't think he could have.

"Julian," Carling said. A pause. Her voice turned icily meticulous. "I am well aware of what we had agreed, but things have changed. The Wyr sentinel Rune and I are pursuing a line of research that is proving to be fruitful—"

Rune gripped the ends of the knife in both hands at the silence that followed.

When Carling next spoke, the iciness in her voice had turned into a whip. "You are my child," she said to the King of the Nightkind. "My creation. I am not yours. I am not coming to you for permission to do anything. You may support me in this last endeavor or you may choose to believe I am chasing desperate dreams to my death. I don't give a fuck either way. What you may not do is interfere with me or try to dictate my actions."

He could hear the quiet click in the other room as Carling gently placed the phone receiver back in its cradle.

Rune lived in a brawl of an atmosphere where profanity was casual, used often and ignored for the most part. Hearing profanity come from Carling, who almost never swore, was somehow shocking, and it lent an odd, raw kind of intimacy to the conversation.

The knife snapped in his hands. He looked down at the pieces. He had bent it so much the time-stressed riveted joints had broken.

It wasn't enough violence for him. He wanted to do damage to something else. Preferably to something with an aquiline Roman profile that said ouch.

He looked out the open French doors as he waited for Carling to step out of the bedroom. She didn't. It was turning to early evening. Icarus had once again caught fire and was falling to the western horizon. Outside, much of the mist from earlier had burned away. What was left behind was a heavy haze that blanketed both land and sea, and turned the peaks of the Golden

Gate Bridge into unearthly spires. Rune knew of an indigenous people who believed that when it was foggy, the veil between worlds became thin, and the spirits of ancestors and other things walked more freely on this land. Maybe they were right. Maybe he was one of those spirits, walking between the worlds.

He really needed to call Dragos now.

But then Carling's Power rippled over the scene.

Instead of daylight, this time the passageway opened to a dark velvet sketch of night that overlaid the bright sunlit suite like a nightmare. He caught the heavy, humid scent of the river and the acrid hint of burning incense.

He stood and stared at the open bedroom door, his hands knotted in fists. Then he grabbed his sheathed knives. He walked to the bedroom. He studied every step he took, every nuance of the experience. He reached the bent place in the crossover passage, the turnaround that led to a different page. It rested on a singular point that was so precise it felt smaller than the tip of a pin. It would be so easy to lose track of that one tiny place, that single moment, in the infinite cascade of all the other moments in time. He tried hard to memorize the turnaround place, just in case he needed it in order to get back.

That is, if he could figure out how to use it. To his frustration, the turnaround place melted away from him, just as every moment in the present did when it slipped into the past.

He went much more cautiously than he had the first two times.

Because what happened in Vegas didn't always stay in Vegas, baby.

Here Carling was, at another cusp.

Each time she reached one of these places, she lost her life. The first time was her childhood life by the river. It always happened by the river.

The second time, she lost her life as a slave, and she went down on her knees every day to offer incense and say prayers of thanks to the strange golden god who claimed he was no god. But he had a sigil for a name, and with a murderous blow and a kiss to her forehead, he had killed the slave Khepri and remade her into Carling, the treasured goddaughter of one of the most powerful priests in the two lands.

Because of Rune's edict, she had enjoyed much more time to herself than almost any other woman she knew, and her father-priest Akil was as good as his word and educated her as well as any man. At twenty-two summers, she had studied *maat*, the order of the universe, and the three types of sentient beings that were made up of the gods, the living, and the dead. She had been privileged to study *heka* as well, or "the ability to make things happen by indirect means," and because she had access to temple libraries, she learned many of the spells that were formally known only by the priests.

Many of those priests were pompous, politically dangerous windbags. She watched them utter spells and perform religious rites, and they seemed like ridiculous buffoons. Sometimes they yelled the spells at the top of their lungs, as if shouting and waving their arms would draw the gods' attention.

She could have told them: no matter how loudly or theatrically they prayed, the spells did not work if they did not have *kneph*, the sacred breath that breathed life into things and gave them form. Only when one had this Power could one awaken the true movement that lived in the spells and hope to call on the gods.

Carling had always had *kneph*, although she had not always known what to call it. When she cast a spell, it worked, although as a woman, it was heretical for her to claim as much, so she kept her studies on a scholarly note and the knowledge of her abilities private. And even though she was treated as a favored goddaughter, she was not a female of noble birth, so she could not become a Servant of God.

She never wanted to be a Servant, anyway, because the female priestesses sang an infernal amount but seemed to do precious little else of note. Carling had no intention of spending her life warbling like a songbird in a cage.

So out of boredom as much as anything else, she had agreed when Akil came to her with a politically brilliant match. It was past time for her to leave the restrictions of this city that was so devoted to the dead, and commence with living her own life. On the morrow, she would go to a minor desert king who had asked for her hand in marriage. Then she would see what she could make of the man.

It was a sensible thing to do, and the offer exceedingly

advantageous for a woman who had once been a slave. She should be thrilled. The king was much older than she, but his breath was not too horrible and he was utterly smitten with her. He had other wives, of course, and many slaves as concubines, but he had not taken any of them as his queen. Yet.

And here she was, like Osiris, dying and being reborn again. She was wrapped in a robe against the chill of the river mist that crept over Ineb Hedj's famous white walls. The night was as rich and wild as wine singing in her blood, and she should be happy and excited. Instead she was drowning in restlessness and confusion. She was about to start on her new life and learn new things. She, who had never been with a man, would be with a man tomorrow night.

A man who was much older, his breath not too horrible.

Her own breath choked in her throat. She wanted . . . she wanted something. She did not know what she wanted, but she wanted it badly. The world was so strange and big, and ferociously beautiful. She wanted . . . she wanted her soul to fly out of her chest again from sheer wonder, as it had when she had been a child.

So she cast her first real spell in secret in the courtyard under the crescent moon's pale smile while her elderly father-priest and the rest of the household slept. She created the words for the spell and crafted them with care, and she burned incense, and gave offerings of milk and honey to Atum, and Bat, and especially to Amunet, the "female hidden one." And then she whispered those crafted words with her breath of Power, and felt them curl into the night along with the smell of expensive frankincense.

> *I give thanks to the gods*
> *Both seen and unseen*
> *Who move through all the worlds.*
> *I give thanks for their eternal wisdom*
> *And the sacred gift of my heart's desire . . .*

For surely the gods would know better than she what to make of this hot, beautiful grief, the gods who had, after all, created her with such a fierce, lonesome soul.

What a wretchedness she had created. Bah. Her fool eyes

were dripping. She sniffed, hugging herself, and wiped at her face with the back of one hand.

Then a wind blew through the reeds and grasses, and it brought with it a scent of fiery Power. Something walked toward her. It moved quietly, but its presence spread absolute silence in the incense-perfumed night. A crocodile hissed from the nearby riverbank, and then there was a splash as it sped away.

Carling reached for the copper knife she had laid at her feet. It was not wise to move unguarded through the night, and she never traveled even to the household courtyard without a weapon. Calm but wary, she backed toward the door.

By the crescent moon's thin, delicate light, a god in black appeared. A god, who claimed he was not a god, great and golden-haired and so intensely formed, his *ka* or life force boiled the air around him.

Carling dropped the knife, staring.

The night was not made for his vivid colors. He was best seen in the hot bright light of day. Copper, yellow, gold, bronze, and the fierce warmth of his ageless lion's eyes.

Yes, that was it. That was exactly how she remembered it. Her soul, winging out of her body, and flying eagerly toward him.

"Rune," she whispered. Her own Atum, who rose from the water to wing his way to the stars and complete the world.

The first time she had seen him, he had been smiling and playful. The second time he had been in a killing fury. This time she saw him made a Powerful three, which was its own completion. Three times, a *heka* number. His unearthly face held a troubled severity, and then it lightened into something altogether different as he saw her, something strange that had to do with the way men looked at women. Whatever that strange thing was, it had her heart racing and her hands shaking and her thighs feeling heavy and full.

"Khepri," he said. His voice was deeper, wilder than she remembered. Or maybe she heard him better now that she was older.

Smiling, she walked toward him, this man who held her soul. "I chose another name when my slave life ended," she said. "I am Carling now. I should have known you would come."

He smiled back at her as she reached him. "Why is that?"

"You always come when I die," she said.

. . .

Shock smashed a fist in Rune's gut.
You always come when I die.

Before he knew it, he had dropped his own knives and
grabbed her by the shoulders. Her head fell back and she
stared at him, and he castigated himself furiously, *Careful,
asshole*. She's a fragile human now. He made himself cup her
slender arms carefully, feeling her pliable warm flesh under
his fingers, and he studied her face.

She had undeniably grown into a woman, but she was too
young to be the Carling that had taken the serpent's kiss, he
guessed by as much as seven or eight years. Her face was more
rounded, less carved, but she still had the same gorgeous long
dark eyes, the fabulous cheekbones, that outrageous mouth.
She looked at him with all the open bloom of wonder in her
face, and her scent held a fragrance unlike any other.

Spiky, beautiful girl. The most beautiful girl in the world.

"What do you mean, I always come when you die?" Rune
whispered. His heart had yet to recover from that one. She had
not shaved her head, as so many early Egyptians had. Her
long dark hair fell to her narrow waist in dozens of small
meticulous braids. He touched one of the braids at her temple
and traced it as it fell away from her face.

"You came the first time, when my life by the river ended,"
Carling told him. Inside, she was stricken. He was touching
her, his hand to her shoulder, his hand to her hair. She had no
idea something could be so utterly lovely as a simple touch.
She had to work to get the rest of the words out. "Then you
came again and ended my life as a slave. Tonight is my last
night in this life in Ineb Hedj. Tomorrow I go to another life,
away from here."

Rune stroked her petal-soft cheek with a light finger. "Is
that a good thing?"

"I think so. I hope so. It is the first time I have had a choice
about it." Carling widened her eyes, tilted her head and lifted
one shoulder in a shrug.

The gesture was so very like the serious, innocent child
Khepri, without warning he tumbled head over heels in love
with her again. He saw the child she had been, this young,

proud beauty, and the amazing woman she would become, and he loved all of them, all of the Carlings past, present and future. He saw her sharpness, her frailties and her strength, and his soul embraced all of it. The feeling was a sword thrust as deep as anything he had ever felt, piercing through his body. It seemed like he had been falling for a very long while, and each time he realized it, he had fallen a little deeper, a little further. He had never known that falling in love could be as helpless and complete as this.

Then just as suddenly, he fell into a panic and he started to shake. It was not simple or quiet trembling, but a violent storm that took him over and rattled his bones. He was really back in time. Really. Back in time. This was not his Carling, not yet. He was not supposed to be here. Another, younger Rune was living his oblivious life in another part of this world.

He couldn't stay. He couldn't protect her, this heart-stoppingly beautiful, fragile, brave human girl. And just by being here, he might have changed history again. He might be changing her even now, so that she made some other kind of choice than she originally did, some kind of new and different choice that got her killed.

Carling—*his* wise and wicked Carling—might have been able to accept the consequences of that, but he never could.

He grabbed her by the shoulders again and hauled her against him, and growled into her gorgeous, unbearably naive, incredulous face, "You *listen to me*. I am not supposed to be here. It is incredibly dangerous for me to even be talking to you."

Carling's expression flared. She gripped his wrists. "Why do you say that?"

"I am not from this time or this place. I am from somewhere else." He could see she did not understand. How could she possibly understand? He struggled to find words that would have meaning for her and still convey the urgency of his message. He said with slow emphasis, "I am from many human lifetimes away, from so far in your future of tomorrows that the pharaoh no longer exists. Where I come from, all the gods have changed, and everything you see around us is either rubble or has completely disappeared."

The wonder in her face was replaced by white shock. "It's all gone?"

"Gone." He got a grim sense of satisfaction from the sharp, sober attention she now gave him. He grabbed her head, his shaking hands cupping the graceful arc of her skull as his thumbs braced under her delicate, stubborn chin, holding her so tightly she could not deny him or turn away. He spoke from the back of his throat, words that were so raw they came from the place where the sword had thrust through him. They fell from his mouth, hissing through the air like dripping acid. "Doorways have been opening in time. I have been falling through them and traveling to your place. In the future, you and I are searching for a way to close them, because they are very dangerous. Other things, dark spirits or creatures that mean you harm, might come through those doorways. That's why we decided I had to come back to warn you. You must take care and learn to guard yourself. There are times, like this night, when you are not safe."

She trembled all over, that beautiful young tigerish woman, and her breath shook out of her, and he felt like such a rotten, stupid bastard to put the burden of all of this on her young shoulders. But then wonder came into her face. "You and I are working together in this future place?"

He tried to think of what would be the best thing to say, but he couldn't because he was in a blind panic, the likes of which he had never before experienced. He said, "Yes. You hold my life in your hands just as surely as I am holding yours now in mine. There is a way for you to live to reach that distant future. You must find it. Do not turn away, or give up, or let anyone take that away from you. *You must live*. Do you understand me? You must live or I will die."

Her mouth shook as she whispered, "You would be there waiting for me?"

He was doing everything wrong. He was only supposed to warn her to be careful. He should have kept his damn mouth shut. But he couldn't stop himself. He whispered, "I will not remember you at first. You will live through your life and meet a younger me, one who has not yet come back to this place to meet you. Then I will see you at twilight, by a river in a place called Adriyel, and I will start my journey toward you."

She studied his face, her forehead crinkled. "But you will remember me some time?"

This is crazy, he thought. It makes no sense. The time slippage is so far out of sync it is working in loops, like a serpent's coils. She and I are drawing each other into existence. If we don't find our way out of this, we may not survive.

He had no cunning for this, no grand plan or intelligent rationale, no established ethical protocol for time travel like out of a sci-fi movie. This was just raw, unvarnished truth, and deadly uncharted territory for how it might carve through history.

And because he had gone much too far to stop now, he gave her everything he had.

He put his lips to her forehead and said against her skin, "I will remember you, very soon after the Adriyel River. And when I do, you will come to mean everything to me. Who I am at this moment, this man who is standing in front of you—I would wait forever for you. *But you must live to get there or none of this will happen.*"

She reached to touch the place where his lips met her skin, murmuring, "It always happens by the river."

He closed his eyes and pressed his lips to those gentle, questing fingers. "What does?"

"The beginning of a new life." She pulled back to look at him, and the expression in hers was grave. "If there is a way for me to live to get there, I will find it."

"There is," he said, pushing all of his conviction into the two words. "You found it once. You got there already. But now I have come back and touched your life again, and every time I do that something else changes, and I am afraid—" His throat closed and for a moment he could not continue. "I am so goddamn afraid that by coming tonight I might have changed something else you do or decide, and you won't be there in my life when I go back. And I have to go back, because I don't belong here."

Her trembling stopped. She stood steady and straight under his hands, her Power a slim, newly minted, adamant flame. She repeated, "If there is a way for me to live to get there, I will find it."

He took a deep breath as he searched her gaze, and the tiger looked back at him, unafraid. Another realization jolted through him, and even as he spoke he knew that the words he said were true.

"This is not all on you. Everything that has happened to me, I have remembered," said the gryphon. "I have held my place and my identity as time and space have flowed around me. The past has shifted twice for us already, and I remember all of it. If you fail somehow—if you die—I swear I will look for a way to walk through time again to find you. No matter where you are. No matter when. I swear it."

He should have known. The joy that filled her face had a keen ferocity that would propel her forward through the centuries. Gods, what passion this mortal had. It filled the chalice of her heart to overflowing.

He thought of his Carling, sitting unprotected in the hotel suite. Time was flowing for her as well. "I have to leave," he said abruptly. "You must take shelter. Go inside. Do not sleep. Do everything you can to protect yourself. This night, for you, is a dangerous one."

She looked around in sharp, quick assessment and gave him a firm nod. "I will take care. It will be all right."

This young woman wasn't his Carling. If Rune and this young woman had the luxury of unlimited time together, realistically he wasn't even sure if they could find anything much to talk about for any length of time. But he still could not resist cupping her soft cheek. "I will treasure the memory of meeting you like this," he said, and he kissed her.

Carling stood frozen and focused everything she had on the touch of his mouth on hers, so fierce yet tender, and filled with the blaze of his Power. It was the first time anyone had ever touched her like that. She knew she would never allow that elderly petty king to touch her on the lips. Then Rune let her go and scooped his weapons off the ground, and she watched as he turned on his heel away from her and faded from sight.

He just faded away, like a dream. Or perhaps a spell-induced vision.

She fingered her lips. They still tingled even though he was gone.

You must live or I will die, he had said. And that could not happen, not to the one who held her soul.

I will treasure the memory of meeting you too, she thought. And wait forever for you.

* * *

Carling opened her eyes and gazed out the open French doors in the hotel bedroom at the rich heavy gold of the westering sun. Morning might be bright and beautiful, but it did not hold the same poignancy as the evening, that had gathered all the day's memories and carried them into night.

She sat on the bed with her legs curled up, her back braced against the headboard. Rune stood at the open doors, facing outside. He leaned a broad shoulder against the frame, his arms crossed. His quiet, strong profile had an uncertain vulnerability she had never seen in him before. He looked proud, self-contained and braced for bad news, a god in black who claimed he was not a god, great and golden-haired and so intensely formed, his life force boiled the air around him.

He was indeed best seen in the hot bright light of day, where he shone with all the colors of creation's fire. Copper, yellow, gold, bronze, and the warm fierce amber of those playful, ageless lion's eyes.

Yes, that was exactly how she remembered it, both so long ago and again just recently on the island. Her soul, winging out of her body, and flying irrevocably toward him.

Some instinct told her he knew very well she had come out of the fade. Why wouldn't he turn to look at her?

She stared out the window again, and thought. The silence of ages lay heavily between them.

I will remember you, very soon after the Adriyel River. And when I do, you will come to mean everything to me. Who I am at this moment, this man who is standing in front of you—I would wait forever for you.

While she was not familiar with the details, she knew that when Wyr mated, they did so only once. Dragos, Lord of the Wyr, had just found his mate. Tiago, Wyr warlord and thunderbird, had mated with the Dark Fae Queen Niniane. Was that what Rune had meant? Was she that lucky—and he that damned?

She straightened her spine and took a breath, and began to speak. "You did not change me this time."

His head jerked sharply to the side, as if she had struck him, but other than that he did not move and he still would not look at her.

"I cast a spell one night and had a vision of you. That was my experience of it, anyway," she said. "I remember you warning me to take care. After that I studied defensive spells, and I put up wards when I slept. I was very careful."

"Why are you telling me this?" Rune asked coldly.

She looked down at the fun, flirtatious outfit she wore and gently smoothed the soft material of her top. She kept her voice calm as she told him, "I'm working through what happened, and what might have been different. I remember agreeing that you needed to go back to warn me and I remember taking responsibility for that. I think we got lucky. I think we changed what we needed to change, and everything else stayed stable."

Everything she told him was the truth. She would not lie to him. His truthsense would be highly developed, and in case, he deserved better than that. But even as her words told him a kind of truth, her soul whispered a deeper, more heartfelt one.

After the first few nights, when the blaze of excitement had died down, doubt had crept in. She couldn't believe he had meant what she thought he had said. She had to have misheard him, or misunderstood. The years passed and gradually turned to centuries, and as she received no other message or sign, she settled into a more mature and balanced "wait and see" attitude. She would not put the entirety of her life on hold for a single spell-induced vision, no matter how vivid or compelling it might have been.

But she had never forgotten how his kiss had burned. She had never let her petty king of a husband kiss her on the mouth, ever, nor had she allowed that liberty to any of her other lovers. Not that she had taken all that many of them, considering the years of her existence. She had stopped after a few hopeful attempts, because they either fell asleep after sex or they ran away, and it was all so relentlessly banal she would rather have walked unshielded into the sun than have to endure one more meaningless, insipid love affair.

Now as she looked at his stiff half-averted form, she told him silently, I fell in love with you earlier today in the hotel lobby. And everything you once said has come to pass. But so much time has gone by. Too much time. So many tomorrows, and tomorrows, and tomorrows, that the pharaohs really do no longer exist, and all the gods have changed and everything I once knew has turned to rubble or has completely disappeared. We have come together too late.

You must live or I will die.

Now I am the one who is dying, and you cannot mate with me and hope to live. What a Gordian knot we have tied ourselves into.

And as Alexander the Great had known, the only solution to untangling an unsolvable knot is to slice through it.

She looked down at the bedspread.

"So let's review," she said. Her voice was under perfect control. "Because of your help, in just a few days I have learned a tremendous amount about my condition, in fact more than I have learned in the last two centuries. And now that Dr. Telemar will soon be here to consult, I am hopeful I will learn even more. I owe you a big debt of gratitude."

He had turned to look at her. She could sense it, that tall powerful black-clad figure standing just barely at the edge of her sight. Underneath the cover of one hand, she curled the other into a tight fist.

"But we both know we can't risk any more of these strange collisions in time," Carling continued. "They are too dangerous for either one of us, and God only knows what we might have changed in the rest of the world." And she knew she could not trust her younger self around him, not for a single moment. If that younger Carling saw him again, she would never be able to contain her joy and she would not know of any reason why she should. "Rune, it's time for you to back out of this now. You've helped me enough. You've certainly done far more than anybody could have expected. I want you to go back to your life now."

The beast that had taken over Rune studied his prey with a critical eye.

Her facade could not have been better. She had no pulse for him to gauge, and she would not show him the look in her eyes. Her beautiful body was arranged just so against the pillows on the bed, like a posed still life, all artifice and composition. She was cool, controlled, rational perfection. She appeared to be a completely different creature than the fierce, eager young tiger he had left just moments ago, and why wouldn't she be a different creature, when that moment was, for her, thousands of years ago?

But her facade was too perfect, and that was her fatal flaw. She should have been reacting more to what had happened between them this afternoon, all that magnificent crazed passion, their laughter and the moments of real intimacy. The memory of what had happened in the fade should have unfolded naturally, as it had the first couple of times. Instead that was the first thing she offered him, only to coolly negate it.

Fury swept a firestorm through him. He sprang across the room, knocked her flat and slammed down on top of her. Shock bolted across her expression as he gripped her lovely throat with long, claw-tipped fingers.

The beast hissed in her face, *"You're such a fucking liar."*

⇒ SIXTEEN ⇐

Carling stared at the monster crouching over her. His face blurred from the tears that had filled her eyes that she refused to shed. His feral gaze tracked every telltale flicker on her face. He knelt over her prone body, his knees on either side of her hips. His bones were all wrong, in his face, across his wide chest, in the sinewy muscular arms. He looked more lion than eagle in this half shift. She could feel his claws against her jugular as he pinned her by the throat. He had driven the claws of his other hand deep into the mattress beside her head.

The monster's powerful body vibrated with violent tension, but while he held her in an unbreakable grip, the heel of his hand pressing down on her collarbone, he hadn't caused her so much as a paper cut.

When Tiago had been like this, he had gutted himself for his mate.

She had done this to Rune. They had done it to each other.

She stroked his strange, beautiful half-lion face, and he snapped at her. His strong white fangs closed around her hand. He could have crushed every bone in her hand in his powerful jaws, but he held her so gently, those sharp fangs would not have cracked an eggshell.

"You know very well I'm not lying to you," she said to him.

She had no idea how she kept her voice calm. "We have been on a weird, wonderful journey together. And I am privileged that you chose to stay and experience it with me, but you must leave, Rune."

Do not presume to tell me what I can and cannot do, the gryphon whispered in her head. *I have not given you the right to send me away.*

I have not given you the right to stay, Carling said, very softly.

An infuriated growl ripped out of him. With a snap of his head, he gave her hand a quick hard shake in reprimand. *Tough shit. I'm not your servant that you can dismiss when things don't suit you. I'm your lover, Carling.*

"And I'm still dying," she said. "I promise you that I will fight and look for a cure until the very last moment I can, but the fact remains, I still might die."

His gaze was fiercely determined. *I get to share this part of the journey with you too. I get to fight for your life too. I get to tell you what I think about it, and how I feel. And if it ever comes to that, I get to hold you at the end and share every last precious moment with you.*

To hold on to him and never let go, no matter what. The thought was so beautiful and terrible, and it caused such a huge swell of feeling in her, she closed her eyes. Two tears slipped away. Once the dam in her emotions cracked, there was no stopping the leaks. Cry me a river.

It always happened, by the river.

She felt the rigid tension in his body soften. His jaws loosened and he let go of her hand, and the pressure at her throat eased. He stroked her temples, wiping the tears away gently with the backs of his fingers.

She twisted at the hips, slipped a knee between them, and rolled to heave him off her. He landed with a crash on the floor against the closet door. She leaped off the bed and strode for the living room. "We fucked," she said between her teeth. "That's all. It was a lot of fun and a nice diversion, but you need to get over it and move on."

Sure he should, just like she had moved on so easily every time she had encountered him. All she had gotten was one kiss, one promise from him back in the distant mist of her youth, and she had never let anyone kiss her again. Not for thousands of years, past all logic or reason. Even when she had moved on in every other aspect of her life, she had held on to that one thing, because he had once looked into her eyes and said to her, *I am waiting for you with everything I am.* Now, no matter how she wanted to, she should not let him stay.

A freight train hit her in the back. It sent her into the wall in front of her with such force she cried out. Before she could react in any other way, Rune had yanked her hands over her head, holding her by the wrists as he kicked her feet apart. He pinned her body against the wall with the hard length of his own, his feet braced between hers, and just like that he had her caged, using only leverage, and his superior speed and strength. His pulse beat pounded against her senses like a sledgehammer, and the blaze of his heat surrounded her.

Shocked arousal roared through her. It pooled between her legs in a liquid gush. She looked up at his hands shackling her wrists and fought as hard as she could to get free. No matter how she struggled, she couldn't budge him.

As long as her mouth wasn't covered, she was not helpless. She could whisper a spell that would at least freeze him temporarily, if she didn't choose something more offensive that might cause actual injury.

And he knew it. He remembered how angry she had been when he had pinned her down, and so he caged her but he left her a way out. The realization that he took such care with her, even in his frenzy, even after she had been so violent with him, pounded in her head. She opened her hands wide to push at the air, as she strained to find the strength of will to whisper the spell that would stop him for those few critical moments while she slipped away. The words were gone, her mind a blank. The sirocco had taken them away.

He was breathing heavily. The thick heavy length of his erection pressed against her ass. As she struggled, he emitted a harsh groan and shoved his hips against her, and another wave of intense arousal sideswiped her. Normally so cool, she felt feverish and started to shake.

He put his lips to her neck and nuzzled the sensitive skin at the nape of her neck, and the strength left her knees. If he hadn't been holding her in place, she would have fallen.

"Here's the thing," he whispered. "I love you. I didn't want to. I fought it. I put up barriers, and they all came crashing down one by one. It wasn't just one thing. It was everything you did, both here in the present and back in the past. It's everything you were, and everything you are. So I just fucking love you, and you are going to have to fucking deal with it. You got that?"

She started to shake her head. She realized she was breathing hard too, great gasps of air as if she had been running hard for a long time.

Rune sank his teeth into the back of her neck, pinning her even further so that a raw incoherent sound spilled out of her. Her mouth tingled again. She bared her teeth. She needed to bite him back and get drunk on his rich, ruby liqueur, but her goddamn fangs wouldn't descend.

He said in her head, *And here's the other thing. I know you love me too. You had a good hand but you played it all wrong, so you might as well admit it.*

"I don't have to admit anything to you," she said.

"Yes, you do," he growled. She had given him all the clues and taught him all her tells, he just had to use them, because she really never did go gently anywhere, and if he had to claw and tear his way into her life, why then, so be it. She needed both his dominance and his tenderness; he knew it, like he knew his own soul. It was just another way in which they fit. "If you don't owe me anything else, you owe me the real goddamn truth."

She cried out again as he yanked her wrists together and held them locked in one hand. She twisted her wrists, trying to break his hold, but his long fingers were like iron. Hunger was not the ache she remembered. Or maybe she had never felt this before, this searing, driving force. She didn't recognize her own voice. She didn't recognize anything about herself. He put his hands on her, and she turned into a crazy person.

With his freed hand, he stroked down her body. He massaged her breast and pinched her nipple hard enough to sting. Then he cupped her crotch in a strong grip, where the need in her spiked the worst, and he yanked her back against him as he pushed his hips harder against her ass. He kissed the graceful bone just behind her ear and whispered, "What we did was more than just fucking. Say it."

A sob came out of her, all the more shocking because she had no control over it. "Yes."

He found the fastening of her jeans and undid them. His voice was as rough as his hand was gentle. "You love me. *Say it.*"

She leaned her hot cheek against the wall. "Yes."

He held still, crushing her back against him, his face pressed into her neck. Then he let her go. She almost slid to the floor but then she managed to lock her knees into place. Leaning against the wall for support, she turned to look at Rune in confusion.

He leaned his forearms on the wall, on either side of her head, his hard, intent face angled down to her. "I know what you're doing," he said. "You're still preparing to die."

She put her hands on his chest. Half-angry, half-despairing, she said, "You can't mate with me and hope to live. I'm trying to save your life!"

The irony of the moment was not lost on him. She was trying to drive him away to save his life, just as he had tried to save Tiago from mating with Niniane. Tiago had said to him, *One of these days, you're going to find your mate. And maybe she'll be Wyr but maybe she won't. Then you will understand just what you almost did to me.*

I get it now, T-bird. I understand.

An eternity of life didn't matter, if he lost her and it became an eternity of desolation. He would trade all of that time away for one day with his mate.

His gaze burned. "I don't want you to save my life. I want you to give me yours."

"Rune—"

He interrupted her. "Do you remember what I told you? For you that happened so long ago I'll say it again. If you fail somehow—if you die—I will search for a way to walk through time to find you. No matter where you are. No matter when. I swear it." He had tried so hard already, but as her last episode faded he lost the connection and the past melted away again.

She closed her eyes. Those words he spoke. She remembered every one. She had held on to them for so long, they had grafted to her bones, until they had spun on an enchanted spindle into a fairy tale of devotion that happened rarely to other people in other lives. To hear him say them again after so long . . . She shuddered. "You can't promise that."

"Shut up," he said. "I can promise any goddamn thing I want." His voice was quiet, even. He watched her put a shaking hand to her forehead, but he was not tempted to relent in the slightest. His long, lean muscled torso moved as he took a deep breath. He fingered the short, untidy hair at her temple and stroked her devastated face. His expression was clear, determined. He looked as steady as a rock, and just as moveable. He said softly, "I will never leave you. I will never let you go. I will not let you fall, or fail. I will always come for you if you leave, always find you if you're lost. Always."

She looked more vulnerable than he had ever seen her as her beautiful mouth shaped the word in silence. *Always?*

It was as if she were too afraid to say the word aloud. Everything inside of him wanted to pounce on her, to cover her vulnerability with his strength, to take her until she screamed with pleasure again. His instincts strained against his self-control.

But she was also a predator. If he did not engage those instincts in her too, no matter how he tried to hold on, eventually he would lose her. And he could not let that happen. He would not.

He whispered back, "Always. But you have to want it too. You have to own up to it and admit you want me."

Own up to it. Like she had taken ownership of her own life. Own it, take it, claim it.

He backed away from her until he reached the bed. His hands went to the buttons of his shirt as he toed off his shoes. His gaze held hers as he stripped off his shirt and tossed it into a corner, and that was when he began to lie. "You have to take me," he said, "or I really will give up and go find someone else."

"You wouldn't," she breathed. Her gaze was riveted to the bare expanse of his broad, tanned chest. The unsteadiness left her as her body went tense. Her beautiful lips parted. She did not look hungry. She looked starving.

It was the most beautiful sight he'd ever seen. He wanted to growl in triumph. It was *his*, that expression was for him. But it wasn't enough. He hadn't pushed her hard enough.

Come on, baby. Get cranky.

"I would," the gryphon lied to his witch. His hands went to the fastening of his trousers. Then they came open. He wore nothing underneath. He pushed them down over his lean hips, the long heavy muscles of his thighs flexing as he kicked them off. "There would be nothing to stop me." He cocked his head. "Maybe after all these years, I've discovered I have a type. Maybe I'll find another dark-haired, beautiful woman. One who doesn't argue about wearing pretty fashionable clothes or wearing makeup."

Carling hissed, and her eyes flashed that pretty, scary red.

He put his hands on his hips and stood there nude, that insouciant alpha male, and he dared to taunt her while the sight of his body drove all the reason out of her head. Her hands fisted as she stared at him. He was built for both speed and power, wide in the shoulders and long, without an ounce of extra flesh anywhere. Washboard abs rippled down to his large erection. His large, tight testicles had drawn up underneath his penis. He was beautifully formed everywhere, with a hard warrior's body that was poetry in motion.

Rune gave her his sleepiest, most disingenuous smile. "Maybe I'll find someone who bites."

A scorching image flashed in her mind, of him caressing an unknown woman who took his vein. She bared her teeth and launched at him.

He fell back on the bed as he caught her, and then she was on top of him, hands planted on the bed on either side of his head as she straddled him. His hard, wild face was flushed with arousal, and lit with a bladelike smile. Carling snarled, "Do you think I don't know you're playing me?"

"My give-a-shit button's broken, baby," Rune said. He cupped the back of her head and coaxed her down toward him. "Kiss me," he whispered. "Take me. Don't let me go—or I'll go." Then he said telepathically the same words he had said to her, so very long ago. *But this man who is in front of you—I am waiting for you with everything I am.*

She looked at him with such feral bewilderment he might have laughed if the stakes weren't so high. "You have legions of women, and I don't share."

"There'll be no one else, ever again. I'm all yours," he murmured. "Body and soul."

The Vampyre sorceress, who had been Queen, hissed in his face, "Swear it."

"I swear it," he whispered, stroking her hair. In this one thing they mirrored each other, for he needed her dominance and tenderness too. He opened his eyes wide again to take all of her in because he didn't want to miss a single moment of this gorgeous, deadly woman.

"I tried to be good. I tried to set you free." But she was a bad woman, of course. It was something she came to terms with centuries ago. His Power roared against her senses, even as he lay stretched out underneath her. She was so slick from wanting him, she felt drenched.

"Why would I want you to be good? I want you to be you."

"If I take you, I will never let you go." Her gaze grew heavy-lidded as she came down to his lips. "Never."

"I will always hold on to you," he said against her mouth. "Always."

He slid his hands under her silken flowing T-shirt, and his clever fingers found their way under the camisole underneath. He eased the material up, and she held her arms up so he could pull it over her head. Then she was naked to the waist, and he almost groaned aloud as her gorgeous full breasts swung free. He fingered the dusky aureoles, watching as the nipples stiffened with pleasure. She caught her breath, and his cock pulsed at the telltale, ragged sound.

Then she lifted off of him. The beast who had been lying in wait for her to take him lunged to the surface to snatch at her, but she was only shrugging out of her jeans. Her hands were shaking so that she could hardly manage it. He sat to help her yank her boots off, and then her jeans were gone as well. Her curved body was unbelievably gorgeous, bearing the twin scars of the whip and flowing with the sinuous grace of a cat, and it was *Carling's* naked body, *Carling's* most private places that were revealed, *Carling* who looked at him with the feral red gaze that was yet still delicate with need, and the luscious, plump, frilly flesh between her strong slender legs was so beautiful, it sent him into a meltdown.

He came down on top of her. She was already wrapping her legs and arms around him as his mouth drove onto hers. His hands were shaking, everything was shaking, and the sound that came out of him was harsh and guttural and completely inhuman. She felt between their bodies and grasped his cock, her palm massaging the broad thick head, and he felt huge and full and in so much goddamn pain, it was like he had never taken her. "Oh fuck, I wanted to take my time with you," he gritted between clenched teeth.

"We don't have time," she whispered. Her head fell back as she guided him to her slick entrance, and as he felt her soft moist cushion of flesh embrace the tip of his cock, he lost the last shred of control he had and came inside of her.

It was torturous, beyond pleasure. He felt huge and burning up, and she was such a tight, wet fit. Need drove him deeper into her. He shoved one arm underneath her waist to clench her lower body more closely to him. He cupped her head with his other hand while simultaneously bracing himself on the elbow, an instinctively protective position. He couldn't get far enough, deep enough inside, and he pushed harder until he was slamming into her.

She raised her hips for every thrust, hands fisted in his hair, and he was so completely sure she was with him the entire way that when she made a miserable, shaking sound, very suspiciously like a whimper, icy shock ran over his skin.

He froze, his heart pounding, and searched her face. "What is it? What's wrong?"

Her face contorted with frustration. Her eyes watered. She looked like she was in actual pain. "I want to bite you. I need to bite, but my damn fangs won't descend."

The image of her sinking slender fangs into his neck as he took her ran through him like a live wire, and he almost came right then and there. He slipped his hand under her slim neck and lifted her head. He said huskily, "Bite me anyway."

"I'll bruise you with these dull teeth," she whispered.

"Promise?" he growled. He was on fire everywhere. In his body. In his soul. He was blind with it.

She keened, lunged up and bit the strong cord in his neck that ran down into his shoulders. At the same time, she clamped down on his cock with her inner muscles, and his climax exploded out of him with such force he groaned with it. He ground his pelvis into hers, spurting hard, and she made a muffled sound, her whole body shuddering as he sent her over the edge. He could feel the rhythmic pulsing in her body, and holy hell, it was more than he ever imagined it could be, but it wasn't enough—it could never be enough—

He rocked with her and clenched her to him with everything he had, and when the pulsing of her body eased, he started to move again. She let go of his neck and fell back to look at him with eyes gone wide in surprise.

"Rune?"

He hissed, "Don't stop."

Then he was beyond seduction, beyond enticement, deep in that place where language had been new and strange, and his need ran like lava, pared down to its purest sense, a hot primal scream.

"You're mine," the gryphon snarled at the witch. He took her by the back of the neck and shook her to make the words go in. "You're mine."

Whatever she saw in him stripped her raw. She looked young again and transfixed with wonder. "Oh God. You're so beautiful."

The compulsion drove him into her. It was so exquisite he tore his claws into the bedspread. She held him tight, her knees high so that she cradled his whole body. She gripped his wide flexing shoulders as his hips moved and moved, and her garnet eyes were filled with some kind of epiphany. Her lips were moving as she made strange sounds. Much later Rune would recognize she had been swearing in ancient Egyptian, and the realization would make him laugh. But that was later when he had recovered the layers of civilization that were now stripped away.

Then she stretched underneath him, and reached above her head with both arms as she lifted up with her strong, graceful hips and legs and he felt it again, felt her inner muscles begin their gorgeous spasm. She climaxed with a shaking gasp, and he hurtled forward again, spilling into her.

And again. This time he flipped her onto her hands and knees. She was mewling into the bed and shoving her ass back to him as he took her from behind. He wrapped his arms around her, his wise and wicked woman, and slammed her into the headboard. She braced herself as best she could and reached up behind her head to clutch at him, and he wrapped an arm around her neck, and this time she was the one who groaned it through clenched teeth. "You've gone and done it now—you're so mine, Rune Ainissesthai—Rune—Rune, oh God—"

Three times, the witching number.

"That spell's already been cast," he said into her hair. And he gave himself to her, spilling everything he had into his mate.

She could not let go of him. He propped himself against the headboard and pulled her into his arms, and she went willingly. She rested her head on his shoulder and only realized she was clenched on his arm when she caught sight of her hand out of the corner of her eye and saw that her knuckles were white. She forced her fingers to loosen and saw that she had left a red imprint on his tanned skin. If he had been one of the more fragile of the Elder Races, she might have broken his arm.

"I'm sorry," she whispered, stroking his bicep.

"Don't ever be sorry," he said. He kissed her forehead. "Bite me, mark me, claim me in any way you wish."

That was when she realized he held her just as tightly too. He rested his face in her hair, and his chest rumbled. It had a low, deep, rough cadence that vibrated against her cheek. She ran her palm across the broad muscled expanse wonderingly. "Are you *purring* at me?"

"I might be," Rune said. His deep voice was rougher, and lazy with intimacy. "Unless you've done something wrong. Then I'm growling at you again."

She tightened her lips to try to keep the laughter in, but it spilled out anyway. "Just because I'm laughing doesn't make it okay," she warned.

"The purring?" He threaded his fingers through her short hair.

"No, the *growling*. I will not be chastised by you growling at me every time you think I might have done something wrong."

"Then I will definitely be purring from now on even when I'm growling." He captured her hand before she had the chance to smack him, and he brought her fingers up to his mouth to press a kiss on her knuckles.

She refused to laugh again. She clenched her jaw against it until the impulse eased. Then she cleared her throat. "About what just happened."

"What about it?" He sounded calm, his purring steady and quiet. It was remarkably soothing.

She looked out the French doors at the wrought-iron balcony they would most likely be too busy to enjoy. The sun had almost set, and the red and gold streaks across the sky were starting to fade. Dr. Telemar would be arriving at SFO soon.

"It was—more than I expected." As old as she was and as much as she had seen, she found herself unexpectedly at a loss for words.

"You mean when we mated."

That was what they had done. They were mating. He was mating with her. She had taken him into her body as she had taken him into her soul, and he had wrung her inside out. Everything ached, pleasantly, although that would fade soon enough as she healed with Vampyric speed. "I didn't know it would be so intense," she said softly. "How could you trust me like that?"

He was silent for so long, at first she thought he wasn't going to answer her. Then he stirred and said, "It just happened. The more I learned about you, the more I cared, and the more I trusted you. Your research, your dog, the way you looked at me and said you took responsibility for how we might change things. You think I don't know you said that to make things easier for me, when I might have been the only one to remember what happened? Then this last time when I went back, I looked at you and panicked at the thought of losing you. I know I told you too much, but I couldn't stop myself. And so you knew all this time that I would come to you some day, and you said nothing, did nothing."

She buried her face in him. "I had a lot of time to think," she whispered. "I thought about time looping back on itself, and about how you said you were from the future and how every time you came back, you changed things in the past. You said it was incredibly dangerous, and I believed you. When I finally met you again and realized who you were, I thought about getting in touch and telling you what had happened. Then I realized that if I did, I might change you too so that you never came back in time to see me. And I didn't want to risk losing those memories, so I waited to see what would happen at Adriyel River, and beyond."

He pushed her onto her back and came on top of her, covering her with his body while he held her tight, pressing his lean cheek against hers. "You thought it through and held steady," he said. "You closed the time loop we created. You held your ground when I don't know of anyone else who would have. Then after *all of that*, you tried to send me away this afternoon, and it was so goddamn loving and extravagantly stupid, how could I not want to mate with you? Of course I trust you. I knew if you laid claim to me, you would hold on no matter what."

"No matter what." She swallowed hard, gripping him as tightly as he held her. They were wrapped around each other, torso to torso, skin to skin, Power entwined with Power, so that she was not sure where one ended and the other began. "I think I can see what my life must have been like before you went back, and everything feels truer now."

He nuzzled her neck. "All the pieces interlock. The thought keeps running through my head that it's like a keystroke password to an unbreakable code. It opens a vault door to a strange new country, and even though it is strange and new, it is all still familiar. All the colors are brighter and more fierce, the song notes more piercing."

She kissed his temple and ran her fingers through his hair. The weight of his body sent his purr vibrating through her chest, and she felt a sudden rush of adoration for him so intense it made her feel drunk, insane. "It's a more beautiful, deadlier world because there's so much more to lose," she said. "Rune, you can't go back anymore. We have to protect what we have."

"There's no reason for me to go back now," he murmured. He kissed her collarbone. "I think I can hold my own and not get caught up in the episodes when they happen. We've warned your younger self to take care, and I also think we've learned everything we can. The most important thing now is to guard you and keep you safe when you're caught in them, while we figure out how to get them to stop."

"You sound so optimistic," she said.

"Are you still the glass-half-empty kind of girl?" he said. "You know, the more things change, the more they really do stay the same."

She shook her head and exhaled a silent laugh. She loved how he could make her laugh.

The more things change. A sudden wave of fear had her clutching him tighter again. She had embraced the changes that had happened to her long ago, but what if something else changed in the world because of what they had done? She would never know, but Rune would. He said he remembered everything. What if they had done something wrong and had somehow destroyed something that should have existed? What if she had decided to do something she shouldn't have, something that she hadn't done originally?

She felt again that sense of hurtling forward, faster and faster, in time. She wanted to turn her racing brain off, to close her eyes and rest against Rune's strong body in a true sleep. Then something else occurred to her.

"I just realized, right after I talked on the phone I went into the fade. I haven't had the chance to tell you," she said. "I'm pretty sure Julian's turned against me. I can take him if we're one-on-one, but as King he commands the support of the whole Nightkind demesne. We need to tread carefully."

Rune came up on his elbow to look down at her. His gaze was sharp, his lean features focused. The fine lines at the corners of his mouth deepened. "Dragos left me a message to call him as soon as I could," he said. "Of course I haven't had time yet. I wonder if he was calling about the same thing. I need to call him back to find out what's going on."

"We have a hell of a lot to untangle," Carling said. "Just set aside the whole dying problem for a moment. Nobody's going to be happy when they find out what's just happened between us. Not the Nightkind demesne, not the Wyr, and certainly not the Elder tribunal."

They were both silent for a moment as they absorbed the enormity of the challenges in front of them.

Then Rune kissed her cheek. He blew a little in her ear, and she cringed away from how it tickled. "It's always something."

═ SEVENTEEN ═

The hotel phone rang, and Rune rolled over to answer it. Full night had fallen, and he switched on the bedside lamp as he did, flooding the room in soft light. Carling could clearly hear the feminine voice on the other end. "Rune, I just arrived at the hotel and I've checked into the room you booked for me."

"Excellent, Seremela," he said. "Please come up to the suite as soon as you are able." He raised his eyebrows at Carling, who nodded in agreement.

"I'll be there in ten minutes."

As he twisted at the waist to hang up the phone, Carling ran her fingers along the line of his bare torso, from shoulder to hip. He turned back to her, his features creased in a smile. "Claiming each other is one thing," she said. "Figuring out how to do 'together' is an entirely different thing."

"We've come out of the gate strong," Rune said. He came over her, bracing himself on one elbow by her head as he leaned down to kiss her. "We've learned to trust each other, like each other and enjoy each other's company. We just have to keep relying on each other as we fight to find a cure for you. Learning about the rest, making life decisions about what comes next, all that can wait."

Carling stared up at him, aching as she thought of everything he was giving up for her. She said slowly, "If we really find a cure that works, then I may become human again. If that happens, I'll die so soon, in just another fifty years or so." After the enormous amount of time she had lived through, fifty years seemed like an eye blink.

"Those fifty years would be worth everything to me," he whispered back. His smiling eyes never wavered. They were clear and steady, right down to the bottom of his soul.

He really meant it, she saw. He really was mating with her, committing to her. He didn't hold back, or qualify or try to dissemble. He would live as she lived, and die as she died. Panic struck her all over again, deeper and harder than before, not for her sake but for his.

She had qualified things and dissembled. Fight to live, he had said to her, and even as she did so, she still prepared to die, still settled her affairs and said her good-byes, still braced herself for the end.

Holy gods, not anymore. She had to fight to live with everything she had inside, because this was no longer just about her. It was about them both. She gripped his wrist hard. "We don't have any time to lose."

"Then we best get cracking," he said.

He rolled off the bed and to his feet in one smooth, lithe motion. She sat more slowly, watching as he picked up the clothes from the floor. His hair was tousled more than ever, his nude muscled body bearing bite and scratch marks that were fading even as she watched. The embers of passion flared in her body as she stared at his neck. As he leaned over to lay her jeans, shirt and lingerie on the bed beside her, she reached up to finger the bite mark.

She felt his breath leave him. He gave her a glittering look under lowered eyelids. Out of the corner of her eye, she saw his penis stiffen. He said roughly, "Behave."

"Do you really want me to?" she asked gently.

His expression turned scorching. "Seremela's going to be here in just over five minutes."

She tilted her face up to his as she took hold of his erection. She rubbed her thumb over the broad head of his cock. He bared his teeth. He looked savage and magnificent, barely held in check and completely inhuman. Gods, how she loved this man. She whispered, "We'll just have to remember where we left off then."

"Bloody hell, woman," he gritted. He grabbed hold of her wrist but didn't pull her hand away. A muscle in his bicep started jumping, he was holding himself so tightly.

She bent sideways to kiss the muscle in his arm. She felt like she was immersed in him, his aroused scent, his hot presence, and yet starving for him at the same time. *She was so starving.* She raked her teeth gently along the skin of the bunched muscle, and he made a muffled sound and went down hard on one knee on the floor beside the bed.

She put her arms around his neck and kissed him. He clutched her to him, kissing her back with every bit as much hunger as she had. "Mine," she whispered against his lips.

"Mine," he whispered back. He ran his lips compulsively down her neck to her breastbone, bending her back. His mind slid on a patch of black ice as he flashed on her incomparable, gorgeous body, those curves, the jut of her ripe nipples, those strong shapely legs as she had wound them around his hips—

A knock sounded at the suite door, and he yanked away from the siren's call of Carling's body with a growl as he snatched up his clothes. She fell back laughing on the bed, her eyes dancing with such wicked delight it nearly broke his head to walk away from her. "*Later*," he snarled at her.

"Oh my gods, yes," she breathed, stretching out her naked body. "Later, and again, and repeatedly, I hope."

He gave her a white-hot glare and bolted from the bedroom. There was another knock at the door. He roared, "Just a fucking minute!"

From the hall outside the suite, a woman said in a startled voice, "I'm sorry, I do beg your pardon."

Rune swore then called out, "No, Seremela, I'm sorry. Hold on, I'll be with you in just a moment."

Carling snatched a pillow, crammed her face into it and rolled around on the bed as she laughed and laughed.

When she heard Rune open the door, she grabbed her clothes and shoved off the bed, and walked into the bathroom for a quick wash before she dressed. She caught a glimpse of her short tousled hair and makeup-smeared face in the mirror and exploded with laughter again.

Here's the spook house/roller coaster mash-up again. Euphoria and glee, sprinkled with outright terror. She turned on the water faucet and splashed her face off. The water felt crisp, cold and good.

Rune raised his voice. "Carling, I'm going to start explaining things to Seremela, if you don't mind. If you would rather, we can wait until you get in here."

She called back, "Not at all. Please go ahead. I'll be right there."

She listened to the two of them talk as she finished dressing. She thought about digging out a caftan from her suitcases but she wanted to put on the exotic jeans and flared silk crepe T-shirt instead, although she chose to remain barefoot. She ran her hands through her choppy short hair then went out to the living room.

She found them sitting in the living area. Rune had dressed in his black clothes and had finger-combed his own hair. He looked burnished and vibrant, and so sexy she pulsed with the dark urgent desire to mark him again. The medusa had taken an armchair, and Rune sat at one end of the couch. He was leaning forward, his elbows on his knees, moodily spinning an iPhone in circles on the coffee table as he talked. Both he and Seremela stood as she entered the room.

Carling strode forward to offer her hand. The medusa watched her approach with a wide, curious gaze. Seremela said with a smile, "It's an honor to meet you, Councillor."

"Thank you for coming on such short notice, Doctor."

"Please, call me Seremela. I was happy Rune called, and it will be my pleasure to do anything I can to help."

Carling watched the medusa's expression closely. "You may find a lot of what we have to say disturbing. We need your confidentiality on this."

"Of course," said Seremela.

Carling glanced at Rune, her eyebrows raised. He nodded. She turned her attention back to the doctor.

As a medusa, Seremela Telemar was Demonkind, although she lived in Chicago, well outside the Demonkind demesne in Houston. She was a pretty woman in late middle age. Carling guessed her to be around three hundred and eighty years old. Her head snakes had grown to the length of her thighs. When she reached old age, they would touch the floor. Her skin was a creamy pale green with a faint snakeskin pattern, and her slitted eyes had a nictating membrane that was open for the moment. Several of her head snakes tasted the air as they peered curiously around her waist and over her shoulder at Carling.

However, most of the medusa's head snakes were more interested in Rune. Carling watched a couple of the snakes slide up his arm. Was she imagining things, or was it actually possible for a head snake to look adoring?

Neither Rune nor Seremela were paying attention to what the medusa's snakes were doing. They were busy in conversation, talking to each other as they focused on her.

Carling cocked her head and pursed her lips.

Snakes.

She strode forward and snatched up the two head snakes, one in each hand. Rune watched her in mild surprise. Seremela jumped and blushed, and began to apologize profusely, "I'm so sorry, I wasn't paying attention. You know they have a mind of their own and, well, they like Rune."

Carling ignored her. She held up the two snakes and looked at them. They looked back at her, their tongues flickering. They did not appear alarmed or disturbed at her handling of them. A couple of other head snakes lifted to twine around her wrists. Seremela gave an embarrassed laugh. "It looks like they like you too."

"Of course it is," Carling said to the snakes.

"Of course what is?" Rune asked.

"You said it was important to go back to the beginning, and it was," Carling said. "The serpent goddess wasn't just an archaic, superstitious Egyptian folktale. She was a real creature named Python who actually existed. So the next logical step is that the serpent's kiss really is a serpent's kiss. Vampyrism became a blood-borne pathogen, and Vampyres are created in a blood-to-blood exchange. But it had to have started as venom."

After she said that, she and Rune had to tell the story from the beginning. Seremela listened intently to everything they told her. She looked shaken at the thought of history being changed, interrupting only to ask for clarification at certain points in the dialogue until she heard of Carling's early sketches of Python. "You *sketched* Python?" the medusa breathed.

"No, I never met Python," Carling corrected, smiling. "I sketched the illustrations of her that were on the cavern wall."

"What I wouldn't give to see those," Seremela said, eyes shining. "Did you know we call ourselves Python's children?"

Carling and Rune looked at each other. She had taken a seat beside him on the couch, and he rested his arm along the back, from time to time fingering the hair at the back of her head. Carling shook her head, and Rune said, "I had no idea either."

The medusa shrugged. "I don't know if there's any historical accuracy in that. If the medusas really are Python's children, that would have happened so long ago it would have predated your Egyptian cavern by thousands of years."

"Do you know what happened to her?" Rune said. He was watching Seremela, his expression intent. "All I heard was that she died."

"She traveled to Greece and was killed at Delphi," Seremela said. "Some versions of the story say she was murdered. In Greek mythology the god Apollo killed her, but Greek mythology is a lot like Egyptian or any other mythology—the myths are mostly strange stories that hold a few kernels of truth. I've heard other stories that simply say she was killed when she fell down a fissure in the earth. She lived in Greece long enough to establish the Oracle at Delphi, though."

"I thought the Oracle was a genetic inheritance, and the Oracle's ability to prophesy was passed down from generation to generation within a human family," Carling said. "At least that's what previous Oracles have told me when we've talked."

The Oracle from Delphi had long since relocated to the States to join the demesne of human witches in Louisville. In each generation of the Oracle's family, there was always a single woman who inherited the title, along with the oracular abilities, whenever the previous Oracle died. She was separate from the main ruling structure of the witches' demesne, which was governed by an elected Head, yet the Oracle was a dignitary in her own right. Carling had not met the newest Oracle. The transfer of Power had taken place just some months before when the previous Oracle and her husband had been killed in a car crash.

Carling had to struggle to hide how bitterly she was disappointed in hearing someone else confirm Python's death. She thought she had control over her expression, but Rune's hand dropped to her shoulder in a bracing grip.

"Well, the ability to prophesy is now passed down from generation to generation," said Seremela. "Just as Vampyrism is now passed from human to human. Where the ability of the Oracle originated is another question entirely."

"Have you consulted an Oracle before?" Rune asked Seremela curiously. He had talked with Oracles just as Carling had, when socializing at inter-demesne functions, but he had never before been interested in talking to one while she was channeling the Power of prophesy. Cryptic ramblings drove him crazy. As he had said to Carling earlier, talking to Python had been like tripping on a bad dose of LSD.

"I consulted an Oracle when I was much younger," said Seremela. "I was barely fifty at the time, and curious. I found it to be a Powerful and disturbing experience. The prophesying is never a controlled thing, either for the petitioner or the Oracle."

"Do you mind if I ask what she told you?" Rune asked.

"I don't mind you asking," Seremela replied quietly. "But it isn't relevant to this conversation, and I would rather not discuss it."

"Time," Carling murmured. Past, present and future. It would seem the Oracle's ability to prophesy was immersed with it. She rubbed her forehead and tried to focus. She looked up to find Rune studying her.

His face was grave, his eyes concerned. When she looked at him, he squeezed her shoulder. He said to Seremela, "What would you say about the properties of venom to someone who is nonmedical—namely, me?"

The medusa regarded him for a few moments. Her head snakes had slipped over her shoulders to pool in her lap in a coiled mass. Most seemed to have gone asleep, although a few still watched Rune and Carling. Seremela ran her fingers lightly over them. "The very first thing I would say to anyone is, this area of toxicology was not my focus of study in med school, so I can't speak as any kind of expert. Given that, the properties of venom are extremely complex and can contain different toxins for different cells and tissues of the body. It can also have some surprisingly beneficial properties, such as bee venom treatments for MS patients, or a derivative of a Malaysian pit viper venom to treat stroke victims. Preliminary studies have also indicated that snake venom can slow the growth of some cancerous tumors. It's a fascinating field of study. So much depends on the venomous species and of course their species of prey."

"Let's focus on snakes," Rune said.

Seremela said, "Mundane snake venoms essentially fall into two categories: the hemotoxic, which is poisonous to the circulatory system, and the neurotoxic, which is poisonous to the nervous system. At the risk of oversimplifying, the snake or serpent species usually intends to subdue its prey."

Carling looked up. "Your head snakes are poisonous."

"Yes," Seremela said. "My snakes carry venom that induces paralysis, although if you take a dose from a single bite, the poison isn't terribly toxic. A human would experience some numbness and lethargy, along with pain and swelling around the area of the bite. Some might get nauseated as well. Generally there would be no need for a dose of antivenin, unless the victim was a child or went into anaphylactic shock. If I was attacked and my snakes were badly frightened, however, they might bite repeatedly, and that could lead to someone dying. Wyr are more immune than humans. If Rune would consent to hold still and let himself be bitten for a couple of days, the venom from my head snakes could eventually stop his heart." She looked at Carling. "And a medusa's snake venom has no apparent effect on Vampyres."

"What about other serpent creatures in the Elder Races?" Carling asked.

"Well, then you add in the extremely unpredictable element of Power," Seremela said. "The venom from my snakes is mundane; the snakes are just attached to my head, that's all. We share a sort of symbiotic connection that has some empathy, a very crude kind of telepathy but no real exchange of language, and the poison is just poison. I really hesitate to speculate about another creature, especially one as Powerful an immortal as Python would have been."

"The Egyptian priestess you spoke to indicated there was some kind of social contract with the serpent goddess," Rune said to Carling. "So Python must have interacted with the group. It sounded like there was some level of caring involved, or at least worship."

"Venom, paralysis, time. Some general themes are coming together," Carling muttered. "As I recall, the priestess talked about Python caring for her children, giving them the kiss of life that was also death. Maybe Python knew her bite would halt the progression of their mortality. Whatever the motivation or reality, it doesn't matter."

"Why do you say that?" Rune asked. His eyes were narrowed.

Carling leaned forward, put her elbows on her knees and dug the heels of her hands into her eyes. She had studied both poisons and sorcery. No wonder her healing spells had only worked to stave off the episodes for a time. The healing spells she had given herself were "cure-alls." In order to create anything more targeted or specific, she would have needed to know the original properties of what she tried to heal. She said dully, "What exists in Vampyres' veins mutated a very long time ago. It's a product of the original source as it interacted with the human immune system. We don't have any of Python's original venom, so we can't create any antivenin."

"What about a more generalized antivenin?" Rune asked, his voice tense.

Carling was shaking her head even as Seremela said, gently, "For something that Powerful and specific, and for the amount of time you indicated you might have left, I'm afraid that would be an exercise in futility. It would take years of experimentation and drug trials. Don't waste your time."

Rune's tension increased. The force of his emotion blasted along Carling's nerve endings. She said to him, "I know what you're thinking. Going back again won't work. I never met Python, and the episodes are too short for you to go looking for her on your own."

He said roughly, "I can keep going through until I learn how to go back on my own."

She shook her head. "And risk further changes to this timeline? That's too dangerous. We said we would stop. We've got to stop."

As Rune opened his mouth to argue, he took note of how her shoulders slumped in discouragement. The line of reasoning in their conversation was a bitter blow to him. How much harder was it for her to hear, after she had borne the brunt of so many disappointments for so long? He bit back what he had been about to say. "Let's set that aside for now. I think our next step is to go to Louisville and talk to the new Oracle. We need to hear what she has to say, especially if she's another one of Python's children."

She sighed and said, "Yes, we need to go."

Seremela said quietly, "Would you like for me to examine you while I'm here? I don't know that I can add any more to what you already know, but this is such a serious issue I really would feel better if we pursued every avenue we have open to us."

Carling nodded. She let her hands drop away from her face. "It makes sense."

Rune looked at his iPhone. He asked, "Do you need me for this? Because if you don't, I've got something I need to do."

Carling turned to him. "No, of course not. What are you going to do?"

"I need to make that phone call," he said.

Carling scooped up her leather bag and led Seremela into one of the bedrooms. Rune listened to the soft sound of their voices as they talked before he picked up his cell. He hit Dragos on speed dial.

Dragos picked up on the first ring, "There you are. What took you so long?"

"This is the first chance I've had to call you," Rune said. "It's been a long day. In fact it's been a long day for a while, and a lot has happened. Carling and I just returned earlier today from an Other land."

Dragos said, "Can she overhear you right now?"

Rune glanced at the closed bedroom door. "No," he replied. "Look I have some things I have to tell you."

Dragos said, "Later. Has she bound you with that favor you owed her, or restricted your ability to act in any way?"

The pointed question threw Rune off track. "No," he said again. "Forget about that, it's no longer important. Listen—"

"All right," Dragos interrupted. "Here's what has been

happening in the rest of the world. I've been consulting with the Nightkind King, and also with other members of the Elder tribunal. Julian had quite a tale to tell. Apparently Carling's been blanking out and affecting the physical landscape around her. Have you seen any of this for yourself?"

Rune set his teeth. "Yes," he said. "That's what we're dealing with right now. What else did that bastard say?"

"He petitioned the tribunal to remove Carling as Councillor for the Nightkind demesne. He claimed she's no longer fit to hold office. They agreed with him. I talked with Jaggar and Councillor Soren. Carling's been removed from the Elder tribunal."

Jaggar was the Wyr Councillor on the Elder tribunal. Soren was the Demonkind Councillor and head of the tribunal. If Carling was no longer a tribunal Councillor, she no longer had the authority or the weight of the Elder tribunal behind her. If anything happened to her, the Elder tribunal would no longer act in retaliation. She was now completely isolated, without anyone backing her. Julian had just set her up to take her out. Rune's hand tightened on the phone. He heard something crack.

He said evenly, "Is there anything else?"

"Yes," Dragos said. "The other gryphons are weirded out. They've insisted three times now that something has changed, twice over the weekend and once today. Only they can't verbalize what that is, they just know something has happened. Graydon said it was like reality had shifted, only he couldn't tell what might have changed. Have you experienced anything like that?"

"Look, you're going to have to let me get a word in edgewise here," Rune said between his teeth. "Yes, Carling and I have caused some things to happen—"

"Three times?" Dragos said. "You and she caused something to happen—you caused *reality to shift* three times?"

"Let me fucking explain what we did," Rune bit out.

But the dragon's anger was roused. He growled, "When Carling blanks out, she affects the landscape around her. Then you and she do something that Bayne, Constantine and Graydon felt all the way from here in New York, and you did it not once but *three times*? What the fuck did you do?"

Rune looked out the window at the spray of stars and electric lights. We changed history, he thought. We changed each other. We changed the world.

"Tell the other gryphons not to worry," he said. "It's going to be all right."

"It better by-gods be all right," Dragos said grimly. "Tell me about the rest of it later. I want you out of there, immediately."

"I can't do that, Dragos," Rune said quietly. He stared out the window as he watched the end of his life approach.

"You said Carling had not restricted your movements," Dragos said.

"She hasn't."

"Then you can do it. Julian's preparing to take Carling out, and I don't want you anywhere near that fallout when it hits."

"She was a good ally to you," Rune said to the male who had just become his former friend.

"Yes she was, but the Wyr can't be involved in this problem too. We've still got border tensions with the Elves, and we've involved ourselves too deeply in the Dark Fae problems for too long. We're overextended, understaffed and short on political tolerance. And anyway, I don't blame Julian. If someone was that unstable and posted that kind of threat to my demesne, I would be making moves to do the same thing. So get out of there and get your ass home."

"No," Rune said.

That was when the dragon's voice got very quiet. "I don't think I heard you correctly."

"You heard me correctly."

"What do you mean, no? Have you lost your fucking mind?"

"I mean no. I quit. Effective right now."

"You can't quit. I won't let you."

"Think I just did," Rune said.

"You're making a very big mistake," growled the Lord of the Wyr.

"What's that you say, Dragos? I can't hear you. You're breaking up," Rune said as he crushed his iPhone.

≈ EIGHTEEN ≈

In the bedroom, Seremela tactfully looked out the window as Carling stripped. Carling had lost all vestige of modesty within her first hundred years of existence, but for the doctor's sake, she slipped on a hotel bathrobe. Then she patiently put up with a very thorough medical examination.

"I'm not sure what to make of this," Seremela murmured. "But your temperature is elevated."

"Is it?" Her eyebrows rose. "By how much?"

"A good five degrees. No doubt you already know that Vampyres tend to reflect the temperature of their surroundings, which in most rooms tends to be around seventy to seventy-two degrees. You're running hot at seventy-six point five." Seremela popped the plastic off her thermometer and tucked the thermometer away in her physician's bag.

Carling bit back a smile. "I have been in close contact with Rune for quite a while, and he's like a furnace."

The medusa looked down. "I imagine so. He cares for you a great deal." There was a trace of wistfulness in Seremela's voice, and more than a trace in her emotions.

Carling's impulse to smile faded. She said quietly, "I am his mate. The timing is inconvenient."

The medusa's head came up. Her eyes had gone wide with a stricken compassion. "Oh gods, this is doubly difficult then."

"Yes."

Seremela sighed. "Physically you appear just fine, Councillor. Your Power is very interesting to me, but since we've just met, I have no way to gauge or assess it. All I know is it hasn't fluctuated while I have been in your presence. And I wish I could take blood and do some testing, but I don't have medical privileges at any facilities here."

Carling said, "At its root, Vampyrism is a blood condition, so it seems highly probable that any original venom would have been hemotoxic in nature."

"That's what I think too," said Seremela.

Carling said, "Ingesting blood is also the only way Vampyres can take in nourishment, at least until they hit the stage I'm in."

"If it's all about the blood, then my guess is that blood will also hold the key."

All about the blood. Carling nodded thoughtfully. She knew very well that feelings weren't scientific, but it felt right to her, felt true.

Seremela studied her. "And you haven't taken in any physical nourishment in almost two hundred years?"

"That's correct," Carling said. "Drinking blood began to make me violently ill. Let me tell you, throwing up gouts of blood is not a pleasant experience."

Seremela winced. "I imagine not. Did your succubus abilities appear before or after you lost your ability to tolerate ingesting blood?"

"Some time afterward. I went through a couple of weeks of feeling weak and lethargic, and I ached all over," Carling told her. She set aside the bathrobe and dressed again in the jeans and flirty T-shirt. "It reminded me a little of when I was first turned, actually. I would get hungry and try to drink, and then it would all come back up again. I finally lost the desire to try. Then some time later I realized I could sense what other living creatures were feeling. The stronger the emotion, the more revitalized I felt. By then I had heard stories of the oldest of us becoming succubi, otherwise I would have been more frightened than I was."

Seremela sat down in the bedroom's chair. "It sounds possible that becoming a succubus was a defense response from your mutated immune system. You lost the ability to process your normal form of nourishment, and your body responded accordingly."

"It certainly sounds possible," Carling said. She liked how the doctor processed information.

"If this progression is as logical as cause-and-effect, if we could find some physical nourishment that you could tolerate, we might be able to put you into a holding pattern," Seremela said. "We need to get you into some kind of remission. Perhaps we can't achieve an absence of all symptoms, but we need to at least try to halt any advancement. It could buy us some much-needed time."

"That's an excellent point," Carling said slowly. "I'll keep it mind. In the meantime, why don't you take a little blood and I'll put it in stasis. That will preserve it until you can get it refrigerated properly."

"Excellent," Seremela said with satisfaction.

After the medusa had drawn a vial and Carling had spelled it, she turned to her leather bag to open it and pull out the tube containing the papyri scrolls of her sketches of Python. She took them over to a dresser and beckoned Seremela over as she unrolled them on the dresser's flat surface.

The medusa breathed, "These are incredible."

Carling watched the other woman's face as she reached out to touch the edge of the top scroll with reverence. Seremela's pleasure was like a keen, bright light. Carling said, "I want you to take these."

Seremela's eyes went wide. Both she and all her head snakes looked so shocked, Carling had to bite back the sudden urge to chuckle.

"I couldn't accept these," Seremela said. Then, in a stricken whimper, "Could I?"

"Of course you could," Carling said. "Talking with you has been incredibly helpful. It's been a comfort as well."

"It's been a privilege to meet you and help in any way I can." Seremela touched the edge of the top sketch again. "You shouldn't feel like you need to give these to me."

"Consider it my way of saying thanks," Carling said. "And honestly I think you'll enjoy them so much more than I do. I haven't thought about or looked at them in centuries, until Python came up in conversation with Rune."

"This is a hell of a thank-you," Seremela said. "Rune had mentioned something about paying me for my travel expenses and my time. If I do accept these sketches, I don't want to hear any more talk of payment. All right?"

Carling said, "If that's the way you need to give yourself permission to enjoy them, I'm not going to argue with you."

Seremela laughed and clapped her hands. "Then thank you, yes, I accept."

Carling smiled as she rolled up the sketches, slid them back in the tube and handed it to Seremela, who perched the tube on top of her physician's bag between the straps. Both women were smiling as they walked out of bedroom to find Rune still dressed in black and armed for war.

He wore two guns in shoulder holsters and a short sword strapped to his back. He had changed out of his sleek dress shoes and now wore steel-toed boots. As Carling and Seremela entered the living room, he was just rolling up his sleeves and strapping leather armbands with throwing stars to his forearms.

After she took one thoughtful look at him, Carling didn't waste time asking for an explanation. Instead she turned her attention to Seremela. "We need to get you out of San Francisco."

"And we need to do that as fast as possible," Rune said. He yanked the straps closed on one armband and began to fasten the other.

"What's happened?" Seremela said. The medusa looked frightened.

"Never mind, Seremela," Rune told her. His expression had turned killer cold, but his voice remained calm. "This doesn't concern you. The less you know about things, the better."

Carling said, "I'm going to call Khalil and use that last favor. He'll see that she gets home safely."

"Sounds good," Rune said. "Then you and I can take off."

A loud knock sounded on the suite door. "Nightkind SFPD," a male said in a voice meant to carry. "Open up."

Rune said to her, "Call him."

She spoke the words that were the spell that sent the call spearing into the night.

The knock at the door turned into pounding. "Sentinel Ainissesthai, we know you're in there. You need to come into the precinct with us for questioning."

"Get in the bedroom," Rune said to Carling and Seremela. He positioned himself in front of the door.

Carling grabbed Seremela's arm and marched her into the bedroom as the cyclone blew into the suite. At the bedroom door, she glanced back to see Rune throw himself at the door, bracing it with his shoulder against the kick from the hall that was meant to break it down.

Khalil materialized in front of her gaze. He looked over his shoulder at Rune then turned to her. The Djinn's spare, elegant features were sharp with interest.

Carling twisted, hauling Seremela bodily around. She shoved the medusa unceremoniously into Khalil's arms, physician's bag and all. "Take her to Chicago," she said. "See that she gets home safely."

Behind Khalil, she saw Rune brace his whole body as another kick slammed against the door. "The doorjamb is breaking," Rune said. "I can't hold it for long."

Khalil raised an eyebrow. He looked mildly incredulous. He asked, "Are you sure this is how you want to spend your last favor?"

"Yes, goddammit, *GO!*" she snapped. She didn't wait to watch the cyclone blow away with Seremela. Instead she sprinted into the bedroom. Moving as fast as she could, she tore into her suitcases, looking for any weapons Rufio may have provided, cursing herself for not thinking to specify what he should pack. She really had relied on Rhoswen too much and for far too long.

Ah, bless you, Rufio. Two stilettos. Her weapon of choice for close fighting. She snatched them up in their leather sheaths. She wished she had a gun as well for backup, but the most effective long-range weapons she had were her offensive spells. She briefly considered shoes and more protective clothing, but then she heard a sharp splintering and the sound of snarling from the other room and she turned to race back into the living room.

Rune was fighting hand-to-hand in a whirlwind melee with a sixteen-foot-tall troll, and three ghouls. Though the word "ghoul" was etymologically descended from *gallu*, the Mesopotamian term for demon, ghouls were nevertheless Night-kind creatures. They blistered easily in strong sunlight, and were inhumanly strong and fast, and if they got someone pinned, their Power could consume their victim's flesh. The massive, gray-skinned troll was not as fast as were the ghouls, but she had a strength that could crush boulders. If she managed to catch up with Rune, she could kill him with a single solid blow to the head.

Rune had partially shifted into the golden monster. He moved with such speed, she could barely track him. He slashed out with both talon-tipped hands, and blood spurted from two of the ghouls.

The troll went down on her hands and knees, fished around with one tremendous hand, and caught hold of one of Rune's ankles. He lifted his free foot to smash his steel-toed boot into her face. The troll blinked and grunted, but held on.

Carling sighed and spoke the words that iced the air, and stillness spread over the knot of fighters. The troll still looked pained, and two of the ghouls bore deep, bleeding claw marks. The third ghoul was in the process of pulling his regulation gun. Carling walked over to appropriate the gun for herself as Rune's Power surged against her spell. He shook his head, swearing, and yanked his ankle out of the troll's grip.

"That spell of yours is beginning to grow on me," he growled. Rune turned away from the frozen knot of Nightkind fighters, his face and body settling back into more normal lines as he walked over to her.

Carling tilted her face up for his swift kiss. "It's not their fault," she said. "I'm assuming they're just following orders."

Rune might no longer look like the monster caught in mid-shift, but his eyes glowed with a flat, wicked light. "Julian's orders," he spat. "He's trying to get me out of the picture and isolate you. He got you fired, baby. You're no longer a Councillor on the Elder tribunal, but I notice he did not come to deliver the news to you in person."

Anger clogged her throat so that she could barely speak. She said, "He can't. He's my direct progeny, and if we get close enough together, I can still command his obedience. I assume you found all this out when you talked to Dragos?"

"Yes," he said. He put his arms around her, and she leaned against him. He was an inferno, throwing off more body heat than ever, and against her mind's eye he glowed molten with rage. "He ordered me home, I quit, and he didn't take it well." He glanced toward the bedroom. "Seremela's gone?"

"Yes." She leaned her forehead against his broad shoulder. "Rune, I'm sorry about Dragos."

A sigh shuddered through him. He rested his cheek on the top of her head. "I'm sorry about Julian. But forget about them for now. Grab what you need to take with you. We've got to get out of here."

She nodded and strode over to take the guns from the other two frozen ghouls. The troll did not carry a gun. Her eyesight was too weak, and her hands too large to make effective use of a handgun. When Carling turned around again, she found Rune had scooped up his duffle and her leather bag. He had also appropriated a butterscotch-colored leather jacket for her, along with matching flat-heeled leather boots.

"Here." He tossed the boots at her. "These're more sensible than the Christian Louboutin boots but alas, not nearly as much fun."

She caught them and bent over to yank them on. "Fun can happen later."

A sudden grin slashed across his face. "Later, and again, and repeatedly, I hope," he said. "You promised. I might have stuffed one of your caftans into my duffle too, in case you want it for later."

She straightened and gave him a lopsided smile. "You know that hairy bespectacled T-shirt you threw in the trash?" He raised his eyebrows and she nodded to her leather bag.

"Then it sounds like we got all we need, baby," Rune said. He gave her a hard kiss. "This next bit is tricky but doable. Climb on my back and I'll take a running launch out the balcony. I'll shift in midair, so you need to hang on."

There was stealthy movement in the hall. Several creatures were approaching. She opened up her arms and gestured to Rune impatiently. "You just get us in the air," she said. "Don't worry about me. I'll hang on."

He gave her that white, wild smile of his, tossed the bags at her and turned his back to her. She slung the bags onto one shoulder and leaped at him, arms around his neck and legs around his waist. As soon as she was firmly riding piggyback, he turned and sprinted for the open balcony doors.

She had seen the power in his running launch, felt the power in his launch from both sea and land. This was something altogether different. This had the roar of a Harrier jet as it shot off the short deck of an aircraft carrier ship. Each of his long, powerful strides shoved them off the Earth, faster and faster, until he took a springboard jump off the wrought-iron balcony and leaped up into the air with his arms outstretched.

It was one of the most exhilarating things she had ever experienced, and possibly one of the most tragic, for even as he shimmered into the shapeshift, and she felt the flow of his body as he expanded underneath her, a massive nylon net unfurled over them, shot with devastating precision from the rooftop of the hotel. They tangled in it and fell.

Even as they plummeted several stories, Rune was unbelievably fast. They turned as they fell and he twisted in midair, keeping his body between hers and the pavement, but the restricting net made his landing horribly awkward. They slammed into the ground with such force they shattered the concrete underneath them. She could hear the massive bones in Rune's front right leg and shoulder snap. The breath left him hard as he collapsed in an uncontrolled sprawl. Otherwise he remained silent. She was the one who screamed with rage and anguish at his suffering.

Her talons sprang out. The nylon net shredded like paper. Within seconds she had it ripped away and she leaped to her feet, standing protectively over Rune. But the net had accomplished what it had been intended to do; it had grounded them. With a muffled groan, Rune shapeshifted back into a man and lay curled on his side around his shattered arm.

She backed in a circle, looking around the open space. They had landed on a sidewalk beside the hotel's large, well-kept grounds. There wasn't any traffic on the nearby bordering street, and there were no passing pedestrians.

There were, however, plenty of creatures dotting the area around them. Julian had set the trap well. Four more trolls, and as many as fifty ghouls, with perhaps twice as many Vampyres, all standing silent, either watching to see what she would do or waiting for orders.

Even if she agreed to go with them, Rune would never accept it. Injured as he was, he would rise to his feet and fight to the death before he would let them get separated.

Her hands fisted. She called out, "You have been my people, and you're just following orders. I understand that. As of this moment, you can all walk away. No harm, no foul, no damage done. But if you're going to go, you need to do it right now."

She was gratified to note that many slipped away in the night. On the ground at her feet, Rune sat and drew a gun. He was hunched over, cradling his arm against his abdomen. He asked hoarsely, "Can you freeze the rest?"

"There's too many, spread over too large of an area." She began to whisper the ancient spell that called all her souls together, gathering all her Power into one compressed weapon. *I call my future selves to me. I call all my desires, all my fears to me. I call all my past selves to me. I call my divine self to me . . .*

Then Julian called across the open space, in his rough, familiar battleground roar, "All you have to do to stop this is keep your promise and return to the island. You can spend your remaining days in peace."

She looked down and met Rune's blazing gaze. "I can't do that, Julian."

"You would really rather go to war? How could you kill your own people?"

"I gave them their chance," she said. "And my give-a-shit button's broken, baby." She didn't recognize her own voice.

Rune came up on one knee. Too many creatures chambered too many rounds. She glanced down, and he nodded to her. He gave her a small private smile. It had been so beautiful for too brief a time. She put a hand on Rune's good shoulder and began to whisper the spell that would rain fire. She poured all her Power into the incantation.

Then the cyclone returned.

It blasted into the open area with such force, the Earth shook. Buildings rattled in a half-mile radius. Later the news channels would state the shockwave from the earthquake was felt three hundred miles away. Many of the Nightkind creatures cried out in fear and fell to the ground to cover their heads.

Rune stood and put his good arm around Carling as a prince of the Djinn formed in front of them. Khalil's strange diamond eyes and elegant inhuman features held a fierce smile.

"Now you will be the one to owe me a favor," said the Djinn to the Vampyre sorceress.

She released all her pent-up Power with a gasp. "Yes," she said.

"Where?"

"The Oracle in Louisville," she said rapidly.

Across the open square, Julian roared orders. His Nightkind forces began to fire. But none of their bullets hit their targets. The cyclone enveloped Rune and Carling and took them away.

The trip was as strange and as chaotic as anything Carling had experienced. She turned and put her arms around Rune to hold him tight as a howling wind surrounded them. In the center of the cyclone, Khalil gripped them to his lean, hard chest. Then the world materialized around them again, in the shape of a hot, humid Midwestern night.

As soon as Rune and Carling's feet touched the ground, Khalil released them. Carling was slow to relax her clench on Rune's waist, and she noticed his good arm was just as reluctant to loosen on her. The Djinn had not disappeared as he had the previous times he had come. Instead, he stood beside them and surveyed the scene with as much curiosity as they did.

They weren't actually in the city of Louisville but instead were some distance out, because the night was dark and quiet, populated with the shadowed greenery of deciduous trees and grass, and filled with the sound of crickets and cicadas. Hundreds of fireflies blanketed the area, winking yellow lights. The scene felt saturated with a very old Power.

They stood in a long gravel driveway that led up to an old sprawling two-story farmhouse. They had to have left San Francisco sometime after midnight, so that meant it was after 3:00 A.M. in Kentucky. A light was on inside the house. They could all clearly hear the sound of a fussing baby. There was the smell of a nearby river. Carling sensed the cool, powerful rush of water.

"Is that the Ohio River?" she asked Khalil.

"Yes," he said. The Djinn stood with his hands on his hips. His head was cocked as he regarded the house.

Even though the dark night outside was lit only by stars and dotted with electric lights off in the distance, Carling's gaze was sensitive enough she could see the lines of pain on Rune's face as he cradled his arm. "We need to get you inside," she said. She walked up the front steps of the farmhouse to the wide covered porch, followed by Rune and Khalil. A motion-sensitive porch light came on as they approached the house. Carling knocked on the door.

Light rapid footsteps approached, then suddenly the door yanked open. A slim, young human woman stood in the doorway with a baby on her hip. The woman was twenty-three or twenty-four years old, with features that might be classified as more interesting than pretty, and she had short flyaway, strawberry blonde hair. She was disheveled and hollow-eyed, and dressed in shabby plaid flannel pants and an oversized gray T-shirt.

The baby was a boy, perhaps nine months old. He looked as disheveled and hollow-eyed as the woman, his small round face splotchy from crying. For a moment he regarded them with as much curiosity as they regarded him. Then he knuckled one of his ears, turned to plop his face into the woman's neck, and emitted a ragged, miserable wail.

The woman looked at them with unfriendly eyes. "What the hell are you doing, knocking at someone's door at three thirty in the morning?"

Carling said, "We're looking for the Oracle."

"This couldn't wait until seven?" the woman snapped. She patted the boy's small back and bounced him with the kind of tiredness of someone who had been doing the same thing for some time now. "Hell, until six? What's the matter with you people, anyway? Can't you see I've got a sick baby on my hands? Go away and don't come back until it's a decent time."

Khalil said, "You're the Oracle?"

The Djinn sounded as surprised as Carling felt, and Rune looked.

"You were expecting a gold shrine and a gaggle of virgins draped in pleated white sheets?" the young woman said. "Yes, I'm the Oracle."

Carling raised her eyebrows and looked beyond the woman at the train wreck of a living room. A scuffed hardwood floor was covered by an old shabby area rug that was littered with toys. Textbooks and coffee cups were piled on the equally shabby furniture. One armchair held a wicker basket piled high with unfolded laundry. The house smelled like sour baby vomit.

The young woman looked around too.

"I know," she said with a bitter smile. "Whoop-de-fucking-do, right?"

⇒ NINETEEN ⇐

Carling said, "You have to give us sanctuary if we ask for it. Let us in."

The woman's weary hazel eyes narrowed. "You're going to pull that card on my ass right now? Really?"

Rune said, "We can go and come back in a few hours."

Carling glanced at him. His face was white, his lips bloodless. His eyes looked bruised. She shook her head stubbornly. "Do you know who I am?" she asked the Oracle.

The human's face tightened. "I recognize you," she said. "At least I know who you and the sentinel are. I don't know who he is." She jerked her chin toward Khalil.

"Rune is injured," she said to the Oracle. "I need to attend to him. As soon as I do that, I can help your boy. If you know who I am, then you know I can do this."

The Oracle took a second, closer look at Rune, and her expression changed to one of reluctant compassion. She pushed the door open wide and stood back.

Carling didn't wait for more. She strode into the house, straight over to the armchair to shift the basket of laundry to the floor. "Come on," she said gently to Rune. "Sit and let me have a look at you."

Rune walked over to the chair and eased into it. His movements were stiff, without any of his usual grace. Behind them,

Khalil strolled into the house. Carling couldn't begin to figure out what was going through the Djinn's mind as he looked around the living room with a speculative gaze, nor did she know why he hadn't yet disappeared. Perhaps he was waiting for his chance to finalize the details of the favor she now owed him.

In any case, she didn't have the energy to waste on mulling over Khalil's odd behavior. Instead she knelt in front of Rune and touched his cheek as she whispered a spell that would numb his injury. Immediately the tight lines in his face eased. He gave her a nod in thanks. "I can wait now," he told her. "Go put the poor kid out of his misery."

"All right." She stood again and turned to the Oracle and the sobbing baby. "What's his name?"

Carling's mild question opened a floodgate in response. The Oracle said anxiously, "His name's Max. I think he's got an ear infection. He was fussy earlier in the evening and didn't want his supper. Then he woke up crying a couple of hours ago, and he has a fever and he just threw up, and he keeps pulling at his right ear like it hurts. I was just trying to decide if I should take him to an urgent care unit, but his sister Chloe's sound asleep and it's just the three of us here and I'd have to either call someone for backup, or set him down to wake Chloe up and get her in the car too—"

Carling shook her head, a little disoriented. In just under ten minutes, they had gone from facing almost certain death in battle to this. She put a hand to the back of Max's head and numbed his pain as well. The baby's crying died away. He hiccupped and shuddered, lifting his head from the Oracle's shoulder to look around in bleary confusion.

"Okay, little man," Carling murmured. "It's going to get better now." She asked the Oracle, "What is your name?"

"Grace," the Oracle said. "Grace Andreas."

"The Andreas family has gone through difficult times these last thirty years," Carling said. A string of ill health and bad luck had decimated what had once been a large, thriving clan. "I was sorry to hear that Petra and her husband died in that car crash. What relation was she to you—was she your aunt?"

"She was my older sister," Grace said, her hazel eyes reddening. "Chloe and Max are my niece and nephew. We're the only ones left."

Carling nodded. She had scanned Max as she and Grace had talked. She said, "You're right, he has an ear infection. It's easily taken care of with a simple healing spell, but he'll be very tired over the next few days."

Grace nodded, the exhaustion in her expression lightening with relief. "That's fine, as long as it takes care of the infection. It's not like he's got to drive or go to work or anything."

In spite of the seriousness of her own issues, Carling had to smile. "No, he doesn't, does he? With your permission, I'll cast that spell for him now."

"Please."

Carling did so and as Grace took the sleepy baby away, she turned her attention back to Rune. He was resting quietly in the armchair, watching her. She knelt in front of him again, glad to see that some color had returned to his complexion.

He gave her a small smile, his eyelids lowered, and said telepathically, *I can't decide which sight of you was more hot, the one where you were getting ready to throw down some kind of Armageddon spell on Julian's ass, or the one where you just healed that little boy.*

She gave a ghost of a chuckle that faded away almost immediately. They had almost died. He had almost died. She closed her eyes and gripped his hand, and his long, strong fingers closed around hers hard.

Time was shoving them faster and faster into a strange, unknown place. The colors may be sharper and truer, and the song notes more piercing, but damn, that fall had been horrific.

"No regrets?" she whispered.

"Not a single one," he said back, quietly steady. "I will miss my friends, but that does not mean I have any regrets. Now heal my arm and shoulder, so we can get on with what we need to do."

She set about doing just that, but healing his injuries wasn't as quick or easy a fix as throwing the healing spell on a sick baby. She had to set the breaks first, and while she had already numbed Rune's pain, getting the bones into alignment was still intensely uncomfortable for him. He braced himself against it, his teeth gritted. The broken edges of bone in his arm grated as they came together. The sensation made her feel ill.

She was wrung out by the time she was able to throw a

healing spell on him. He sighed as the spell sank into his body. He looked as tired as she felt. Then he leaned forward to enfold her in both good arms, and a warm kernel of rightness found its way into her cold, stressed soul. She put her head on his shoulder and they held each other.

"What I want to know is, what kind of trouble did you bring to my doorstep?" asked Grace, who had returned from putting Max to sleep in his crib. Carling lifted her head to look at the other woman. Grace stood just inside the living room. The human was staring at all of Rune's weaponry. The relief from Max's healing had disappeared, and fear had taken its place. "And how much danger have you just put my niece and nephew in?"

At that Khalil stirred. The Djinn had moved to one corner of the room to watch everything that happened with his arms crossed. His long raven hair was pulled back severely from his face, and he wore a high-necked black tunic and trousers. He said to Grace, "I cannot speak to what the other two may have brought here. But I will see to it personally that the small ones are not in any danger. You have my word."

Carling narrowed her eyes on Khalil. That was why he had stayed, instead of blowing off as soon as he had dropped her and Rune on the Oracle's doorstep. He had heard the baby crying. Oh, Khalil.

Grace gave Khalil a leery glance. "Is that supposed to mean something to me, like your word is somehow supposed to be reassuring? Because it's not. I might be new to this Oracle gig and I might have a lot to learn, but at least I've figured out that you're a Djinn, which in and of itself is not reassuring in the slightest. And I still don't know *who* the hell you are."

Carling said to her, "Khalil is one of the oldest and strongest of the Demonkind, and if he promises to keep your children safe, he will keep them safe."

"You're telling me my kids now have a demon bodyguard?" Grace muttered. "Are you telling me my kids might *need* a demon bodyguard? That's just freaking great. That's the best news I've heard all week. All month."

Khalil raised an eyebrow. Other than that, he looked supremely indifferent to the human's opinion.

Rune said, "No one will intentionally bring any harm to

your children. No matter what our conflicts are, children are precious to us. We don't put them in harm's way."

"I have a problem with the 'intentional' part of your statement," Grace said. "So excuse me if I'm still not reassured. Why are you here?"

"We need to consult with the Oracle, of course," said Carling.

After that, there was no stopping Grace. She dug out a notebook to consult an on-call roster of phone numbers from the local community of witches. Carling knew that the witches provided help to the Oracle whenever she was called to act in the capacity of her office. It was part of the witches' tithe to community service, but apparently the help was not enthusiastically given.

"I know it's not even five in the morning, Janice," said Grace. "But this is an emergency, you're next on the roster and you know I need somebody to stay with the children whenever I have to do this."

The unhappy witch on the other end of the line promised to come right over, and Grace hung up. She said to them, "We can do this as soon as Janice gets here, in about fifteen to twenty minutes."

Rune said, "We could have waited until morning."

Grace shook her head. "The laws of sanctuary that are supposed to protect this place only work on those creatures that are law-abiding. How many weapons do you have strapped to your body? After the two guns and the sword on your back, I lost count. The sooner we do this, the sooner you leave and take your trouble with you, and that means the safer we'll be. Janice is unhappy I got her out of bed. She'll get over it."

Khalil scowled. "I could have sat on the children."

"Sat with the children," Carling murmured, as she fought the sudden urge to laugh. "With, not on." She set their two bags at Rune's feet and shifted toys and a college calculus book to sit on the end of the couch closest to the armchair he occupied.

The others ignored her. Grace said to the Djinn, "Do you have a list of references for all the times you have babysat very small, fragile human children?" She waited a heartbeat. Khalil's scowl darkened but he remained silent. She continued, "No, I thought not. They didn't start out as my babies but they're mine now, and you're not looking after them." She paused again as if reconsidering what she had said, then added, "Ever."

As Khalil spat out an angry comment and Grace snapped back, Rune and Carling looked at each other. "She's right," Rune said. "The sooner we leave, the better."

"I know," she said quietly. Would Julian pursue their dispute over demesne borders? She would have said no before the confrontation outside of the Fairmont. Now she was no longer sure of anything. "I'm not the one arguing with her."

Rune worked one-handed to loosen the fastening of one of the armbands. His energy was still roused from what had happened earlier. He appeared calm but felt battle-ready, still burning with an edged anger at both Julian and Dragos. The sensation jumped along Carling's nerve endings like an ungrounded electrical cord.

He said quietly, "I haven't had a chance yet to ask you how the examination with Seremela went."

She held open both empty hands to him, and he offered one forearm to her. "The exam itself wasn't any surprise," she told him as she worked to undo the armband fastenings. "The conversation proved useful. She's really bright. I think she's a talented pathologist, and you were right about her bringing a unique perspective to the whole thing. We may not find a cure, at least not right away. Our first priority has to be to buy some time."

"Did you come up with any way how we can?" Rune asked. His head was bent close to hers, his gaze intent on her face.

Carling murmured to him, "I need to try to get in some form of remission. Seremela also took blood to run some tests—"

A sharp staccato knock sounded at the door. Grace threw up her hands in a "We're done here" gesture at Khalil and turned away from him. Out of the corner of Carling's eye, she saw Rune put a hand on one of his guns as Grace opened the door to reveal an unhappy, disheveled witch. The woman was middle-aged and comfortably rounded, and wore jeans, sneakers, a hooded University of Kentucky sweatshirt and a sour expression. Grace stood back and let her step into the house.

The woman jerked to a halt, her sour expression fading and eyes widening when she took in Rune, Carling and the Djinn.

"You got here in record time," Grace said to the woman. She sat on the opposite end of the couch from Carling to jam her feet into a battered pair of sneakers. "The kids are in bed where most sane people are right now, and you know how this goes, Janice—it'll take however long it takes."

Janice's fascinated gaze bounced around the room. Then she focused all her attention on Grace. "I'll make a pot of coffee."

Khalil crossed his arms and informed Janice, "And we will both sit on the children to make sure they remain safe."

The older human witch's eyebrows went up. She stared at Grace, who said, "Pay no attention to anything this Djinn might say to you while we're gone. I've never met him before tonight, and he has no authority to dictate anything here. I don't think he understands that, so apparently he's not a very bright one either."

"And she is an impudent, disrespectful child," said Khalil between his teeth. "Who does not understand the value of what she has been offered."

Janice said to Grace with a bright, fixed smile, "In the meantime, you'll hurry back as fast as you can, right?"

"Right," Grace said. The bitterness was back in her voice. She turned to Carling and Rune. "Are you ready?"

Rune and Carling exchanged a glance then stood. "Of course," Carling said. "What do we do now?"

"You come with me." Grace turned and walked out, leaving the front door open for them to follow.

Rune scooped up their bags and gestured for Carling to precede him. They caught up with Grace, who was waiting for them in the front yard. She led the way around the house and along a well-worn footpath that cut through overgrown grass and a tangled line of trees and undergrowth. After twenty yards or so, the human's gait turned uneven until she walked with a decided limp.

"How much land do you have?" Rune asked.

"About five acres," Grace said as she slapped at a mosquito. "The Ohio River runs along the western border of the property. It's been in the family ever since we came over from Europe in 1856. We couldn't afford to buy anything like this now. I'm not even sure I'll be able to pay property taxes when they come due."

"There is a very old Power here," Carling said. "Did it come with you to the States?"

Grace sent her a shadowed glance. "Yes," said the human. She didn't elaborate further.

She led them across a meadow to an old doorway that had been built into the side of a rocky incline. The sense of an ancient Power grew stronger as she took a small rusted coffee can from the top of the wooden lintel and withdrew a key that she fitted into the weathered wooden door to open it. Rune studied the structure. It looked like the opening to a mine shaft. It must have been constructed when the Andreas family originally settled on the property over a hundred and fifty years ago.

Grace said over her shoulder, "Your weapons are not welcome. You need to leave them here at the doorway."

"Okay," Rune said slowly.

Carling had been content to remain silent and study the land during the walk. She could tell by the aggressive spike in Rune's emotions that he didn't like the idea of disarming, but he set their two bags by the door then he stripped off his short sword and shoulder holsters with the guns and set them with care on the bags.

"Are we going into a cave?" Carling asked curiously.

"Yes," Grace said. "There are cave systems all over the area, from Bluespring Caverns, Marengo Cave, and Squire Boone Caverns in southern Indiana to the Mammoth Cave system in central Kentucky. This is a very small system by comparison."

The human stepped inside the doorway and felt along the inside wall. She flipped a switch and a naked light bulb went on over her head. It revealed an area large enough for them all to step into comfortably with two sturdy Rubbermaid storage cabinets, and a roughly hewn tunnel that sloped downward.

Grace opened up one of the cabinets. She drew out two flashlights. She handed one to Carling and kept the other one. "I don't know if you'll need this or not," she said. "Your eyesight is a lot more photosensitive than a human's. It gets pretty black down there though."

"We had better take it, just in case," said Carling.

Grace reached into the cabinet for something else that was wrapped in a protective cloth. "Pull the door shut behind you," she said to Rune. Then she turned on her flashlight and led the way down the tunnel.

"So much for talking over a cup of coffee," Rune muttered. He pulled the door shut, and they turned to follow the Oracle.

"Talking over a cup of coffee is not what you asked for," Grace said over her shoulder. The light from her flashlight bounced off the roughly hewn rock walls and the packed earth floor of the tunnel. The temperature dropped sharply as they went, and the cold air felt faintly damp and smelled of the river. "You wanted to consult with the Oracle. Well, this is how you do it. The Oracle has always spoken from the deep places of the earth. What we channel demands it."

Carling got the sense of space opening in front of Grace before she saw the tunnel walls widen. She and Rune followed Grace to step into a large cavern. Rune turned in a circle with the flashlight and then he flashed the light upward. The light did not touch the cavern walls, and it only glanced off the nearest part of the ceiling.

"It's remarkably dry for being so close to the river," he said. His voice echoed strangely.

"It has the same basic structure as the Mammoth Cave system. There's a strong solid sandstone caprock layer over limestone. On the far end of the cavern there's a natural tunnel that leads a bit farther down. The sandstone layer is damaged down there, so there's some stalactite and stalagmite formation and the river leaks in before the cave system ends. There's been some falling rock too, so that area's not safe. That's why we lock the door, to keep out exploring kids."

Grace set her flashlight down and unfolded the cloth from the item she had brought with her. She let the cloth drop to the ground and as she turned to them, she held the item up for them to see.

It was a Greek mask. Ancient gold gleamed in the beam of the flashlight. The face was androgynous, beautiful and blank, with holes for the eyes and the mouth.

Carling murmured, "Oh my. That's stunning."

"The Oracle has worn this mask for thousands of years," Grace said. "As you can imagine, there have been many reasons for that and they have fluctuated over time. Sometimes it has been worn with a great deal of ceremony. My grandmother taught my sister and I that we now wear it for two reasons. The first is tradition and honoring our past. The second reason is to remind the petitioner, when you consult with the Oracle you will no longer be talking to me, Grace Andreas."

"Do you remember what is said?" Carling asked.

"I've heard that sometimes we can, but sometimes we just go blank." Grace's head was bent. She said quietly, "But I'm no expert. I've only been called to do this once since Petra died." She lifted her head. "Are you ready?"

"Yes," Rune said.

Grace raised the mask to place it over her face.

Something vast stirred the cavern air. The ancient Power that haunted this land began to coalesce. A dry sound scraped at the edge of their hearing, like the sound of scales sliding along the cavern walls. The sound surrounded them as the Power coiled around.

Already unsettled, Rune's hackles raised. He found himself growling low in his chest. Carling moved near until her shoulder brushed his arm. In the slanted beam of the flashlight, her face was composed but her eyes were wide and wary. Rune turned so that he stood back-to-back with Carling, facing outward.

A voice spoke from behind the golden mask, but it was not Grace's voice. It was something else, something older and much wilder than a human's voice.

"There you are, gryphon," said the old wild Power. "I have looked forward to this conversation we have had."

Looked forward, to a conversation in the past. Rune shook his head sharply. Yeah, there was that bad dose of LSD again, tripping on his ass like a flashback.

"How you doing?" he said to Python. "You old crazy, dead whack-job, you. Long time no see."

The Power chuckled, a sound that brushed against their skin. "Have you seen Schrödinger's Cat yet, gryphon?"

Rune knew of Schrödinger's Cat. It was a famous physics hypothesis that described the paradox of quantum mechanics. Place a cat in a box with some poison along with some twisty scientific mumbo jumbo. Rune had lost patience with the mental exercise long before he bothered to learn all the physics involved. What he remembered was, the cat was supposed to be both alive and dead in the box, until it was observed to be *either* alive or dead.

Part of what the hypothesis was supposed to illustrate was, in quantum physics, the observer shapes the reality of what he observes. What did she mean by asking him that question?

Behind him, Carling hissed and bumped into his back. She said in his head, *How could she possibly know to refer to Schrödinger's Cat? That hypothesis wasn't invented until the 1930s, and she died—if she really did die—thousands of years ago.*

He said, *I've lived a whole long life filled with weirdness. But this is weird even for me.* He said aloud, "I'm not nearly drunk enough for this kind of conversation, Python."

Something rushed up to his face. He jerked back, staring at the pale indistinct lines of a face. The transparent face bore a resemblance to a human female, but only in the same kind of way a chimpanzee or ape might. Its features were too sharp and elongated, with more of a snout than a nose, and it flowed back to a hooded cobra-like flare of a neck before falling into the body of a serpent as thick as a man's waist.

He steeled himself and passed his hand through the apparition. "You're a ghost. You're not really here."

The woman's smile revealed a wicked curve of fangs. "I am not here," she said, "like a dimly seen island overlaid on the ocean. I am not here, so perhaps I am there, lost in some Other land."

"Are you dead or aren't you?" he demanded. Cryptic ramblings—gods help him, his head might spontaneously combust.

"Like Schrödinger's Cat, I am both dead and alive," said Python, coiling and recoiling her ghostly body through the cavern. "I was alive in the past. I died in the past. Who knows what I will be next?"

Carling gripped Rune's arm before he could explode. She had turned to face the apparition too. She asked, "Are you traveling through time?"

The ghostly apparition turned to her, and Python's smile widened. "I have traveled. I am traveling. I will travel."

"Is that why, even though you have died, you're not altogether gone?" Carling asked.

"Either that," said Python, "or I'm just a crazy whack-job ghost." That feral transparent face drew closer to Carling and softened. "You're one of mine. My children are so beautiful. I want you to live forever. That is why I gave you my kiss."

"Your gift has lasted a very long time, and I am grateful," Carling said. "But now I am dying, unless we can figure out how to stop it. We came to ask for your help."

"I can't give you the kiss again," said Python. "That time is past." Her coiling and recoiling increased in speed as though she were agitated. "I took away the day but gave you an unending, gorgeous night. What you make of that is not up to me. A mother cannot live life for her children."

"That's not what she's asking you to do," Rune said. Desperation edged his voice. He hadn't known what to expect, but he sure had not expected this. To actually be able to talk with Python was more than he could have hoped for, but it might end up being one useless, psychedelic nightmare. "She doesn't want you to live her life for her. We're asking you how to keep her from dying."

"Wait," said Python. "I'm confused. Hasn't she died yet?" Her face came around to Rune. "Why have you not gone back to save her?"

Python's words seared him. She's crazy, he thought as he stared at her. She's a crazy ghost. That's all. He fought to find his voice and said hoarsely, "She hasn't died, Python, she's standing right here in front of you. But she is my mate, and she will die if we don't find a way to stop it. So will you please, just fucking please make some fucking sense for once in your *goddamn fucking life*!"

The feral ghost looked at him with surprise. "Well, you don't have to yell at me," she said in a plaintive voice. "You're not as far along as I thought you would be by now."

"Where am I supposed to be?" he asked dully.

"Right here, gryphon," said Python. "Remember what we are. We are the between creatures, born on the threshold of changing time and space. Time is a passageway, like all the other crossover passages, and we have an affinity for those places. We hold our own, steady against the interminable flow. That's what I tried to give all of my children. That's who you are. The Power of it is in your blood."

"It's all about the blood," Carling whispered. "The key is in the blood."

"The key has always been in the blood," said Python. "You are perfect for each other. Nature could not have created a more flawless mating. You have everything you need to survive. If you survive."

Python faded as they watched. The Power that had filled the cavern ebbed away.

Rune threw the flashlight to the ground and dug the heels of his hands into his burning eyes. He felt demented.

"We have everything we need to survive—if we survive?" He roared, *"What the hell did that mean, you crazy whack-job bitch!"*

Carling came around to face him. She grabbed his wrists to drag his hands away from his face. Her eyes were shining. "Rune, I think she told us everything we need to know."

He stared at her, breathing hard. After a moment he was able to speak more or less sanely again. "Well, do you mind explaining it to me?"

"I didn't get a chance to tell you everything earlier," Carling said. "Seremela and I had talked about looking for ways to get me into some kind of remission, at the very least try to reach a holding pattern to buy us some time to do more research. She said it was possible that becoming a succubus had been a defense response from my immune system when I could no longer keep down the blood I drank."

"A defense response," he said, frowning. "When you frame it that way, the transition would not have been a good thing." Victims of prolonged starvation ate things out of desperation, often things that had no real nutritive value. Their bodies started to consume themselves until eventually their organs began to shut down.

Carling nodded. "Seremela suggested I try to find some kind of physical nourishment that I could tolerate, in the hope that it might slow down some of the symptoms. I wasn't looking forward to trying to drink blood again, but I'm willing to do just about anything, so I said I'd think about it. Python just said you hold your own against the flow of time, Rune, and that it's in your blood. The key is in the blood. Those are the exact words Seremela and I said to each other."

Gradually he calmed, stroking her hair as he listened to her. "Could you have been starving all this time?"

"I don't know," she said. "Eventually I stopped feeling hungry, then I began to sense emotions from living creatures and started to feel better whenever I did. From everything I had heard, that sounded like a natural progression of the disease."

"Well that might be so, but it still sounds a lot like starvation to me," he said. "Much as I want this, I'm afraid to believe in it. It sounds too good to be true."

"But it could fit," she said. "Your blood could have what it takes to put me in remission. This whole strange journey you and I have been on has been as a result of your Wyr attributes coming into contact with my Vampyrism."

He closed his eyes. "And that has never happened before," he whispered. A sliver of hope worked its way into his chest, lightening the dull panic that had taken him over when Python had disappeared. He bent his head to kiss her, savoring the soft curve of her lips as she kissed him back. "We need to start trying this."

"Yes."

"We're not going to give up if you hork a couple of times," he said sternly. He yanked her close to hug her fiercely. "You haven't eaten for a helluva long damn while. It may take some doing to get your system to accept anything. We'll keep at it."

She put her arms around his waist and leaned on him. "Agreed. We can even try giving me blood intravenously if I can't stomach it."

Some fifteen feet away, Grace said in a rusty-sounding voice, "I sure hope you got everything you needed from that session, because I'm cooked."

They turned to find the human on her knees. Carling pulled out of his arms to go over to Grace. "Are you all right?"

"I think so."

As Carling helped the human to her feet, Rune collected the flashlights and wrapped the gold mask in its protective cloth. He asked, "Do you remember what happened?"

"No. I feel like I've been hit over the head with a blunt object." Grace squinted at them.

Carling said to her, "It was a very Powerful, very strange session, but hopefully we learned what we needed to."

"Good, because I don't think I can do that again in a hurry," said Grace as she pulled away to stand on her own. She moved as if every muscle in her body hurt. "Let's go."

They climbed the tunnel, moving more slowly than they would have otherwise in deference to Grace's halting stride. As they went, questions and doubts began to crowd out Rune's relief.

Hasn't she died yet?

His blood began to pound in his ears. What were they missing? What piece of the puzzle had not yet formed? Or had Python just had one of her little diagnostic moments? He managed to keep from growling but he wanted to lash out at something or someone. He wanted to do some damage in the name of something good.

They helped Grace tuck the things back in the Rubbermaid cabinets. Carling pushed open the door to the gray light of a warm, humid summer predawn. She stopped so abruptly Rune ran into her. Then he saw what had brought her to a standstill.

A great bronze dragon the size of a private jet dominated the meadow. His gigantic horned head lay on his paws with the appearance of relaxation, except that his Power was a smoldering volcano and his eyes burned with hot gold.

Dragos had found them.

Rune put his hands on Carling's shoulders and tried to ease her back inside the tunnel. She dug in her heels and refused to budge, keeping her body between him and the Lord of the Wyr.

A whippet-slender woman with a long blonde, disheveled ponytail leaned back against the dragon's snout. She wore cargo pants, high-end running shoes, and a cherry red tank top. Her arms were folded across her chest, and she had one foot kicked over the other. At their appearance, the woman met Rune's gaze and shook her head.

"I've got to hand it to you, slick," the blonde woman said. "You've really pissed him off this time."

≈ TWENTY ≈

Carling felt Rune's energy spike with adrenaline and aggression. She felt his grip on her shoulders tighten, the fingers lengthening into claws. He picked her up bodily and shoved her back through the doorway. She didn't have a chance to resist. She fell into Grace, who had been right behind them, and both women went sprawling. The human woman made a muffled sound filled with pain.

Carling sprang around as Rune grabbed hold of the door. She didn't bother wasting time on trying to get upright. Instead she thrust out her foot. She managed to get a boot wedged in the opening before Rune could slam it shut.

"Goddamn you," she said between her teeth, so furious she could hardly see straight. She twisted to grab hold of the edge of the door with both hands. Rune couldn't shut it now without hurting her, and he couldn't both guard her and at the same time waste energy on fighting with her to get her inside.

He realized it too and gave up. She leaped to her feet and pushed outside to find the golden monster standing between her and Dragos and the woman.

The dragon had lifted his head. Both he and the blonde woman with him were staring at Rune. The blonde woman's wide gaze was stricken with dismay. "Oh God, you didn't," said the woman.

"I did," Rune said. He was growling, a low menacing sound that warned them off.

The blonde woman said to the dragon, "You're too much of a threat to him this way. You have to change."

Dragos considered, thoughts shifting behind his huge, fierce gaze. Carling put a hand on Rune's shoulder as she stepped to his side. She watched the dragon carefully as she brought her Power to the ready. She may not have studied which spells would work best against a gryphon, but she had studied spells to use in battle against a dragon, because she and Dragos had not always been allies. It appeared they were not allies now either.

"All the Elder Races agreed this was to be a sanctuary," Grace said sharply from behind Carling and Rune. "Violence is forbidden here."

"People can be taken from this place," said Dragos. "And violence done to them elsewhere."

Underneath the grip of her hand, she felt the golden monster take in a sharp breath. Then the dragon shimmered and changed into the figure of a six-foot-eight male with black hair, golden dragon's eyes, and rough-hewn features. The dragon's Power boiled in the air around him, just as Rune's did. Dragos put his hands on his hips and stared at Rune, his expression tight.

The blonde woman looked at Carling. "I'm Pia, Dragos's mate," she said. "Are you Carling Severan?"

"Yes," said Carling.

Pia said gently to Rune, "We understand better now. We don't intend any harm to your mate."

"But that won't be true of those who are coming," said Dragos.

"What do you mean?" Carling asked. "What's happened now?"

"More consultations and an agreement. You are under an order of execution. What you have been going through has some sort of effect on the environment around you, and you have refused to remain segregated from others. You have too much Power, Carling. You've been deemed too dangerous to live. Julian and several members of the Elder tribunal are on their way to imprison you until the sentence can be carried out." Dragos looked at his former First. "You need to snap out of it. Start coming up with reasons why they shouldn't carry out what they plan to do, and you need to start talking now."

Dread and rage were a clenched fist in Rune's stomach. He fought to even his breathing and after a few moments of struggle, he managed to come out of the partial shift. He needed reason and diplomacy now more than ever.

Carling said to Dragos, "We think we have figured out what has been happening to me, and we believe we have found a way to stop it. It would be premature for the Elder tribunal to execute a kill order until we know that for certain."

"That still doesn't tell me what has been happening," growled Dragos. "And why it has my other gryphons so freaked out."

Carling and Rune looked at each other. Rune said telepathically, *The other gryphons are between creatures too, and they have a right to hear what that might mean about their nature. But I'll be damned if I paint a target on their backs for every desperate aging Vampyre. Whatever we tell them should remain confidential.*

I think we should wait to say anything, Carling said. *I'm not saying no. Let's just think about the consequences of full disclosure first. Dragos is barely on our side right now, and we need him. We can't risk alienating him by telling him you went back in time and changed the past. Even if we don't think you changed things by much, the fact that you could do it at all is a huge threat to everything we know in the present.*

Rune nodded in agreement. *As far as I'm concerned, that's why we can't say a thing to any of the others,* he said. *They would freak out just as much as Dragos would, and this is none of their goddamn business.*

I agree.

Rune turned to Dragos, who had been watching them with an expressionless gaze. "It doesn't matter what happened," he said. "That was an accident and it's not going to happen again. The important thing is if we can stop what Carling is going through, then the reason for the kill order goes away."

It was clear Dragos didn't like what he heard, but after a long moment, he said, "Agreed."

Even as he spoke a whirlwind blew into the clearing. The whirlwind materialized into several figures that were well familiar to Carling and Rune.

Five were members of the Elder tribunal. The first was Soren, Demonkind Councillor and head of the tribunal, with his white hair and the piercing white eyes like stars. Soren had been the whirlwind that had transported all the others. The second was the tall, pale blonde figure of Olivia Dearling, the Light Fae Councillor. The third was the Elven Councillor, Sidhiel Raina. The fourth was the witches' Councillor, Archer Harrow, his frail elderly body housing one of the strongest Powers in the witches demesne. The fifth was the Wyr Councillor, Jaggar Berg. Jaggar was a kraken of immense age and strength, who normally dwelled in the Atlantic Ocean off the coast of New England, but he consented to walk the land in the form of a man for periods that were long enough for him to execute his duties as tribunal Councillor. The Dark Fae Councillor, Arandur Daeron, was absent, no doubt still in Adriyel attending the many governmental functions surrounding Niniane Lorelle's coronation. Apparently no one had had time to appoint and approve of the next Nightkind Councillor.

The other three arrivals were Vampyres. They wore protective cloaks in preparation for the sunrise within the next half hour, but for the moment they wore their hoods back. Julian Regillus stood flanked by his second-in-command, Xavier del Torro, and Rhoswen.

Carling looked at Julian thoughtfully. His dark hair was kept customarily short, with sprinkles of white at the temples, and he returned her regard, his strong aquiline features inscrutable. Both his Power and his anger were palpable things. Xavier was much less easy to read. He had shoulder-length nut-brown hair pulled back from pleasant nondescript features. His pleasant demeanor was a deadly camouflage. Xavier del Torro was one of the keenest hunters in any of the Elder Races.

Carling was not surprised at the appearance of either male. Rhoswen, though. Rhoswen was a bit of a surprise. Carling looked at her last. The blonde Vampyre did not meet her gaze but instead stared directly ahead, her youthful face a perfect composed mask.

Wyr Councillor Jaggar said to Dragos, "You should not be here."

"My First is involved," Dragos said. "Of course I should be here."

Light Fae Councillor Dearling said coldly, "The Wyr have been cropping up in conversation far too much of late."

"Forget that I am Wyr," Rune said. "That holds no place here. I am not here in any official kind of capacity. For this discussion, I am merely a man."

"We agree on one thing," Soren said. "Who and what you are is irrelevant." The Djinn's white starred eyes turned to Carling. "The tribunal has come to take you into custody."

"Under what charges?" Carling said.

"Since the Wyr Lord managed to arrive before we did," Soren replied, "I'm sure you know very well why we're here and what we have come to put an end to."

"Actually, I don't," said Carling. She forced herself to remain sounding calm and logical. Rune felt like a powder keg of violence beside her, needing only a random spark to make him blow. He stared at Rhoswen with a cold expression that promised violence. He needed her calm, and she knew from experience that logic would be the only thing that could persuade such a diverse group. "I've only heard supposition about why you might be coming, and gossip about decisions that might or might not have been made in my absence. I have not received any official declaration from the Elder tribunal itself."•

Restlessness stirred in the group, and both Sidhiel and Archer looked uncomfortable. Good, Carling thought. This should be difficult for you to do.

It was Julian who spoke next. "Carling, I've petitioned to have you removed as Nightkind Councillor, and my petition has been granted."

When Julian spoke, Rune's rage spiked. He bared his teeth as he stared with naked hate at the Nightkind King. As Carling nodded, she pressed hard on Rune's shoulder. *Hold on*, she whispered gently in his head. *We must make them justify what they've decided, and put them on the defensive.* She said aloud, "That's all very well and good, Julian. That certainly is the Nightkind King's prerogative"—although it wouldn't have been if she'd had five minutes alone with him—"but what does that have to do with the tribunal wanting to take me into custody?"

She sounded reasonable, intelligent, even tolerant. Julian watched her closely. Was that a flicker of confusion in his hard face?

"We have heard a detailed testimony of your condition," the human witch Archer said, not unkindly.

Don't I know who that was, Carling thought, as she stared at Rhoswen.

Archer was continuing. "We know that it is due to your advanced age. You are suffering from periodic episodes of increasing severity that are causing your Power to fluctuate and affect the world around you, yet you refuse to remain isolated to protect others. You are too Powerful and the results of that are too dangerous and not well understood. This can't be allowed to continue, Carling."

"I agree," Carling said.

"And so do I," said Rune. He projected all of his faith, all his passionate hope into his next words. "Which is why it is a very good thing we have discovered how to make it stop."

The stirring that passed through the group was even greater, as the tribunal members looked at each other. All of them were looking increasingly uncomfortable.

Rhoswen's perfect, composed facade cracked. Her eyes flashed up to meet Carling's. Carling met her gaze coldly. Julian moved, a sudden betrayal of astonishment, his expression arrested.

Off to one side, Dragos and his mate stood side by side, watching the proceedings intently, Dragos with his arms crossed.

Soren asked, "You are sure you have stopped them?"

Rune shrugged. He appeared far more casual than he was. "She hasn't had an episode since California, and we don't expect her to have any more."

That was stretching the truth all out of proportion, but he still made it sound completely sincere. Carling pushed the advantage and turned her next words into a delicate whip. "But this issue is far too serious to take any one person's word for it." She paused to let that sink in. Julian's gaze flickered to his left, toward Rhoswen. Ah, that was all the confirmation she needed. She said, "Time will tell this tale. It would be an easy enough matter to set up a household where we can watch and wait."

"You are willing to stay quarantined for an undetermined amount of time?" Soren said.

"Of course," said Carling. She focused on Julian. "I didn't leave the island just to be willful. I left with a clearly defined purpose."

Rune interjected. "We're willing only if we're together. Carling is my mate, and I am not leaving her."

And there drops the other shoe, Carling thought, as a fresh argument erupted. She almost found it in her to be amused.

Julian no longer wanted Carling in the Nightkind demesne. Carling gave him a heavy-lidded smile. She said gently, "That is perfectly fine with me."

Her smile said to him, *I know what you have done and tried to do. Exile me and turn your land into a prison. I may no longer come to the Nightkind demesne, but take one step out of your jurisdiction, and you are still my progeny, my child, and I may still command you. And now you have no idea how long I might live, or where I might be. You tried to take me down, and you would have killed me, and maybe you did all of that sincerely for the good of your people, but you also did it because you thought you would finally get out from underneath my authority. And while I understand all of that, I will not forgive you, because I know how to hold a grudge with all of my heart, and one day I will remind you of that. One day.*

Then Dragos stirred and said, "This is a stupid conversation. Rune, of course you can come home to New York and bring your mate with you." He gave Carling a machete smile. "We'd love to welcome you into the fold."

"I'll just bet you would," she said to the dragon, with a blade in her smile every bit as keen and bright as his.

The argument that erupted at that was more vociferous and impassioned than ever. It turned out nobody was in favor of that option.

The morning was brightening. Streaks of yellow and pale rose lightened the dark purple sky. The sun would crest the horizon soon. Rune took Carling by the shoulders and turned her to face him. He stroked the short choppy hair off her face. He looked as tired as she felt. *I'm not sure anybody could really stop us if we did live in New York*, he said. *Although there is a great deal of pressure on Dragos right now.*

No matter how strongly they had spoken to the tribunal, they still did not know if they had found a solution. She did not say it. She preferred, as he did, to look ahead with hope. Instead she asked, *Do you want to go back to New York?*

He took a deep breath and shook his head. *No. I haven't*

forgiven him for the last conversation we had. I also think he's yanking everybody's chain right now. I don't believe he would let me go back and pick up my duties as his First with you as my mate. He would always wonder if having you in my life skewed my motives, and he would be right. Maybe he and I can repair our friendship over time, but for now I think the only thing you and I can really do is start somewhere fresh and new.

She smiled up at him. *What in the world are we going to do with ourselves?* The thought of the unknown was exhilarating and frightening. There was her good friend again, the spook house/roller coaster.

Rune's face lightened and he smiled back. *I have no clue. It's going to be fun to figure it all out.*

As long as they could buy themselves time.

She squeezed his hands. *I have a few things I need to say to a couple of people.*

She watched as he struggled with himself. There were too many Powerful and dangerous people around, and they had skated too close to the edge for him to let go of her easily. But he had to know it was not a good thing to try to hold on to her too tightly, because his grip loosened. *All right.*

She turned and walked over to her wayward children, Rhoswen and the Nightkind King. They stared as she approached, noting the changes in her hair and dress. Julian asked in a low voice, "Did you really do it? Did you find a cure?"

Carling let her gaze travel over Julian's rough, intelligent features one last time. They had been close friends once, long ago, and political partners for far longer. He was another one like Rune, an alpha male born to command. Perhaps she had simply ruled him for too long. Maybe like Rune and Dragos, when this anger of hers had died down, they could achieve peace, but she wasn't going to hold her breath.

"That question may grow to haunt you over the next thousand years or so," she said. "But you're going to have to find your own salvation."

She turned her attention to Rhoswen, who grew more and more agitated under her steady regard. "You went straight to Julian, didn't you?" she murmured, low enough to keep her words from everyone else but not so low that Julian couldn't hear. "What did you tell him—how unstable I'd become, how dangerous I was, how it made no sense that I would send my most loyal and devoted servant away and latch on to that manipulative Wyr? I know what you told him. You told him everything he wanted to hear to justify doing the things he did. Then you told the same things to the tribunal."

Rhoswen straightened and held her head high, while her eyes glittered with angry tears. "I spoke my truth."

Carling's contemptuous expression never wavered. "What a poisonous little snake you turned out to be," she said softly. There were too many fractures in Rhoswen's behavior. Carling no longer believed the younger Vampyre was stable. If they were anywhere else, Carling would have taken her head. But Rhoswen was not worth breaking the laws of sanctuary over. Carling and Rune had come too far, through too much, to throw it all away.

As she turned away, she said to Julian, "She's your problem now."

She watched Julian's face undergo a drastic change even as she felt a sharp stabbing pain in her back. She arched and tried to turn away, to keep the blade that was sliding into her body from striking a critical, mortal blow to her heart.

But then Rhoswen's arm came around her neck. The other Vampyre was so much younger than she, so much slower and weaker, but Rhoswen didn't have to hold her in place for long. She just had to hold her in place for long enough.

"I loved you," Rhoswen hissed in her ear. "I gave you everything."

The blow hit home.

Rune, Carling said, and even though he was twenty feet away talking with two Councillors, he could still hear her.

He spun. The shock and horror that filled his face and emotions saddened her terribly.

She still had so many things to say to him. She reached toward him and watched her own hand dissolve.

She still had so many things . . .

*R*une, Carling said.

And he turned to see the tip of a short sword burst through her chest, just like the spear he had once watched burst through her father's body. Behind her, Rhoswen was crying even as she thrust the sword. Julian had lunged forward, but there was nothing the Nightkind King or anyone else could do.

All Carling had time to say was his name. She looked so sad, so loving, and it was *Carling* that looked that way. That was his look; that look was for him.

She had shone so brightly, for so long. Then she crumbled to dust. And everything in Rune's fierce, remarkable soul began to scream.

Every little thing is going to be all right.

Except sometimes it wasn't, Bob. Sometimes things got so fucked up you couldn't even send them home in a body bag.

Screaming.

Wait, I'm confused.

Hasn't she died yet? Why have you not gone back to save her?

Have you seen Schrödinger's Cat? Like Schrödinger's Cat, I am both dead and alive.

Screaming.

I cannot live in this universe. I cannot live this way.

If you die, I will find you.

I will never leave you. I will never let you go. I will not let you fall, or fail. I will always come for you if you leave, always find you if you're lost.

Always.

Each moment in time was the tiniest of things, the most precious of things. Each moment held the potential for change, a turnaround that led to a different page. It rested on a singular point that was so precise, it would be so easy to lose track of that one miniscule place, that single moment, in the infinite cascade of all the other moments in time. Each turnaround melted away, as every moment in the present slipped into the past.

Every moment slipped away until he reached back, not too

far, just far enough, reached for the last definitive place when she was *there* instead of *not there*, and he threw all of his screaming soul at her.

And there it was.

The keystroke password to an unbreakable code.

As Carling turned away from Rhoswen, she said to Julian, "She's your problem now."

And suddenly the golden monster was in front of her. He was *right there*, even though Rune also stood twenty feet away talking to two Councillors.

The golden monster contained a nightmare that was so far beyond emotion, it whited out Carling's senses. He yanked her to him while at the same time he lashed out with all his killing claws extended.

Rhoswen fell, her body in ribbons. Everyone in the clearing spun around to stare as she crumbled to dust, until all that was left was the short sword that had fallen from her hand.

Rune sank to his knees, dragging Carling down with him. He clenched her so tightly that if she had been human she would have been in trouble. His body shook with convulsive shudders. He breathed in great sobbing gulps of air, like a drowning victim who had just been rescued. Other than that, he made no sound.

"Rune," Carling said. She framed his wet face in both hands. He wasn't looking at her. He was staring at something else. He wore an expression of someone looking at damnation. She dared a quick sidelong glance around. Everyone was staring either at them or the place where Rhoswen had stood. Julian strode over to pick up the sword. He looked furious.

The other Rune had disappeared. Had she imagined what she had seen?

"It's all right," Rune whispered. "It's all right now."

"Bloody hell," Dragos muttered from across the clearing. "I don't know what the fuck that was, but something definitely happened."

TWENTY-ONE

Two weeks later, Rune still couldn't speak of what had happened.

She realized what had to have occurred, of course. The brief glimpse Carling had gotten of Rune in two places, the sword Rhoswen had hidden underneath her cloak, the appalling state he had been in after he had killed her. It did not take a huge stretch of imagination to figure out what that meant. Carling tried a couple of times to get him to talk, but he looked so haunted and sick, she didn't have the heart to push it. Instead she held on to him tightly when he woke in a sweat, and she teased him gently whenever he had stared into space for too long.

As for Rune, it felt like part of his soul would always be caught in the horror of what happened, in the loop that went around like a serpent's tail coiling in on itself. But gradually he began to see how he could reach a point where he could set it aside and get on with the business of living.

After much discussion, and more argument, it was decided that Rune had not broken the laws of sanctuary that were meant to protect the Oracle and all who came to petition her. While several people besides Dragos were well aware that "something" had indeed happened, and it made everyone uniformly unhappy, no one else admitted to seeing Rune in two places for that brief moment in time, so no one understood what really had transpired.

Everyone agreed it was a mystery how Rune had gotten from one place to another so fast, but as Jaggar said, Rune was famous for his speed for a reason. As for Rune, he wouldn't talk of it. At that point, Carling suspected he couldn't. In the end they admitted that he had acted in defense of his mate. Since he did not instigate the violence, acting in defense was deemed acceptable. Meanwhile Julian swore he had no idea Rhoswen would do such a thing. Carling didn't think many people actually believed him, but nothing could be proven one way or another.

They relocated to a beachside villa in Key Largo while Carling remained under quarantine and observation for three months. As far as prisons went, it was luxurious enough. Two-story windows along one side of the villa overlooked an infinity pool beside the ocean. The villa had an acre-length private beach, four bedrooms and four baths, a great room, a family room and a kitchen filled with a fortune in black granite countertops and Wolf appliances, including a Sub-Zero refrigerator and a wine storage unit. Rune cooked himself some mighty fancy-ass hamburgers and steaks in that kitchen.

There were two guesthouses on the property where Carling's observers, the Demonkind Councillor Soren and the Elven Councillor Sidhiel, stayed along with a few of their attendants. Their mission was simple: to monitor Power activity in the area immediately around Carling. Often lights stayed on in either one or the other of the guesthouses, and the quiet sound of conversation drifted through open windows into the early hours of the morning. Occasionally Soren and Sidhiel ate dinner with Rune while Carling kept them company with a glass of wine, but more often than not the Councillors kept to themselves.

"This is much better than exile to my island," Carling said to Rune. They were in the sitting area of the villa's master bedroom. She was curled at one end of a couch with several books, and she had just hung up after an hour-long talk with Seremela.

"Hells yeah," Rune agreed lazily. He wore cut-off jeans and nothing else, his long muscular legs and bare feet propped up on the opposite end of the couch. The sunshine loved him. Already he was burnished all over with a deeper golden tan. He sprawled on the rest of the couch, his head pillowed against her thigh as he channel surfed for cable movies on a fifty-six-inch flat-screen. "Got ESPN and SPIKE TV right here, baby. And I'm DVRing both *Escape from New York* and *Escape from L.A.* later. Snake Plissken is my man. Booyah."

Carling made a note on her new iPad to remind herself to do a Google search for a definition of *booyah*. She told him, "I had in mind a rather different reason than cable TV."

"I know what you had in mind," Rune said. He reached behind his head to capture one of her hands and pressed her fingers against his mouth.

They were in daily talks with Seremela. Carling had FedExed her research to Seremela, for whatever good it might do, and Seremela was pouring over everything with a fine-tooth comb. The medusa had become obsessed with the medical puzzle they had given her, and her phone conversations were littered with her excited inquiries. She had just arranged for a vacation so she could come out to the villa for a prolonged visit.

"I think we need to lure Seremela away from her position as ME for the Cook County Morgue," Carling remarked. She looked out the windows at the moonlight sparkling on the ocean water. "She's underutilized there. I think she would be much happier focusing all her attention on research."

"I think that's a bitching idea," Rune replied. "We could set her up in her own lab. I'd want her to be much closer though. I wonder if she might like to move to Florida?"

"We'll have to ask her when she comes," she said, smiling.

The Key Largo villa was a temporary arrangement for quarantine purposes, but the warm climate was so attractive to both of them, they were already talking about the possibility of settling somewhere in Florida. They just hadn't agreed on where yet. Perhaps Miami Beach. It was on the ocean, connected to a major metropolitan area, and it was also just fifty miles away from a 720,000-acre Everglades preserve, which was quite an attractive thing for an active Wyr to consider. The one consideration was finding a place to live—or building somewhere—that had plenty of space providing shelter from the sun.

Because it was two weeks later and Carling had not had another episode.

On Seremela's advice, they had started out very carefully. Small watered-down amounts, sipped frequently. The first time Rune slit his finger and bled a few drops of blood into a small glass of wine. After having gone so long without drinking anything but wine, they hoped it would help Carling make a transition back to drinking blood again.

She found it unexpectedly difficult to take a swallow of the blood-infused wine, but managed after a brief struggle. It almost knocked her to her knees. She had thought his blood would taste spectacular, as burning and as intense as the rarest liqueur. It was so much more Powerful than she had imagined.

That one mouthful made her feel drunk, dizzy. She leaned on the kitchen counter, gasping. Rune snatched the wineglass out of her hand as it tilted sideways. He studied her worriedly. "How do you feel?" he asked. He put an arm around her waist. "Are you sick?"

She shook her head, and the world spun around her. Holy hell. She clutched at the counter.

"Are you going to throw up?" he demanded.

"No!" She tried to focus on him. "At least I don't think so."

Then euphoria hit. A wave of heat washed over her skin like a sheet of flame. When she turned around to face Rune, her eyes had gone garnet red.

His own expression flared. He whispered, "Hello, beautiful spiky girl."

She growled, launched at him and took him down to the floor where they made love in a frenzied white heat.

Now she was able to ingest as much as a quarter of a cup of his blood at a time, mixed in a glass of wine. The Power in his blood knocked her nearly senseless every time, although she felt more energized than ever. There were side effects other than "crazed monkey sex" as Rune so eloquently put it. She was beginning to lose her ability to sense other creatures' emotions. She also became more grounded in a way that she had forgotten. Her own Power was no longer revved at such a constant state of high velocity, and she tired more frequently. She was not able to hold her spell of protection against the sun for longer than an hour at a time. As soon as she had lost that ability, Rune had gone shopping online for cloaks, SPF +100 sunblock, and other protective gear.

And just that afternoon she had taken a half-hour nap. It was such merciful refreshment, she woke with tears in her eyes. Rune stretched out on the bed beside her, his head propped in one hand, watching her as she slept. She turned to him and surprised a look of such tenderness on his face, her eyes watered more than ever. They moved at the same time, and held each other tight. He rocked her a little, his face buried in her hair.

Maybe it wouldn't last. Maybe it was just a reprieve, and her symptoms would return. Neither one of them wanted to take the ghost of crazy Python's word for anything. The wisest, most prudent thing they could do was continue to pursue all avenues of research, which was why they wanted to recruit Seremela to work on the project full-time. But for now they were holding steady, against time and everyone else. They held their own.

Other people got in touch. Carling had Duncan petitioning Julian to allow him to oversee the safe removal and transport of her library. She was almost certain she had managed to coax Duncan into opening a law office in Miami. She might even convince him to relocate. She was talking to other people too. She suspected Julian would miss several highly talented people from his demesne very shortly.

Aryal called Rune daily to tell him how much ass he sucked, and how much she hated him. Once she called to tell Carling how much ass she sucked too. Carling laughed and invited the harpy for a visit. The other sentinels called, sometimes to ask work-related questions and sometimes just to shoot the shit. Dragos never called, and Rune never called him.

Carling watched Rune carefully as he talked and laughed with the sentinels who were his friends. She ached that she couldn't make that better for him. But no matter how much she looked for it, she never saw a hint of anything other than what he had told her. He missed his friends but he really did have no regrets.

Still, it would be good to get a better picture of what they might do next. As Rune told Constantine one day with a grin, "I think I might have to buy a Don Johnson suit while I'm down here. You think you're suav-ay, brother? Johnson was suav-ay. You don't hold a candle to him."

Carling was not a big fan of TV, so she had to Google that reference too. She found herself chuckling at the photos of the 1980s *Miami Vice* series. Then she turned thoughtful.

For now she set aside her iPad and her books, and she ran her hand down Rune's arm to ask silently for the remote. He handed it to her, tilting his head back to give her a sleepy-looking, sexy smile. She turned off the flat-screen and asked him, "Are you all right?"

"Of course. Why wouldn't I be?"

"We've both had quite an abrupt change of lifestyle," she said carefully. "It's a lot to adjust to."

"I know. It's going to take a while. The answers will unfold over time."

"I just want to be sure they unfold fast enough for you," she said.

"Are you kidding? This is the best vacation ever. It's too bad we've only got the villa for two and a half more months. I could use a good six months more of this. Besides, we've figured out a lot already. We should start looking at houses in the greater Miami area, and we're going to open up a research facility and coax Seremela to come on over to the dark side. You've already got your baby boy Duncan half-convinced he needs to move out here, and Rasputin and Rufio are arriving tomorrow evening. As for me . . ." He shrugged and ran his fingers along her arm. "I might look into consulting opportunities with the local police force as a temporary gig while we sort everything else out. That won't hold my interest forever, but it will be enough for now, so stop fretting."

Her gaze narrowed. "I do not fret. I consider all angles."

He started to laugh. He tugged at the shirt she was wearing. "You're so full of bullshit sometimes. You're fretting, darling Carling. It's cute. You also swore you would never wear a T-shirt with a hairy, bespectacled man on it."

She looked down at herself. She was wearing his old Jerry Garcia T-shirt, a pair of panties, and nothing else. "This is the ugliest item of clothing I have ever seen," she said. It had also become her most favorite item of clothing. "It's a good thing I don't have to look at myself very often when I wear it."

"It looks much better on you than it ever did on me," he told her, his voice turning husky.

"We'll have to agree to disagree on that." She set the remote on the back of the couch and ran the palm of her hand over his hard muscled chest. His skin was always so gloriously warm.

Hunger stirred, both sensual and otherwise. Her gums tingled. He raised himself on his elbows and lifted his face as she bent over to kiss him. She whispered against his mouth, "I want to bite you so badly."

Raw sexuality flared hot in his aura. "So bite me," he murmured.

Her eyelids felt too heavy. They drifted closed as she drew her lips along the side of his neck. She nipped gently at his skin and got a frustrated growl in response.

"You call that a bite? That's not a bite." He rolled off the couch and yanked her to her feet. He muttered, "I'll show you a bite."

She started to laugh. She felt drunk again, and saturated with his presence. She put her arms around his waist, cuddled against his bare chest and nipped at his nipple. "Promise?"

He put his hand under her chin to turn her face up to his for a scorching kiss. Then he led her to the bed. She pulled away long enough to drag his T-shirt over her head, and then he was on her.

She fell back on the bed as he came down on top of her. He tore off her panties in one impatient yank. Then he started biting her.

He suckled at her beautiful breasts, tugging at the plump gorgeous flesh of her distended nipples with his teeth, while he fingered the juicy softness of her labia. His hands were shaking. He moved lower and sank his teeth into the soft flesh of her side, just under her rib cage, biting sharp enough to sting but not enough to bruise.

Hunger and arousal pulsed through her. She was becoming accustomed to their companionship. She had forgotten how much the appetites of the flesh were also things of the spirit. They twined up her body, as Rune settled between her legs and put his mouth to her.

He ate at her as though he could never get enough, with a patience coupled with ferocity that caused her to pull up her knees as the pleasure stabbed deep. Her climax started gently and built in intensity as he licked at her with a steadily increasing rhythm. She stroked his hair as she shook with it. Then she coaxed, "Come here."

"No," he said. He bit her again, hard on the sensitive skin of her inner thigh, while he rolled his thumb over her clitoris.

That one would leave a bruise. The second climax punched through her, and there was nothing gentle or sane about it. She cried out and her torso arched off the bed. He pleasured her, yet she felt so empty, and she was starving again. "Come here," she growled.

"No, I don't think so," he said. He parted her flesh and suckled strongly at her.

The sensation was so piercing, and yet she was so damn empty, and *starving*, that she came up on her elbows with a hiss, and for the first time in two hundred years her fangs descended.

She rolled over to her hands and knees and prowled toward him across the bed. *"I said come here."*

Rune's face was hard angled with desire, his lion's eyes glittering like polished stones. He stared at her mouth, frozen. Then he purred, "You going to come take me now for real, baby? Promise?"

Insouciant alpha. She sprang at him and struck, sinking her teeth into his neck. They both groaned as the wild liqueur taste of him exploded on her tongue. She whined at the back of her throat and started to shake.

He held her with a hand at the back of her head and pushed her mouth harder against him, impaling himself on her fangs while he hauled her onto his lap. She went willingly, spreading her legs to sit astride him. He positioned his erection at her slick opening and pulled her down. Then he was filling her aching emptiness with the hard warmth of his cock as his hot blood filled her mouth. He clenched her to him and rocked in her as she drew on him and took in his nourishment.

She grew drunk again with pleasure. She was always so surprised at how generous it was, that pleasure. He filled her to the brim with laughter and constancy, and such a rare bountiful passion, her soul unfurled and flourished.

She realized he was whispering in her ear. "I will always come for you, always hold on to you. I swear it."

The mouthful of blood she had taken was more than enough. The vitality of it already sang in her veins. She pulled out her fangs and whispered back, "I will never let go of you, never fail you. I will hold steady, no matter what."

He began to shudder with his own climax, and he gave himself over completely to his mate again.

She held on to him tightly, with all of her heart. She had made a promise to do so.

Early the next evening, Rufio and Rasputin arrived.

"Let's try to get through this without anybody growling, okay?" Carling murmured to Rune as they watched the rental car pull into the driveway.

"Don't look at me. I'll be purring the whole time," said Rune. He blinked at her with his best innocent look.

She tried to scowl at him. She didn't have it in her. They had spent the afternoon dozing. She had drifted in and out of dreams with her head resting on his shoulder. It could not have been more precious or perfect.

Rune opened the front door as Rufio climbed out of the car, followed by the little brown and sable dog on a leash. Rasputin caught sight of Carling as she stood in the shadow of the doorway. He barked, high pitched with excitement, and strained at the leash until Rufio laughed and let him go.

The dog hurtled up the path with a manic grin. He danced and twirled and jumped, and when Carling bent to pick him up, he leaped into her arms and tried frantically to lick her face. Rune greeted Rufio, asked him how their flight had been, and showed him to his room so he could settle in.

When Rune returned, he found Carling and Rasputin in the kitchen. Rasputin was exploring the corners of the kitchen floor, his plumed tail wagging. Carling had pulled out a package of raw chicken breast tenders, muttering to herself as she sprayed some PAM in a skillet. She glanced at Rune. "I'm going to cook Rasputin some chicken for supper. Would you like for me to cook some for you as well?"

Rune pinched the bridge of his nose. He said, "Ah, I have to come clean about something."

"What's that?" Carling asked. She turned on a burner, squinted at the flames, and adjusted the temperature down.

"I don't want to hurt your feelings," said Rune. "To me, you are perfection personified in so many ways. But darling, you are a terrible cook."

Carling narrowed her eyes on him. He gave her an apologetic shrug and a smile. He watched her gaze fall and her expression change. She covered her mouth with one hand.

He looked down too. The dog had come over to him and lifted its leg. A tiny stream of urine sprinkled Rune's shoe.

Rune angled out his jaw. Both he and Carling squatted down to regard the Pomeranian thoughtfully. Rasputin sat and scratched energetically behind one ear.

"What do you suppose he's feeling right now?" Rune asked.

"I don't have any idea," said Carling. Her face creased with laughter, her long almond-shaped eyes dancing. She looked completely alive, completely happy. "But from now on, you're taking him out."

Turn the page for a special preview of
the next Novel of the Elder Races
by Thea Harrison

ORACLE'S MOON

Coming March 2012 from
Berkley Sensation!

Grace dreamed she was running along a dark paved road. The night was full of shadows, the new moon hidden from the naked eye. The full moon at its zenith was a witch's moon, a time for incantations and Power. The new moon, at its darkest, was the Oracle's moon, a time when the veil between all the worlds and all the times thinned. A brilliant spray of white stars like Djinn's eyes pierced the dark purple sky, and the wind whispered secrets to the shadowed, swaying trees.

Her running shoes slapped the ground rhythmically, striking a pagan tempo for the song in her coursing blood. She loved how her body felt, sleek and strong as it moved smoothly along the paved road. Perfect. She felt perfect.

A gigantic black panther ran along beside her. His broad shoulder was as high as hers, and his long powerful body ate the distance with effortless fluid grace. As soon as she became aware of him, the panther turned his head and looked at her with strange diamond eyes that were as piercing and shining as the stars. Shocked, she jerked and stumbled—

And she slipped into another dream. This time she climbed the side of a steep rocky bluff. She had to use her hands sometimes, and the burn in her muscles felt good. The sun was high in the sky and beat down on her head, and she was so hot she dripped with sweat.

An immense black dog climbed at her side. He was easily twice the size of a mastiff, all muscle and power, yet he climbed up the side of the bluff with impossible grace. As she stared, he turned to look at her with radiant diamond eyes that startled her so badly, she lost her grip on the rocks.

Gravity yanked her. She fell, and the ground hurtled toward her.

She woke with a start, her heart hammering. Her T-shirt and flannel pants were clammy with sweat. The sun had shifted, and she was alone in the living room. The television was off. There were so many things that were not right with the scene, but before she had a chance to panic, she heard Max and Chloe giggling in their bedroom.

"I want you to be a doggie now," Chloe said.

A male voice said, "But at the moment I am a cat."

Grace knew that voice. She had only heard it for a brief time, but she would never forget it. It was the voice of the Bane of Her Existence, deep and clear with a kind of purity that somehow hurt the heart, and it held the Power of a cyclone.

And it belonged to a creature that was visiting with her kids.

She was off the couch and moving down the hall before she fully knew what she was doing.

Chloe said, "I want to ride the doggie!"

"I believe what you want would then be called a horse," said the Bane.

Max shrieked, a happy sound that escalated so high it could shatter glass.

Sharp pain shot up her leg. Just as it threatened to give out from underneath her, she reached the children's bedroom and grabbed on to the doorway as she looked inside.

Max stood in his crib. He couldn't walk on his own yet, but he could stand when he held on to something. The single wisp of dark brown hair at the top of his head waved as he bobbed up and down. He was grinning from ear to ear and watching Chloe, who sat on the floor along with a black cat, who sat in front of her.

The cat had to be the Bane of Her Existence. The Djinn. Khalil Somebody Important. Visually, it looked like a normal, fairly large cat, perhaps twenty pounds or so, but to her mind's eye, it felt immense with a smoky, dangerous Power.

The cat said, "For something so small, you emit a great deal of noise."

Chloe grabbed the cat's tail and yanked on it. "Doggie!" Chloe shrieked. "Doggie! Doggie!"

"That is my tail," the cat remarked. The little girl stabbed at his furred face with a plump finger. "Now you have discovered one of my eyes. Oh look, you have discovered the other one. I think you have awakened your aunt. I told you we should be quiet."

The trio turned to look at her as she stood frozen. Two delighted children and what appeared to be a normal black cat but was instead an alien, enormously Powerful, infinitely dangerous being.

"Look, Gracie!" said Chloe. "It's the doggie-cat! You said we can keep him."

The cat's strange, wrong eyes narrowed. "Did you?" he said. His triangular face looked distinctly unfriendly, whiskers held awry. "That wasn't what you told me earlier."

Grace lunged forward to snatch up the cat, and he allowed it. His body hung boneless from her grip just like a real cat would. "I had no idea you meant this doggie-cat, Chloe," she said, her voice hoarse. "That changes everything."

"Which other doggie-cat could she possibly have meant?" said the cat. "You don't exactly have a plethora of them hanging around."

Grace growled to Chloe, "Stay here."

Chloe pushed to her feet and whined, "But I want to play with him."

Grace looked at the little girl. "I said stay here, young lady."

Something in her expression must have made it clear she meant business, because Chloe kicked her toys on the floor. "You never let me do anything fun. I'm never going to live here again."

"Fine," Grace said between her teeth. "Just do as you're told."

She limped out of the bedroom. Max gave a wordless yell, clearly displeased at recent events. Chloe shouted, "Horrible! He's *MY* doggie-cat! I found him first. You're not fair! I hate everything and everybody!"

Grace hissed at the Demonkind. "Thank you. Thank you so much for that. There are so many things wrong with what just happened. What the hell is the matter with you anyway? Have you got no sense?"

"You are every bit as impudent and disrespectful as you were this morning," the Djinn said in a cold voice.

The cat grew as she walked down the hall, until suddenly she was holding on to a weight that was much too heavy for her to carry. She dropped him, and he continued to grow until he was the massive black panther from her dream. A thrill of shock iced her skin. Her gaze slid sideways to look at the impossible behemoth slinking along beside her. He was the size of a small horse, and yet he still seemed small compared to what her mind insisted was the immensity of his Power.

She would not give in to what she was feeling. She would *not*.

"Stop it," she snapped.

"I have no idea what you're talking about," said the monstrous creature. He turned his head to look at her with those bizarre eyes that sparkled with malice.

They reached the living room. Grace rounded on him. She used her fury to propel her forward. She shoved at the giant creature. It was like trying to push a mountain. She shoved at him again. "You're trying to intimidate me. Well, guess what, asshole? It isn't going to work. This is my home. Those two kids are my niece and nephew. And I did not give you permission to spend time with them. You are trespassing and it is not okay."

The giant panther morphed into an upright figure of an angry man, and finally she came face-to-face with the Djinn she had met so early this morning.

The form he wore this time was tall, somewhere close to six and a half feet. Long raven-black hair was pulled back from an elegant, pale face. That face had all the same things that a human face had, two eyes, a nose and a mouth. It was even lean-jawed and handsome, yet somehow it was clearly not a human face. His strange eyes were the same in every form he chose to wear, crystalline and diamondlike. He had a lean, graceful frame that matched his face, and he wore a simple black tunic and trousers, and a fierce, regal pride.

This was, as much as anything was, his real physical form. At least it was his go-to form. At his essence, he was a spirit of air and fire. No physical form could contain him in his entirety. His Power filled the house.

My gods, there's so much of him, she thought as she stared up at his sparkling angry eyes. What a calamity he is. Standing in front of him, she felt absurdly young, very small, and stupidly, excessively fascinated.

"I offer you a gift beyond price, you foolish creature," the Djinn said between his teeth. "And you throw it back in my face."

"What do you think you're offering me?" she asked. "I wake up and I find you with my kids in their bedroom. And I'll say this again—without my permission. Do you realize how offensive that is? Maybe you don't. Maybe that's something Djinn would do all the time. You know what, I don't care. And I'm not even going to get into all the wrong lessons you were teaching them. Wait a minute, yes I am. You were a talking cat with children who are much too young to differentiate between that and reality."

His eyes narrowed. "What nonsense are you spouting, human?"

"What do you think is going to happen the next time Chloe sees a black cat?" Grace demanded. "Do you think she's going to say to herself, oh this is not like the freaky black cat that talks to me and lets me yank its tail and poke it in the eye? No. Do you know what she's going to try to do? She's going to try to talk to it, and pull its tail and maybe poke it in the eye. And you know what *that* cat is going to do—because it's a real goddamn cat? It's going to scratch her. It might bite her. Cat bites are filthy things. Usually the puncture wounds go deep and they get infected. And then suddenly I'll be taking a confused, crying three-year-old girl to the ER for a three-hundred-dollar doctor's visit to get antibiotics all because of your ignorant arrogance!"

The Djinn regarded her with a supercilious expression. "Do all your thoughts proceed in such a fashion?"

"What are you talking about?" Grace blinked, thrown off balance. "Do my thoughts proceed where?"

The Djinn gestured with a long, white hand. He made it look impossibly graceful. "To conclusions of disaster, of course. No doubt there will also be brain-eating parasites in the cat bite, or perhaps a troop of rabid monkeys will escape from a nearby zoo and cut a path directly for your house."

She stared. "You think I'm making this stuff up? That cat bite happened to me when I was little. I have the scars to prove it. Do you know what I caught Chloe trying to do yesterday? She was climbing on top of the kitchen table. She was about to jump off and fly like Clark Kent, because we had just watched an old movie rerun with Christopher Reeve, and if Superman could fly, she thought she might be able to too. Maybe she wouldn't have broken her leg if I hadn't caught her, but she probably would have hurt herself somehow."

The curve of the Djinn's elegant mouth turned cruel. He looked around the living room, his gaze cold and judgmental. "How unfortunate then for your children that you choose to nap in the daytime instead of watching out for them the way you should."

She flinched as if she'd been slapped, and she looked around the living room too. Her textbooks were stacked on the coffee table. Toys littered the floor. A basket of unfolded laundry sat on the floor by the armchair. Chloe had spilled some of her Cheerios on the area rug in the living room then walked over them. Crushed cereal crumbs were everywhere.

She thought of the tangle at the back of Chloe's head that she still hadn't brushed out. Embarrassment and fury clogged her throat so that she couldn't speak. After a moment she managed to whisper between clenched teeth, "You have no idea what you're talking about. You have no real understanding of me, my kids or the issues we have to face. That lack of understanding alone makes you dangerous to us."

"How dare you?" He thrust his angry face close. "*I would never cause harm to a child*. The whole reason I stayed was to protect them!"

His rage curled around her, manifesting as black smoke. She felt as though she were staring into an inferno.

She would not flinch. She would *not*.

There was simply no point in trying to reason with him. They were too different from each other, and he was too arrogant to listen to anything she said. She dug down deep and found enough composure to say, "I get that you don't mean us any harm. Thank you for staying this morning to make sure Chloe and Max were protected. If you don't wish to petition for a consultation with the Oracle, I'm telling you now to leave my house."

He scowled and opened his mouth, clearly intending a scorching reply, but a small, sad voice beat him to it. Chloe said, "No more fighting. Don't be mad anymore, okay?"

Khalil's diamond gaze flickered. He looked down as Grace did, at Chloe's worried face. Then Grace witnessed a remarkable thing, as the Djinn's elegant, malicious expression gentled. He went down on one knee so that he could look at Chloe face-to-face. The girl regarded him gravely. Something in Grace's chest twisted. He was so enormous, and Chloe was so tiny.

"I will not be mad anymore," Khalil said. He did something to throttle back the Power in his voice and spoke quietly.

"Promise?" Chloe asked.

His gaze slid sideways and up at Grace. He looked sour. Wow, Grace thought on a sudden spurt of hysteria, he really doesn't want to give up on his grudge. But he wasn't talking to Grace any longer. She raised her eyebrows and nodded toward Chloe, telling him silently, you're answering to her, not to me.

His bizarre, unfriendly gaze pledged something to her, but she didn't know how to read unspoken Djinn messages. With an air of decision, Khalil turned to Chloe. He said, "Yes, we both promise."

Wait, what? Grace straightened. She hadn't given him permission to speak for her.

"We will not fight anymore," he continued. "It is too upsetting for small people."

Chloe said strongly, "It's upsetting for big girls too."

"Indeed," said Khalil. He held out his hand and Chloe put hers into it.

Chloe was so small, Grace thought, biting her lip. She held herself so tensely her muscles were starting to ache again. So fragile, so precious.

The Djinn brought the girl's fingers to his lips and kissed them. Then he let her go, and straightened to his full height before he vanished.

Grace stared at Chloe, looking for some kind of reaction to the Djinn's sudden disappearance. Other than wiggling the fingers Khalil had kissed and looking intensely thoughtful, the little girl didn't appear to have much of one. Maybe Chloe was concentrating on trying to disappear too, and she was discovering that she couldn't do that either.

Max shouted angrily from the bedroom. Normally good-natured, he'd apparently had quite enough of being left out.

Grace sighed and went down the hall to collect the little man. Chloe had had her Cheerios snack, but she and Max had missed out on lunch. He had to be starving. She knew she was. She changed Max's diaper and tickled him until his bad mood vanished, and he kicked and giggled. Then she settled him on the hip on her good side and turned to Chloe, who had followed her into the bedroom to watch.

"Think it's about time we had some supper?" she asked.

Chloe gave that proposal due consideration. "Indeed."

Khalil reformed on the roof of the house, not necessarily because he felt any particular desire to take physical form again but more to give his roiling energy a focal point. He crossed his arms and leaned back against a dormer. The roof was shabby and missing a few tiles, he noted with disapproval. The land was as unkempt as the house, with grass that was too long and weeds sprouting around fence posts. They were overtaking once well-tended flower beds. Everywhere he looked there was evidence of neglect, while the lazy, contentious human napped. He did not approve, either of how the property was maintained or how she cared for the children. He tapped his fingers on his biceps and thought.

The Djinn were among some of the first creatures that came into being at the Earth's formation. Born of magic and fire, they were beings of pure spirit. They gained nourishment from the energy of the sun, from of the living things of Earth and from sources of Power. Any form Khalil chose to take was like donning a suit of clothes, a facade without real substance. This body he currently wore had no organs and would not grow hungry, or grow old and die. Easily assumed and easily discarded, it would fade into nothing as soon as he let go of it.

He was not the oldest of his kind, that first generation of Djinn that were born at the keen, bright morning of the world, but he was of the second generation and therefore considered old among his people. He was an authority in his House and a voice to be reckoned with among all the Houses of Djinn. This young human creature was nothing more than a single breath of time in his ageless existence, and the fact that she called *him* ignorant was insupportable.

While he certainly knew why she irritated him, he did not know why she interested him. Her facial features and physical form were pleasant enough, at least as far as humans reckoned such things. She was pale and wore shadows on her face like the haunts of memory. Those shadows were intriguing. They told a tale but in a language he couldn't read. He wondered what they said.

Her hair—now her hair interested him. It was a light reddish blonde, like captured fire and sunlight, and her eyes held flecks of green and honey brown. She had a temper as fiery as her hair, and she held Power in that slender body of hers too, a great deal of it. It was an odd thing, that such a young creature held a Power that felt so old to him. The land itself held echoes of the same Power. He wondered what it meant.

He sensed movement and other flares of ancient Power in the nearby city. He knew that several of the entities from the early-morning confrontation were still in the area. Carling and Rune, several of the tribunal Councillors, the Nightkind King, and the dragon were somewhere close by. Khalil was curious to discover who might leave, and if any might return to speak again with the Oracle.

Shadows lengthened across the land. The Midwestern air felt heavy and full of water, like it was pregnant with some kind of storm. From his position on the roof he could see the Ohio River that bordered the western edge of the property. One of the great rivers of the North American continent, the water captured the sunlight along its surface until it seemed to shine with its own light.

He listened to the sounds from within the house, small domestic things like the clink of cutlery against dishes, the baby's infectious giggle, Chloe's light voice. The child chattered about anything that took her fancy and when she wasn't talking, she sang. She asked questions unceasingly. Despite the fiery temper Grace had displayed to him, she always answered Chloe's questions with patience.

They were like a small nest of birds. Khalil grinned when he thought of it. Chirp chirp chirp. Then there was the sound of water running, and much flapping of wings. The chirping grew louder. Much giggling was punctuated with Chloe's *tra-laing* and Max's cheerful yodel. The noisiness moved from the kitchen to another part of the house. Grace was putting the children to bed. She lavished love on those babies. While he did not approve of her, and he was almost certain he didn't like her, he would have to give the human female credit for that.

He thought back to a time long ago, when his own child Phaedra would have made such light, happy sounds. Djinn children were not born as humans or other embodied creatures are born, but were occasionally formed as two Djinn mingled energies. All forms of children were rare to the Elder Races, as if nature were compensating for giving the Elder Races such long lives, and the children for Djinn were no exception.

Phaedra's mother Lethe had been even more Powerful than Khalil, a first-generation Djinn who remembered the dawn of the Earth. Over time he and Lethe had become enemies, and to hurt him, Lethe took their child and tortured her. Khalil, along with a select few allies that included Carling, had rescued Phaedra and torn Lethe to shreds.

His daughter lived but didn't laugh any longer, not like these bright innocents. Phaedra's energy was jagged and twisted. She shunned contact with others and was quick to lash out and cause damage. He did not know how to help her. He had never known how to help her.

At last Grace left Max and Chloe's bedroom. He heard her move back to the kitchen. She ran more water, and there were more sounds of dishes clinking and splashing. Then she moved to another room, the left room in the downstairs. That would be the dining room. She was silent for a while and then she went into the living room. He noticed how her gait changed at times. She would start walking at a smooth pace but she quickly slowed down, and her footsteps became arrhythmic, ungraceful. It was another oddity.

She turned on the television and that was when he slipped silent as the summer breeze through the open window into the children's bedroom.

The toys had been picked up. The floor was clear, and the room tidy. The bedroom was not quite dark because the door was open and indirect light shone from the living room down the hall. The two cribs were at opposite sides of the room. Posters of puppets adorned the walls. A cheerful green frog hung over Max's crib, and a pink pig wearing a blonde wig and pearls hung over Chloe's.

Khalil added the pig in the blonde wig to the growing list of things he did not understand. He hated to admit it, but the human female might have had a point.

Khalil moved silently over to check Max's still form. The baby smelled clean and was fast asleep again, his round cheeks flushed. Khalil picked up Max's hand and studied it curiously. It was even smaller and more delicate than Chloe's, a soft little starfish of flesh. These humans were such odd creatures.

When he moved over to Chloe's crib, he saw that she lay on her stomach, sucking her thumb. She smelled clean too, and her curls were combed. Then he saw the shadowed sparkle of her eyes, and he realized she was awake and watching him as he watched her.

He crouched to look at her through the bars of her crib. She smiled at him around her thumb. He whispered, "Do you know that I am the doggie-cat?"

She nodded.

"Clever girl." He thought a minute, trying to come up with words she might understand. It was surprisingly difficult to try to think like a small, new human might. "Do you know that I am not really a doggie or a cat?"

She nodded again.

Good. That was good. He reached over the bars to pat her back. She felt warm and soft, and a little lumpy under a light summer blanket. "Do you know that you should not pull a real doggie's tail, or a real cat's tail either? And you should not poke them in the eye?"

She popped her thumb out of her mouth and whispered, "Indeed?"

He frowned, suspicious. "Do you know what that word means?"

She shook her head.

He sighed. "I see we have things to work on."

She asked, "Can you be a horsie too?"

Ah. Small, noisy and remarkably tenacious. He was learning a great deal about new humans.

"I don't think we should be having this conversation right now," Khalil whispered. He wanted to pick her up and hug her but restrained himself.

She snickered sleepily. "Indeed."

He patted her back again.

Indeed.